Praise for
STONE SONG

"A WORK OF GENIUS AND COURAGE . . . ONE OF THE GREAT BOOKS OF OUR TIME . . . one of those RARE UNIVERSAL works that touch the souls of all peoples."
—Richard Wheeler, award-winning author of *Cashbox*

"FAR ECLIPSES everything that has been written about Crazy Horse . . . a man whose spirit has become a sacred symbol to all Native Americans . . . IT TOUCHES ITS READERS DEEPLY WITHIN THEIR SOULS."
—*El Paso Herald-Post*

"*Stone Song* is a CLASSIC EPIC, fit to stand beside Frederick Manfred's *Lord Grizzly* and A.B. Guthrie's *The Big Sky.*"
—Kathleen O'Neal Gear and W. Michael Gear, bestselling authors of *People of the Lightning*

"Blevins expertly delves into the psyche of a warrior guided by mystic visions. . . . MANY-LAYERED AND COMPLEX: Blevins reveals a TRULY HUMAN Crazy Horse, and a COMPLETELY BELIEVABLE tribal life."
—*Kirkus Reviews*

STONE
SONG

≈≈

A NOVEL OF THE LIFE OF
CRAZY HORSE

WIN BLEVINS

A TOM DOHERTY ASSOCIATES BOOK
NEW YORK

STONE SONG: A NOVEL OF THE LIFE OF CRAZY HORSE

Copyright © 1995 by Win Blevins

Maps by Ellisa Mitchell

A Forge Book
Published by Tom Doherty Associates, Inc.
175 Fifth Avenue
New York, NY 10010

Forge® is a registered trademark of Tom Doherty Associates, Inc.

ISBN: 0-812-53369-0
Library of Congress Card Catalog Number: 95-6934

First edition: June 1995
First mass market edition: March 1996

Printed in the United States of America

0 9 8 7 6 5 4 3 2 1

mitakuye oyasin

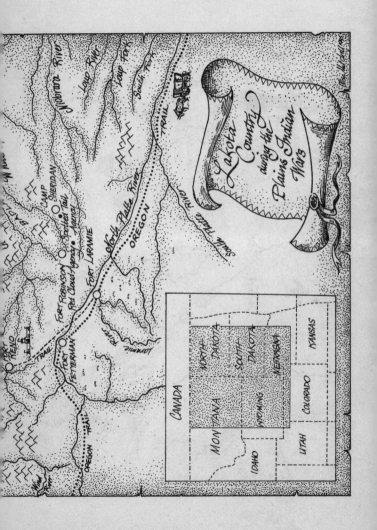

Look at the real reality
beneath the sham realities of things.
Look through the eye in your heart.
That's the meaning of Indian religion.

—LEONARD CROW DOG

Nothing lives long,
Nothing lives long,
Nothing lives long,
Except the sky and the mountains.

—THE DEATH SONG OF WHITE ANTELOPE

PART **ONE**

SEEKING
A
VISION

A sundance ground:
It is twilight.
The dance ground has not been
*   used in years.*
The shade branches of the arbor
*   are brown.*
Dead pine needles lie in the dust.
The sundance pole in the center is
*   gone,*
the gaudy prayer flags gone.
The circle of prayer sticks is gone.
This place is empty, physically,
except for you, and me, and others
standing under the skeleton arbor
perhaps in hopes of . . .

Is that the whisper
of ghost moccasins against the
*   earth?*
The darkness deepens a little,
*   plush.*
The evening star glimmers.
From somewhere beyond the
*   horizon,*
or beyond all direction,
or within the earth,
to the ear of the mind and spirit
come once more pulses and throbs,
*   supplications,*
the drums and songs of the sacred
*   dance.*

Where the sundance pole once was
suddenly comes a shift in the air,
a flux, a breath, a whirl of dust.
To the eye of the heart only
    appears . . .
the shape of a man.
He stands at middling height,
in his thirties,
boyish in his slimness.
Except for a deer-hide breechcloth
he is naked.
His face is daubed with white
    paint,
like hailstones.
He may be an Indian,
but his skin is not dark,
and his hair, falling to his hips,
is the brown of river sand.

He is not ordinary:
See his assured carriage,
the look of aliveness in his eyes,
the unnaturally bright colors
of his body and paint, and,
when he moves,
the illusion of looking
through him
into eternity.

He fixes us with his eyes,
commands our attention with his
    gaze.
At this moment the drum starts
    thumping,

the open, hollow pong
of a wooden drum,
slow, hypnotic, insistent,
a seducer of spirit.

The man slaps the ground hard,
once, in a ritual manner.
The drum punctuates the slap.
He begins to speak
in a voice clear but soft.
We must listen attentively
to hear his words:
Tasunke Witko tanagi he
    miye,
malakota, na Hunkpatila
    Oglala.
Though he speaks in his language,
    Lakota,
somehow we understand what he
    says:

"I am the spirit of His Crazy
    Horse,
from the Hunkpatila Oglala of the
    Titunwan Lakota.
I look,
and I tell you truly what I see."

The drum throbs.
The spirit disappears.
Light blazes,
as though the world is being born,
    or ending,
and the sun is rising at sunset.

Where a shadowed sundance
ground lay unused
now stands a village of buffalo-hide
tipis.
The air is filled with
the smoke of campfires,
the babble of children,
and the yaps of dogs.
A youth approaches one lodge,
lifts a door flap,
and enters.

Hawk was restless in the youth's chest. She turned and turned, uneasy on her perch. Sometimes she beat her wings against his ribs. He was afraid she would lunge against his chest wall and scream.

He couldn't tell anyone.

He had to talk.

He looked around the shadowed lodge desperately. His home where he never felt at home. The robes where his father and two mothers slept at the back. His father's willow backrest. Weapons hanging from the lodge poles, women's things hanging from other poles. Beside the lodge skirt, parfleches with the family's belongings. On one side the robes where he and his brother slept. Opposite, his grandmother sitting on the robes that made a bed for her and his sister, Kettle. A home, but not his home.

Hawk stirred.

He had to talk.

"My Grandmother," the youth Curly said, "Unci," in his language. "Unci, will you come sit with me?"

She didn't respond. She never did. She hadn't spoken for ten winters, or responded in any way to words. She acted deaf and dumb. But he thought she knew things.

Light Curly Hair walked sunwise around the center fire to the side of the tipi where she always sat on her robes, staring into the shadows. He sat next to her and thought he heard her sigh. Though she didn't speak or act as if she knew anyone else was there, sometimes he thought the way she moved showed some awareness. And she was not feeble. If you called her name, Plum, or addressed her as Unci, she didn't respond. But if you gave her a spoon, she would stir the stew. If you gave her the knife, she could cut up a rabbit. She could get up and go outside to relieve herself.

He thought maybe he was crazy. Was he going to talk to someone who couldn't hear or speak? Except he thought she could hear and could speak but chose not to.

He scooted directly in front of her, took one of her bony hands between his hands, and held it. He studied her eyes, which were blank.

She will never tell my secrets.

"Unci?"

Now, because of another dying person, he had to talk. He had seen them moving Bear-Scattering-His-Enemies this morning. Curly's brother by choice, Buffalo Hump, his *hunka,* was helping. Curly had squatted and looked between Hump's legs and seen the chief. And smelled him. Bear-Scattering was rotting.

Whenever Curly saw death, *she* came back to him from ten winters ago, his blood mother, Rattling Blanket Woman. That death had silenced his grandmother, and perhaps destroyed her mind. Grandmother Plum and Curly had walked into the lodge and found his mother, Grandmother Plum's daughter, hanging from a lodge pole by a rope around her neck.

Grandmother Plum had screamed, a terrible outburst full of all the evils of the black road of this world. At its loudest she cut off the scream so violently she seemed to choke on it, as though a great hand had seized her throat and was strangling her. Somehow the silence was louder and more awful than the scream. She had never spoken since. She didn't lose her voice and her mind, not in Curly's opinion. She threw her voice away. And maybe her mind was still there, in the shadows.

He held his father responsible for that suspended body.

Was he a fool to talk to Grandmother Plum? He shook his head, uncertain. She held her eyes blankly toward the shadows. There was no one else to talk to.

She will never tell my secrets.

It was time to force himself to speak. He sat there and held her hand and breathed the air she was breathing and tried out different beginnings in his mind. There was no way but to blurt it out. "Sometimes I feel a bird in my chest. Beating her wings."

He looked hard at her face. Maybe now she would laugh at him, or her eyes would mock him. Her lips didn't move, though, and her face was as blank as ever.

He plunged on, like a fallen tree being washed down-river by a rushing current. "Ever since I can remember, since I was a small child, I've felt it. Most of the time things are quiet. When things are hard, and I get scared, I feel it. A bird in my heart. A red-tailed hawk, female, I think, beating her wings." The female was normally bigger.

No response. He imagined a glimmer in his grand-mother's eyes, but her face was shadowed.

"Hawk gets jumpy sometimes. Sometimes . . . When people make demands of me, she's like one of those eagles the Sahiyela men trap and raise. They keep the legs teth-ered to perches, so the eagles lunge against the tethers, shrieking, and lunge again and again. Sometimes Hawk lunges and shrieks until I can't stand it."

He just sat there for a moment. "Unci, does everyone have that feeling?"

He didn't know what answer he wanted. Maybe he was ordinary, which he didn't like. Or maybe he was very strange.

Surely he was strange. He never forgot for a moment how conspicuous he looked. Not only did he have light skin, but his long hair was the tawny color of sand. In his people's dances, with their blue-black hair and earth-dark flesh, he stood out like a candle flame in darkness. He avoided dances.

They called him Light Curly Hair, a name he didn't like. He heard the whispers: Somewhere in his family, maybe, they said, was *wasicu* (white-man) blood. Not only the *wasicu* on the Holy Road noticed his hair and pointed at him rudely and said he must be part *wasicu*. His own people did, too.

He never answered in any way. Never. But the whis-pers made him angry. He would say to himself, *My father is the Oglala called Tasunke Witko, His Crazy Horse, a name* revered among the Lakota. He is the son of a father also called His Crazy Horse, later known as Makes the Song. My blood mother bore the honored name Rattling Blanket Woman, because she could make her blanket crackle and pop when she danced. She was the daughter of Lone Horn, one of a line of chiefs, all named Lone Horn, of the Mniconjou band. My uncles are honored warriors and leaders. I am utterly Lakota.

In camp he wore his light hair braided. On the warpath, where they gave him only boys' duties, he let it flow free. It hung not to his heart, where most Lakota men cut their hair, but to his waist. The sun made it gleam like brass. In the village he felt ill at ease. On the warpath Hawk was always calm in his chest.

He repeated the question softly, more to himself than Grandmother Plum: "Does everyone have this feeling in the chest?"

Grandmother Plum seemed to be looking off into the past.

He said loudly in his mind, *I am confused. I don't know whether to feel proud or fortunate or peculiar. I only know that in my spirit I am Hawk. I feel fully at ease alone, and only in solitude. With Hawk.*

Now he looked into Grandmother Plum's face again. He wanted to provoke her into speech. So he asked the other big question: "Unci, shall I cry for a vision?"

Nearly sixteen winters old, he was powerless. He had no wing feathers of the war eagle, or tail feathers, no whole wing to be used in prayer. He had no coups, no vision, no power. When he let himself think of that, shame blotched his spirit like boils.

Out of his shame and weakness he had been thinking of going onto the mountain to cry for a vision, to enact the great rite *hanbleceyapi*.

From early boyhood he had been taught that seeing beyond, into the spirit world, is a man's medicine, his personal power.

But he had not gone to an older man for counsel about

this crying for a vision. He was afraid the counselor would say he was too strange, too peculiar. The refusal would humiliate him.

"Unci, shall I cry for a vision?" Crying to see beyond had been on his mind all summer. His friends and comrades and rivals were doing it. Both the twins from the Bad Face band had sought visions this summer, and found them. He had been waiting for . . . he didn't know what.

No answer.

Now Hawk turned in his chest. He felt a faint flutter of her wings against his ribs.

All right, he told Hawk silently. *Wait. I will take care of you in a moment.*

He looked at Grandmother Plum. Her face was unreadable, blank as a dried-up mud puddle.

He hadn't solved anything. She wouldn't speak. He knew that when he came here. But talking to her had soothed his hurt.

He got up, put her hand back in her lap. *"Ake wancinyankin ktelo."* Until I see you again. The Lakota did not say good-bye, like the *wasicu,* unless they meant good-bye forever.

He had no answers. Maybe no one could give him any answers. Maybe his way was to find all answers by himself, alone. A hard way.

He lifted the door flap and looked back and said softly, "Thank you, Unci."

HANBLECEYAPI

He kicked his pinto away from camp, along the river bluffs.

Often riding alone calmed him, and Hawk.

He had nowhere special in mind, just a ride. He didn't pay any attention to the river or the bluffs, but he did notice the old eagle pit, a little way up the hill. It was a *wakan* place, one of holy power, that cavity in the ground where dedicated men trapped eagles to earn some of the power of this all-seeing bird, closest of all creatures to Wakan Tanka, his people's word for Spirit, Power, Mystery. He had sneaked out there a couple of times and lain in the pit, his senses alert to the spoor of Spirit, trying to see and feel and hold the power.

His father, a holy man, had talked to him about the *cante ista,* the single eye that is the heart. It meant, said his father, the whole and true way the heart sees and comprehends. This stood in contrast to the way the two physical eyes worked, a double seeing, the sight of the mind and not the spirit, and often false. The eyes of the head saw only horses and magpies, said his father, while the single eye of the heart saw Horse and Magpie.

When he had lain in the pit trying to see with the *cante ista,* little had come to him. He was only a boy then and had no power. He still didn't.

He ought to have power. His people needed his help. Bear-Scattering's wounding and dying were just a symptom. Everything was askew—this whole time on earth, his time for being alive, was aberrant.

Three years ago the Lakota had signed a big treaty, which had brought many obligations, no rewards, and starvation.

Now new troubles. The Oglala and the Sicangu had gone to Fort Laramie in late summer to get their annuities, the beef and cloth and other goods the government had promised them for signing the peace paper. They were hungry. For five winters now buffalo had been scarce. In the winter camps some people actually had starved to death. They needed those rations desperately. But the goods were late, and the people were sick of waiting.

While they waited, a Mormon cow wobbled right into the village of the Sicangu, their brother Lakota band. Seeing that the beast was about to die anyway, a visiting Mni-conjou killed it for food. The people worried that the sol-diers might make a fuss, but they couldn't speak unkindly to one of their guests.

The soldiers made more than a fuss. They refused to accept the payment the Sicangu offered for the cow. They damn well would arrest the culprit, they said.

They didn't know what they asked. The Sicangu's obli-gations to a guest were sacrosanct. Besides, every Lakota knew what was done to a captured enemy. They weren't about to turn over one of their own cousins to be tortured and killed. Or jailed, which was worse. All because of a cow that was already dying when he shot it.

So the soldiers came blustering among the lodges, led by the loud, arrogant Lieutenant Grattan. The Sicangu chief, Bear-Scattering-His-Enemies, was the one who had supported the treaty so strongly that he was named the big chief by the *wasicu*. This time he stood his ground about not surrendering the Mniconjou. Somehow the firing started. For his courage Bear-Scattering got shot.

The Sicangu warriors wiped out the soldiers to the last man, all twenty-nine of them.

A-i-i-i, bad trouble.

Both bands rode hard away from Laramie and the sol-diers. "Don't wait for the rations," said the wounded chief. "Run. Get as far you can from the soldiers."

They fled here to the Running Water River at the mouth of Snake Creek, Bear-Scattering suffering with every step. The women gathered berries, currants, and plums, and the young men and boys shot small game, and Chief Bear-Scattering got on with his dying.

The people needed the power of every Lakota, espe-cially the young men.

For no reason Curly stopped the horse. He looked around. He noticed the sun warm on his skin. He felt the slight breeze. Then it stopped, and he sensed something else.

He could have been in any of a thousand places nearby on these plains. Beyond the old pit, by a sunpole tree, a cottonwood, a plain lifted into a hill. The dry slope was full of loose stone, prickly pear, and low bushes. Below a dry watercourse started, finger-joint deep, a crack in the earth breaking its way toward the creek. The plain rolled away from him in every direction, broken by dry gullies, dotted with sagebrush. Each direction from this junction of earth and sky was home to every kind of creature, animals and plants, all earth's children, so many that only the high-flying *wambli,* eagle, Wakan Tanka's emissary, saw them all.

This place was not exceptional. It was anywhere and everywhere. Yet Curly sensed something.

He looked around. He had a queer strangled feeling. In his chest Hawk fluttered her wings.

The four first spirits were here too: Wi, Skan, Maka, and Inyan—Sun, Sky, Earth, and Rock. Their companions Moon, Wind, Contention, and Thunder were here. The four winds were here. This place was nothing special, but it was every place, and the powers were as much here as anywhere.

"Mitakuye oyasin," Curly murmured, acknowledging his kinship to all living things.

A peculiar avidity clutched him. It was a voracity, a lust, and it had him by the throat.

He looked up the hill. He hadn't seen it at first. Off to the left, more than halfway up, a rocky projection with a flat top jutted out from the hill, like an altar. The kind of place where Lakota . . .

He saw, suddenly. Saw himself on the prayer mound walking back and forth, arms lifted to the sky. Heard himself crying out to the universe. The picture and the cries danced in his mind, entrancing him. In this dream he was crying for a vision, trying to see beyond.

His mind railed at him. *Hanbleceyapi* was a most serious step. If you saw beyond, it would determine everything about your life. Normally, it would give you an animal guide. It would tell you how to paint yourself, how to make connection with medicine. In it you saw how to conduct your life, whether your nature was to be a warrior, a councillor, a leader, a father, a holy man, a healer.

You would spend the years of your life discovering how to live this vision. It would be the defining experience of your existence.

In his mind Curly yelled at himself: *You do not take this ritual on yourself lightly, fool!*

When you asked for help, a *wicasa wakan,* holy man, took you into the sweat lodge, prayed with you, gave you a *canupa,* a pipe, dedicated to this ritual, and helped you prepare your mind to go four days without food, water, or sleep. He took you onto the mountain, made sacred gestures, and left you there. When you came down, he took you back to the sweat lodge and helped you understand what you had seen.

To cry for a vision was high seriousness. For a mere youth to try it without preparation would be foolish and arrogant.

Yet Curly had a feeling that was so strong, so violent. If he did it, Hawk would be truly peaceful within his heart. Hawk wanted him to cry for a vision.

He dismounted, tied the pony, and stripped himself naked.

By sunset he was thoroughly muddled.

He had hobbled the pinto by a sunpole tree close to water. He had stripped and left his clothing and gear by the tree. He went up the mountain naked, unprepared, uncertain, vulnerable.

He acted as he thought he should. He had no *cansasa,* tobacco, as an offering, no *canupa* to send breath to Spirit, no sweetgrass to burn as a sacred gesture, no white sage for a bed. He wasn't so sure exactly what criers for a vision did anyway.

He felt agitated. You couldn't see beyond the evident, the apparent, world on your own, without guidance.

Surely he was being ignorant and disrespectful. If the Wakinyan Tanka, thunderbirds, flew to him here, they would probably hurl lightning and kill him.

He blamed himself. He was always that way. He couldn't accept what others said but had to try everything for himself. He cursed himself for always having to be different, for being a stranger among the people.

So he had made this choice and he would live with it. He thought back. He would follow through, regardless of what came, and he would accept all consequences.

"You can do anything, be anything," his father often said, "if you're willing to accept what comes with it."

All day Curly had done what he'd heard about and what made sense to him. He set stones at the four directions and drew one line from the north to the south, another from the east to the west. His father had explained these signs to him: The east-west line was the black road, the path of warfare and destruction for human beings. The north-south line was the red road, the path of harmony and fruitfulness. The circle was the wholeness of life itself, unifying the red and black roads. This was the meaning of the most common of all the icons, the four-winds wheel.

Now Curly stood where the red and black roads crossed, at the center of this circle, the center of himself and of the universe. One by one, he walked to each of the four directions and back, his feet naked against the earth, his body naked to the wind, and he prayed.

He walked first to the west, the home of the thunder powers, the Wakinyan Tanka. As he prayed, he kept in his mind the spirit of the west, Yata, and the powers he sends—the swollen clouds, the mind-dazzling lightning, which is harbinger of the rain, and its thunder, which in Curly's language was called lightning-gives-birth-to-sound.

> "Hiye haya!
> Hiye haya!
> Hiye haya!
> Hiye haya!

Grandfather, I am sending a voice.
Grandfather, I am sending a voice.
Grandfather, I am sending a voice.
Grandfather, I am sending a voice.
Hear me.
Hear me.
Hear me.
Hear me."

Ceremonially, he repeated each line four times, a sacred number.

As he cried for a vision, he watched especially for winged creatures that might fly to him. Of all animal messengers they were the closest to the powers Wi and Skan, Sun and Sky, and so the most powerful. The animal aides of Yata would be hawks or bats. But the skies looked empty.

Curly walked to the north, the home of the white giant and the north wind. Whenever the white giant breathes hard, things freeze. Whatever this god touches withers and dies. If the white owl, the raven, or the wolf appeared to Curly, that would be a message from the white giant.

He walked to the east, where Yanpa lives on an island whose shining yellow sands are the home of the sun. The east is the path of insight and may send a nighthawk with wisdom.

Curly walked to the south, the home of Okaga, the giver of life and the maker of flowers and other beautiful things. His breath is warm, he is kind, and he always brings goodness. His messengers are waterbirds, meadowlarks, and cranes.

Curly called out to these powers and to Tunkasila, Grandfather. He lifted his voice in a thin, wavering cry, respectfully, mindful of his boyish weakness, and he asked for help.

He saw nothing, he heard nothing.

It was like an upside-down miracle, not seeing but blindness. Any bird might have spoken to him, any one at all. The sky was miraculously empty. A squirrel, a chipmunk, a coyote, a deer might have appeared. A spider, an ant, any insect might have crawled by. He saw nothing–Mother Earth acted unnatural, dead.

He knew he might not be blessed enough to get a song or a dance or even thoughts or words. Still, just by what it did, or its presence alone, any messenger would give him something. He had heard wise men say that any appearance of any creature whatever mattered, no matter how seemingly insignificant. If you cried for a vision, you had to remember everything and report it to your guide.

Since this was an ordinary piece of plain, rolling, jumbled, indistinguishable from a thousand others, it should have been as abundant and various with life as all the others.

He was half-angry, half-shattered by its emptiness. Life itself seemed taken from him, Spirit taken from him, as though part of the world could be perfectly empty of *skan,* the force that moved the world, the force that made all the peoples alive, two-legged, four-legged, rooted, crawling, swimming, and winged, that made water flow, that made everything vital.

It was a sign, a miracle. He was answered. Answered in emptiness, blackness, a void.

He snorted.

He cried for a vision and the answer was his blindness.

He cried for a vision and the answer was his deafness.

Wild self-accusations stampeded in his head.

Worse, far worse than no answer.

Here was an answer, and it was death.

He made a deliberate effort to control his trembling. Carefully, he lay down with his head where the black road met the red road. The ground was rough and uncomfortable. It was almost dark. He would not sleep–he refused to sleep–he would follow the rules. But the darkness was a blessing. In the darkness he would not have to face the awful answer Spirit was giving to his plea. The nothingness.

He woke in the blackest part of night. He shook himself with shame. His mind accused him: *You slept. Only the cold woke you up.*

The Seven Sisters said it was halfway between midnight and dawn.

He sat and thought a little. What was in his spirit? Determination, tenacity. He would persevere, persevere doggedly. He would not accept this pretense at an answer, this silence of the universe. He would bull onward until he got a glimmer of insight, a hint of power.

His grandfathers, his father, the uncles he called *ate* (his father's brothers), the uncles he called *leksi* (his mothers' brothers), his friends all came back from the mountain with something. It was usually a waking dream, they said. Your eyes were open, but what you saw was not the ordinary world. It was the world within this apparent world, the real one. A creature might appear to you, not an ordinary creature, maybe a meadowlark, but the true meadowlark, the one the earth's meadowlarks imitate. If you were fortunate, the bird might give you a word or a song or a dance. Or you might see it do something. Whatever it was, you were to hold that gift in your mind for the rest of your life, a sign, perhaps difficult to interpret or to follow, but a sign.

Sometimes one seeker would wear an eagle-bone whistle in his hair because of what he saw. Another would dangle the paw of a kit fox around his neck to help him remember that animal's ways. Another would put the skin of a raven in his medicine bag as a revered object.

Something, you would be given something.

Occasionally a seeker came back with nothing. Empty-handed. Empty-minded, Curly guessed. Or was it full-minded, too full for the powers to add anything new? Then you simply went again. The universe was a place that gave men guidance. It always spoke. You had only to open your mind and wait.

Except him, maybe, except Curly. Right now its answer was a thunderclap of silence. The universe refused Curly.

He would show the powers. He would seek in a rage, he would claw and scrape and rip, he would demand of the universe until he tore from its heart a response.

I am lost! his mind screamed at the powers. *Show me the way!*

He began his prayers again, his solicitations to the west, home of the Wakinyan Tanka, north, home of the bald-headed eagle, the east, Huntka, the path of the rising sun, and the south, where we are always facing, home of the white swan.

When the sky began to grow light, he walked toward the stone at the east slowly and prayed in that direction until the sun was well up, beginning:

"Hiye haya!
*Grandfather, I am sending a voice.
Hear me,*"

repeating each line the sacred four times.

When he had finished praying aloud, Curly sat at the center of the sacred circle and turned his thoughts to matters of reverence. He pondered the four ages of life on this earth, which are also the four ages of the life of a single man—rock, bow, fire, and *canupa*. He dwelled on the buffalo that stands at the west, holding back the waters that will flood the world and end this age of mortal life on earth. He knew the buffalo was almost bald now and stood on only one leg, as the last days approached. He shaped a buffalo with his right hand, his thumb and outer fingers the legs, his middle finger the hump and head. He made it stand on one leg, like the buffalo that holds back the waters of the final destruction. He looked at his own buffalo flesh and reflected.

When the sun was well above the horizon, he turned his prayers again to the four winds. He spoke to each of them, one by one, addressing each with a plea, ending his prayer with the words, *"Unse la ma yelo."* Take pity on me.

As he walked to each of the directions, he kept his restless eyes down. He tried not to notice that the world was still empty of life, the sky empty, the earth empty.

His hunger did not bother him. His thirst did not bother him. His weakness did not bother him. Even the way his tongue was swelling up in his mouth did not bother him.

This answer to his prayers—nullity and void—was driving him into a blackness beyond despair.

All day he prayed. "Take pity on me."

All day the answer never changed. Nothingness.

As darkness fell, he wondered if the red and blue days were coming, the time when the moon would turn red and the sun blue and the world would come to an end.

He rejected this notion. Earth and Sky refused to answer one pleading boy—so what? That didn't mean Earth and Sky were mute forever. They were just giving the one boy, a contrary, mule-headed boy, what he deserved.

The second night Curly didn't fight sleep. It silenced the accusing voices in his head. Instead his dreams became galloping accusations.

Nothing changed on the third day. Sunup to midafternoon of eloquent praying. Sunup to midafternoon of eloquent silence.

He waited most of the day. Sometime between midafternoon and sundown he sat down and blew his breath out. He breathed in deeply, and out. Once more.

Then he surrendered.

He quit.

He had failed.

Walking, stumbling down the hill toward his pony, he seemed almost to be hearing two voices, both of them his own. As he fingered his light hair, one voice told him being different had nothing to do with it. He was not part *wasicu,* that wasn't it. He wasn't so strange. True, he didn't like paint, he didn't like beads, he didn't like dancing. He didn't want to trick himself up in fine clothes, the way most Lakota men did. That didn't matter. The loneliness he felt, the need always to be alone, didn't mean he was alien.

Even having Hawk in his breast did not mean he was a monster. Didn't other men feel the yearning to be out hunting, out raiding, free?

So he stumbled down the hill telling himself that he wasn't an alien, he was a Lakota.

The other voice didn't answer directly. It only whispered: *Failure, humiliation.* This voice would tell everyone, instantly, it would blurt out his shame, he knew it would, he could not imagine it doing otherwise. He would be unmasked, exposed as a fraud. Powerless, spiritless, a nothing, a void.

Which was what he deserved.

When they heard his tale of nothingness and silence, they would mock him, they would throw spears of laughter.

He had been foolish to go unprepared, to try without the guidance of his elders.

Unprepared? His mind threw the word back at him in echoes. *What arrogance! To assume preparation would make a difference. It's not preparation. It's just you.*

As he neared the river, he limped toward his hobbled horse. He was aching all over and dizzy. After three days without food or water, he felt giddy and weak. He took the pony by the bridle, but he felt too woozy to mount. Besides, his belly hurt. He sat against the sunpole tree. He would be stronger in a moment, clearer-headed in a moment.

He leaned back. He let his body flop against the tree and on the ground. He gave up. He shuddered with surrender. He had hurled himself into the maw, and he had failed. He gave up.

His eyes fluttered.

Gently, he felt a release of some kind, a loosening of grip, a lightening of heart.

Suddenly he . . . was it dreaming? Or seeing? He was wide awake. His eyes were open, and he felt intensely aware, and he saw . . .

SEEING

The horse trotted lightly, appearing to float, seeming not to touch the earth.

Now Curly saw it was his hobbled pony running free, trotting toward him, legs prancing, neck held high.

On its back a rider sat leaning forward, perfectly motionless on the moving mount, except that the fringe on the heels of his moccasins trembled.

What Curly saw seemed more real than real. The colors were brighter, edges sharper, motions more vivid, sounds clearer, the air somehow brilliant, the world radiant. Sight, hearing, and touch were keener, consciousness itself more vibrant.

Curly knew: This earth, this horse and rider, these grasses and trees, this sky and clouds were not the ordinary ones of every day, but the ones that live . . .

He was seeing beyond, seeing in a sacred way.

As though to offer proof, the pony changed from his pinto, the one hobbled by the sunpole tree, into a bay. And then into an appaloosa, a slate-blue grulla, a strawberry roan, and other colors in succession. Like a statement: "I am not a horse, but Horse. And luminous—aglow—for you who have eyes to see."

Curly looked closely at the rider, bright as a shining stone you held in your hand, one you turned to study its every facet. His hair was the color of light sand, and he wore it long and loose far below his waist. His hair was ornamented by a few beads and only one eagle feather, a feather hung upside down, in the position of the war eagle when it is about to kill. The rider's face and body bore no paint. He had on a shirt of pale deerskin and blue leggings, both unadorned. Yes, unadorned, though he seemed to be a man in the fullness of maturity.

He did have medicine. Behind his left ear was tied a small stone, Inyan. Beneath his left shoulder, slung over a thong from the opposite shoulder, one eagle feather adorned another stone creature, Inyan.

Into shadows rode the rider, forever and forever into shadows.

From the velvety blue-gray of these shadows came enemy fire, streaks flashing toward the rider, fast and dangerous, maybe arrows, maybe bullets. They flashed toward him, ominous in the air. But before touching his flesh they disappeared. Like raindrops from a high thundercloud over desert, they evaporated before striking the earth's flesh None tore his skin, none broke his bones, none shed his blood.

A man of great power, bullet-proof. Then why unadorned?

Now the rider—Rider—was stripped to nothing but a breechcloth and rode harder, faster, in a martial vigor. But hands flailed at him, clutched at him from behind, slowed him down. He tossed his arms backward like a man slinging off a tangling shirt. The hands kept pulling at him, holding him back, the hands of his own people. He felt threat in them. He shook them off and shook them off and rode on and rode on, but the hands did not relent. Rider shook and shook and shook at them. He feared the hands behind more than the bullets before.

Behind Rider a thunderstorm erupted. Dark clouds boiled, lightning flashed and gave birth to sound. A zigzag of lightning marred Rider's cheek like a wound. Hail spots welted his body.

Into clouds and shadows rode the rider, forever and forever into clouds and shadows.

The storm cleared, the hail spots faded, the day shone bright as polished metal. Horse and man flew forward. A hubbub of people rose up around him like a storm, his own people, talking and murmuring and grabbing at him. Over his head flew a hawk—a red-tailed hawk—and she cawed forth her warning to the world, KEE-ur, KEE-ur, KEE-ur, harsh and atavistic.

On flew Horse and Rider into the shadows, hooves floating above the earth, forever and ever on, as the hawk cried KEE-ur, KEE-ur above Rider's head.

In his chest Curly felt Hawk lift her wings and turn into the wind. She merged with the red-tailed hawk, and they were one. The weight within his ribs eased. In the whip of the wind, reckless and free, his heart ringed up the sky.

LOOKING AT THE SACRED DREAM

He lay there limp, his body profoundly stilled, his mind filled with a wonderful clarity, sweet and cool, like floating underwater in a crystalline stream.

It had not been a dream. He saw it all with his eyes open. He didn't see it obscurely, as if looking through a shard of creek ice, as he did some dreams. On the contrary, it was more vivid, brighter, more colorful than the world. More real than the world.

He lay there seeing it again in memory, savoring the details. He didn't try to decipher it yet, to sort out whatever meaning it might have for his life. He looked at it, over and over, feeling its textures and nuances, getting to know it.

He noticed Hawk in his heart. For once she was not aquiver, not restless, but at ease. But now he knew: Hawk did not have a song. Hawk was a predator, a creature wild and rapacious. Her cry was not music, but a war shriek.

It reminded him of once when they were going without food and water for a day. His *hunka* Buffalo Hump wet a stone in the creek and gave it to Curly to suck on. It was a smooth, flat rock, red as pipestone. Curly held it in his mouth and felt it with his tongue, sucked at its small shapes and curves and nuances. Later, when he took it out and looked at it, he realized that he knew much more about the stone than his eye could tell him. His tongue knew. And did not know *about* the stone. Knew the stone.

Buffalo Hump smiled at Curly, holding the stone in his fingers, and said it would make his mouth feel wet long after it had lost the film of moisture that came with it.

Remembering, Curly felt warm toward his *hunka*. That's what an older brother by choice did, guide his younger *hunka* toward becoming a man.

It was a grand way of being related, this custom of relative by choice, brother, uncle, aunt, father, son, daughter, any kind of relative.

Curly stretched, the feeling of his body and of the earth coming back to him.

Curly wanted to tell Buffalo Hump his vision; he wanted to share everything with his *hunka*.

He didn't know whether he should.

Again he blamed himself. If he hadn't gone onto the mountain without guidance, he would know what to do.

Now the feeling of clarity altered subtly. He had another feeling, shame. It was seeping into him like muddy water onto a fallen leaf.

He had come crying without preparation, without understanding. For three days he had been punished—the world and the powers that move it had turned their backs on him utterly. Then, abruptly, a vision had been thrown at his feet like rotten meat to a dog.

It was a difficult vision. He didn't know what it might mean. But he knew it was a curse, a well-deserved curse.

For the first time since his vision he stirred a little. It was as though his spirit was beginning to inhabit his body again. He shifted, wiggled, half-turned. Hawk was more or less calm on her perch in his heart.

"E-i-i-i," he said to himself, a murmur of regretful acceptance.

He recognized himself even in his curse. This was his way, to go alone, to do things his own way, which was often the wrong way.

A rueful smile glinted in his eyes.

RETURNING TO THE WORLD

The clappety-clap of horses' feet. Two horses, walking. Not far from the camp, not sneaking. Friends.

Curly saw no reason to rise. He felt, somehow, that if he didn't get his body all the way up, Hawk would sit easier. He wanted to feel tranquil a while yet. He wanted this freedom a little while longer.

Tasunke Witko looked down at his older son. The boy lay there limp, his body oddly loose and pliant, his eyes on his father, with a faraway look. The boy so often had a faraway look.

The father's first impulse was to vault off the pony and touch his son and make sure he was whole, still breathing, not bleeding. But he wasn't the boy's mother. Also, his older son kept his distance, wary, blaming.

He sat his pony and looked down. Buffalo Hump, his son's *hunka,* sat on the mount next to him. He didn't look into Buffalo Hump's face.

Tasunke Witko shuddered. "We've been looking for you for two days," he said. It sounded gruff even to him. He thought of adding that for two days his throat had clutched tight with fear. "There are Psatoka war parties everywhere." The Psatoka, Crows, their bitter enemies. He couldn't help making it sound like an accusation. No, they hadn't worried the first night Curly didn't come home. A youth might do that. But when he didn't show up the next day, they rode all over the countryside, looking not for the boy but for his body.

"I didn't realize," Curly said softly.

"You didn't realize." He nodded in exasperation. *Didn't you know that Bear-Scattering is dying? That there's no telling what the wasicu soldiers will do now? I was looking for your corpse.*

Tasunke Witko repeated, "You didn't realize."

Curly looked up at the face of his father and saw the anger. Hawk beat her wings nervously. His father was a holy man, a diviner. Did he know that Curly had seen beyond? Curly wanted to clasp his vision to his chest and turn his back, shield it from alien eyes.

You didn't realize. He heard not the words his father spoke, but the spirit, the hostility. Curly knew Tasunke Witko treated his sons with respect. That was why a small rebuke cracked like a whip. Curly felt the sting.

As for Buffalo Hump, no, his *hunka* would never let his anger toward Curly show. So the careful neutrality of his face was eloquent. He must agree with Tasunke Witko that Curly had acted badly.

"I'm sorry," Curly muttered. He let his voice show no emotion. He kept his face down. Were his secrets, his personal life, safe against his father's divination?

Curly got to his feet. He walked to his pony weakly, almost staggering. He knelt for steadiness while he took off the hobbles. He mounted without a word or a glance at the people closest in the world to him and looked at them, waiting.

"Let's go home," Tasunke Witko said.

Curly ignored his placating tone. He did not bother to say, "Yes," but he meant it. Yes, he would attend to the everyday world now. Yes, he had to, for now.

He would remember, every moment, the feeling of being Hawk in flight. He would hold her close, cherish that feeling.

He forbade his head to swivel back and look at the man he called *ate,* father. Curly would not tell that harsh man his vision. Or even that he had tried to see beyond. Certainly not what he had seen. He had never felt close to his father. Now he was furious at this man who kicked him with words, like kicking a camp dog.

He trembled. *Can I hide from a man who is a* wicasa wakan, *a seer?* he wondered.

In fact, he would not tell anyone about his vision. Not even his brother by choice. He would tell no one on earth.

His shame wouldn't let him. His pride wouldn't let him. His sense of sanctity wouldn't let him.

A LITTLE DEATH

Everyone was glad to let him have his privacy. Bear-Scattering was near death. The two bands were grieving, the entire Sicangu camp and the entire Oglala camp. Some were also politicking, trying to fix the blame.

Curly paid as little attention as possible. With Buffalo Hump he slept in a brush shelter and spent his visiting time at the lodge of Sinte Gleska, Spotted Tail, his uncle, the brother of his two mothers. Mostly he stayed to himself, so he could be still and peaceful inside and turn what had happened to him over and over, like a stone in his mouth.

Spotted Tail's lodge was full of grumbling. The people of both camps were divided. Everyone knew it was trouble. The soldiers had come into camp and the people killed all twenty-nine of them. Whatever the justification, that was the fact. The other soldiers would take revenge, that was the way it was.

The Sicangu had killed the soldiers. The Oglala had stood by and hadn't fought. That caused hard feelings between the peoples.

The soldiers would come after both bands, you could count on that.

Blame flew like blood during butchering. "This is what comes of making yourself a big, big man," Bear-Scattering's enemies said. At the big council three winters ago at Fort Laramie, he had let the Indian Superintendent appoint him big chief of all the Titunwan Lakota.

"You know he didn't want it," his relatives answered. "He tried to tell the *wasicu* it wouldn't work, the people didn't want a chief of chiefs. He said over and over that if he was chief of chiefs, someone jealous would kill him."

Everybody did know. In his short acceptance speech, they remembered, Bear-Scattering mentioned his impending death seven times. Funny thing was, he did what the *wasicu* wanted and kept trying to do it, and they were the ones who killed him.

Remembering was inconvenient for Bear-Scattering's enemies, though. They were stirring people up to drive his relatives out of the Sicangu camp. "The Bear-Scattering family has brought grief on our heads," they said. "Let them live with the Oglala. Those Oglala who didn't fight."

Bear-Scattering's male relatives answered that Bear-Scattering had been trying to make peace. That was why he was out in front, why he got shot.

But the women knew they were going to be kicked out of their own circle of lodges now.

Some people wanted to go back to Fort Laramie. Curly had heard the conversation a dozen times in a dozen forms:

"We've been around there for twenty winters."

"Sure, and it was trouble from the start."

"We need to trade."

"Blankets, pots."

"Guns, powder, and ball."

"Cloth and awls." No one said so, but some women would hardly be able to sew with bone awls anymore.

"Whiskey," said the opposition.

"Bull Bear." The head of all the Oglala had been killed in a drunken fight. Oglala killing each other, a terrible business. Most said that the one who shot him was Red Cloud, Mahpiya Luta, and that the old Bad Face chief Smoke was behind it. Regardless, Oglala killing the Oglala leader—

many people still resented and distrusted the Bad Faces because of it.

"Maybe now the *akicita* will come back." The warrior societies.

"All the old ways."

"And we can fight against the Psatoka," Crow enemies.

In the twenty winters the old ways had weakened. Ceremonies seemed half-hearted. Because the people had made an absurd bargain with the *wasicu* not to fight the Psatoka or the Susuni or anyone else, the *akicita* had lost members.

"*A-i-i-i.* How can a man make his way now?" Without combat as a field, a man would have no way to gain honors. A leader would have no way to harden and temper. The tribe would have no way to discover which men had strength of spirit.

The people who wanted to revive the old ways even said the bands should go far away from the Holy Road, to the old hunting grounds, and stay there. "Out of reach of the soldiers," they added ominously.

Curly brought himself back to now. Here was grief. Weeping, the women of Bear-Scattering's family packed their belongings in silence. When Bear-Scattering died, they would strike their lodges and go to the Oglala. It was terrible, the animosity of your neighbors in your time of heartache.

"Let's go help Black Twin," said Buffalo Hump.

Curly was sitting out along Snake Creek alone, worrying. He was pretending to straighten a shaft for an arrow. Work like that kept Hawk quiet and let Curly think. But actually he was worrying about Wakinyan Tanka, the fact that he'd dreamed of thunder and was too scared to say anything about it. He'd rubbed dust on his face and his clothes this morning, the way a *wakinyan* dreamer did to make himself look poor. Curly wondered if anyone would notice.

"Up!" said Hump. "Go!"

Hump was always full of enthusiasm. He also didn't mind those Bad Face youths. For some reason that band had a group of ambitious young men—glory hunters, Tasunke Witko called them—youths in their mid- and late teens who considered themselves destined to be leaders. Curly avoided them, all except He Dog, whom he liked. He Dog lived with Curly's band so much he seemed like a Hunkpatila anyway.

The truth was, Curly felt rivalry with the Bad Face youths. He thought they would compete with him for every honor, deprecate his achievements, and try to hold him back. Now that he'd seen Lakota hands hindering him in his vision, he suspected that the hands belonged to these Bad Face young men, Black Twin, White Twin, their brother No Water, and the brothers Pretty Fellow and Standing Bear, sons of Chief Bad Face.

Hump hoisted Curly up by the armpits and got him going. They walked from the circle of the Hunkpatila to the circle of the Bad Faces, stepping around and through the bustling life of the village, small children and dogs underfoot, women working and calling to each other and yelling at the children, a benign pandemonium. Here was a woman scraping a buffalo hide stretched on a pole frame. There Bad Heart Bull painting an elk hide. Here a grandmother forcing an awl through thick buffalo hide to make winter moccasins. There a man lashing a stone point to a spearhead with sinew and glue. Here a girl whipping a cur away from the stew pot. There two women building a low, smoky fire under a high rack loaded with raw meat to be jerked.

Curly liked the smells of a village, the odor of wood smoke and lodge covers of buffalo skin, the pungency of green hides being scraped, dehaired, or tanned, the aromas of food being butchered and prepared, the strong scent of blood being let. Even the excrement smells of the dogs and horses and people were part of it, and as long as you didn't camp too long in one place, not rank. He had never been more surprised than when a trader out of Laramie told him the worst thing about an Indian village was the stink. To Curly what stank was Laramie, with its outhouses.

He Dog stood next to the others, a thick, chunky fellow smiling at Curly. Tall and imposing, Black Twin held a piece of rawhide shaped for a shield and waited with a glower. Hump wouldn't mind. Hump kept himself genial toward everyone. He was tall, good-looking, somehow glorious—everyone liked Hump.

"Why did you bring him?" said Pretty Fellow teasingly, inclining his head at Curly. "He can't make anything beautiful."

The young men all chuckled, but Hump said gruffly, "Enough."

Though Curly had not heard any report, what was happening was obvious. Black Twin had seen beyond. Now he had made a shield and wanted to paint it with a picture he'd seen in his vision. Hump was good with paints and would mix fine, bright colors easy to apply to the rawhide.

Curly felt a pang. The Bad Face youths who had seen beyond hadn't sneaked away to do it and so could proclaim it. Black Twin would be honored now, an honor Curly deserved but couldn't claim. The twins were a couple of winters older than Curly, but still . . .

Hawk was quiet.

Hump set a hide on the ground and unfolded it. Pretty Fellow crowded close to watch—he liked to wear good-looking clothes and make handsomely decorated weapons and ceremonial objects. The *wasicu* at Laramie were always telling him how handsome he looked all decked out. They also treated him as important, the son of a chief. Pretty Fellow was one who probably would not want to leave the fort permanently for the old hunting grounds.

In the bundle Hump had red, ocher, and white clay and bitterbrush, lichens, raspberries, and blueberries to make other shades. Plus fat to mix the pigments with, forming thick liquids you could brush on with the softened and pounded tip of a bird's wing bone.

"There's a trick to getting colors to take to rawhide right," said Hump, and began to show them. All the young men watched keenly, except Curly. He was only half-interested. He had seen no shield in his vision. One day he would be painting black slashes of lightning and blue spots of hail on his face and body, but not yet. To do that would be to admit he was a *wakinyan* dreamer.

The young men were busy mixing paints under Hump's instruction.

"Brother," said Hump enthusiastically to Curly, "try it."

Curly took some blueberries and fat and pretended to work. This would make the color of his hail spots one day. He didn't want to think about it now. He was scared.

Lightning and thunder—called lightning-gives-birth-to-sound—were dangerous. If you dreamed of *wakinyan*, its power was in you. In ordinary life it was two-faced: It brought the rain, yes, but it struck people and killed them. In the life of a *wakinyan* dreamer, it could likewise be grandly benevolent and madly destructive. Dreaming of *wakinyan* was riding the whirlwind.

Curly remembered scrupulously what he saw:

> Behind Rider a thunderstorm erupted. Dark clouds roiled, lightning flashed and gave birth to sound. A zigzag of lightning rose on Rider's cheek like a wound. Hail spots welted his body.

Curly knew what a *wakinyan* dreamer had to do. He had to tame the terrible power a little. He had to make offerings to the Wakinyan, to win their benevolence.

That would require him to give a *heyoka* ceremony, at least. It might require something more. The Wakinyan could make a demand of you, and you had to carry it out. It could even be that you killed someone. It could even be that you were *heyoka* and did things backward your whole life.

Curly would hate that.

On the other hand, you got power. Sometimes a *wakinyan* dreamer could make an approaching storm split in half and go right around a village, leaving it dry and peaceful in the midst of a storm.

Black Twin said coolly, "Hey, friend, are you going to make that blue or not?"

Curly looked at him. Both the twins were quick to see insult in whatever Curly did. Sensitive about being shunned as Bad Faces, they took offense at everything.

"He doesn't want to learn to mix paints," said Pretty Fellow. The handsome youth sang lightly:

"Our cousin is poor, terribly poor.
He dresses so plain, the same as naked.
He doesn't love beauty—
He has nothing, owns nothing,
He makes nothing beautiful."

Curly turned his back to the teasing, but he still heard the snickers. Hump always said they were just chuckles, but Curly heard snickers.

It was worse now. He had dreamed of Wakinyan. He had to dress shabbily, he had to diminish his body, play down his appearance.

Hawk was kneading Curly's heart with her claws.

Curly backed off and watched. His mind was far away. His watchfulness was on Hawk, who was calming down.

He asked himself, *So why don't you set down your burden? Tell your father about your vision. Then tell the dream interpreters he sends you to. Then you'll be ragged-looking, but people will respect it.*

Because I wouldn't throw my vision in the dirt before these idiots, Curly told himself.

The youths burst into laughter at something Hump said.

No, that wasn't right. Curly wasn't mad enough to lie to himself.

Because my father gave me a tongue-lashing I didn't deserve.

You can do better than that.

Because I was an idiot and went unprepared.

Closer, but only half-true.

Because I've never felt close to my father.

That's part of it.

Because I am ashamed.

You're stalling.

Because the dream is too big for me. It will overwhelm me.

That's pretty close. You know, since you won't hold a heyoka ceremony, the Wakinyan may kill you.

Hawk prodded at his heart with her claws.

Cries, women's cries. All the young men looked toward the far end of the Sicangu lodge circle, their work limp in their hands. Women were running around like foolish prairie hens. Their wails intensified. Bear-Scattering's women.

So the chief was gone. The smell of his dying came back to Curly's nose. Rottenness, foulness. He felt himself quiver a little.

All the young men stood there, helpless, foolish.

Now they would put the one who was a chief on a scaffold for his journey to the northern land beyond the pines. Women would chop off their hair. His wives might hack off fingers or slash their arms in grief. They would keep his spirit in a special lodge for a year and then release it.

Yes, Curly would rather die than tell his dream.

His own death stank in his nostrils.

APPRENTICESHIP

"Unci," he began.

He sat on her robes in front of his grandmother and looked into her eyes, blank and indifferent. Then he launched forth, pushing a canoe into an unknown river, the roar of rapids audible.

"I have seen beyond." He waited, he didn't know why. "I have seen beyond." Maybe the lightning would strike him dead. Hadn't he seen the lightning power? He felt his stomach lurch. Forward into the rapids now.

"Unci, I saw and heard *wakinyan*." He let the memory come and the terror of these awful powers of the west. "Lightning and thunder. But I am not to be a contrary, Unci. No, a warrior." He held this thought still for a moment. He was afraid. Lightning and thunder—what did it mean? He didn't want to spend his life as a clown made sacred by a *wakinyan* vision.

He fumbled his way forward. "I saw myself as a warrior riding into battle. I appeared to be at the height of my powers. What was strange, Unci," and the word "strange" chilled him, "was that I, he, wore almost no adornment. One eagle feather, a few beads, nothing more. No scalps. No paint to show my deeds. Like a man who had done nothing. Or never revealed what he'd done."

He hesitated and then blurted it out. "Except hail spots on my face." The fearful powers of the west again.

He had decided before he started not to mention the two Inyan creatures. You always kept something back for yourself alone.

"I had a great power, Unci," he said in a whisper. "Bullets and arrows couldn't hurt me. I rode in front, and they didn't touch me." He was awed by this. "But my own people's hands grabbed at me from behind, and I was afraid of them."

Suddenly panic hit him. He looked hard into his grandmother's eyes in the half-light of the tipi. Did she understand? Maybe she would walk around the village telling everyone at the top of her voice. Maybe she would say for everyone to stay away from the one who might bring *wakinyan* down on the village.

Her face was unmoving, stonelike.

But this was a botched job, a bad idea. He couldn't tell what he had seen beyond, not really, not yet, not . . . He wanted to be finished, done, outside, out in the sunlight. He jumped to his feet.

He made himself stop. He touched his grandmother's arm. "Thank you, Unci," he said softly. "Thank you."

* * *

He took a tone that set aside the bantering, the comradeship, the fun. He needed Hump to take him completely seriously. *"Kola,"* he said, "listen to me. I want you to teach me to be a warrior."

Buffalo Hump looked at him strangely. Hump had been teaching Curly the advanced skills of the warpath and the hunt steadily for two winters. Curly looked at his *hunka*'s handsome face and his heroic physique and took confidence. Hump could do things.

"I mean a warrior beyond what any good man is, far beyond. I mean . . ." He hesitated. "There's something I cannot say here." He looked into Hump's eyes and saw only understanding and willingness. "Your *tunkasila,*" Grandfather, "taught you secrets, you said, secrets of the warrior's mind. Great secrets. Will you teach them to me?" He didn't have to say that the men of his own family were *wicasa wakan* more than warriors.

Hump got to his feet. He grinned down at Curly. "You want to start now?"

"Stillness and watchfulness," said Hump. "Breathing and awareness. Two ways of saying the same things."

He got Curly to sit beside him on a rock in the sun. They made no effort at all to conceal themselves. "Pay attention to your own breathing," said Hump.

They sat. Curly fidgeted. Curly paid attention to his breath, in and out, in and out, and sat more still. After a while he felt very, very still, like part of the rock.

Then he noticed the changes. The winged and the four-legged peoples began to stir again. Though at first they had fallen silent, now the birds were singing, the squirrels darting about, the chipmunks and rockchucks feeding nearby. It was like being part of a village of animals.

They sat. Breathed. Sat. Breathed. Kept very still. And from that stillness Curly began to see. He saw everything, even the slightest change in the world in front of his eyes. A hawk circling in the hunt. A deer slipping out of the trees to graze. A duck feeding quietly, undisturbed. Insects crawling. And he knew that when he saw the pattern of the life in front of himself, he would see the telling changes in it. A flight of ducks that had been scared up—by what? A silence of squirrels that meant they were wary—of what? And he began to know what he was not seeing.

That first day he didn't get far. After several days, though, Curly was amazed at how keen his perceptions had become. Hump said that with daily practice they would become much, much more keen. Then Curly could use them in war. Become so still that no man could see him, so aware none could approach him, and learn to move as invisibly as the wind.

They worked every day on breathing and stillness and awareness, which Hump said were the greatest of the warrior secrets.

Curly already had the skills of making weapons. He could make a bow from the best bow wood. He could straighten the shafts of arrows and fletch them with feathers. He could flake arrowheads and the heads of spears. He knew how to lash a point onto an arrow or spear or a heavy stone onto the end of a war club.

So now they practiced fighting skills. Curly and Hump worked on getting four arrows in flight before the first one hit and putting all four into a small circle. They threw the metal tomahawk at measured distances and then at random distances, putting on the right spin to make it strike blade first. They hurled the spear at trees. They swung the war club so that the strength of the arm truly went into its head at the moment the blow struck. They practiced a little with Hump's rifle, but powder and lead were too precious to waste. Curly decided he would trade for a pistol as soon as he could.

Curly wanted to practice actual fighting, but since Hump and Curly were *hunka,* they couldn't fight each other, even in play. So they got other young men to practice the kicking game and wrestling and other kinds of combat with them, sometimes the youths of their own Hunkpatila band, Young Man-Whose-Enemies-Are-Afraid-of-His-Horses,

Black Elk, and Lone Bear, and sometimes the Bad Faces, the twins and their brother No Water, Pretty Fellow, and his brother Standing Bear, and He Dog.

Curly was the smallest. He was short, skinny, and stringy-muscled and envied the splendid body of his *hunka*. No Water was the biggest of the bunch, tall and thick like a tree, maybe a little slow.

The play fighting got rough sometimes, and Curly got the impression that Pretty Fellow wouldn't have minded hurting him a little. Maybe none of the Bad Faces would have minded. But Hump urged Curly to understand that such hidden feelings hurt the warrior. The warrior's love was not the damage he did to his opponent, but the qualities the combat brought forth in him—high courage, precise and rhythmic movement, the joy of risk.

Hump showed him how the honors of a warrior reflected these excellences. The highest honor was not to kill your enemy, but to strike him with your hand, which made you most vulnerable. The second highest, to strike him with your coup stick. Killing was honorable but might show a desperation to end the danger to yourself. All honors, Hump taught, reflected not what you did to your enemy, but the power, the medicine, the spirit you exhibited within.

Curly loved it all. When he practiced for war or for the hunt, Hawk was peaceful in his chest.

Sometimes Curly and Hump simply talked about the qualities a warrior cultivated. Hump emphasized the four virtues, courage, generosity, fortitude, and wisdom, and how each should be manifested by the warrior. The warrior's concerns were more personal, more individual, than those of the *akicita* men and the Big Bellies, Hump said. The warrior fought and hunted to find exhilaration of spirit. The *akicita,* warrior societies made responsible for orderliness and the welfare of the band, sometimes had to control the impulses of the warriors. Likewise the Big Bellies, the chiefs, thought not of the glory of the individual warrior, but of how that spirit could be used to benefit the band. When a young man had finished his years as a warrior, he might become a Big Belly and be obliged to think of these larger issues.

"I don't think I will ever see the end of my warrior days." He looked at his friend with mixed feelings. He didn't want to tell even Hump about Rider and his seeing beyond. Yet . . . Curly said, "All my life I have known in my heart that my destiny is war."

Hump nodded, waited, nodded again. Curly could see that he was wondering whether Curly had a spirit guide that instructed him, or had seen beyond. But Hump gave his *hunka* the respect of not asking questions.

Curly thought of all the maneuvering Bear-Scattering had done, consulting with his own people and with the *wasicu* agent and the soldier chiefs, persuading people, getting people to agree, planning—conniving, as it seemed to Curly. He thought, worse, of the maneuvering done by those who wanted to replace Bear-Scattering as leader when he died. "I don't want ever to be a headman," he said.

Hump just nodded again. "Some men are born for the rapture of the fight itself," he said.

When Curly and Hump were riding back from a long day's hunt with no meat, several Bad Face youths fell in with them.

"The deer are gone," Pretty Fellow complained. He didn't like to hunt anyway. At the fort he hung around the soldiers and their wives a lot. He was learning English. He was the son of the leader of the band, Bad Face. He said the new leaders of the band would need to know English.

"The deer are around," said No Water. "Just spooky."

Black Twin and White Twin nodded. The twins had a rivalry to see who was the best hunter. Those two had a rivalry for everything.

Curly didn't like the way Pretty Fellow was looking at him. He was deliberately wearing poor clothing again and had rubbed dust on himself in the manner of a *wakinyan* dreamer. Pretty Fellow seemed to think Curly was comical.

Curly wished he and Hump could stay clear of these Bad Faces in general. He kept thinking of the hands of his own people in the dream, somehow bringing him harm. But he couldn't tell Hump that.

The Bad Faces asked Buffalo Hump if things had really changed, and Hump said they had, for sure. The last five winters, since all the *wasicu* started charging through the country like madmen, headed for the country by the western water, everywhere to get the yellow metal, the game had been scarce and elusive. Without game, people were going to go hungry this winter. Not only the Lakota, but their friends and allies the Sahiyela and Mahpiyato—whom the *wasicu* called Cheyenne and Arapaho—too.

"*A-i-i-i*, Curly," said No Water, "can you put your ear to the ground and hear the buffalo?" The people had run off from Laramie without their rations of food, and they needed a good fall hunt. "*A-i-i-i*, Curly," the big fellow repeated, grinning at his comrades, "can you? Can your father, the *wicasa wakan?*"

Curly had nothing to say. He didn't have the medicine of seeing things far away, and No Water knew it. Neither did Curly's father. Tasunke Witko was not that kind of *wicasa wakan.*

"When we find the buffalo," No Water went on, "I'll get one my size, and Curly will get one his size." No Water thumped his big chest, and all the youths but Hump and Curly laughed.

Pretty Fellow was making mocking eyes at Curly now. Then he tossed his head around in the air with a grin and began to hum. Everyone wondered what he was doing. Finally he crooned a teasing song:

> *"Our cousin has hair the color of dust.*
> *His fathers,*
> *Were they shaggy, hairy, dirty wasicu?"*

All the Bad Face boys grinned and looked sideways at Curly. The boy felt his face flush. He gripped the reins until his knuckles turned white. They were almost into camp, and Curly thought someone might have overheard the song. Tomorrow it would be all over the village anyway.

Then he saw that Buffalo Hump was looking at him differently, too, challengingly. Curly understood. Hump wanted to see whether he handled this like a grown-up or a child.

Hawk lurched at her leg ties, flapped her wings, and shrieked.

Hump wants me to ignore this teasing, thought Curly, *but Hawk wants me to fight.* He spoke in a casual tone. "Maybe one of you Bad Faces would like to practice fighting a little."

The Bad Face youths looked at each other, all smiled, and all said at once, "Me."

Hump was not surprised. He held up a hand. "Wait," he said. He studied everyone. "Bad Faces, you pick your champion. Curly will pick the weapons."

The Bad Faces all looked at each other again and as one said, "No Water," and laughed.

Hump nodded. As he expected, they had picked the biggest, to take the most advantage of Curly's slightness. Now Hump wanted to see how wise his *hunka* would be when confronted with this challenge. "Weapons?" Hump asked.

"Knives," said Curly.

Hump smiled at his *hunka*. His anger was not running ahead of his wisdom.

The preparations took a few minutes. The combatants wrapped their blades with strips of deer hide, so neither would get cut. They stripped to breechcloth and moccasins. Hump went into the village circle and came back with a handful of wet ashes. "Here," he said. "Put this on the knife edges. That way we can see when someone gets hit." They rubbed the soot on the deerskin coverings.

Hump backed off and gave the sign to begin. The fighters circled each other. The Bad Face youths looked on in a group, smirking. Black Elk, Young Man-Whose-Enemies, Lone Bear, and Horn Chips came up to watch the fun.

Yes, yes, Hump thought. Curly was staying well away, knife held low in his left hand. He would dart in and out. No Water's strength would do him no good this way, and his size would make him slow. Curly had chosen perfectly.

Hump wondered what Curly's being left-handed would do to No Water. The Bad Face might not have faced a left-hander before. Hump had taught Curly to take advantage of that.

No Water jumped forward and thrust. Curly knocked the blade hand aside, slid to the left, and flicked his blade at No Water's face. The big man jumped back, a black slash on his cheek. He looked furious.

The Hunkpatila, Black Elk, Lone Bear, and Young Man-Whose-Enemies, let out a cheer. Horn Chips looked on impassively.

Hump thought, *Don't build up the fire in him.* Hump wasn't sure whether Curly had gone high because the left arm was protecting the gut or deliberately to shame No Water by marking him.

His knife well down, No Water suddenly charged.

Curly kicked the knife arm away. "Beautiful!" Hump wanted to shout. No Water hurtled past, carried by his momentum. Curly cut a black gash down his side.

Hump looked hard at Curly's face. Yes, his *hunka* was full of cold fury. Hump wondered who would win, Curly or his anger.

"Be careful," Hump wanted to warn Curly. "The bull may charge again. He is not tricky, but he is dangerous."

Curly stepped slowly toward No Water, feinting left and right with his hips and head. The knife blade stayed still, point up.

Uncertain, No Water backed up.

In a flash Curly knocked No Water's blade aside and hit him twice on the chest. Soot blackened each nipple.

Hump was thrilled at his pupil's quickness.

Black Elk and Young Man-Whose-Enemies minced like women and made the trilling sound mockingly.

No Water exploded. He gave a huge yell and bolted forward, straight at Curly, knife high this time.

Curly ducked under the blade. He came up under the armpit and let No Water ride onto his shoulder. They toppled, Curly going backward. Into the dust they fell, No Water on top. The big man's gut bounced off the point of Curly's knife.

"That's enough!" yelled Hump. No need to say that Curly had won, that with an exposed tip the blow would have been fatal.

Rolling off Curly, No Water jabbed him in the face with an elbow. "Didn't mean to," he said baitingly.

Hump saw Curly start to flash in anger and then control himself. Good.

"That *hurt*!" complained No Water, rubbing his gut and scowling at Curly.

Curly said nothing.

"Did you come to gloat?" Black Twin asked Young Man-Whose-Enemies challengingly.

But the youth was not the son of a chief for nothing. "No," he said, "we came to tell you that Horn Chips has looked into Inyan and seen that the buffalo are at the forks of Rattlesnake Creek. We're going with the wolf," scout, "to make sure."

"Why don't some of you Bad Faces go, too?" said Chips. He was related to both bands but lived with the Bad Face people.

"I'll go," said Black Twin quickly. White Twin said the same. They looked at their brother expectantly, but No Water walked off with an angry look, rubbing his belly.

* * *

As the group headed back toward camp, Horn Chips said to Curly, "Come with me."

Curly started to speak, but he didn't know what to say. He shrugged. He started to speak again, and nothing came out.

Chips just turned his back and set off for the Bad Face circle.

Scared, Curly followed Chips to his lodge. The *wicasa wakan* sat behind his center fire and got out his *canupa* and lit it. Curly noticed how he watched the shifting shapes of the smoke as they wafted toward the center hole. He wondered if Chips saw the future in the smoke, which was the breath of the earth.

Chips patted the ground and Curly sat next to him. Chips burned a little sweetgrass to invite the presence of the spirits. Curly accepted the *canupa* and smoked. When he was finished, Chips said, "You must tell your father what you dreamed."

Curly gushed his breath out. He had been afraid Chips would make him tell his vision right now, to Chips. He was half-afraid of the *wicasa wakan*. The man had power, and all power cut both ways, for good and ill.

Curly's throat tried to squeeze shut before the words could get out. "I understand, Cousin." Having to tell his father was not a bit better.

"When you've told your father," Chips said, "come to me. I have things to show you."

Curly felt riven. Fear, panic, excitement, he couldn't tell his own feelings. Hawk was clasping and unclasping her claws in Curly's heart.

Chips knew the spirit power of Inyan, Stone, a great power, hard to control. Curly hoped that wasn't what Chips wanted to show him.

"That's all, Cousin," said the holy man gently.

Curly hurried across the Bad Face circle through the darkness toward his father's lodge. His legs felt unsteady. He kept an eye out for the Bad Face youths other than He Dog. Curly was sure they would dislike him more now.

It showed what gaining power did to you, any kind of power.

Hawk pranced within him, tense.

At the Hunkpatila camp he stopped and let himself be aware of standing within the circle of this village, of sleeping in the circle of his family's tipi, of living in the big circle of the Oglala and the bigger circle of all the Titunwan Lakota. He looked up at the moon. He lived within the circles made by Moon and Sun every day. This was all a sacred hoop, and it was his life.

He murmured into the infinite night, "I should tell my father my *wakinyan* dream."

Curly stood there looking up, waiting for an answer.

He heard nothing.

Hawk dug her claws into his chest.

So he wouldn't tell, not yet. He didn't know why, but he didn't think Hawk wanted him to.

Yes, for Hawk I will defy Horn Chips.

LEAVING HOME

The hunt was good, lots of meat and robes for the Oglala and Sicangu. Curly got a four-teeth, a four-year-old, the best for robes. When his two mothers had the meat on a travois and headed back to camp, he nudged his pony alongside Buffalo Hump. His *hunka*'s eyes were glittering. "They say the Sahiyela and the Mahpiyato are hungry." Their friends the Cheyenne and Arapaho had stayed back at the soldier fort after the troubles. "The *wasicu*'s rations weren't enough." Hump's eyes glanced toward Curly with a smile and went back to their restless watching.

Curly just nodded. *Hunka* didn't have to put everything into words. When you loafed around the *wasicu* fort, you starved. When you got away from them and hunted in the old way, your children were so full their bellies pooched out.

Tasunke Witko rode up alongside. They were heading back to camp slowly.

Curly's father had that look, the one that meant "I'm worried about my older son." Curly could read his looks instantly. He knew them all, and they were all objectionable.

"You did very well hunting," he said. "Corn will make you a fine robe from the four-teeth." Some young men would get their mothers or sisters to paint the robe or bead or quill it. Curly would keep his plain.

"We will eat the tongue tonight," said Tasunke Witko. Tongue was Curly's favorite cut.

The youth still didn't look up, keeping his eyes on the ground, flicking them around toward the horizons but not toward his father. "I'm going to eat with Spotted Tail," the boy said. "I'm going to stay with Spotted Tail for a while." He kicked his pony to a canter, and Hump followed.

Tasunke Witko looked after Curly, the slim form fading in the dusk. This wasn't like his elder son. First he stayed away from camp for three days, scaring everybody, and acted remote and indifferent when they found him. When he came back, he lived with his brother by choice and seldom visited his parents' lodge. He wandered around camp distracted, looking broody. He dressed as though he belonged to a very poor family. Now the boy was going to live with his uncle Spotted Tail. Anywhere but home, it felt like.

This boy . . . One day a great name would be passed down to Curly, father to son. Tasunke Witko, His Crazy Horse, the third consecutive eldest son of that name.

He had to earn it, naturally. Tasunke Witko knew the boy would earn his name, many times over.

But why was he so odd? Always courteous but never really present in his mind. Thirsty to learn, but never satisfied, never pleased with himself. His eyes far away, always listening for something in the distance. Troubled, as though with a pain he never spoke about.

Tasunke Witko thought he knew part of why the boy

was strange. The woman who gave birth to him was dead. He had two mothers now, and it was all the same, they were real mothers. But Tasunke Witko thought Curly was constantly remembering the woman who gave him birth, longing for her.

Tasunke Witko held her face in his mind. He would never speak her name again, but her face was with him all the time and sometimes the feel of her next to him in the robes at night. Rattling Blanket Woman, that was the name he would never speak and Curly would never utter again. A Mniconjou, the daughter of Lone Horn, a chief, but that was not why he had married her. She was an imp. Her face, round as a plate, was all mischief and play. Even respect for her husband didn't stop her practical jokes. To her everything was play, even what went on in the buffalo robes. Especially what went on in the robes. The children loved her. Tasunke Witko loved her.

Curly was just six when she died, his sister, Kettle, two years older.

The trouble came when Tasunke Witko's brother He Crow got killed by the Psatoka, the enemies the *wasicu* called the Crows, in battle. He was just two years younger than Tasunke Witko, both in their early thirties. Tasunke Witko took an oath of revenge and cut a bloody path through the Psatoka men for six moons. When he got back from slaking his blood thirst the last time, Rattling Blanket Woman was dead.

She had gone crazy, they said, in her grief for her brother-in-law. Or from loneliness, thought Tasunke Witko, from missing the husband who was never home anymore, even when he was in the lodge, a husband who had abandoned her in mind and body to keep company with the dead. Either way, she killed herself.

The six-year-old Curly came into the tipi with Plum and found his mother hanging from a lodge pole by the neck, her head twisted, her body twisting slowly.

Tasunke Witko knew what the faces of hanged people looked like, what Curly must have seen. But he could never get the boy to talk about it. And Plum dropped into madness.

It was not so bad for Tasunke Witko. He married Red Grass and Corn, two Sicangu women, sisters of Spotted Tail, whom everyone admired. Together they gave his children mothers, and one bore him a second son. But Tasunke Witko had never stopped worrying about Curly. The boy seemed half here and half . . . somewhere. Tasunke Witko imagined sometimes that boy had a melancholy spirit song in his head and even when he talked to you, he was always listening to that music.

Tasunke Witko wondered if the one who once gave Curly suck was singing the song.

For whatever reason, the boy's mind was always somewhere else. Now it was worse. He was sure Curly was avoiding him. Tasunke Witko hoped it was just the surliness of a boy in the becoming-a-man time.

He hoped so, but he didn't think so.

He called in his mind after his riding-away son: *Stranger, stranger, come back!*

Curly sat in the lodge of his uncle Spotted Tail, listening to the men, his uncle and Little Thunder, the war leader and the chief of this band of Sicangu. Curly liked to be able to sit quietly behind the men, between them and his uncle's four wives and all the children, in the dark away from the fire, where no one would look oddly at him.

The men were busy with reports of troubles. The *wasicu* were furious about the killing of the twenty-nine soldiers. The bands would have to stay away from Laramie, which meant losing this winter's annuities. Some of the people wanted to go back to their old northern hunting grounds for good. Others, even those who thought the soldiers had gotten what they deserved, wanted to make up with the *wasicu* and get the gifts and be able to trade.

"We're entitled to those goods," said Little Thunder. The annuities were what the *wasicu* paid them back for the disappearing buffalo. That was the deal of the big papers signed at Fort Laramie three years ago: The *wasicu* could keep the Holy Road and travel on it. For all the game the emigrants killed, the *wasicu* would pay wagonloads of goods. It amounted only to a dollar or two per Lakota and often was paid late, short, or not at all.

"If they don't deliver them, or too little and too late," said Spotted Tail, "we'll go take them." He smiled in a bloody-minded way. "Or just take the money."

Little Thunder chuckled when Spotted Tail said this. He and several other warriors had robbed a mail coach this autumn. Among the valuables they had found was lots of paper money. Not knowing what it was, they had scattered it in the wind. When the traders told them in an incredulous tone that it was $20,000, they had a good laugh. The *wasicu* and his money. But you could use it to get the annuities they cheated you out of.

Back there in the dark Curly liked his uncle's attitude. Simple. Clear. Strong. Based on what was right.

Spotted Tail had a fine contempt for *wasicu*. Something in Curly celebrated this contempt.

"We'll talk to the agent next summer," said Little Thunder, getting ready to leave.

"You talk," said Spotted Tail with a smile. "I'd rather go hunting. And stay sober."

Spotted Tail hated whiskey. Curly did too. He'd seen it make Lakota kill each other.

He moved up beside his uncle next to the fire. Spotted Tail lit the *canupa* and without a word handed it to Curly. One thing Curly liked about this man was that he knew how to share a companionable silence.

After a while Spotted Tail spoke up. "Would you like to spend the winter with us?"

"Yes." He was grateful to his uncle for understanding.

"Give it to me." Curly handed Spotted Tail the *canupa*, which had gone out. "What do you want to do this winter?"

"Keep working with Hump on the skills and spirit of a warrior. And with you."

"Here." Curly took the *canupa* filled with *cansasa*, tobacco. "You want to go live near the fort and learn the *wasicu* ways?"

Curly shook his head. "They're disgusting and dangerous."

"Anything else you want?"

Curly picked up an ember with sticks and dropped it on top of the tobacco. He drew in hard, watched the fire glow, and let his mind go upward in a prayer with the smoke.

"I don't know." He shrugged.

He did know. He would remember what he had seen beyond, picture by picture. He would ponder the old ways, which were disappearing, the ceremonies less often performed, the *akicita* weakening, fewer men gaining fighting honors. He would consider the danger of the *wakinyan,* and Chips' instruction to tell his father. He would try to figure out why he wasn't going to tell anyone.

"Hu ikhpeya wicayapo!" the young men cried, meaning, "Let's whip the enemies so bad we could bugger 'em." And they smiled fiercely at each other and slapped shoulders.

Curly watched with envy. He wanted to go to war and wasn't invited. He thought he had prepared himself meticulously under Hump's tutelage. He had seen himself as Rider, riding into war. In war Hawk would be at ease in his breast.

Some Lakota were concerned that they'd promised the *wasicu* when they signed the paper that they wouldn't go raiding against the other tribes anymore. To Curly that was no issue. To begin with, the *wasicu* didn't keep their promises. More important, how else could a man show his spirit, show he was a man? How could a young man with a vision calling him to war . . . ?

The Bad Face warrior Red Cloud took some of the young men against the Psatoka, all Bad Faces, including He Dog, the twins, and No Water, going as warriors.

Though he was He Dog's age, sixteen, Curly wasn't invited.

It was the Moon of Shedding Ponies. Not until after the moons of lightning and rain, the sun dance, and into the Middle Moon, July, Wicokannanji, did he get his chance. Then Little Thunder and Spotted Tail decided to go east, where the Two Circle People, the ones the *wasicu* called Omaha, would go away from their reservation for their summer buffalo hunt. Aside from the leaders, all the raiders were to be youths. "Why don't you come along?" said Spotted Tail.

Curly stood rigid in the sunshine, waiting for the words he was afraid of. Such as, "You can hold the horses," meaning wait while the others fought. Or, "You can go for water," meaning sneak to the creek at night to fetch drink for the real warriors.

The words didn't come. So the invitation was to fight for the first time. This was his mothers' brother offering, the man who traditionally helped teach you shooting and tracking and hunting and war. He was one of the men you called *leksi*, a mother's brother. Now his uncle was saying, "Come show us you are a warrior." Curly was barely able to murmur, "Yes."

Curly ran fast to his lodge to tell Tasunke Witko and his mothers that he was going raiding against the Omaha. When he got inside, he looked at them and couldn't say it. He sat down. He shared a little food with them, and his parents talked idly. Hawk was restless on her perch. They said they were going in to Laramie to see about the rations.

Finally Curly said softly, "My mothers' brother has asked me to go with him to fight the Two Circle People."

The three parents looked at each other. Curly supposed they were happy but also afraid for him. They didn't understand.

He stood up. "I think Hump and I will stay with my uncle the rest of the summer," he said softly. He pushed the lodge flap open and walked into the sunlight. He felt set free.

FIRST WAR

They went to war this Middle Moon in the spirit of a lark. Spotted Tail and Little Thunder took their wives with them, as though to say, "These Pani and these Two Circle People," whom the *wasicu* called the Pawnee and the Omaha, "they're nothing. There's so little threat in fighting them, we'll even take our women along." Buffalo Hump went, too, and Young Man-Whose-Enemies, Lone Bear, Black Elk, and from the Bad Face band He Dog.

Spotted Tail was a genial man, strong, stocky, with a slow, wide, easy smile. He loved to play practical jokes on his brothers-in-law and his nephews. He seemed to think everything in the world was an occasion for fun.

He seemed so big, so burly in the upper body, so friendly, so protective that Curly always felt small and taken care of around him. Curly saw his father's brothers constantly, the ones he called *ate,* "father," in the Lakota way, Long Face, Spotted Crow, Bull Head, and Ashes. Of his mothers' brothers, he saw Spotted Tail most often. Curly's other favorites, the Mniconjou brothers of his blood mother, Rattling Blanket Woman, Lone Horn and Touch-the-Sky, usually camped far to the north. But the Hunkpatila were often with Spotted Tail's band. The first time Curly rode among the buffalo, he had felt sure that if a herd father, a big bull, fell on him, Spotted Tail would simply lift it off, chuckling at his own strength.

Sometimes Curly had trouble realizing that this man was not only one of the main war leaders of the Sicangu, but a shirt wearer as well, one of the four men not yet Big Bellies but responsible for the welfare of all the people. It was a hard job, putting the whole tribe before your family, even before yourself. Spotted Tail seemed too much interested in having fun for all that.

When the party got near the Loup River, Little Thunder and some others said they wanted to ride to the Pani earth lodges to steal some horses. The Sicangu thought the Pani truly a vile people. What marked them irredeemably as savages was their taste for capturing girls of the Lakota and Sahiyela and sacrificing their lives to Morning Star.

But Spotted Tail looked at Curly and his Hunkpatila comrades. Everyone was holding horses or getting mounted. Spotted Tail grinned, seeming to ponder the fun of committing mayhem here against the fun of committing mayhem there. "Let's not overwhelm the poor Pani with numbers this time," he said. He jerked his head sideways and smiled with one corner of his mouth. "Let's go against the Two Circle People." He seemed to have something delicious in mind.

They found the camp easily enough—the Two Circle People were away from their river cornfields to hunt—and Spotted Tail said they'd try stealing a few Two Circle mounts, just for fun. "This time we'll ride Two Circle horses, next time Two Circle women," he joked.

Curly got his wish: Spotted Tail chose him to help sneak up on the herd, his first warlike deed. In the middle of the night he and his uncle slipped quietly toward the pony herd. They sat still in moon shadows. Curly used his eyes silently. And his ears—he took in all the sounds of the night birds, the wind, the thumpings and snufflings among the ponies. Before long he knew where the two guards were, knew that one was motionless but alert, the other still and asleep.

Spotted Tail and Curly crept toward the herd very slowly, easing from shadow to shadow, blending in with the wrinkles in the landscape when they moved, sitting still as boulders when they waited. At each pause they sat still until the birds stirred again, and until the herd stopped stirring.

Curly breathed slowly, fully aware of himself, his body, its motion, of everything around him. He could walk with perfect certainty, knowing he would not make noise. He was sure he could sit still while a sentry looked right at him and go unseen. He was a tree, a bush, perhaps a coyote, but not an enemy.

They did it the hard way but good way. They took the time to approach a dozen of the hobbled horses without disturbing them. These would be the most valued mounts. Silently, one by careful one, they cut the restraints. Just before first light they mounted swiftly, yelling and waving their blankets. As they hightailed it out of there, Spotted Tail laughed and whooped like a maniac.

For the first time Curly felt himself a warrior.

Then Spotted Tail got serious. He and the youths drove the horses hard half the night, left them in a gully with a watch, and rode fast back to the Two Circle camp. At dawn, hidden, they watched to see how many warriors were in camp. Spotted Tail gave a big smile of satisfaction. "Goddamn few," he said to Curly. When he wanted to act silly, Spotted Tail would say his favorite *wasicu* word: *goddamn*. The Two Circle men were mostly gone after the stolen ponies.

Curly, Hump, and Young Man-Whose-Enemies lined up in a flank next to Spotted Tail. When the leader nodded, the warriors charged as furiously as dust devils, whooping and yelling and kicking up dust and creating every kind of havoc.

That was when Curly felt it, the lifting of Hawk from her perch in his heart, the rise toward an attitude of flight.

He toppled the ear-flap poles of one tipi and threw his spear through the hide of another. He vented the cry of the red-tailed hawk, KEE-ur, KEE-ur, fierce and primordial, a yawp of predation. Now he felt it, the leading edge of her wing catching the wind.

He saw Hump touch an armed older man on the head with his coup stick and yelp out his victory. Spotted Tail knocked down a tripod holding a medicine bundle. Excited, Curly trampled the bundle with his pony's hooves. He saw a fat woman fleeing with a duck waddle. He chased her on his pony. When she heard the clap of hooves, she waddled twice as fast. He laughed and circled his pony so hard they both almost fell.

KEE-ur, KEE-ur. His heart's cry, not a musical sound like some birds', but raw and bloody.

Two Circles ran like spooked prairie hens. Some of the youths and older men got into some brush along the creek and started a defensive fire, arrows and a little lead.

Curly heard the whu-up-up of lead near his ear, too near.

KEE-ur, KEE-ur.

Whoa. Death is here. A warrior must watch himself or catch a little of it.

He held up his pony. The thought of Rider's invulnerability against enemy fire skittered across his mind. He felt for it in his heart. He couldn't find it.

Uncertain, he decided to rest a moment at the far end of the village. Most of the fire was in the center. Spotted Tail was riding around like a dervish, screaming. Curly saw him push a running man down with his coup stick and whoop with laughter. The Sicangu shot at no one.

Then Curly saw it. Yes, movement. Buckskin. A warrior in the brush not forty yards away, creeping close enough to shoot an arrow.

KEE-ur, KEE-ur.

Riding close enough for the hand coup crossed his mind, but Curly realized he was far from that size of spirit yet, and unprotected against enemy fire.

He slipped off his horse. He wanted to make sure of his aim, not show off with a wild shot from horseback. He waited.

Motion again. The left arm of the figure raised.

Quickly Curly aimed just below the arm and squeezed the trigger. The warrior half-rose and pitched forward.

"Hu ikhpeya wicayapo!" Curly bellowed, calling bloodthirstily for the complete defeat of the enemy and then humiliation heaped on the dead body.

He left his horse and dashed to the body, scalping knife in hand, and touched it, his first coup.

Noticed uneasily that the hair was brown, like his sister's, and in braids, like a woman's.

Jerked the head back to take the scalp. Saw he had killed a woman.

His mind and heart were fluttered with wing beats.

Take the scalp! his head shouted at him.

Some of the people would judge a woman's scalp more of a trophy than a man's, a greater blow to the pride of the enemy.

Don't touch it, his heart said. *Like Rider, take nothing for yourself.*

But Curly hadn't intended to kill a woman. Shame ran in him like bile. If he had identified her as a woman and deliberately attacked her in front of her man as an insult to him, that would have been fine, but . . .

He dropped the lifeless head.

Mounted. Trotted off. Wing beats pounding furiously against his ribs. Hawk's agitation.

Should he have trusted in the protection against enemy fire? Should he have done this, should he have done that?

He heard Young Man-Whose-Enemies whoop as he took the woman's scalp.

Suddenly Curly didn't want to be in the fight but simply to take it in with his senses. He trotted his pony off to a little knoll.

The fracas was ending. The other warriors joined him, no one hurt, four scalps in hand.

Curly saw Spotted Tail look back at the village keenly, bowing his horse's head back that way. The Two Circle men were set and ready now. The village was dangerous.

Spotted Tail jumped his horse forward. Curly had the impression of a fury of energy, like a huge boulder bounding down a hill.

Spotted Tail raised no weapon. He charged straight at the firing Two Circles.

He rode untouched through the barrage. He turned his horse and rode parallel to their line, lead and arrows flying all around him. Untouched.

Rider, Curly thought. His blood surged.

From behind them on a bluff Spotted Tail's wife Spoon made the trilling sound, rejoicing in her man's medicine.

Spotted Tail kicked his horse hard back toward the Lakota on the knoll. His warriors shouted their exultation. Curly yelled, for once full of words.

Spotted Tail whirled and looked back at the village. Curly felt his muscles arch with eagerness.

Again! The shirt wearer bounded horseback toward the village. The Two Circle men fired frantically. Spotted Tail seemed to ride in triumphant pulse to a grand, measured, heroic music.

Curly felt not a quiver of fear for his uncle.

Spotted Tail was invulnerable.

Oddly, now, in the midst of Curly's uncle's whirlwind, it came back.

That sense of himself as possibility, riding the wind, in the fury of the whirl of life, yet at the same time above it, observant and serene.

In this high awareness, Curly smelled again the blood and excrement of man and beast flowing. The acrid dust dried his nostrils. The sounds of the battle streamed through his consciousness, separate and distinct. He saw his uncle's charge and the previous fight not as a tumble of distinct impressions, but as a slow parade, all events simultaneous, prolonged, suspended in time.

This must be the way Hawk sees the world, he thought. He heard the trilling of Spoon on the bluff behind as a kind of martial flute music. He felt at home.

Spotted Tail let his nephew maneuver the two of them off by themselves. They sat cross-legged chewing on pemmican, a dried, sausage-like meat. Spotted Tail saw that the boy was distressed. For Light Curly Hair the hardest thing seemed to be asking other people for things, anything.

At last Curly began, "Where does that power come from?" The boy forced himself not to mumble the second sentence: "You couldn't be touched by enemy fire."

"A gift," Spotted Tail said. He looked his nephew in the eye.

"From . . . ?"

Spotted Tail shrugged. He was not a philosopher, did not trust words for the big things everyone knew. He waited.

Curly seemed to turn the words over and over and look at them carefully. "You saw beyond?"

Spotted Tail shook his head. "No. I didn't. I seldom do."

The boy's face spoke a thousand words. Always so serious. "But how do you know you're safe?"

Spotted Tail looked within himself. He didn't want to give a facile answer. He wanted to look at the reality and describe it simply and accurately. At last he spoke. "You are prepared. You listen to your spirit helper. You feel . . . everything. The sun, the wind, everything. Sometimes you feel something rise in you, and you know."

He waited. "When you are truly thirsty, drink deep. When you truly feel the drum, dance." He said it this way even though he knew his nephew didn't dance. "When you feel the power, swim in it, feel it like a big river in spring flood." Spotted Tail smiled a big smile at his nephew. "That's all."

He hoped Curly had the simplicity and the truth within him to accept this explanation, to feel its surfaces, to suck on it, to hold it in his heart. For there was nothing more to say, really.

Curly sat. Words lit his face and went away. He struggled not to fidget. He stared off into space. Finally, he got to his feet, murmured, "Thank you," and left.

Yes, thought Spotted Tail. *It's hard to be young.*

A DIFFERENT KIND OF WAR

A quarter-moon later Curly awoke to the sound of the rain-slides-off-the-feathers bird, the owl. Two calls, he remembered now. Maybe even three.

Without sitting up in his blankets he looked around the camp. It was half-shadowy, the first hint of dawn light.

Another hoo-oo, hoo-oo.

Other young men were stirring, reaching for their weapons. They heard what Curly heard—men imitating owls.

Suddenly Spotted Tail burst out of his little travel tipi, brandishing his spear in one hand and his war club in the other. He yelled, "Who wants to fight a true Lakota? Who is man enough?" He dashed around like an incensed goose looking for someone to bite.

Curly flushed with shame. His uncle was playing the fool and would get himself killed.

It came from the gully, fast. Hit Spotted Tail. Knocked him down. Two bodies tumbled over the ground like boulders hurtling downhill. Arms thrashed. Blows, strangled cries, probably bites. The bodies poised, writhing, struggling.

Curly ran toward his uncle, an arrow notched.

A brawny chest rose up above Spotted Tail. A thick arm hefted a club.

Curly knelt quickly and drew his bowstring.

At that moment a dozen riders whipped their mounts into camp, bellowing their battle cries.

Curly held the tip of his arrow on the brawny chest.

Then he lowered it.

The enemies were yelling in Lakota.

A rider tapped him on the shoulder with a coup stick, very lightly.

No Water's thick arm plunged a knife into the dust next

to Spotted Tail's ear. Spotted Tail's guffaw filled the camp.

No Water's face lifted to the sky above the mock-slain Spotted Tail. His voice roared in triumph. Curly couldn't take his eyes off No Water's hands.

Spotted Tail gave a death rattle and then cackled.

Then everyone sat down with stories to tell.

No Water, the twins, Pretty Fellow, several other Bad Face youths, and some young Sahiyela had gone out looking for Two Circle ponies, too. Not until they saw the tracks did they realize the Sicangu and Hunkpatila young men had already had their fun with these people.

"It's nothing to brag about, whipping such unworthy foes," said Black Twin, "but we want to hear what happened anyway."

Little Thunder spoke for his young men, Spotted Tail for the gang Curly was in. "We got some horses," Little Thunder said, not making a big deal of it. "The ones you see there," he said, nodding toward a rope corral. "The Pani know nothing about horses."

The chief was bragging by understatement. They had fifteen or twenty good-looking ponies.

Spotted Tail told briefly about stealing the Two Circle ponies and the doubling-back raid. He mentioned Curly's first coup. This was not a formal telling, like the one they'd have back at the village. Hump sat next to his *hunka* and looked at him happily.

Curly hated to talk in front of groups of people, but it was necessary. He spoke simply. "We surprised the village, got five first coups and four scalps. When the Two Circle warriors began to shoot back hard, we rode off onto a little knoll to rest the ponies. It was then that my uncle, Spotted Tail, showed the strength of his spirit.

"Invulnerable in his power, he charged his pony straight into the fire. He did not fire, because he had no need. He rode like a whirling wind, furious power but nothing to hit. He circled in front of the enemies, gave them his back to shoot at, and rode dancing back to us, his comrades."

Curly hesitated. He felt a little foolish doing all this talking. "Then," he went on, "Spotted Tail felt the spirit rise up in his heart once more, and he rode down the mountain at the enemies again, like a storm. They were afraid of his medicine, and he returned to us untouched."

When Curly finished, the young men gave Spotted Tail the respect of silence.

The camp of the Sicangu was half a sleep away, the visitors said. Tonight they would ride into camp ceremonially, in the manner of victory. They would tell what had happened. Curly's first coup, Spotted Tail's great rides, and the other deeds would be told formally to the people. Everyone would dance.

"Co ho! Co ho!"

Curly and Hump rolled wearily out of their blankets and stood in front of the wickiup. The dance had lasted until nearly dawn.

"Co ho! Co ho!" came the chant again.

Young Man-Whose-Enemies and the others crawled out of their brush huts and looked around warily, eyes blinking at the rising sun.

None of the young Lakota men was early up from his blankets, and maybe the smiles on the faces of the young Sahiyela men were partly because of that. But not entirely, Curly knew.

"Co ho! Co ho!" came the chant over and over. It was the young Sahiyela visitors, singing an incantation in their language.

"They want to fight," said Hump, grinning.

Curly wasn't good at the words of any language but his own, and not much good with those.

"The kicking game," Hump said.

"Co ho! Co ho!" came the chant, low, insistent. There were half a dozen Sahiyela youths and three times as many young Lakota, plus adults. Curly smiled to himself. Probably enough to make a Lakota winner likely. The guests, the Sahiyela, got to pick the game.

Hump slipped sideways to Young Man-Whose-Enemies and murmured softly, "Yes, the kicking game."

Young Man-Whose-Enemies nodded happily. Though it was mainly a Sahiyela game, all the Lakota knew it. The Sahiyela liked to pit one warrior club against another, with wild enthusiasm and violence, but all in good sport. It was a fine way for the Lakota to have fun with their Sahiyela guests.

The game was tricky. You couldn't use your hands at all, not even to fend off the other fellow's feet. You had to learn to dodge kicks, knock them aside with your arms, or slip them with your torso. And the maneuver the Sahiyela were best at, leaping into the air and kicking with both feet together, was very difficult.

All the young Lakota grinned at each other. *"Hokahe!"* said someone. It was a joke, a call for violent war against friends.

"Hokahe!" cried Buffalo Hump. He was always ready for a war, play or real, and always a wild man. He was the most experienced Lakota and so might do well.

He jerked his head at Curly, meaning, "Let's go."

Curly felt it. Hawk in his chest was uneasy. Not lunging at her perch straps, but restless.

He would have to think later about what it meant. Later.

Now he eyed Pretty Fellow. The Bad Face was stronger than Curly would have thought, and smart. He looked slighter than he was. Somehow he'd taken Young Man-Whose-Enemies out of the competition, which got a reaction from the crowd. Two old enmities met, one chief's son faced the other, and the Bad Face won.

Pretty Fellow was smiling crookedly. It was one of those smiles that said, "This had to come sooner or later, and I welcome the opportunity."

Curly was surprised. He didn't care about a killing that had happened when he was one winter old. He didn't like the way resentments still festered. And he didn't feel that he represented the Hunkpatila.

Hunh-hunh-he!

Curly jerked away from three right-foot kicks from Pretty Fellow, head high. They were feints, but Curly flinched backward. Pretty Fellow smiled more crookedly, and the crowd chuckled. Then the silence of high anticipation. This Pretty Fellow wasn't just playing.

All right, Curly wouldn't play either. He searched in himself for the serenity and concentration Hump had taught him. It wasn't there. And Hawk in his chest was fidgety. Why didn't she fly free? Was mock fighting not enough? Or . . . ?

Curly circled to the left. He liked going sunwise, what the *wasicu* called clockwise, the way the sun moved. Somehow he thought Pretty Fellow didn't. Like most people, Pretty Fellow was right-handed and felt better going to the right. Funny, that was against sunwise. Every dance, all sacred steps of any kind, went sunwise, the natural way for left-handed people like Curly. But a fighter could get his betters a little offtrack in a fight by circling sunwise. Curly had done it in wrestling lots of times.

"Hey, boy," said Pretty Fellow mockingly. "Why didn't you take the Two Circle woman's scalp? Nice scalp, can't tell it from a man's."

They circled each other.

"What do you say, boy? Something wrong with your knife? It's dull, maybe?"

Curly paid no attention. He kept his eyes on Pretty Fellow's middle and legs. That was what would tell.

It was the best two out of three knockdowns. Red Cloud and Spotted Tail settled disputes about whether you had slipped or got knocked down.

The two fighters circled each other.

Everyone still standing was a little older and a little stronger than Curly. Hump was fighting No Water, tall against husky. Black Twin was kicking against a lean, agile, muscular Sahiyela named Little Wolf, who looked like a winner to Curly. Five of the six fighters still standing were Lakota—not bad.

Time to get even for being teased.

Curly made a feint in, just one step. Pretty Fellow didn't back up, didn't flinch, acted like he would welcome Curly's kick. From his cocky look, he would welcome any kick Curly could launch at any speed from any direction. Curly thought Pretty Fellow might even let Curly kick him deliberately, just to show it didn't affect him, to show that what a younger, smaller boy tried didn't matter.

Which might be a mistake.

Curly had a thought. He feinted in again.

Then he laughed out loud and called, *"Hokahe!"* and glanced sideways at Spotted Tail and his wife.

No move from Pretty Fellow. He wasn't fooled. He knew Curly's attention wasn't wavering.

Maybe Pretty Fellow wouldn't expect what came next. One kick without any preparation, a shot at one quick fall. A rush, both feet in the air, body as high as he could get it, a two-footed kick to the head.

It would have to knock Pretty Fellow down, because Curly would be vulnerable afterward, half on the ground, unready. And the next two falls, they would have to take care of themselves.

Hawk in his chest lunged against her ties. *Why?*

He bounded. One huge step, a terrific lift—

Pretty Fellow turned sideways, bobbed his head, and threw up one arm.

One of Curly's feet grazed the upper arm. The other flipped a braid of hair aside.

Whumph! He crashed down onto his back.

Wheeze. Wheeze.

Pretty Fellow laughed, and the crowd tittered.

Finally Curly's lungs sucked, and air rushed in. Cool, sweet air. He took a moment to start getting up.

"No knockdown," came Spotted Tail's voice. Curly could hear keen interest in his uncle's tone.

Curly was fine. Sort of. Hawk was flapping her wings against his ribs, and he didn't understand that. It was a distraction.

Suddenly came laughter from the two women, and Curly wondered why. He looked around at the others.

As he got his feet under him, Curly noticed that the Sahiyela Little Wolf had whipped Black Twin and was waiting for a new opponent.

Pretty Fellow charged.

Curly slithered sideways.

The kick got him hard on the side of the ribs in front but slipped off. He spun but didn't fall.

The next kick got him square on the side of the hip. He went down in a clump.

People laughed. Pretty Fellow chuckled, and his eyes gleamed.

Curly looked up at Pretty Fellow, towering over him. His attention was drawn to Pretty Fellow's hands, dangling. Again he felt the hands of his own people clutching at him from behind, dragging him back. That's why Hawk was agitated. Well, at least hands couldn't hurt him in this game.

Curly thought before he got up to fight.

The last kick had come much too fast after the first one. Pretty Fellow was first-rate. He saw that the bear grease Curly had rubbed on his torso would help the youth slip kicks and maneuvered Curly for a kick to the pelvis, which couldn't slither.

It was good. Curly's skill was moving his body so subtly that few blows ever struck him center. Pretty Fellow knew that and had a good counter.

Curly crouched, balanced on his toes, ready to blow in space like a leaf, so that all kicks would glance off.

How could he get Pretty Fellow off balance?

He circled to the left.

"Pretty Fellow will whip you," his opponent crooned. "One look at your skin, and everyone knows why. It's white." He sang tauntingly:

> *"Curly is a white man,*
> *Curly is a white man."*

Curly felt a touch on his elbow. "Look at me! Look at me!" Curly recognized the voice of Standing Bear, Pretty Fellow's brother. He didn't look around.

Hump said softly, "Stay calm, stay clear, relax."

Curly wasn't calm, clear, or relaxed. He almost looked Hump's way.

Smash!

Curly stumbled backward, fighting for balance. His head and neck screamed. And one eye. He touched its edge and pulled away blood. There was a trick to drawing blood from tender skin with your feet. You flicked your toe on impact, using the sewn edge of your moccasin to scrape.

Pretty Fellow was laughing scornfully. He turned his back and waggled his bottom at Curly. The crowd laughed. He waggled it bigger.

Rage took Curly—two steps, the highest and hardest kick he'd ever launched, right at the back of Pretty Fellow's head.

At that moment Pretty Fellow turned his face.

Heel rammed nose.

Pretty Fellow howled.

Blood spurted over his face and arms and chest. Pretty Fellow bumped to earth, and blood gushed into his lap.

Curly backed away. Hawk's claws were gouging at him.

Rage, he told himself. He hadn't meant to kick Pretty Fellow in the nose. Rage takes over the man and works its ill.

People rushed to Pretty Fellow.

"You broke my nose!" the Bad Face wailed.

"He did that on purpose," snapped one of the twins harshly. Curly couldn't tell their voices apart.

"I'm sorry," said Curly softly, ineffectually. "I was aiming for the back of the head." But he knew he had lost his calm, had let rage take over.

"Pretty Fellow turned into the foot," said Hump.

No Water was lunging at Curly, and Hump's hands were holding him back.

"I'll be ugly," mewled Pretty Fellow in a scalding voice. In his voice Curly heard those earlier mocking words:

"Our cousin is poor, terribly poor.
He dresses so plain, the same as naked."

But he wasn't glad. He felt a pang of sympathy.

"I'll remember this," said Pretty Fellow, his voice clotted with self-pity. He was struggling to his feet. His voice took on an edge of anger. "I'll get you." He pointed at Curly, and blood ran onto his nice breechcloth of blue strouding. "You and your *hunka,* too." One of the healers started to lead Pretty Fellow away. He wheeled and pointed at Spotted Tail. "You want me to be ugly like him."

Curly was only paying attention to Hawk. Hawk was lunging at her tethers and screaming.

He walked away. "Come back here!" yelled No Water. "When I finish Hump, I get you!"

Curly kept walking. He noticed that people stood aside from him, making way, as though they didn't want to be around him.

Curly slipped through the watchers. From the back he observed for a little. Hump was in high fierceness now, attacking and attacking. It was a style No Water should have liked, but the spirit was huge in Hump. His kicks seemed to come from all angles, and his energy was immense. The Bad Face must have felt assaulted by a herd of buffalo. He was on the defensive, bewildered by this wild man.

Curly walked on. He wanted to quiet Hawk down.

He walked toward the nearest rise, overlooking a creek, moving gently in the way that always seemed soothing to Hawk. He could walk or ride a horse for a quarter-day, a half-day, all day, not thinking actively about anything, just being quiet and feeling the rhythm of the motion of his body. When he did that, he never felt Hawk inside him beating her wings against his ribs. She was still, satisfied.

He heard the cries of the crowd and looked back. No Water was on the ground. Hump and the last Sahiyela, Little Wolf, were stepping toward each other, beginning to circle. Good. Curly's *hunka* was doing well. The spirit was big in him.

Curly walked awhile. He saw a rock and sat. He wondered. Was Hawk agitated today because Curly had fought with his own people? In his mind's eye he once more saw hands clutching at Rider. He didn't know.

More cries, big ones—the match was over.

Curly looked back from the little hill. Hump sat in the dust. He wasn't moving. Since he was sitting up, though, he was all right. He was holding his belly with both hands.

Little Wolf was making a joke of it. He put his foot on Hump's shoulder, pretended to grab his hair tight, and mimed taking the scalp. Laughter carried on the air.

Curly smiled. He wondered how Hump had gotten whipped. If Curly knew his *hunka*, it was with recklessness.

Curly wondered if Buffalo Hump had a spirit animal inside him. He wondered if everyone did, and no one talked about it. Maybe everyone had something he should do, hunt or scout or paint shields or make healing chants or, if you were a woman, dig roots or suckle children or make beautiful things. When you were doing that, whatever it was, you felt free. Doing anything else you felt indifferent or uncomfortable. Or trapped, or even anguished.

Maybe everyone was like that.

So what should he, Light Curly Hair, spend his days doing?

Not loitering around other people. Not facing whatever they expected of him. Especially not talking—he would never make a strong man in council.

In his mind, shining and more vivid than even the creek below, he saw Rider galloping through eternity. That picture made him know: Light Curly Hair should always be in vivid action. Riding hard or drawing back an arrow held on a buffalo or especially fighting, galloping toward the enemy, facing the arrows and bullets that would become as puffs of wind before they reached him.

Then Hawk would soar up from his breast and fly over his head and ring up the sky.

For him that would be a feeling . . . It was beyond words.

He had gotten the feeling strongly when he went against the Two Circle people. It had made a throb in his heart.

Today Hawk had surprised him. Though he was fighting, Hawk was fitful.

Curly didn't understand. Was it that Lakota shouldn't fight each other, even in rough play?

Maybe he didn't have to understand. Maybe he only had to listen to what was within him. Listen and act accordingly.

A STORM

They spent most of August, the Moon When All Things Ripen, out hunting, going into camp only to take meat in. Spotted Tail was fun. In the evenings he would tell wild jokes about sex and pissing and shitting, extravagant fantasies, very funny. He could even bring Curly out of his pensiveness.

Spotted Tail acted as though Curly's inclination to disappear into his thoughts or feelings was kind of funny. He started calling his nephew "Strange Man." It was one of those names meant as both tease and truth.

Spotted Tail was the best of hunters. Curly already had the skills of patience, silence, and marksmanship. Spotted Tail taught him much more, taught him subtleties of tracking beyond what Curly could have imagined. Seeing horses' hooves, Spotted Tail could tell whether the riders were red or *wasicu*, whether it was a village or a war party or wolves—scouts—how fast they were moving, where they were going, and if it was a small party exactly how many there were.

He could tell whether a deer was grazing at its leisure, grazing but uneasy and inclined to move on, traveling fast or slow, spooked, whatever. Sometimes he could say what a deer's urinating meant. He could watch a creek bed from a bluff while the sun moved halfway from midday toward midafternoon and tell you about the animal life up and down the creek as far as you could see. His knowledge dazzled Curly. But Spotted Tail was too fun-loving to inspire awe in anyone.

Near the end of the Moon When All Things Ripen, heading back to camp empty-handed for once, the two hunters saw a wild buckskin horse, probably a yearling, running along across a ridge.

"It looks like Long Spear's buffalo runner," said Curly.

"Yes," said the uncle, sounding excited, too. They were horsemen, and from here they could see the conformation of a horse with unusual ability.

"Let's catch it."

Spotted Tail hesitated. *"Goddamn,"* he said. "You catch it." He stretched lazily and gave a big grin. Curly knew his uncle was offering him an adventure on his own. "It's been a long time out here. I feel like being with my women tonight."

Curly smiled back at his uncle. The youth was seldom eager to be back in camp. Besides, he wanted the wild horse.

Toward evening, with the buckskin on a lead now, Curly watched the clouds nervously. They were closing in. He'd been lucky—he hadn't been near a lightning storm since the lightning-gives-birth-to-sound in his waking dream. Maybe this was the time the *wakinyan* would come for him.

First he wanted to get to Little Thunder's camp. It might be safer there, yes, down along Blue Water Creek and off these ridges. Mostly he would be with people, and they would see what had happened and tell his parents. Maybe he could say he was sorry he hadn't told anyone his dream and hadn't offered the spirits a *heyoka* ceremony.

He kept an eye on the buckskin. It would lead nicely for a while and then get unruly. Jerk its head at the lead rope. Rear. Once it even tried to run ahead. Curly had to make it feel the stubbornness of the rope. They were pussyfooting their way along narrow ridges. He didn't want the buckskin to blow up here and send them all tumbling.

He liked the pony. He didn't know yet if it would make a buffalo runner. In some ways the buffalo horse was the most important mount a Lakota could have, with a good burst of speed from a standing start, the courage to get you close, the intelligence to respond quickly on its own, the agility to avoid the horns, and plenty of surefootedness.

A Lakota needed a warhorse, too, a mount of utter obedience, courage, the agility to cut in and out of a melee of men and beasts, and speed in short bursts.

His secret hope was that it was a traveling horse, one that would keep going forever, cross the distances day and night and take him from enemy country back home. When a Lakota went to war, he needed those two horses, the warhorse and the traveling horse.

There was a tradition in his family of traveling horses. An honored family name came from such creatures, and it was Curly's formal name now, the name no one used, though Curly preferred it, His Horse Sees. It came from an old family story:

One of Curly's ancestors was saved by a horse. He was riding home in a snowstorm and got lost. Plains snowstorms could be terrible. The flakes fell so thick you couldn't see, sometimes couldn't see as far as your moccasins, or even your hand in front of your face. White world, visibility zero. Sometimes it was not flakes falling but being blown up from the ground. Maybe it was such a storm for Curly's ancestor. You couldn't travel in weather like that—you might ride into a deep drift or even walk off a cliff. You had to stop and hunker down. Then you might freeze to death.

Curly's ancestor did something desperate—he gave the horse its head. Maybe it was a conscious decision: *I can't do it, let the horse try*. Maybe it was just giving up: *It's hopeless, I'll drop the reins and hang on until we die*. No one knew now what his desperate thought was.

The horse then demonstrated the wisdom that animals sometimes have. Or was it just impulse, the screaming of equine muscles and sinew to save themselves, to live another day? In any case, the horse floundered into no drifts, walked over no rimrock edges, lay down on no flat, just found its way back to the village. By dim sight, by instinct, by hit and miss, by chance, by animal knowing, by whatever means, the horse delivered the man to his lodge, to family, fire, hot food, warm robes, friendly hands and voices.

The people didn't think it was by chance. They thought it was by horse awareness of some kind. Brothers to the horse, they did not make themselves out superior to it, but knew the horse had powers they lacked.

Mitakuye oyasin—we are all related.

So they gave the man the new name Tasunke Ksape, His Horse Knows, or His Horse Sees. And the family passed the name to other young men to honor that horse and its rider.

Tasunke Witko, meaning another kind of horse, was an even more honored family name.

Witko was a tricky word in the Lakota language, kind of like *crazy* or *mad* in English.

Sometimes *witko* was used for women who lost themselves and started loafing around Fort Laramie all the time, begging for whiskey and selling their bodies for a dram to any *wasicu* who came by. Sometimes it referred to women like Curly's birth mother, women who so lost their way, usually through grief, that they committed suicide. Sometimes it referred to a horse ridden until it could walk no more. These meanings seemed to be that the creatures had lost their spirit.

But in another way *witko* meant men or women abundant with spirit, those who could dance wildly and all night, or who could ride forever and at furious speed, or who went into battle as though possessed by spirits, whether gods or demons. These people were energized by a kind of holy zeal or diabolic rage in war. Risky for themselves, and wildly dangerous to their enemies.

In one more way it meant "acting in a sacred manner that is preordained." Perhaps that came from the days when the Lakota first got the horse and one of Curly's ancestors excelled in training his horses, getting them to act in a certain way, his power seeming sacred.

This last was the meaning in the name Tasunke Witko, acting in a preordained sacred manner.

It was a name handed down in the family from father to son, Curly didn't know for how many generations. Seven generations, perhaps, the Lakota way of counting what the *wasicu* called a century.

For sure Curly's grandfather had been named Tasunke Witko. Then this man gave the name to Curly's father and took the name Makes a Song for himself.

If Curly could make himself a true Lakota, then his father, Tasunke Witko, would take some other name and call Curly Tasunke Witko.

Curly wanted to earn this name.

Curly snapped back into the present. The buckskin was jerking nervously at the lead rope. It didn't want to go on.

Curly looked around. Was the horse afraid of the storm? The clouds were getting ominous, but there was no lightning yet. The village, low down in the creek bottoms, was almost in sight.

Then he saw the smoke. It was black and ugly. It smelled like grease or hides or flesh. It was coming from the valley of the Blue Water.

The village was burning.

He smelled gun smoke, too.

Lightning exploded.

When the *wakinyan* smacked him, his skin shuddered, and his stomach lurched.

The storm was roaring when he got to the creek. Thunder and lightning. Smoke everywhere, and a scorched smell. The smoke was from burning lodge covers—that was the acrid smell—but it came from upwind.

Squatting in a little wash, he started on what he had to do. A deep breath, and another, and another. If he was going to die now, he simply would. Whatever the *wakinyan* did, kill him or not, he had to find out what had happened to Little Thunder's village. To Spotted Tail, his aunts and his cousins, his grandmother.

He hobbled his horses in the wash and went to where the circle of lodges had stood and looked at the tracks. He studied them carefully.

He wasn't thinking about the *wakinyan*. He had made some sort of decision without words, some acceptance.

Probably the people were all dying anyway, and he would die with them.

Hundreds of Lakota horses and hundreds of shod *wasicu* horses had been everywhere. A riot of moccasin and boot tracks. Walking soldiers had come from the east, riding soldiers and wagon guns from the west, a trap.

Some people got their pony drags headed north, up the creek.

Some people went into caves on a hill on the west side of the creek. The tracks showed where the wagon guns had bombarded the caves. Even from below Curly could see that the caves were destroyed—half the hill was torn up.

Many villagers left on foot, maybe even *opawinge,* a hundred, walking toward the Shell River and flanked by the pony soldiers.

Captured.

He squeezed his stomach to keep it from churning.

The only big outfit of walking soldiers and mounted troops in the country belonged to White Beard, called Harney by the *wasicu*. The agent said White Beard had been sent out to punish the ones who had killed Grattan and his men. The agent said the peaceful Lakota would be left alone.

Little Thunder had always spoken strongly for peace. He supported the big talk paper from three winters ago, supported it so firmly that some of his own people disapproved. Yet the camp White Beard hit was Little Thunder's.

Suddenly, unpredictably, as he was looking up at the cannon-smashed caves, the urge to kill shot through Curly. He noticed how it felt, like swallowing a red-hot stone. For a moment it was in his pores, in his hairs, in his finger- and toenails, in all of his existence. He hated the feeling. So did Hawk.

The tracks said the walking soldiers and the wagon guns had gone downstream with the captives, toward the Shell River, which the *wasicu* called the Platte. The pony drags and most of the people had gone upstream. So had the mounted soldiers.

Curly followed the people who were fleeing. Slowly, in the seep of light remaining, the pony picked its way along the wash.

The *wakinyan* sounded.

Malign spirits were everywhere. You could feel the air where their wings pushed it into your face.

Before he got to the place, it was black night. He couldn't see. By the stink he knew it was the place.

Crack! The lightning made a cannon-burst of light, and Curly saw more than he wanted to see.

Then nothing. His eyes were blind after the blast of light.

The world emerged from his blindness.

He saw carnage.

Here at the foot of a sandstone bluff Little Thunder's people had made a stand.

Carnage.

The lightning boomed again.

Curly waited to see. Soon he could make out a few details, humps on the ground. Rolled-up lodge hides, he thought, parfleches full of food and others full of clothing, robes, everything the people owned except what they wore, all of it scattered across the foot of this slope, most of it burning.

Now the smoke wasn't so much, but the stench was awful, burning fat and meat, smoldering hide.

Mixed with the metallic smell of blood.

A whack of light.

At first he only guessed what he'd seen. Then his eyes adjusted and brought to him crumpled bodies slung across the sand, torn like rags and abandoned. Cradle boards here and there, some with flesh in them that once was human.

He rode up the slope where the soldiers had chased the people. Bodies of his people everywhere, shot, hacked with swords, blown to pieces, men, women, children flung down like garbage.

He retched.

He felt thankful his belly was empty.

He walked among the lifeless forms, turning them over to look at their faces. One might be Spotted Tail. Or one of his wives or children. Or Spotted Tail's mother, Curly's grandmother.

He recognized the dead face of a maiden from last summer's sundance pole. Her skirt was pulled up, and she had been scalped between the legs.

He felt that he was walking in a nightmare. The ghouls and monsters always just on the other side of the thin membrane between the physical world and the spirit world—they had passed through and were running amok.

He shivered, a long spasm of cold, not the cold of physical death, but the death of spirit.

From a stone's throw away, lightning knocked him down.

Lightning-gives-birth-to-sound bashed him.

He felt the air on fire. It singed his nostrils. His guts wrenched hard.

He grabbed for his pony's reins. The horse was evidently too stunned to run off.

Curly got to his knees and looked around, blind, seeing nothing, his head reeling. He thought he remembered that the lightning had hit up the ridge a little, maybe a hundred yards. It had pounded the earth. Maybe there was a big hole where it had hit or a litter of powdered rock.

He would go on. He had surrendered his life already to the *wakinyan*. He wanted to find his grandmother. Somehow he was sure he would find the body of his grandmother.

He led the horse along the ridge.

Movement at the edge of a boulder, a ghost.

No, a coyote.

No, his grandmother's mangy old dog.

Curly wanted living warmth. He called and reached, but the animal ran from him.

Or was it a spirit dog?

Suddenly he saw. His waking dream of a winter ago gushed into his eyes and his ears and his heart. In ten or a dozen consecutive flashes of lightning, Rider galloped through a rain of arrows and gunfire, untouched. The horse's hooves were the roll of *wakinyan*. The figure on the horse was motionless, save for a fringe of buffalo beard on his moccasins. Now for the first time Rider had a distinct face, the visage of Light Curly Hair, properly known as His Horse Sees, son of Tasunke Witko, grandson of Makes the Song, Hunkpatila Oglala Lakota.

The lightning stopped, and for a moment the world was dark. Low bursts of light danced at the rim of the circle of the world. Distant *wakinyan* beat the drum-pulse of the earth.

Light Curly Hair rode into enemy fire, but the bullets and arrows didn't touch him.

Hawk flew high.

The rain came now, slashing, cold as hail.

He didn't care.

He would ride toward the people and the soldiers, untouched.

The people were moving fast, the tracks showed, and the soldiers hard after them. After a while, though, the soldiers' ponies were walking, not running. Finally their tracks veered off to the west. The people pushed on north.

Find the people, that was Curly's first job.

Dropped robes, broken travois poles, and the occasional body of a horse marked the way.

And then a small figure next to a dropped bundle of robes.

He dismounted and looked carefully. A little boy, no one he knew. Dead, shot through the chest, cold.

Curly bent over the body.

And heard a mewling. There. From that pile of robes.

"Tanke," Curly said softly. Sister. It was an offer to treat this woman like an older sister.

She was huddled pitifully under the robes, soaking wet, spinning out a soft whine.

"Tanke," he said again, and touched her shoulder tenderly.

She didn't respond. Her face was to the ground, her back to him, and she was shivering uncontrollably. Her crying was distracted, bizarre, perhaps lunatic, *witko.* A picture of his birth mother lightninged into his mind, *witko* with grief, hanging from a lodge pole by the neck.

He scourged the picture from his mind.

He rolled the woman back gently to see her face.

Then he saw what was beneath her. A baby, sucking at her breast. A just-born baby, still glistening with the juices of the womb.

Lightning smacked the ridge. It was so close Curly thought his hair must be singed, the white ends burning.

He ignored it absolutely. The *wakinyan* would do as they pleased.

The woman whined louder when the *wakinyan* ka-boomed.

A good sign, he thought. She was aware of the world around her, at least a little aware.

He wiped tenderly at her cheek. In the flash of lightning he had recognized her. She was not Lakota but a Sahiyela, visiting in the village with her husband. Curly didn't remember her name.

He could see in his mind what had happened. Somehow she had gotten separated from her husband—maybe he was among the dead back at the bluff. She must have carried her dead son here, moving as fast as she could but falling behind, utterly unable to set the body of her son down, unprotected, naked to the storm and tomorrow to the birds and coyotes.

She would have slipped badly in the mud, been chilled by the rain, been terrified by the lightning. And hardly able to walk farther as her unborn child began to force his way into the world.

Curly turned the child slightly and saw that it was a boy.

She had lain here on the ridge, with the rain cutting at her, the lightning battering the earth all around her, the lightning-gives-birth-to-sound exploding in her mind. Alone. Terrified. Riven by these great forces, and the greater force that made her grow life within, she had brought forth a man-child.

The *wasicu* soldiers had taken one son from her. Life, its force rising within her belly, had given her another one.

Miracle.

Curly looked around at the dark earth, wet with rain and blood, scourged by lightning, and reached down without looking and touched the miracle child.

A great feeling rose, a wave cresting.

"Mitakuye oyasin," he said softly but clearly to the universe. *"Mitakuye oyasin,"* he repeated. We are all related.

* * *

He went back down the ridge and hunted until he found two usable travois poles. He hauled them back up to where the Sahiyela woman lay, quiet now, as though her spirit was soothed a little.

He tied the poles onto his pony to make a drag and lashed a robe across them for a litter. When he lifted the woman onto the robe, she opened her eyes, looked into his face, and said tentatively, "The sandy-haired one." He could not tell whether recognizing him made her more or less afraid.

He covered her and the baby with the other robes, except for one. He moved the dead boy to some rocks, wrapped him in the last robe, put him into a crevasse, and stacked rocks over the whole bundle. Now, when she was better, she could come and send his spirit on its journey in the proper way.

He led the pony on, following the trail of the people's horses, not knowing where they would make camp. He didn't care where. He didn't care about the rain or the cold, or even the lightning and *wakinyan*. As Rider, he advanced into danger without trembling.

He was exhausted from riding all day and walking all night. But he felt useful, useful to the woman and child and to the larger forces that coursed through them and himself, useful to life.

He would deliver this woman and her son to the village. His act, his gesture, his service.

Toward dawn the rain stopped. The tracks split in many directions into the sand hill country. Curly knew the people were dividing, making it hard for the soldiers to find them all again, offering a fragmented target.

On one trail he saw big hoofprints that might be the tracks of a big American horse, maybe Spotted Tail's favorite traveling horse. He followed these tracks.

Before long lookouts saw him. They led him to a village circle by a little lake. They took the woman and child to her family.

The hubbub of voices spoke the people's mood—grief, wild grief. And fury, vengeful fury.

Curly headed for what they said was Spotted Tail's lodge for a little sleep. When Curly woke, he would rise in anger too. He would fight back too. But something in him was a more private feeling, something of consequence. He would keep quiet about it but hold it and watch it: When he helped people, especially in desperate circumstances, Hawk was still, at peace.

AN ANGRY WASP

When he woke, his aunt Sweetwater Woman signaled him to stay quiet and brought him some soup. The hump in the buffalo robes must be Spotted Tail. "Wounded," whispered Sweetwater Woman. Seriously, from her manner.

Curly looked around for the other wives, the children, and his grandmother.

Sweetwater Woman's face contorted with a spasm of grief. "Spoon, Yellow Leaf, and Willow have been captured."

Curly's head jerked toward her. Sweetwater Woman's face was impassive again. Willow was his grandmother. Spoon was Spotted Tail's sits-beside-him wife, the eldest of the four sister wives. Yellow Leaf was their seven-winters-old daughter.

Taken by the soldiers! A picture lurched into Curly's mind, the young woman scalped between the legs. Immediately he blacked it out.

"Many captured, many dead," Sweetwater Woman said softly.

Curly's heart twisted like a piece of hide wrung in the hands.

He decided to visit the Sahiyela woman and her boy-child while his uncle slept.

* * *

The boy in the cradle board held Curly's finger and tried to suck it. His eyes didn't go beyond the finger yet. Newborn babies seemed to have trouble seeing this new world, as though their minds were still wherever they came from.

Lark hovered. Lark was the sister of Yellow Woman, the Sahiyela mother. Her husband, Stick, was off talking with the men of the Badger Society. Curly was sure the men of all the societies, Foxes, Badgers, Brave Hearts, White Badges, Crow Carriers, Silent Eaters, and Wand Carriers, were meeting. They would be badly divided in their minds. They would want to make *wasicu* blood run like rivers in spring flood, and they would want the women and children back. *A-i-i-i*, they would need some wisdom now.

Yellow Woman was sleeping. Her Sahiyela husband, Lark said, had been killed by the wagon guns at the caves on the hill.

Curly nodded. It was as he'd guessed.

Curly looked into the eyes of the infant without thinking, just opening his eyes and his heart. He felt like a gift, this newborn man-child, a solace.

When Curly was small, during one Cannanpopa Wi, the Moon of Popping Trees, he had been shivering in the robes. A terrible storm raged outside in the darkness, wind and snow, the breath of Waziya, the white giant, blowing fiercely, trying to kill all it could touch. The one who gave him birth, Rattling Blanket Woman, heated two stones in the center fire. Then she wrapped them in deerskin and gave them to Curly and his sister. "Hold this to your chest," she said softly. Curly hugged the warm stone and slept the night through.

Sometimes in his sleep now Curly still heard Rattling Blanket Woman's loving voice. Sometimes she would touch him gently and he would start suddenly awake, and then remember. The sadness never left him, like dark, cold water pooled at the bottom of his heart.

Last night the *wakinyan* had sent warning blasts at Curly.

The soldiers' big-fire guns had shot terror among the people. But in the midst of these storms had emerged a warmth, this infant, newly come to the earth. The little boy was a heated stone to wrap in hide and hold against the chest on a bitter winter night. Not a reward, for Curly felt he'd done nothing to earn a reward. Instead a gift.

Curly had picked up this gift of life and brought the boy and mother to camp. Because Curly had treasured the gift, they would live.

Lark woke Yellow Woman gently, took the child from his cradle board, and laid him at his mother's breast.

Yellow Woman noticed Curly and covered her surprise with one hand to her mouth.

"I'm glad you're well," he said awkwardly. "And your son."

She inclined her head in acceptance.

He went out of the lodge. He stood in the open air and looked around at the ragged circle of the village. Families were living under bushes or in wickiups or small travel lodges. Their real homes had been destroyed down on the creek. It would be a hard winter now. The hoop of the people was not broken, but it was much tattered.

When times were terrible, that was when you needed truly to act like a Lakota. He had done that. It felt good. He liked the feeling, being one of the people.

Spotted Tail was shot in two places and saber-cut in two others. His wounds looked scary, but his spirits were martial.

"I'm not whipped," he said. "Tomorrow or the next day I'm going to kill soldiers."

Curly heard that gruff tone and looked into the face of his genial uncle and swallowed hard. Spotted Tail was grizzly-bear furious. The soldiers had hurt the bear just enough to enrage it.

His story was appalling. White Beard had come up with the troops and said he wanted to parley. In the talk he had demanded that Little Thunder give up everyone who had helped kill Grattan and his men.

"This cannot be done," Little Thunder had explained. "The Mniconjou who killed the cow has gone back to his village in the north.

"Of the Sicangu," Little Thunder had gone on, "who could say who the fighters were? The soldiers came right into camp, shot Bear-Scattering, and the fighting was hand-to-hand. Every decent man defended his lodge." Sometimes you really did have to explain to the *wasicu* like children.

"I have always wanted peace, still want peace. I offered to pay for the cow. But when soldiers came straight into camp and started killing people . . ." Little Thunder shrugged.

White Beard answered with roars and accusations.

Before long Little Thunder, Spotted Tail, and the other Sicangu in the parley realized the soldier chief only wanted to fight, so they left. Halfway back to the people, they saw that they'd been tricked. White Beard had used the parleying time to get his men into position for a trap.

The first charge came even before the peace talkers could get back to their lodges. Spotted Tail had to fight empty-handed.

The wounded man managed a grin. "I took a sword away from a horseback and started knocking heads," he croaked.

Sweetwater Woman chimed in, "He knocked thirteen soldiers off their horses. I saw."

A look passed between the man and the woman. Sweetwater Woman was lovely, and the two were very much attracted to each other, a love match.

It had been the second love match among Spotted Tail's wives. Everyone knew the story. The young Spotted Tail had courted Spoon, the eldest sister, and she had wanted him. But Spoon's parents had promised her to an older man. Finally the two suitors had argued and then set to fighting with knives. Spotted Tail killed his rival and claimed his woman.

Parents decided on husbands for their daughters, and that was good. But once in a while, when a young warrior was filled with passion, when he was willing to throw his life away for a woman . . . Then the people smiled at each other and envied the young couple.

And now Spotted Tail, a mature man more than thirty winters old, an admired leader in war, had his heart made young a second time by Spoon's sister. It made the camp's other wives titter.

"Yes, woman," he said in half-reproof, "I lent you my horse, but you stayed and made the trilling."

Curly saw what mixed feelings were in that comment, what pride and grief.

Spotted Tail's sits-beside-him wife, his daughter, and his mother were being marched away, no one knew where. Even talking to Curly was a pretense. Spotted Tail and Sweetwater Woman's hearts were with the prisoners. They knew what happened to captives. The Lakota's enemies had taken captives for centuries. They kept the women for breeding and tortured the men with exquisite deliberation until they died. The Pani even made human sacrifices of the girls.

Last night, Spotted Tail said, the men had tried to hold off the soldiers while the women escaped up the creek with the lodges, but many women had been killed or captured. Little Thunder and Spotted Tail had been wounded, and many more.

There were maybe eighty captives, And probably a hundred people dead, many of them women and children.

Curly saw his uncle's eyes wander to the half-light of a corner of the lodge, and then into the twilight of the desperate stand by the bluff last night, and then into the darkness of the death of nearly a hundred Lakota men, women, and children. Families ruptured, the hoop of the people battered, the band maimed in a way that would last seven generations, a hundred winters.

Men were gone toward the river, following the prisoners, seeing what could be done. They would be back soon. Then the warriors would talk, and decide.

From the hooded look in Spotted Tail's eyes, Curly guessed what they would do would be to kill *wasicu,* a barrel of white blood for every drop of Lakota blood shed.

But he didn't know. Whatever it was, Curly would fight by his uncle's side. The terror of the lightning and *wakinyan* and cold rain was still in his flesh. But the birth of the manchild warmed him, and a lust for *wasicu* blood set him afire.

Some men came back from Laramie, and their news buzzed around the circle of lodges. They'd run off with fifty soldier horses, which made everyone smile, but the rest of the news was bad. The prisoners hadn't gone upriver to Fort Laramie but down the river, no one knew where until the men who followed them came back.

And there was even worse news. Everyone would hear it in the council lodge tonight.

"Circle of lodges," murmured Spotted Tail, who was well enough to sit outside a little. "Council lodge." Even the words were mockery. Most of the lodges were brush huts. The council lodge was a brush roof without sides.

Light Curly Hair sat with the men in the council lodge. He was seventeen winters old, and he had counted coup. It was not a coup he boasted about, but he had been first to touch the Two Circle woman. The eyes of the men in the lodge told him where he should be, at the place of lowest rank of men. The women sat huddled in their blankets at the back. There was no question of his speaking in council, a mere youth.

White Wing sat behind the center fire next to Little Thunder, to give witness for the men who had gone to Laramie, and Reeshaw sat next to him to confirm certain matters. Reeshaw was a trader's son and understood the *wasicu* language. Spotted Tail was next to Little Thunder.

He had long been a war leader. He was a shirt wearer. Now he was becoming like a chief.

White Wing spoke in the formal way that meant, "This is a serious matter and I tell exactly what happened." First, he said, the prisoners had not been taken to Fort Laramie. The soldiers had marched them downstream. Some said they were going to Fort Kearny, which was farther from Lakota territory. Young men were following. They would send word back.

The people were silent except for the *e-i-i-i* of lament in the back, from the women. Everyone had admitted to himself, mostly silently, that these loved ones would never be seen again. They hoped the *wasicu* were not such devils as to torture women and children.

Second, the Wasp (their new name for Harney because he stung them) was bragging about the fight and treating it as a great victory.

The Lakota looked at each other in wonder and disgust. What kind of man attacked a peaceful village and slaughtered dozens of women and children and called it a victory? What kind of man thought it honorable? To have a skirmish, yes, to show valor in the face of danger, certainly—but to kill nearly a hundred, capture nearly another hundred, take the people's food, and burn the lodges they lived in? Why?

Some of them wondered for the first time what kinds of beings they had to struggle against in these *wasicu*. They didn't seem human. Warriors looked at each other in puzzlement. All a man knew was that he could never figure how *wasicu* would act.

Reeshaw had something to add. Marching toward the Platte, he said, the walking soldiers made up a song about the battle. He chanted it in English so the people could hear the rhythm of marching feet:

"We did not make a blunder;
we rubbed out Little Thunder
and sent him to the other side of Jordan."

When Reeshaw translated the words, the people thought the soldiers were like adolescent boys given weapons before they were responsible for where they pointed them.

Third, because of the trouble, Harney had ordered the agent not to give out any rations this autumn.

A murmur went through the lodge, mixed with the *a-i-i-i* of anxiety. It was already the Moon When Leaves Turn Brown, also called the Moon of Ten Colds, September. Buffalo were scarce again, and the people were counting on the rations promised by the *wasicu* under the paper signed four summers earlier. Now the soldiers had captured most of their pemmican, or burned it, or scattered it over the prairie. Unless the band was lucky, like last autumn, and came upon a big herd, this would be a hungry winter.

Finally, Harney had talked to the Lakota in a way no other soldier chief had ever dared to talk. He ordered the Lakota to surrender the men who had robbed the mail coach a year ago. He ordered them to bring back the fifty horses. He said he'd attack other villages in the spring if they didn't. He spoke sharply, like a man snapping at a dog to get out of his way, not as one spoke to human beings.

There was some talk about what to do, but the main point was clear:

Ordered. Lakota. No one had ever dared to do that.

Little Thunder made White Wing repeat several times the part about giving up the men who robbed the mail coach. It was perfectly clear:

"The Wasp regards those men as murderers.

"He intends to hang them by the neck.

"Until they are turned over, there will be no more rations. The Wasp will destroy villages at will—not just make war against fighting men, but against women and children and lodges and even food."

White Wing said it softly, firmly, without variation. The Wasp had been absolutely clear.

Everyone knew who had robbed the mail coach. Spotted Tail, their main war leader. Red Leaf and Long Chin, the brothers of Bear-Scattering, the chief killed by Grattan. Two boys, who didn't count.

Little Thunder guided the talk away from these mail-coach raiders for a while.

"Why doesn't the Wasp demand any longer that the ones who killed Grattan and his men be turned in?"

In the Grattan fight twenty-nine soldiers came into the Sicangu camp, and all died. But the mail coach? That was done in anger afterward, in revenge for the killing of Chief Bear-Scattering. Yes, three *wasicu* died, and their wonderful paper money got thrown to the winds. (The people were still tickled about this.) But why did the Wasp demand blood payment for this and not for Grattan?

"I don't know," said White Wing.

Reeshaw had something to say. "I talked to the other interpreters. They said when he got to Laramie, after he hit the village, the Wasp heard the truth about Lieutenant Grattan from the soldier chief at Laramie. Grattan was spoiling for a fight, the soldier chief said—he'd boasted he wanted to take on 'the entire Sioux nation.' And besides, he was drunk, the soldier chief said."

Murmurs filled the brush arbor. Yes, Grattan had been looking for a fight, and deserved what he got. Whether he was drunk they didn't know, but his interpreter had been drunk and hadn't told the officer the truth about what Bear-Scattering was saying.

"Something else," Reeshaw added. "Some of the newspapers back in the white-man towns are calling the Wasp a squaw killer. They say his attack on Little Thunder's village was cowardly."

Heads nodded.

White Wing spoke up again. "But the Wasp demands that the ones who attacked the mail coach be given up. Or he will attack other villages, any villages anywhere."

Eyes grew large. No one said anything because there

was nothing to say. The *wasicu* wouldn't admit they were wrong. Instead they'd do some more killing and give any flimsy excuse. What kind of people were they?

So everyone waited to see what answer Little Thunder would send to the Wasp. Give up Red Leaf and Long Chin? They were living with the Oglala now—what could Little Thunder do about that? Give up Spotted Tail? Outrageous.

But if Little Thunder refused, more women and children would die.

You didn't ask if a wasp gone wild was right or wrong. You couldn't placate it. You killed it if you could. Or got away from it.

Little Thunder didn't look at his friend Spotted Tail. "Everyone think about the Wasp's words," he said, "and we'll talk more later."

SPOTTED TAIL'S DECISION

Spotted Tail disappeared.

The morning after the council, still slow-moving from his wounds, he went alone to the far side of the little lake in the sand hills, across from the camp, and built a sweat lodge and spent the day there.

He didn't come back that night.

Sweetwater Woman acted rattled. Spotted Tail must have talked to her. "One goes onto the mountain," she said quietly to Curly, telling him in the oblique way that was polite that Spotted Tail would cry for a vision. She didn't need to say he'd probably be gone several days. Her voice sounded pebbled, and one hand trembled.

Curly would never have asked—it would have been an intolerable breach—but Sweetwater Woman suddenly added the words herself. "Spotted Tail will see whether he should turn himself over to the soldiers to be hanged."

Curly flinched as if she had slapped him. His tongue

thickened so that he couldn't respond. Her language was shocking. She had specified the decision with indelicate directness, and she had said that terrible word for the way of death. An ugly picture tried to rise in his mind, but he forbade it.

Then Curly realized she wasn't slapping him but herself.

The awful picture rose again, his uncle hanging by the neck, fouling himself, his face swelling up grotesquely. Or was it his mother?

He levered his mind into the present. He thought of Spotted Tail alone in the place where Curly had been last year in this Moon When Leaves Turn Brown, in that queer space between this world and whatever else there was, and sitting still and facing, alone, the question: Live? Or throw away your life?

Curly saw his uncle in imagination, the man's big arms and his huge chest and his amused eyes and his hearty laugh, and could not make the picture fit, this man so . . . vital, sitting and thinking of choosing to die.

Sweetwater Woman suddenly said she was going to be with her two sister wives and their mother for the night.

Curly decided to sleep in the lodge alone, preferring solitude to family, another reason his people were calling him "Our Strange Man." When Sweetwater Woman left, Hawk flapped her wings within his breast.

Spotted Tail was entirely different from him, fixed somehow like a tree with roots in Mother Earth and her ways of copulating and birthing and excreting and bleeding, a man who planted his big, flat feet on the earth and looked around and said inside his head, *This is mine*.

Alone in the lodge this night, Curly told himself that Spotted Tail was made to live in the world and he, Curly, was not.

Sweetwater Woman and her two sisters didn't come back for three days. Nor did his uncle.

The whole time Curly brooded, and Hawk pranced on her perch, restless.

On the fourth day Spotted Tail came back. He strode in calling out to his friends, hollering for his children to come and play. He threw the two small ones into the air and spent a while helping one of his daughters paint a piece of buffalo hide she wanted to stuff for a doll. When his boys came back, he played war with them, both boys on one side and Spotted Tail on the other. The weapons were sticks for flinging gobs of mud.

That night Curly heard the sounds of love from the robe of Sweetwater Woman and later both of the other robes.

His uncle seemed clear, light, at ease. Apparently he had made his decision.

Curly felt dazzled. And he wondered what it was.

The next morning Flat Club came back to camp drunk. Everyone wondered where he had gotten the whiskey, but there were places. Flat Club liked to get drunk. It made him amiable and amorous. He was well known for chasing his two wives around when he drank too much. Most people were embarrassed by his behavior. Even eye contact between a man and woman was brazen, and public touching entirely improper. But when Flat Club was drunk, he acted like a lustful bull among the cows, all in good humor, and only toward his own wives.

Spotted Tail always enjoyed this vulgar behavior. Since Flat Club was married to two of his own half sisters, he treated Club like a brother-in-law. Which is to say Spotted Tail teased him.

This time Spotted Tail solicited Curly's help. Flat Club was carrying on comically in front of their lodge, one of the few buffalo-hide tipis left in the village. "Come on," he said over and over to one wife and then the other, "let's walk under the blanket together." And he would stumble toward one of them, hands outstretched lecherously. The women kept to their tasks and avoided him easily enough—he kept falling down—but they were acutely embarrassed.

One of them told Flat Club that his *œ*, penis, wouldn't work any better than his legs.

"Show her!" yelled Spotted Tail, laughing. "Show her your legs work!"

He whispered to Curly, and the youth scurried off.

Flat Club ran around the tipi at high speed, with unbelievable balance for his state of inebriation.

"Let's dance!" yelled Spotted Tail, and started in. Spotted Tail chose a ridiculous sage grouse strut, an imitation of the bird's mating dance. Flat Club thought this was hilarious and joined in fervently. The two puffed out their chests like the silly-looking birds, waggled their tails, and looked sideways sneakily to see if the females were watching.

Now a crowd was gathering to see Spotted Tail's fun. Even Flat Club's wives were starting to enjoy the show.

Curly slipped back into the lodge with a big bundle of something wrapped in a blanket.

"Ho, Flat Club!" yelled Spotted Tail, looking around to make sure his audience was appreciative. "Remember what we did that time with the crazy old woman?"

Flat Club slapped his belly over and over until he fell down. He rolled onto his back and waggled his feet in the air.

Many people remembered. This old woman, who'd gotten very prickly with age, had badgered the teenage Flat Club and Spotted Tail until they vowed vengeance. The youths ran up the slanting side of her lodge until they could grab the lodge poles, hang on, and sit in the crotch of the poles. Then they rocked the poles back and forth until the hides began to tear along the seams, poles broke, and finally the whole lodge toppled. All the while the old woman yelled like a wounded she-bear, but none of the adults interfered—they thought she had it coming.

The boys crashed down with the lodge and capered off laughing.

Now Flat Club began to reenact their great moment. Up the side of his own lodge he ran. And slipped back. And backed up and ran harder. And slipped back. On the third or fourth try Spotted Tail grabbed the cooking tripod, applied it to Flat Club's bottom, and boosted him up.

The man clawed the lodge poles desperately and hauled himself to the top. He looked over the gathered crowd impudently and shook a fist in triumph. Some of the women trilled mockingly.

Spotted Tail hollered at him to take off his breechcloth. "Show us your *œ* is up to it!" he yelled. Flat Club took off his breechcloth and waggled his erect penis at everyone.

Some laughed, some made sounds of disapproval.

His wives had had enough. "Get down here!" they shouted. "You're making a fool of yourself!"

Flat Club looked at them insolently and ceremoniously sat down, bare-bottomed, in the crotch of the poles.

Spotted Tail darted into the lodge.

The wives harangued Flat Club—"Come down, get off there, you fool; get back down here. . . ."

Inside the lodge Curly had the dry grasses and sedges ready, in a big pile next to the center fire. He'd built it up to a small flame.

Spotted Tail's eyes rolled wildly.

He tossed the grass on the fire.

Furious flames shot up—and up—straight up the tie-down rope, straight up toward the center hole and out, in a wonderful, whipping rush.

Spotted Tail burst out of the lodge, Curly right behind.

A wail to remember—"Ye-e-o-o-w!—a once-in-a-lifetime shriek, a truly inspired scream, a bellow to touch the clouds.

Flat Club jumped up. He grabbed his scrotum and penis with one hand and tried to cover both buttocks with the other. He did a dance. With the divine agility of the drunk, he did another dance, right on the tips of the lodge poles, a tribute to the muse of drunkenness.

Then, still holding his tender parts, he leapt. Perhaps only a drunk could have leapt so high. His legs kicked furiously, and he seemed to swim up through the air. Sadly but inevitably, he descended. He hit the lodge cover about a third of the way down. He rolled, he tumbled like a buffalo bull to earth. Roaring, he catapulted down the lodge cover, cartwheeled across the hard earth, and at last came to rest in a pile of fresh dog droppings.

Everyone was laughing, especially the two wives. But no one enjoyed the spectacle as much as Spotted Tail.

The big man laughed. He held his belly and laughed. He sat, shook, and laughed. He lay back full-length, beat his heels into the ground, flailed his arms, and laughed and laughed and crooned his delight. Tears of joy flooded down his face.

Curly's belly twisted and squeezed.

On the way back to the lodge, Curly blurted his question to Sweetwater Woman. After all, she'd broached the subject. "He has decided to dare the soldier chiefs to find him?"

His own blood burned his face. It was a wildly intrusive question. Curly's stomach wriggled with self-disgust. But he still waited to hear the answer.

Sweetwater Woman's face ran with feelings. "After one half-moon," she said softly, "he will throw his life at the feet of the *wasicu*."

She walked away, her back rigid.

Curly looked hard at his uncle, walking behind.

Spotted Tail was holding his face in both hands, shaking, relishing, basking in, wallowing in the fun of his own joke.

THE MOOSE BIRD

The entire village went to Laramie to watch Spotted Tail turn himself over to the soldiers—up the Running Water River and down the familiar trail toward the Shell River and the fort. Spotted Tail must have told Little Thunder of his decision privately, but he never mentioned it otherwise, not even within the lodge.

In the way that village people have, everyone knew, and

whispered about it. Some of the men muttered disputatiously. "I wouldn't do that," said one.

"Let the Wasp buzz all he wants," agreed his friend. "We will fight."

Other men bragged the same way under their breath. "Lakota men do not give up their lives because a *wasicu* says so." They cast at each other dark looks that meant, "Lakota die as warriors—we do not submit to being hanged by the neck."

"Let's go kill Harney," several grumbled.

But everyone remembered what White Wing had said in the council lodge. The Wasp had promised to sting any village of Lakota he could find, hostile or peaceful, sting them anywhere, anytime, sting women and children as well as men. Everyone would suffer until the five men who attacked the mail coach surrendered themselves. And the Wasp had said that if the Lakota killed him, The One They Used for Father, the President of the United States, would send ten more armies, or a hundred more armies, until the Lakota obeyed and gave up the five offenders.

Some men muttered, but the people knew that Spotted Tail was showing greatness in this decision. He was acting like a man who belonged not to himself or even to his family, but to the entire tribe. Spotted Tail was showing himself truly a shirt wearer.

The sandy-haired youth wondered about this. He wanted to be a warrior, a guardian of the people, and as a warrior to make sacrifices. But to become a leader and be owned by the people . . . He thought he needed to find his own good, red road, the road purely of a warrior, and hold resolutely to it. He wished he could talk to Hump about this, but his *hunka* was gone north to visit his Mniconjou relatives.

A-i-i-i, would Harney really hang Spotted Tail? For stealing the mail and the paper money and flinging it all over the prairie and shooting the men who fought back?

And what about the other two warriors who had gone on that raid, Red Leaf and Long Chin? They were living with all the relatives of the dead chief Bear-Scattering among the Oglala now, since the Sicangu had kicked them out. Would they give themselves up? Spotted Tail was a big-spirited man, but the people weren't so sure about the other two. And what about the two boys who had gone along? They didn't have anything to do with it, really. Surely Little Thunder wouldn't tell the soldiers who the boys were.

If Spotted Tail threw his life away and the others didn't, would the Wasp be satisfied? Or would he murder all the Lakota women and children? What if only Spotted Tail surrendered? What if the three warriors gave themselves up and the boys didn't?

When you were dealing with a *wasicu* you never knew.

"You take the shot," whispered Spotted Tail.

Curly held his point on the deer, but the arrow missed. He was missing too many shots. He had no inner stillness. All day long every day he squirmed with one thought: Spotted Tail was throwing his life away—what were Spotted Tail's thoughts about that? It was anguish for Curly not to know.

On the way in to Laramie they'd gone hunting every day. They rode out ahead of the village or far to one side, pushing their ponies pretty hard, trying to jump deer out of the cedar breaks.

Maybe Spotted Tail was making a last stab at feeding the people, self-sacrificial to the end. Curly didn't know. The big man seemed focused on hunting but not on making meat.

Curly's uncle stopped his big American horse and looked over the country intently. He studied sign with a deep concentration. Was he distracted by fears of his approaching death? By thoughts of his family and their survival?

Spotted Tail seemed absorbed simply in the things of the hunt, game trails, the lie of the land, water here and none there, rimrock that way, what grasses spread this way and that, the wind, the sun, the myriad creatures of the earth. He insisted that Curly take all the shots and didn't mind when the youth missed.

Maybe the one concession Spotted Tail made to his imminent death was that they went back to camp every sunset. Spotted Tail spent the evenings and nights in his own lodge. He saw no one but his family, talked with no one but his family. He seemed relaxed and didn't seem to notice their anxiety. Before dawn each morning he and Curly headed out again to hunt.

Curly cramped with wanting to know.

Toward evening they were walking their horses gently back to camp. It was their last hunt. Tomorrow the band would reach Fort Laramie. The people would greet their Oglala cousins already camped there. Curly would see his father and mothers. The three men who were throwing their lives away would spend a last night with their families.

Spotted Tail seemed to want silence. He rode looking around at the rolling plains, here and there broken by rimrock, sometimes marked by the dark lines that were wet or dry watercourses. Curly had the impression that Spotted Tail was breathing deeply, heartily. His uncle seemed content.

Suddenly Spotted Tail broke the silence.

"Nephew, do you know what it means when we say it is a good day to die?"

Curly took a long look at the one he called uncle, and Hawk stirred. Finally he shook his head no.

"Here is something we have over the *wasicu*." Spotted Tail grinned. "Their minds are clever, they can make guns and knives and little round things that tell the time of day or the four directions." This last was a half-joke. With sun and moon in the wide sky, who could need to tell the time? Who would not know what direction west was, or north or east or south? "Yes, their minds are very clever."

Spotted Tail rode in silence for a moment, smiling broadly.

"But they are afraid to die. They understand how to make a far-seeing glass and how to make the powder that explodes, but life and death they do not understand.

"Dying is natural. To the rooted people, the grazers, the fliers, the crawlers, the swimmers, to us and *mitakuye oyasin*"—all our relations—"dying is natural." He paused.

"We like to live, and dying is part of living. We enjoy Mother Earth—birthing and dying are part of her way. As we love her, we love them.

"A Lakota likes living and is not afraid of death. He accepts it." He looked sideways at Curly. "That is what a death song says. I love the earth and am ready for death. On an evening like this," he said, "you feel it strongly. I love the earth and am ready for death. They are part of the same feeling."

Spotted Tail tossed off the next thought idly. "*Wasicu* are afraid to die. It makes their sweat bead out, their guts clench, their bowels go loose." He flashed a grin at Curly. "I would hate to be a *wasicu*."

The horses clopped along for long moments. Spotted Tail lifted a finger to make a last point. "Remember always, Nephew, you can fight for life. But you cannot fight against death."

Curly had a small thrill of comprehension and then a blanch of uncertainty. *You can fight for life. But you cannot fight against death.* He looked sideways at his uncle, not quite sure.

The next evening Curly sat in front of his mothers' lodge with his father and brother. He was glad to see Little Hawk, who was a husky fellow for eight years old. Since Curly and Tasunke Witko were slight men, it would be nice to have a big fellow in the family.

Their sister, Kettle, was at her own lodge. Earlier this summer she had married Club Man. Already she was making life within her. It was hard for Curly to think of her as a wife and mother. To him she would always be the friend who helped him through the terrible months after she-who-gave-them-birth died.

When he scratched at the door flap of the lodge this afternoon, like a stranger, no voice had invited him in. Later he had discovered that the family was at the fort, trading. But at the time he had felt a pang. Homelessness . . .

He sat and thought. He was aware of his father's glance at him and Little Hawk's wondering at his older brother's silence. They thought he was broody, probably. He couldn't help it. His mind was on Spotted Tail. Tomorrow his uncle and two other men would ride to the gate of the fort singing their death songs.

When it came out, it felt blurted, even to Curly: *"Ate,* what does it mean, 'You can fight for life, but you can't fight against death'?" He fell silent a moment. "The words say something to me, but . . ."

Tasunke Witko was quiet for a while, thinking. Curly waited nervously, respectful but impatient. Finally Tasunke Witko got up, went out to the tripod holding the pot, and dipped his fingers into the stew for a fatty piece of meat. He walked away, nodding for his sons to follow.

They went to a boulder on the edge of camp, a high one you had to climb with your hands. Curly helped Little Hawk up. Tasunke Witko motioned for his sons to sit at the other end of the rock from him.

Tasunke Witko tore the fatty meat into several pieces and put them on his legs. Curly knew what he had in mind. Often Tasunke Witko would feed the moose birds that gathered around camp. He'd start with fat near himself, get the birds avid, and then put it on his body. After he'd fed birds in one camp for several days, as now, they would peck at meat on his hands, his head, his shoulders, even his bare toes. Curly had seen his father get a moose bird to light on his upturned chin and feed off the tip of his nose.

Once Curly had seen Tasunke Witko get up and walk around the camp, singing an honor song to these birds as they flitted from his head to his hands to lodge poles and back to his hands. It was a memory of his father that Curly loved.

Now Tasunke Witko held a piece of meat up with one

hand, high over his head. Immediately one moose bird fluttered up from his leg, landed on the heel of his hand, and pecked greedily.

Tasunke Witko's eyes lit up. He waggled his arm in the air, he made his hand dance, yet the bird stayed on and ate. When it knocked the meat off the hand, Tasunke Witko picked the morsel up and raised the hand once more. He grinned at the bird as it returned to eat.

When it finished, it cocked its head at Tasunke Witko. Mockingly he cocked his head back. He made a bird-chirping sound. Then, suddenly, but gently, he closed his hand on the bird.

It squawked. It bellowed. It pecked. It clawed.

Tasunke Witko opened his hand, and the moose bird flew away. It nattered at him from a nearby branch.

"You can dance with life," he said. "You can play with it. But you must always hold it lightly. If you squeeze, it rebels. If you get scared, it will hurt you. If you squeeze desperately hard, you'll kill it."

He smiled, and his eyes flashed light at Curly.

DEATH SONGS

Sweetwater Woman helped Spotted Tail dress. Since she was the youngest of the four sisters and the newest wife, she was pleased that he had asked her to be his helper. She found it hard now, the way he expected her to hand him his clothes and fix his hair and act calm and steady. He smiled at her, and she knew he expected a smile back. It was hard to give one, but she did.

She set the fully beaded moccasins at his feet. He would be riding, not walking, to the fort, and then he wouldn't walk anymore, not on this earth. His feet would swing in the air. She felt that she would gag on the thought.

He already had his war shirt on, the one fringed on the underside of the arms with scalps he'd taken. He was wearing his full-length breechcloth, the one of red strouding, and the long leggings over it. He had not accumulated many possessions, not yet. He would have, for he was a leader. But he was also a generous man. Since he thought of others first, he didn't have much.

He was painting his face. She began tying eagle feathers into his hair. Spotted Tail could do this perfectly well, but she knew it pleased him on his last morning to feel her fingers pulling against his scalp. When she had tied the feathers, she would wrap his braids in ermine tails. As a last gesture she would wrap them.

A tear ran, and she brushed it away.

Her two sisters busied themselves. They would all ride to the fort with their husband. Sweetwater Woman wondered if his thoughts were with his sits-beside-him wife, their daughter, and his mother, all three captured and taken to the soldier house far down the river. He would never see those three again.

At last she held the piece of polished wood with the shining glass in front of his face so he could see. "You look splendid," she said.

"Splendid," echoed her older sisters.

Spotted Tail smiled at them tenderly.

It was a cool autumn morning, half-sunny, half-clouded. Curly saw his uncle a long way off. He knew that big American horse. Curly was riding from the Oglala camp behind Red Leaf and Long Chin, who were also throwing their lives away. They would join Spotted Tail in a procession, their wives riding close behind and then the rest of their families. They would leave the river and the three would go through the gates of the fort and that would be all.

Curly intended to be far away tomorrow, probably fasting and thirsting, alone for sure. He refused to look at the body of his uncle swinging from the *wasicu*'s rope by the neck. He wondered how long the soldiers would make it swing. Sometimes they kept a body hanging for days, people said, maybe wanting to flaunt this obscenity in everyone's face.

When they rode close, the three warriors looked at each other, and their eyes held. Curly found the faces unreadable. The only one who seemed at ease to Curly was Spotted Tail. For a moment he turned his face upward, as if he was enjoying the sun on his flesh.

They turned three abreast and started toward the fort. Spotted Tail's voice lifted in song first:

"Hiye, haya!
Hiye, haya!
Hiye, haya!
Hiye, haya!"

Red Leaf and Long Chin joined in chanting this preparatory phrase, their voices strong. Then each man began his own death song, perhaps a traditional one of his warrior society, perhaps something he had composed himself over the years, perhaps a spontaneous response to the moment. Spotted Tail sang:

"Hiye pila maya.
Hiye pila maya."

"Thanks," it meant, in words saved for ceremonies.

*"I rose from the earth.
I return to the earth."*

His voice soared high in the first line, fell on the second, plaintive and quavering.

*"To my mother I return.
With all my relatives
I go gladly to her."*

He repeated this simple song over and over, mesmerically. Curly wondered if his mothers' brother had come to that place where the face of this world meets the face of the other, the one Curly knew only in the waking dream. He looked at his uncle, so solid, so corporeal. Yes, surely Spotted Tail had arrived at that place. Otherwise what he was doing was impossible.

Curly also heard the words of the other men, mentions of the six grandfathers and the powers of the four directions and of their spirit helpers. But he concentrated on the voice of Spotted Tail.

"Hiye pila maya.
Hiye pila maya.
To my mother I return.
With all my relatives
I go gladly to her."

The walls of Fort Laramie loomed above them, shadowed. Curly saw soldiers in the blockhouses in the corners. Other soldiers swung the gates wide.

Without hesitating, without looking back, Spotted Tail, Red Leaf, and Long Chin rode through the gates. In the opening they rode into a swatch of sunlight. The colors of their blankets and feathers and beads grew brighter, as from a last pulse of life.

As though by plan, the families stopped outside the gates, sat their horses, watched, listened. At the last moment Sweetwater Woman kicked her horse hard and burst through the gate as it was closing. Evidently she could not bear to be apart from Spotted Tail, or even his suspended body.

Inside, the three men sang their songs, all flowers of the same tree of Lakota teaching. Spotted Tail sang:

"I bear death within me.
It is my old companion.
I have loved life on Mother Earth.
I accept death."

As the soldiers closed the gates behind the warriors' horses, rage flash-flooded Curly. Sitting on his pony, he felt as though he were reeling.

"Hiye pila maya.
Hiye pila maya.
To my mother I return.
With all my relatives
I go gladly to her."

LOVE OVER DEATH

In the village he saw Black Buffalo Woman. His head snapped around and his eyes shot at her.

It was wondrous, like seeing someone you had never seen before. She looked radiant, as White Buffalo Cow Woman must have looked when she came to the Lakota three times seven generations ago, bringing the *canupa,* sacred pipe, as a gift.

The girl half-turned, as though she knew his eyes were on her. Her eyes flicked up at him and quickly back down to propriety.

He swallowed his astonishment. She was flirting with him, flirting brazenly. Suddenly she turned and went her way.

Curly shuddered with cold.

He shuddered again. It was his uncle's impending death, he knew. The families were just back from the fort, and the whole village was waiting for the awful news: three bodies dangling from the gallows.

Everyone was acting strange. They would shake their heads and avoid each other's eyes. The unspoken words were: Only *wasicu* . . .

None of them would ever speak the name of any of the dead men again. The ones who threw their lives away, they would say. The one who was your mothers' brother.

The one who rode magnificently against the Two Circle People. Spotted Tail's actual name, Sinte Gleska, would never be used to designate him again.

Curly took only his blanket onto the hill where he would fast and thirst and pray.

He tried to think about his uncle, but his mind was on Black Buffalo Woman. He sat on the rock on the hill high above the camp. He spoke to the six grandfathers and asked the blessings of the powers that make the world. "You make life," he said in their honor. "You make the life continually being born into the world, two-legged people, four-legged peoples, rooted people, creatures of the air, all that is, *mitakuye oyasin*. You bring life onto the earth every day."

He tried to remember carefully, one by one, the good times he had spent with Spotted Tail. *The one who was my mothers' brother,* he corrected himself. Probably Spotted Tail was already dead and his name now forbidden. Curly repeated to himself over and over what his uncle had said to him about dying: "You can fight for life. But you can not fight against death."

His mind kept lurching back to Black Buffalo Woman.

He knew now what had been different about her. She wore her braids in front like a woman, not in back like a child.

He had known Red Cloud's niece all his life but hadn't seen her since spring, when his band and hers, the Bad Faces, were camped together. She must be fifteen winters now.

She was wearing her braids in front. That meant she was ready to take on life within her. It meant she spent time in the hut for women during her *isnati,* bleeding.

Pictures stampeded through his mind. Black Buffalo Woman walking under the blanket with a man he couldn't see. Black Buffalo Woman giving suck. Her sitting at the center fire beside a shadowy man. The pictures gave him a feeling like fever.

He pushed his mind back to the matter at hand. He said in his mind to the powers, *You make life. In the face of death you offer life, ever birthing into the world.*

Spotted Tail's death crept into his mind like a dark spirit. He could wrestle with it, or he could dream of Black Buffalo Woman.

A touch on the shoulder.

Curly jumped.

Black Buffalo Woman. Her face close to his, eyes alight with mischief.

Quickly she turned her face away from his. But she sat down next to him. Close to him. It was wildly, unbelievably brazen.

He felt his face flush with fear and anger. To get sneaked up on from behind! Even while praying! By a woman!

She smiled at him, proud of herself.

He wondered if she was feeling a fever, as he was.

What did she want? Why was she here?

Ah, she was crazy right now, living in the shadow of the body of Spotted Tail swinging on the end of a rope.

He was crazy, too. The shadow was very black. His mind was blacker than blindness.

They said nothing. They sat.

Curly wondered why Black Buffalo Woman had chanced in his direction at this time. True, she had acted enamored of him, the way girls do before they wear braids in front, smitten by an older boy. That meant nothing. The girls themselves forgot it in a moon or even a quarter-moon. She had watched him and sometimes hung around him at the camp of the two bands on the Running Water last winter. He had pretended not to notice, being polite.

The fever ran through him.

She turned her face into his and looked into his eyes. Astonishing for a Lakota woman anywhere. Alone on a hillside, away from people's eyes, mad and frightening.

The fever coursed through him.

Her face was alive. It looked to him somehow like the

surface of a small stream, still if you weren't paying any attention, flowing if you were. And sparkling here and there with sun glints. And full of things you couldn't see, the darting shadows of fish and other living creatures. Sometimes they touched the surface in a flash of color.

She was much amused.

She raised a hand and touched his face.

Fever raged in him.

She held her hand to his face for a long, long time. Curly had never been touched like this.

Time writhed.

His arms goose-pimpled.

They looked into each other's eyes.

She eased her face close to his. The breaths from their nostrils mingled.

The fever was a runaway horse.

She touched her lips to his, very lightly.

Curly reached up with his right hand and touched her breast, a caress.

She put her hand over his on her breast and slowly lay back on the earth.

In the fever he took her. There on the hill, embraced by the sky that arched over his uncle's body and their living forms, his mind shadowed by the dark spirit, he took his first woman.

He wanted to do it as he had always dreamed, slowly, tenderly, with gentle explorations.

Instead he erupted like a fire-spewing mountain.

She seemed not to be sorry. She did her best to make him erupt.

When he was finished the first time, they lay spent, silent, soaking up what was happening. Then he took her again.

Later he held her hand and led her farther away from camp, onto the back of the hill in a little clump of trees.

He wanted to take her again and again all afternoon.

It was madness, but it was what he raged for. Hawk was

still, at peace. If Hawk could be stroked and truly gentled, it would feel like this.

With all their clothes finally off, they ravished each other. Ravished each other over and over.

When he rolled off her, the picture of the dead Spotted Tail lightninged through him. The dark spirit in his mind shoved him back on top of her. Over and over.

Toward sunset they walked back to camp together. He wondered if he was her first man. Surely so. Surely. He didn't know for certain.

It was impossible. It was madness. They wouldn't be able to set up a lodge together for years. At seventeen Curly was much too young to marry. Black Buffalo Woman, fifteen, was barely a woman.

Yet he had to have her. Today, tonight, every day and night he had to have her. That urge cascaded through him.

If she took on life within her, it would be a disaster. She would be disgraced. Probably she would be given as a wife to an older man, one who could take care of her child.

Impossible. Disaster. Impossible to mate with her body and spirit, impossible not to.

He shook with joy. He spasmed with fear.

A short way from camp they separated to walk back to their lodges separately, so people wouldn't see them. As they parted, she spoke. Curly realized that all during the sex, in a compact they didn't need to name, neither of them had said a word. Her words of leave-taking were, "My Strange Man."

A SPY

Hatred clotted in No Water's throat.

He watched them touch hands one last time, lingeringly, and finally start to the village on separate and deceitful paths. He almost choked on his loathing for the two of them.

He had seen it all. Fools. What fools they were, both of them, thinking they could commit such crimes almost within sight of the village and go unnoticed. And unpunished.

He had been watching Black Buffalo Woman carefully since her Buffalo Woman Ceremony a quarter-moon ago, when the *wicasa wakan* helped her over the threshold from girl to woman, giving her ritual instructions, singing the traditional songs, giving voice to the prayers. It meant she had had her first flow. She had spent time in the lonely tipi, so that the power of her trickling blood and the dangerous spirits that attended it would hurt no one. She had taken the cloth where that flow dripped, wrapped it in hide, and walked out alone to find a plum tree, because plum trees bore fruit bountifully. She had put the hide into the tree and left it forever, where the coyotes could not eat it and no man would dare touch it for fear of the malicious spirits that hovered nearby.

Then, because she was much prized, her parents sponsored a buffalo ceremony for her. The *wicasa wakan* asked the blessings of the good spirits on her, gave her defense against spirits that might make her act crazy, instructed her in the virtues of womanhood, and prayed for her fruitfulness. Her mother braided Black Buffalo Woman's hair, put the braids in front, and made a red line down the part in the center of her head. She was a woman now.

Hah! She had just spent the afternoon acting completely crazy. No Water had witnessed her madness with his own eyes. He snorted at the so-called power of the *wicasa wakan*. He knew what kind of person Black Buffalo Woman was. He had known for a long time. He knew, and he wanted her for himself.

True, right now he hated her. True, she was wild, like a dog not trained to drag the travois. He would break her to his will. The need to break her, to make her move to the touch of his harness, pumped through him like hot blood and bile.

No Water wouldn't break Light Curly Hair—he

wouldn't have to. He knew that one's heart, which was weak. Taking the woman the boy-man wanted would be enough, and more than enough. Light Curly Hair would walk through life feeling like a rag was stuffed down his throat, No Water's rag.

What a fool. Light Curly Hair had not even known she wanted him. Or known himself well enough to realize he wanted her. The sandy-haired boy knew very little about life. But No Water had known. He had always watched, and had seen the way they looked at each other, like it made them dizzy. Now he would take what Light Curly Hair most desired.

No Water smiled with twisted pleasure.

From his spot on the hill he watched them disappear from view, approaching the village from different paths. He didn't even like the way Light Curly Hair walked, though it was like Black Buffalo Woman's way. They were both coltish creatures, a quality attractive in a woman, repugnant in a man. No Water felt alien to these people with sapling bodies. They seemed to him ephemeral, shifting here and there on the breeze. They were flowing liquid, not solid rock—tricky Coyote, not staunch Buffalo Bull. A man ought to be big and solid and immovable, like a boulder, like himself.

The worst was, the sandy-haired boy thought himself better than anyone else. The other youths were always together, having fun, each doing what young men did, following along, participating. Light Curly Hair was always standing off to himself, aloof. Or he was gone away alone, wandering, pretending he was on a mission no one else knew about. Even when he was in the group, his eyes looked far away and his head sometimes seemed half-cocked, listening to a voice no one else could hear.

Because of the airs he took on, some of the old people said he was something special, someone sacred. No Water thought he was flimsy as mist on the river, mysterious at dawn but gone when the sun rose. The sun in this case was No Water.

Oh no, it wasn't just because the sandy-haired boy was Hunkpatila and not one of the scorned Bad Faces. Or because the *wasicu*'s blood clearly ran in his veins. Or even because he'd kicked No Water's friend Pretty Fellow in the nose and broken it. No Water had despised the light-haired boy for a long time, and his enmity was beyond needing reasons.

Today was hard, though. He'd seen how Curly touched Black Buffalo Woman's breasts delicately, and helped her unwind the hide belt that circled her waist and ran between her legs to protect her innocence and coiled down her thighs. He'd seen her fling that chastity into the bushes. He'd seen his woman topped for the first time, and then many times. He'd watched her make herself a wanton.

He hated Light Curly Hair today. He knew he would hate the son of Tasunke Witko many nights in the future, when lascivious pictures of the two of them invaded his dreams.

But he also saw in his mind Black Buffalo Woman with himself, doing the same things, doing them when she desperately wanted to, and doing them when she wanted not to but was commanded by her husband. He preferred the pictures of her submitting half-willingly. They were delicious.

The two were well out of sight now. He got up from behind the stump. He knew what he had to do. He knew where the power over Black Buffalo Woman lay. He must seize it. He must go to the plum tree where she'd put the bundle of her first flow, lay his hands upon it, and claim it for himself.

This was dangerous. The evil *tonwan* would be close by. They would attach themselves to any man who touched the bundle and give him boils, or worse. It could be nasty.

But a man who dared nothing gained nothing. No Water would go to Red Rock, the bone keeper. Bone keepers conjured with dangerous medicines. Sometimes they even killed their fellow Lakota with their spells. But Red Rock had the power to chase away the *tonwan* with his incantations. When he was paid with even more horses, he would take the blood of Black Buffalo Woman's new womanhood and turn it into a powerful potion and . . .

Then No Water would possess the soul of the woman he wanted.

He thought of possessing her in every way. He thought of flaunting his possession in the face of the Strange Man. He smiled. He almost laughed out loud.

He set off toward the plum tree.

A SURPRISE

Tasunke Witko came walking across the circle of lodges toward Curly. A-i-i-i, Curly thought, *will my father reprimand me for being away from my mothers in their grief, for disappearing on this day of all days?*

"Spotted Tail," Tasunke Witko began, and paused. He was letting the message sink in.

Curly got it. His mothers' brother was still alive.

"Spotted Tail and the others who threw their lives away," Tasunke Witko went on, "have been taken down the river. They will go to a fort far away, the soldiers won't say where. They will not be hanged. They will be punished by being kept away from us. No one knows how long."

"Why?"

"No explanation." Tasunke Witko paused for effect. "Also, the hundred prisoners will be released."

Curly looked into his father's eyes. They were bright with happiness. The women and children would come back to their families.

He wanted to throw his arms around Tasunke Witko, to hold his father and be held. He wouldn't do it. He was no longer a child, to be embraced by his father, and they had never been close. But right now he wanted to.

They turned and walked toward the lodge.

He realized it was not his father's body he wanted to touch. The memory of Black Buffalo Woman's body was in his fingertips, his lips, his *ce,* his skin all over.

He saw the two of them atop one another all afternoon, dancing the dance all creatures make to create life.

He smiled to himself. Maybe they'd loved Spotted Tail from the shadow world back into this world. Maybe this afternoon they'd made life, the two of them. On his way to the land beyond the pines, where spirits live, Spotted Tail had seen them making love and laughed his big, bawdy laugh and come back to earth to enjoy making life some more.

Curly half-believed it.

They'd raised Spotted Tail from the dead by dancing the mating dance.

A miracle, that dancing.

Curly felt grand.

PART **TWO**

Earning
A
Name

The spirit of His Crazy Horse—
or is it Rider, or are they the
*   same?—*
stands where the dance pole once
*   stood.*
From a beaded bag
he takes the two pieces of the
*   canupa,*
the stem,
which represents Mother Earth,
and the bowl,
which represents the circle of the
*   universe.*
He fills the canupa with
*   cansasa,*
and lights it with an ember.
Without words he offers the smoke
*   ritually*
to each of the four directions,
the sky,
and the earth.

He slaps the earth with an open
*   hand,*
"I, His Crazy Horse," he says,
"From the Hunkpatila Oglala of
*   the Titunwan Lakota,*
I look, and I tell you truly what I
*   see."*

The drum throbs.

"E-i-i-i," Curly said to Buffalo Hump, and lifted his eyebrows mockingly. Tasunke Witko was walking away from the wickiup where the two young men lived alone except during the coldest months. The eyebrows protested one of the thousand things fathers did to irk grown sons. That was one of the reasons unmarried young men lived in wickiups and stayed away from the village as much as they could on hunting trips or raids. The older men shook their heads a lot and murmured that the young men needed to be married. But the older women said they weren't ready to support wives and children.

"Hoye," said Buffalo Hump, "right." He had a father, too.

Curly looked after his father and shook his head. Yes, maybe he was exaggerating his impatience for his *hunka.* But he really couldn't talk to Tasunke Witko these days. Not about his vision or much of anything else. *Fathers.* For that matter, *parents.*

"Let's ride," he said. Buffalo Hump grinned and nodded.

It was their way. Sometimes they called it scouting, sometimes hunting, but usually they just rode over the country, looking. Often they talked about the warrior spirit. More often they simply kept a companionable silence. Buffalo Hump was the only person in the world, it seemed to Curly, who let him be silent without asking what was wrong. Curly preferred silence. The sound of his own voice threw him off inside. When he talked, he couldn't hear his own interior voice, couldn't tell how Hawk was responding.

Half a day later they staked the horses downhill from a long slant of stone and picked their way carefully through the cedars to the summit. It was one of their favorite places, a sandstone bluff shelving up and out into an awesome emptiness of air. You could see so far here, a couple of sleeps' worth of country to the left and right, across to another upthrust opposite, and the meandering bed of the creek in the middle.

They had come here first because it was a learning place for Curly. At one end of the bluff was a nest of *wambli,* war eagles, wing flappers, bearers of the feathers the people prized most. That alone made it a special place. Here you could see *wambli gleska,* the spotted eagle, the young golden, highest-flying and farthest-seeing of all creatures, the representative of Wakan Tanka, the first Spirit.

This place was Curly and Buffalo Hump's retreat, a place for solitude, contemplation, and the companionship of *hunka.*

They slipped through the small twisted trees to the summit and lay flat. They were careful. If you silhouetted yourself against the sky, an enemy might see you, and your haven would become a trap.

They slid into a big fissure in the sandstone and down. Below, down twice the height of a very tall man, was a shelf wide enough to put a tipi on. Here they often camped. At their feet stretched nothing but space. If you tossed small limbs down the big fissure, you could build a little fire. You only had to bring water and a little pemmican. The timid would never be comfortable here. It was a home for the daring.

This time they lounged out on the edge, rambling through big talks, looking at the void beneath their swinging feet, the air Mother Earth gave as space for birds but not for men. Underneath their words whispered a small song in the voice of death. They heard it whenever they looked down.

They spoke first of their resentments and dislikes, but soon of their hopes, their dreams for their lives, then even of their nighttime dreams and their fantasies, the lives of their spirits. They felt they understood each other intimately, in a way no one else could understand them.

When dark fell, Buffalo Hump again pointed out to Curly the emerging stars and their constellations. He knew well the positions of the stars and assemblages of stars, at every time of year and every time of night. He told the time of night and the season of the year by the stars. He knew where the star creatures had come from, where they were going, who they were chasing, what they wanted.

It was not winter, the time for telling stories, so the young men did not retell the tales of the star gods and goddesses. Hump knew all these stories. Though some people said the stars were evil, for they fled from the sun, Hump's grandfather had said otherwise and had passed his star lore to Hump.

So they talked also of the men of power like Hump's grandfather, Lakota who knew the stars, the sun and moon, the flowing winds and the powers that live to the west, north, east, and south, the rain and lightning and lightning-gives-birth-to-sound, even the rocks. Many people were afraid of these powers and of the men who approached them closely enough to gain added understanding. These people had been afraid of Hump's grandfather. They were afraid of men and women who could seduce or suck an ill spirit out of someone's body, of men and women who could heal people (or maybe make them sick) with herbs and potions, even of *wicasa wakan* like Tasunke Witko and the Bad Face Horn Chips.

"Do you know anything about the Inyan Horn Chips wears around his neck?" asked Curly. Stone medicine, Inyan power, was the most ancient and powerful medicine the people knew, for Inyan was the most ancient of creatures. Horn Chips wore Inyan near his heart and kept others in a hide bundle.

"It comes from the Maka Sica," said Hump. The badlands along the Earth-Smoke River. "It's the body of an ancient water creature." He stopped, and Curly didn't ask more. The youths were daring even to touch on the subject. "He sings the songs Inyan has taught him," finished Buffalo Hump, meaning their power flowed through him.

They spoke softly, because this power was dangerous. None of the people would ever reprimand Chips—they were Lakota and had utter respect for the path of every man's spirit. But they feared him and subtly avoided him.

Buffalo Hump shook his head. He smiled ruefully at Curly. "Such Lakota," he said.

Curly smiled, too, but he didn't look up at his *hunka*. They'd often chuckled together about these cowards, people who stayed away from Lakota men and women of medicine. Cowards, yes—they feared to connect themselves to power, to use it, to live it. Surely such people were barely fit to call themselves Lakota.

Curly looked between his feet at the empty space below. His mind looped outward and down, a spiraling drop through nothingness. Just the spinning and floating drop, not the death at the end of it.

He felt himself a coward. He had not told his *hunka* about what he saw beyond. Or anyone. He was not living his vision.

Even now he wasn't going to tell Buffalo Hump about seeing Inyan in his vision, the small stone Rider wore slung under his left shoulder, or the other one behind his ear. Even knowing—knowing somehow—that it was one of Horn Chips' Inyan creatures, he would not tell. Could not tell.

Instead he started talking about Black Buffalo Woman.

"We were like this," Curly said, "like small grasses that grow near springs, that grow braiding around each other." He made his fingers intertwine, lacing away from his body and into Buffalo Hump's eyes.

Hump pictured in his mind those fragile tendrils. They grew so close together, weaving through each other like vines, that you couldn't pluck one alone, but only a bunch entwined, always the most delicate of greens. He felt a lightning bolt of fear for his friend.

Curly talked on. He had told Hump already about the mating, there on the hill and later in the glen, his *hunka* Curly and the blossoming girl-woman Black Buffalo Woman coupling over and over. Curly didn't speak of their bodies but of feelings, of reachings and surgings of emotion, of intuitions, of stirrings of soul, of spirits and the journey of body and spirit in riding the stallion and mare of sex. Though the words were ordinary enough, Buffalo Hump felt like he was hearing one of the old, old stories.

"*A-i-i-i,*" said Curly, "being away from her makes me ache. I ache just walking around the village. I ache in my loins. I ache in my heart. I ache in my spirit."

"If she's been with the *wasicu,*" said Hump, pointing to his penis, "a woman will make you ache, starting three or four sleeps afterward." Then he saw from Curly's face that the joke was dumb.

"When I see Black Buffalo Woman," Curly went on, "I get a fever. Half the time I sneak around trying to see her on the sly, spot her gathering wood for a fire or helping her mother paint a parfleche."

He took a deep breath and let it out. "The other half I run from seeing her like a husband encountering his mother-in-law."

Hump smiled painfully at this foolish comparison.

"When I see her," Curly went on, "I feel like I'm about to drown. Glug, glug, glug," he said mockingly.

Buffalo Hump looked up sharply and saw that his *hunka* was not exaggerating. Curly's eyes said it was all real. He could not have Black Buffalo Woman and could not stay away from her. He could not shoot at an antelope without wanting Black Buffalo Woman to see his prowess, but he could not take her his kill, for she belonged to her father and her brothers. He could seldom talk to her and could not stand to see her speak with any other man, even one of the grandfathers. When she stood in a blanket with another man in the evening, even for a moment, it drove him mad.

The two sat in silence. Buffalo Hump watched Curly's eyes play in the space below their dangling feet. The younger man had always been intrigued by this emptiness in a way that eluded Buffalo Hump. Like being fascinated by the spirit world or by death. Himself, Hump liked life, not this eerie-airy stuff. He liked a good woman, and her body more than her spirit. He liked a fire, not for its meaning or whatever the *wicasa wakan* saw in it, but for its warmth. He saw Spirit clearly enough. Like all Lakota, he was habitually conscious of it. But he was a little impatient of talk about it. This was the world, this was life. It was enough and more than enough.

He did see, though, that his younger brother lived nearly in another world.

Buffalo Hump had a jolt of thought. He looked at his *hunka*. Then he knew. He turned over in his mind what Curly had said about his love for Black Buffalo Woman. He knew. Not from Curly's meaning, but from the kinds of words he chose. So Buffalo Hump asked, "Little brother, have you seen beyond?"

Curly's look told all. The boy's eyes shot into Hump's, startled and ablaze with something. Then he turned his head away.

A-i-i-i. Curly had had a vision. And told no one.

Buffalo Hump gazed at his friend, his heart dancing with excitement and dread and sorrow. He knew now. . . .

"E-i-i-i," moaned Curly. "Those who see beyond must speak. And change their lives. Or suffer terribly."

Yes, or suffer terribly, thought Hump. The boy's eyes flitted away, pretending to skim over the landscape or read the earth.

Hump wondered. In the last year—or was it two years?—Curly had dressed shabbily and sometimes seemed unnecessarily dusty or muddy. Was this deliberate? Was it the gesture of the *wakinyan* dreamer? Maybe his *hunka* had had the most powerful and terrible of visions and was afraid to tell? Cold quaked up and down Hump's spine.

He tried to remember. No, Curly had been neat as a boy, not careless, like many children. Yes, he'd gotten slovenly. It had happened in the last year or two. Was this just from the odd feelings of the time Curly's body became a man's? Lots of boys got sloppy then. But Hump would swear that Curly was not sloppy. He was deliberately shabby, dirty, as though he were from a poor family. There was a difference.

Buffalo Hump could not ask. That would be a violation of another man's way. But . . .

Hump writhed. His *hunka* was suffering. What could Hump do?

He breathed in and then out and finally took an awful chance. He said, "Do you have anything you need to tell your father?"

After a long pause Curly shook his head very slightly. No.

Hump knew Curly would resist talking to his father seriously about anything. Bad blood between those two.

Hump pondered. He would take one more chance, a bigger one, more dangerous.

"Have you heard about the one who ran like a duck?" he asked.

Curly shook his head no.

"This youth who ran like a duck," Hump began, knowing that Curly would understand from the avoidance of the name that the fellow was no longer living, "he was my mother's sister's husband's uncle, a *wakinyan* dreamer."

Buffalo Hump let that sit a little. This was the most dangerous moment. Curly might get up and leave. This was the most antagonistic behavior you might ever show toward your *hunka*. Hump waited, giving Curly a chance to choose. He stared out across the sagebrush plain far below their feet, not glancing anywhere near Curly's eyes.

The young man said nothing. Maybe he wanted to hear this cautionary tale. Maybe he needed to. Leaping into the dark, Buffalo Hump went on.

"The one who ran like a duck was scared to death of storms." Hump shrugged self-consciously. Curly would know that the youth either hadn't told anyone about his dream of *wakinyan*, hadn't done the ceremony necessary to put himself on the side of the powers, or hadn't done it properly. "He was only nine when he had his dream. He was sick for many days, near death, traveling far in his dream. After that he was afraid to tell."

Hump waited, thinking of the fear in this silence.

"For several years the Moons When the Geese Return and When the Ponies Shed were terrible for him." The months of spring, when the *wakinyan* brought rain back to the plains. "Whenever a storm would come, this fellow would run from lodge to lodge, trying to hide. At first everyone just thought it was funny, to be so afraid and run so hard. He ran like a duck on the slick mud, his feet flat and splayed apart.

"At first they thought, *He's just a child.* Then people began to suspect. Even if he hadn't had a dream of *wakinyan,* they said, somehow he was not all right with the *wakinyan* tanka, or else he wouldn't be so scared. Now when he splatted from lodge to lodge in a storm, looking for a safe place, people began not to let him in. They thought he would bring the lightning there.

"After a while, during a storm, he would just scratch at door flaps or even try to crawl under lodge skirts and people would drive him away. As he left, running splayfooted, they would call after him that he ran stupidly, like a duck."

Curly would know they said that because they wouldn't speak of the more serious matter, the way he was endangering the whole band.

"Finally a *wicasa wakan* got him into a sweat lodge and nearly sweated that boy *dry.*" Hump took the risk of smiling sideways at his *hunka.* "He didn't let the boy out until he told what he had dreamed. After that he was a sacred clown all his life," meaning one who obeyed the *wakinyan* by doing everything backward. Hump chuckled a little. "He walked pigeon-toed after that."

Curly felt his breath catch again. He didn't know what to do.

So Buffalo Hump knew about him.

Shame pumped through Curly's veins like a dye.

Buffalo Hump knew Curly was bringing danger to his people every moment. Curly was inviting the anger of the *wakinyan* tanka. Grandmothers and grandfathers could be killed because of him. Children. Warriors, fathers, mothers.

Curly stood up on the edge of the precipice. He looked down.

Once, maybe one winter ago when they were here, he'd taken off his red breechcloth, thrown it over the edge, and watched it curl and twist and float through the long seconds. He'd felt every lilt and lift and flutter all the way down, a dance in the air. He'd felt in his knees and spine the dance his body could never do. When the breechcloth came gently to rest at the bottom on Maka, Earth, he looked at the bloody spot for too long a moment.

Then he and Hump laughed, alive, and started climbing down to get it.

Hump asked again. "Do you have anything you need to talk to your father about?"

It was beyond decency for Hump to ask twice, really, but Curly could not be angry. He felt a water-flow of relief. He turned back to his *hunka* to speak. The words should have begun, "When I went beyond, I saw Rider. . . ." They gushed up into his throat. They clotted into a ball, like thick, gooey blood.

He could not speak. The words were strangling him.

Curly turned to the edge of the cliff. He looked out into emptiness. His eyes danced downward as his breechcloth had danced, as a leaf would fall. The dance made his knees queasy.

Curly felt Buffalo Hump's hand on his arm, warm, friendly.

He looked into his *hunka*'s eyes. His knees steadied.

"Spirit does not expect us to do what we can't do," Hump said companionably.

He seemed sure.

Curly clasped his *hunka*'s forearm.

"I have an idea. Why don't you wait for me here?"

What did Hump mean? Normally Curly loved to stay here alone. But was Hump saying he should stay here and make the decision to tell what he saw beyond? Was Hump pushing him?

"It's something we might do together," said Hump lightly. "I want to talk to some people in the village."

Curly nodded.

Hump began to climb. From the top of the cliff Hump looked back and smiled. Curly felt afraid. Afraid to think about telling what he saw beyond. Afraid to think of his mad love for Black Buffalo Woman. Almost for the first time in his life, afraid to be alone.

Hump came back in the predawn light. Curly heard the call of the hoot owl and answered it with the same call, twice. Then came the scraping sounds of Hump's feet and hands on the rock as he climbed down.

"Want something to eat?" asked Hump.

He handed Curly some pemmican. Curly chewed on it. They sat on the edge of the cliff, wordless. They dangled their legs and smiled to themselves and watched the light of the sun seep into the world.

When they'd eaten plenty and the sun was fully up, Hump said, "Did you know the Sahiyela woman Yellow Woman and the child are going to join their families on the Red Shield River? With Stick and Lark?"

Curly jerked his eyes into his *hunka*'s face and smiled. The woman he had saved in the lightning storm and her son, plus her sister and brother-in-law.

His spirits lifted.

"You want to go adventuring to the Sahiyela?" asked Hump, his eyes merry. "You and me?" It was another country, far to the south.

"To!" Damn right!

Curly felt the power in the beat of the drum. Subtle and insistent, this was the pulse of the dancing, the life force of the ceremony.

This was the eighth day of the medicine lodge ceremony of the Sahiyela people. All the people were gathered here on Beaver Creek in this land the Lakota called Fat Meat Earth, far to the south and east of the country of Curly's people. All the Sahiyela were here, dancing and singing and drumming as the sun came back to its full strength.

It was a ceremony for all the tribe held every Moon of the Ripening Berries, which the Sahiyela called the Time When the Horses Get Fat and the *wasicu* called June. The people gave thanks to Maka, Earth, for the things that grew, the things that nurtured and fed human beings. They gave thanks to Power for the great pattern of birthing and growing and dying that was the energy of life on earth.

Some men made private gestures during this ceremony. Having made pledges to Spirit during the year, they danced and fasted and thirsted for the final four days. They gazed at the live sunpole tree cut down and planted, still green, at the center of the sundance ground. They called it the sun pole and filled its leafy branches with to-bacco ties of buckskin, each representing a prayer. They shed their blood through cuts on their chests or backs. They tied themselves to the sun pole by their bloody breasts or dragged buffalo skulls around camp by the wounds in their backs.

But these were private matters. The great matter was the welfare of all the tribe, the sustenance of the great cycle of nurturing between the Sahiyela and Earth.

For that reason all the Sahiyela were here each year—

every tribe, every band, every village, and every lodge.

It was a year of change. All sun cycles were times of change, for change was the nature of life. But this time the changes were sharper, and caused by *wasicu*.

This Fat Meat Earth lay between two great rivers, the Shell River, which the *wasicu* called the Platte, on the north and the Feather River, which the *wasicu* called the Arkansas, on the south. These *wasicu,* whom the Sahiyela people called *veho,* as the *wasicu* called them Cheyenne, were running up the trails on these two rivers like ants to carcasses, as many *wasicu* as buffalo in one of the greatest herds. This was what was happening in the *wasicu*'s summer of 1857.

But it was one of the endless summers that the Sahiyela did not number, in one of the endless circle of years that made up time, yet spiraled beyond time, and what was happening was the medicine lodge ceremony. It renewed the ancient way, the earth's giving the people sustenance.

The drumbeat, ever-present, inexhaustible, eternal.

Curly looked sideways at Buffalo Hump. Both the young men felt the spirit of the Sahiyela pump like blood into this dance. They had talked about it. For one more than twenty winters now, since the *wasicu* who came for the beaver had built the big lodge they called Fort Laramie where the Swimming Bird River flowed into the Shell River, the Lakota had not given this kind of spirit to the *wiwanyag wachipi,* the gazing-at-the-sun-pole dance. Instead many people loafed around the fort. They brought in hides and traded them for the *wasicu*'s knives and pots and beads and bells and guns and powder, and *mni wakan,* holy water, whiskey. Especially whiskey.

Curly and Hump's band, the Hunkpatila Oglala, had stayed close to the fort too, but now they were keeping away. Otherwise you might become dependent, helpless, willing to do anything for the *wasicu*. Women might become every man's women in exchange for a drink. Worst of all, when you drank, you lost control of your spirit. You had no power and no connection to Power. You had no spirit to give to the great ceremonies and could take none. So the strength of the ceremonies among the Lakota had waned these last twenty winters.

Curly and Hump thought it was grand to see the Sahiyela still so strong, so fervent, so united in their awareness of the sacred, their connection to Earth and Sun. They thought now that traveling all these many sleeps and spending these moons among the Sahiyela was beyond doubt worth it: They knew that the Lakota people must stand as unified in spirit as the Sahiyela.

Now Curly began to wonder: He had had a vision. He thought of it as his own, and how he triumphed or suffered through it was his own business. But was that so?

Here he saw that visions and all connectedness to Power in some sense belonged to the people. Individual power was the people's power.

Did Curly have a right, however weak or strong his vision might have been, to keep it secret? To not live it? Did not all the people own the strength in it?

The medicine lodge ceremony was basically like the sun-gazing dance of the Lakota, but not exactly like it. Curly and Hump had been learning the differences every day. The first four days were a kind of building up, and the camp moved each day. The Sahiyela built three lodges, what they called a gathering lodge, a lonely lodge, and at the last camp the medicine lodge. The first two were tipis, but the third was an arbor of poles, with a sunpole tree in the middle, the sacred center.

In the gathering lodge, as far as Curly and Hump could tell, the leaders planned the ceremony. In the lonely lodge people who had pledged to offer the ceremony, two men and a woman this time, got instruction from experienced medicine lodge givers. The medicine lodge itself was the sacred heart of the ceremony, with its center sun pole, its buffalo skull, its prayer mound. It was a circular arbor supported by poles, with an opening to the east. In and around this lodge was done the painting of the makers and the dancers, the praying and offering, and singing and dancing, ever to the drumbeat.

The drum throbbed now, the voice of Earth herself, her pulse. The pulse that sounded in the streams, that made the winds blow, that pushed life through the trees until buds came out, that brought the grasses back, that birthed the buffalo. Thump, thump, thump, the beat of Earth.

The dancers were making their final ceremonial homage to both Earth and Sun. Curly and Hump had watched their mentors prepare them. They were already painted, many with red suns on their chests and crescent moons on their left shoulder blades, others with white spots of hail or long forks of lightning. Now the instructors made smoke from sweetgrass for each dancer, rubbed and blew on the bodies of each one, put dried grass in their hair, showed them just how to salute the sun pole or the sky itself.

To the beat of the drum they danced. They blew their eagle-bone whistles. Four days ago the sound had often been energetic, jubilant, defiant. Now it was faded, thin, forlorn. The dancers had taken neither food nor water for four days. Their only energy now came from the drum-throb itself. Curly could feel their weakness in his knees, their dizziness in his mind. The women sang stoutheart songs to keep the dancers going. He could see in their dances and feel by sympathy in their bodies what was happening to them: The heartbeat of the drum moved their legs and arms, its force kept their bodies upright, its spirit entered them, animated them, and became them. All of existence became the thump of the foot on Mother Earth and the beat of drum, which was the pulse, the rhythm of the blood, the body, the rivers, the earth.

Curly felt it primally. He felt it in the soles of feet, in his legs, his balls, his belly, heart, and brain. He wondered: *Is this the song of Inyan? Is this the song of Maka, Earth?* But it didn't matter. He felt it.

Yet another pause came. Most of the dancers, all except those who had dreamed of *wakinyan* and wore hail spots, wiped off their paint and left the medicine lodge wrapped in blankets. Yellow Woman slipped up beside Curly and Hump. Her son, the one saved in the thunderstorm, toddled behind her. "This is the last dance," she said softly. Only the lodge givers and the hail-painted dancers, those who had dreamed of *wakinyan*, were left. They were being painted one final time.

One of the men put four bundles of white sage on four sides of the sun pole, to the southeast and southwest, then the northeast and northwest. One by one the lodge givers led two hail-painted men in dancing from the bundles to the sun pole and back, waving their right arms as they advanced toward the pole, left arms as they retreated. As they danced, each lodge giver dropped his clothing and it was wrapped back around him.

Then the mentors of the lodge givers did similar dances.

Now the sun was just down. The throbbing of the drum spoke climax.

A command was shouted.

One of the mentors stood just east of the sun pole, hail dancers to his left and right. He held a peeled willow stick as tall as a man, with a scalp tied to the tip.

Driven by the drum they danced forward toward the east entrance. Then stopped and danced in place. Thump, thump, forward to the door again, and again in place. Thump, thump, once more forward and in place. The fourth time they charged out onto the prairie to the east, circled the lodge, and dashed back to the pole.

Out they charged three more times in different directions, the leader waving the willow stick like a lance, running back to the pole, bursting out again.

Just before full dark the voices fell silent and the drum ceased. Curly could still feel it from Earth herself.

The dancers sat on the ground in the lodge and washed their paint off. The ceremony was over.

"Come eat with us," said Yellow Woman. She was remarried, to her older sister's husband, Stick.

Curly and Buffalo Hump smiled, nodded yes at her, and looked at each other. They held each other's eyes. Neither needed to put the lesson here into words: *We'll take this spirit home, this sense of unity, all the people as one beating heart, its pulse the pulse of the drum, which is Earthbeat.*

A RING, A CIRCLE

Everyone had a grand time, the moon after the medicine lodge ceremony. First all the camps stayed together to hunt buffalo. The Lakota visitors found out that everyone called this Fat Meat Country for a reason. And the young Lakota showed that they were good guests—they hunted as fiercely as anyone and gave the meat to the families who had shown them hospitality.

When the big herds began to wander east, where the grass was deeper, the people hunted deer and antelope. The Sahiyela would have plenty to eat this year.

They might not have their ease, though. The agent had told those who went in to trade that the *wasicu* soldiers were determined to find the Sahiyela and fight. Horse soldiers, walking soldiers, wagon-gun soldiers, they were all coming.

"Why?" everyone wanted to know.

Incidents along the Holy Road, where the wagons traveled.

"But we were the ones who were wronged, not the *wasicu*," the people complained.

The agent just shrugged. "The soldiers are going to look for you this summer," he warned.

So they kept the wolves out, and sure enough, soldiers were coming from the Feather River to the south and the Shell River to the north. Everyone would be able to tell them where the medicine lodge had been, and the trail of pony drags would be easy to follow from there. It was just a matter of time before the soldiers blundered close.

The Sahiyela were all camped together, though—at their

strongest both physically and spiritually. Surely the soldiers wouldn't dare strike them now.

That was why Curly and Hump were glad when other young Lakota showed up to visit. Young Man-Whose-Enemies, Black Elk, Lone Bear, and He Dog. Curly was even half-glad to see the twins, No Water, and Pretty Fellow. If war came, the youth would feel better with Lakota at his side and not just strangers.

Everyone talked about what to do. The young men wanted to fight—men weren't men if they didn't stand up for their rights. The older men wanted to find a way to keep the peace. Nothing was decided, and everyone was buzzing about what would happen.

So they went hunting and waited and traded news and waited and gossiped and waited. The young men competed at fancy riding and trick shooting, or played the team sport of hitting the ball at a goal with a stick, or the kicking game. Young women gathered plants together, showed each other what they had quilled and beaded over the winter, or traded secrets about what young man had an eye for what young woman.

Curly noticed that the young women of the Sahiyela were freer than those of the Lakota. They wore the hide belts between their legs to keep lovers away, naturally, but they were not so closely chaperoned, and they talked with the young men more. Sometimes a woman would stand in a man's blanket with him for a long time, their faces close, their eyes deep into each other's. Supposedly the talk was not personal—just what the band would do, where the buffalo were, how the weather was changing, whether the berries were ripening early or late—but who knew? Who knew how many of them slipped off for an afternoon together, as Curly and Black Buffalo Woman sometimes did?

The Sahiyela had a custom Curly had never heard of but liked. A young man and woman who wanted to marry exchanged rings. Traditionally, these were made of horn, sometimes of metal, not new rings but ones made precious by wearing. They might wear these rings for a long time before being allowed to marry. Sometimes they weren't allowed to marry at all, or one of them had a change of heart. Then they sent the rings back.

Curly saw one young woman, Three Small Stones, throw a ring away. When she was helping her mother cook in front of the lodge one evening, wearing a man's ring, Three Small Stones saw the man's grandfather lead a string of horses into camp. She stood up straight, expectant. Curly saw her smile, but she and her mother both pretended to be totally absorbed in the cooking, acted like they didn't see the horses coming.

The old man led the horses right past Three Small Stones and staked them in front of a neighboring lodge, where another eligible young woman lived.

Three Small Stones' eyes went flat, her body rigid. She looked at her mother by the cooking tripod, but neither said anything. Suddenly the girl slipped the man's ring off her finger, cocked her arm, and threw it into the willows—viciously, the way she would throw a hunting stick at a rabbit. Curly thought the young man was lucky she didn't crack his head with the ring. Then Three Small Stones called raucously at her younger brother to get those *tipsila,* those prairie turnips, on over here, and in her voice Curly could hear how she would sound as a crabby old woman.

But Curly liked the ring-giving custom, and thought of Black Buffalo Woman.

Sometimes he fevered with the thought of her. Sometimes he dwelt on the details of their times together—the touching, the kissing, the passionate coupling, yes, and even more the sense of union of spirit. Sometimes he just imagined them sitting in a lodge together, just the two of them, eating quietly, sharing the hours, each knowing the other's thoughts without words, connected in their separateness as a man and woman are when their bodies are joined, in too deep a knowing for talk. For Curly all knowing was too deep for talk. Black Buffalo Woman was the same way, so they would be perfect together.

Perfect together after the years they had to wait. He found that hard to imagine. He had been here with the Sahiyela for eight moons, and the pain of missing Black Buffalo Woman was sharp. If he saw her every day, it would be worse. It was terrible during the half-moon he had stayed in the Oglala camp, before he left with Yellow Woman and her family. The evening before the trip, he had spoken only a few words to Black Buffalo Woman. As she was gathering sticks in the woods, he called softly. She came. They looked into each other's eyes for a long moment. Finally he said, "I'm going to the Fat Meat Country to visit the Sahiyela."

She blinked her eyes as a kind of nod. She'd surely heard the news already. She would know that, leaving this time of year, he would stay the winter. He wanted her to kiss him but knew she would not, not here where some other woman gathering sticks might see them. She looked at him soulfully.

He felt that she was wringing his heart in her hands.

She turned toward a downed tree and picked up more sticks.

Light Curly Hair thought that people who needed words to communicate were handicapped.

No, he had not run from her, he told himself, not really.

Another thought slapped him lightly, the way a man slaps a lumpraiser, a mosquito: No, no, he had *not* run from his responsibility to Rider, and to his vision.

Curly wore no rings—his vision forbade him ornamentation. So Blue Ear showed him how to carve one from the base of an elk antler. Curly shaped it to fit his smallest finger, polished it with fine white river sand, and brought it to a high gleam by rubbing it with back fat from a *pte,* a buffalo cow he himself had shot for Yellow Woman and her family. Yellow Woman gave the hoof bones to her small son, the one whose life Curly had saved.

He carved the top into a circle, like a hill with a flat top. He borrowed an awl from Yellow Woman, and in the circle he carved three simple lines, representing Hawk, who perched always in his heart, Hawk who would one day fly over his head as he went into battle.

He wished he could wear the ring. But he just put it away. His ring now, Black Buffalo Woman's ring soon, and the sign of their oneness in spirit, a circle, a whole.

BATTLE

Curly stopped at the edge of the turquoise lake. He looked to the east, where the sun was just bubbling over the horizon. Its first light, not yet full-strength, played on the clear water, glimmering off the surface, flashing into his eyes. It was a dance, this sunlight reflecting off water, a bedazzling whirl of spirit.

Curly slowly and gently dipped his hands into the cool water, left and then right. He dipped them once more, together, held them high, and watched the water trickle home to the lake, catching the sun's rays as it went, so transforming itself from liquid into light.

Miracle, this water. So said Hail and Dark.

Curly looked sideways at Buffalo Hump, also dipping his hands. Farther away, doing the same, stood the other young Lakota.

All around them several hundred Sahiyela fighting men were dismounting, coming to the bank of the small lake, dipping their hands, mounting again. From this upland they could see for a couple of sleeps in every direction, including the valley of the Mahkineohe, the Creek of Turkeys, where they would meet the soldiers today. Power was big in the Sahiyela warriors, and the water of this lake made it huge.

More sun stabbed through a cloud, and Curly saw the new light on his skin, and Hump's. *Hokahe!* he said to himself. *It is a good day to die.*

Now the Sahiyela riders reorganized themselves into their warrior clubs. They had ridden here behind Hail and Dark, the two *wicasu wakan* who had foreseen power for today and who sang and danced and prayed it into this world. The fighters would leave here riding not behind their medicine leaders but behind their war leaders.

The dispute about whether to avoid the *wasicu* or fight them had been solved by Hail and Dark. The two *wicasu wakan* were young enough to be full of courage and seemingly too young to know power. These men wanted to fight, not run like cowards. They had discovered two kinds of medicine to make the Sahiyela invincible against the *wasicu* and gave it to the people in ceremonies.

Everyone understood then that fighting was the right course, for victory was guaranteed. The people would teach the soldiers a lesson.

Now the men were renewing the power Hail and Dark had given them.

The first medicine gave power to the Sahiyela weapons. The men had only poor firearms, some smooth-bore flintlocks and old-fashioned Allen six-shooters. These weapons were scarce in camp, and they were inaccurate anyway. Hail and Dark blessed the powder the fighters loaded their guns with. Now, said the seers, every shot would strike home.

The second medicine was even stronger—it would turn away the soldiers' bullets. When the soldiers fired, their bullets would dribble out the ends of their muzzles and plunk to the ground, harmless. Or a Sahiyela need only lift a hand and the lead ball would bounce off like a pebble thrown by a boy. This medicine was the key. Instead of being overmatched, the warriors now were fighting an unarmed enemy.

The men had danced to these powers. They had sung the songs taught them by Hail and Dark. They had connected themselves to strengths larger and mightier than the merely physical. The last gesture the seers had required was that they dip their hands in this small turquoise lake.

Everything was in order. The Sahiyela had chosen the field of battle for their advantage, the broad valley of the Mahkineohe. Here they had plenty of room to maneuver. They were a day's travel from camp, not so far they had worn out their ponies getting here, but far enough to protect the women and children. They could feel their own might rising in them.

Curly had studied Hail silently, for this man was Yellow Woman's brother. Curly wanted to understand a young Sahiyela who took the way of the *wicasa wakan,* as his own father had, the path of spirit sight more than the path of war. That was not Curly's way, but he wanted to understand it. Unfortunately, Hail said little except in public, and Curly found his face unreadable.

The Strange Man had another reason for wanting to understand. Hail was evidently a *wakinyan* dreamer—thus the name. He must have gone through a *heyoka* ceremony, but he was not one of the sacred clowns.

Curly was a *wakinyan* dreamer, too, but he didn't let his mind wander in that direction, now by the lake or any other time. He stood up, mounted his traveling pony, checked the spare pony on lead, and followed the Sahiyela to meet the soldiers.

They waited in the sunpole trees at the east end of the valley. The soldiers would come at midday, said the Sahiyela wolves, or maybe not until mid-afternoon. Letting the horses graze, the Sahiyela lay in the shade, ate a little dried meat, and rested. They had painted themselves in camp this morning. Each man had long since invoked his personal medicine.

Curly felt queasy. He had seen beyond and learned of powers that would help him. He should have been wearing lightning on his face, as Rider did, and hail on his chest. He should have mounted the skin of a red-tailed hawk on top of his head and an eagle feather pointed downward in his hair behind. He had done none of this. He wondered whether, because he went naked into battle, he would die today. He looked at the hands he had dipped into the lake, uncertain. He felt Hawk tremble in his chest.

Suddenly men cried out. Everyone was looking at the bluffs at the west end of the big valley. The wolves were coming back at a gallop. From time to time they would ride their horses in a circle, the sign meaning the horse soldiers were here. The walking soldiers and the wagon-gun soldiers would follow.

Quickly the Sahiyela formed into a long line and started forward. Then they separated into loose ranks across the width of the valley, the warrior societies together. Curly and his friends brought up the rear with the unproven Sahiyela youths. Finally the warriors stopped and waited for the soldiers. The hot wind made thousands of feathers flutter.

Curly's mind was on the carbines the horse soldiers would be carrying. The Sahiyela bore only bows and arrows and those pitiful few firearms. He reminded himself of the medicine Hail and Dark had given them. Then he thought he should be in front, like Rider, galloping boldly toward the enemy fire, his fellow warriors trailing behind. He swallowed hard.

Buffalo Hump looked sideways at Curly. *"Hokahe!"* he barked.

From a swollen throat Curly answered, "It is a good day to die."

Curly saw the horse soldiers canter forward across the flat valley floor. Two Sahiyela soldier societies rode off to the right and left in flanking movements. The soldiers rode out to force them back toward the center.

A bugle sounded, an unfamiliar call. Suddenly sun flashed off the soldiers, bright slashes of light.

The bugle sounded again, a different call, and familiar—the charge.

The big cavalry mounts came to a gallop.

The Sahiyela galloped straight at them.

Soon they were close enough to see individual soldiers. Onward charged both sides.

Suddenly Curly realized what was so strange. Over the roar of the hooves of hundreds of horses should have been another and different roar, a thunder—the sound of rifle fire.

No such sound.

Curly saw why. The horse soldiers were charging with their carbines put away and their swords raised.

The medicine of Hail and Dark protected against bullets, not blades.

All the Indian warriors seemed to make that observation at once. The men in front slowed, skittered about, turned. Others began to mill. Then the largest throng of fighting men the Sahiyela had ever put together bolted.

The powers said this was not a day to fight.

Warriors scattered in every direction.

A SECRET PLEDGE

Curly thought about that day all the way to Bear Butte. The Sahiyela broke and ran, which was simple judgment. They were not defeated, not routed, not terrorized. They were bewildered.

No one had ever seen the horse soldiers make a charge with sabers instead of firearms. On the single occasion when the warriors were protected against lead, how did the *wasicu* soldiers know to choose steel?

Nobody knew what it meant, but everyone could read a sign as plain as that.

After the first moments, it had been a workable retreat. Arrows kept the soldiers mostly at a distance. The warriors scattered to give the soldiers plenty of fast-moving targets, not a single mark. Curly, Buffalo Hump, and the other

Lakota rode a long way hard before they rested. When they circled around to the village later, families were dragging lodges as fast as they could go to the four directions to make many small camps. In their hurry they were leaving packs and packs of belongings on the ground. The soldiers would burn them. Even after the big hunts, people were poor again.

But when you can't fight, you have to run.

The young Lakota men rode north with one Sahiyela village and kept going north toward their own country. It was nearly time for the big council at Bear Butte anyway. The council had been two winters in coming. What had just happened to the Sahiyela only made it more urgent.

The Sahiyela in that village talked only of one thing—the impossibility of what had happened. Right after the medicine lodge ceremony, when the people's hearts beat strongest as one, how could their power have failed so utterly?

Some of them blamed Hail and Dark, seers too young to understand the power they conjured. Others spoke bitterly of betrayal—someone must have talked loosely about the invincibility against bullets, and the soldiers heard it. Only betrayal could have led to such a calamity, they said.

Curly thought about it all through the long ride to Paha Sapa, the Black Hills. He thought often about the possibility of betrayal from within. Sicangu themselves had told White Beard where Little Thunder's village was, he knew, and the husband of a Lakota had guided White Beard to it. He remembered what he had seen beyond—Rider's own people clutching at him from behind, pulling him back. Yes, your own people might betray you.

And Curly wondered: *If I'd gotten to charge into the* wasicu *soldiers at Creek of Turkeys, would Hawk have flown, and would my heart have soared with Hawk?*

But he didn't know. All he knew for sure was appalling—medicine had brought the Sahiyela to disaster, and no one knew why.

That didn't help him much. You didn't abandon power because it failed. Bowstrings broke, but you didn't give up your bow and arrows. You fixed the string.

Sometimes Light Curly Hair's heart trembled with other thoughts: Maybe all Indian medicine was simply getting weak, like a person who was too old. Maybe the Lakota and Sahiyela people's connection with power was feeble. Maybe the hoop of the people was broken, the Lakota and their allies the Sahiyela, too. Maybe for the Lakota it was the way they'd let their ceremonial life weaken the last twenty years. Maybe Spirit didn't move in the world as much, and the field was left to the *wasicu*'s strange gods.

Curly wondered about some things. Life was a changeling. There were old stories about how people used to live. Curly's long-ago ancestors had had few buffalo and no horses, the tales said—they had lived by planting along the river bottoms. Then White Buffalo Cow Woman came and gave them a new way to find food, a better way.

The *wasicu* didn't always have fire boats and iron horses—they once had lived by planting and by herding sheep, so their stories said. The blackrobes told these stories.

Life was a trickster, like Coyote. Maybe this was one of those times on the earth when the changeling life smiled at everyone and shrugged and shed its skin and took a new, unimaginable form. Curly thought such things happened. And what if, in the new form, Power abandoned the Lakota?

A man couldn't hold back the wind with his fingers.

But Curly didn't know. At the big council at Bear Butte he would look and listen, with his eyes and ears and with the *cante ista,* the single eye that is the heart.

What he saw lifted his spirits as the invisible, rising, circling wind lifts the eagle.

All the people were here together, all seven tribes of the Titunwan Lakota—his own Oglala, whom the *wasicu* called the Sand Throwers, his mothers' Sicangu, the Burnt Thighs, the Mniconjou of his birth mother, Those Who Plant by the River, the Hunkpapa, Those Who Camp by the Entrance of the Circle, the Itazipicola, Those without Bows, the Oohenumpa, Two Boilings or Two Kettles, and the Sihasapa, Blackfoot, all within the hoop of the people.

The big difference from the Sahiyela, who had all gathered together for their medicine lodge ceremony, was simply numbers. The Titunwan Lakota were a much larger group, and the Dakota lived to the east, between the Muddy Water, which the *wasicu* called the Missouri River, and the River of Canoes, which the *wasicu* called the Mississippi. Though the *wasicu* soldiers' numbers approximately matched the Sahiyela fighting force at Creek of Turkeys, they could never match the Titunwan Lakota, much less the warriors of all the Lakota and Dakota.

Curly could feel power throbbing in the pulse of his people. Power was in the circle after circle of lodges, in the beat of the drums night and day, in the babble of all the children playing, the murmur of the women talking, the men conferring, in all the embrace of the hoop of the people. The *wasicu* would not be able to push the Lakota around if the people stuck together.

Curly also saw here for the first time the leaders he had heard about—Four Horns of the Hunkpapa, Long Mandan of the Oohenumpa, Crow Feathers of the Itazipicola. Little Thunder of the Sicangu and Lone Horn of the Mniconjou, one of his uncles, Curly already knew. He was glad to see these men and the Oglala's Man-Whose-Enemies-Are-Afraid-of-His-Horses respected along with the other leaders. No one spoke of Bear-Scattering-His-Enemies, killed by the *wasicu*.

The younger men were here, too, many of them shirt wearers, those who would be the leaders when they aged beyond the winters of war—Sitting Bull from the Hunkpapa, the seven-foot Touch-the-Sky from the Mniconjou, who was one of Curly's uncles, and others. Red Cloud of the Bad Face Oglala was not a shirt wearer but was a strong leader in war.

Across the meadow Curly heard the rising, heroic tones of an honor song:

> *"Spotted Tail,*
> *your deeds are known.*
> *The people praise you."*

Spotted Tail, his uncle! The Sicangu were riding into camp across the way. As the melody repeated, Curly ran toward the line of horses dragging travois.

> *"Spotted Tail,*
> *your heart is big;*
> *your farseeing eyes are wise."*

Curly had heard that Spotted Tail was out of the soldier prison, back among the Sicangu. But Curly had been living with the Sahiyela and hadn't seen him. Few of these people of many council fires had seen Spotted Tail since he went east in shackles.

Spotted Tail rode past the Itazipicola camp and into the grassy area where his people would pitch their tents. As Curly caught up, he could see some people walking behind Spotted Tail, showing their esteem for him. The honoring song lifted once more, and this time some of the walkers joined in. But Curly could see that some of the Itazipicola turned their backs as his uncle rode past. Some of the Sicangu pushed their ponies to the far side, away from Spotted Tail, so they wouldn't seem to join in the praise.

Curly quickly covered his mouth in surprise. What way was this to treat Spotted Tail, the shirtman who threw away his life for the people?

When he caught up to his uncle, Spotted Tail was dismounted, and the song ended. The big man didn't seem to mind whatever had just happened. He grinned broadly and said, "Hello, Nephew. Do you want something to eat?"

Though Curly wasn't hungry, he sat and ate to spend a little time with the family. He was relieved to see the man utterly unchanged—big, hearty, full of fun. Curly had heard that prison undid men, made them gray of spirit, weak, uncertain, confused, no longer men. Spotted Tail seemed himself.

He had been taken all the way to Fort Leavenworth and had stayed there the winter. He said everyone treated him well. He wasn't penned up in a guardhouse or forced to wear chains. He lived with Sweetwater Woman. He went where he liked in and around the fort, talked to everyone freely, got to know many of the officers and even some of the wives. After a year they had let him come home, but Curly was off visiting the Sahiyela.

Spotted Tail said the whites were lots of fun because they were so gullible. He himself had gotten a young white officer to eat mud. Truly, to eat mud. Spotted Tail's eyes gleamed mischief. But he would have to tell that story later. Tonight—a-i-i-i, it seemed every night and every day, so there was no time for fun—he had to spend all his time consulting with the leaders of all the Lakota bands.

Curly slipped away politely. He hadn't gotten any clue why some Lakota people would not want to honor his mothers' brother.

The people built a double council lodge, and the leaders went there every day to speak of what was happening and what they would do.

Since youngsters had no place at the big council lodge, Curly sought out Black Buffalo Woman. But he didn't want to stand outside her lodge wrapped in a blanket, among other young men similarly wrapped, waiting for her to slip in beside each one (to pass one man by would give offense) and talk to each awhile in that way, with other young men and her family watching, especially her sisters.

He had heard she had plenty of suitors and knew most of them would be older than he, men of more coups, and his standing there would cause talk. He wondered if any of his rivals among the Bad Faces went to court her, Pretty Fellow or No Water or Black or White Twin. They were all a winter or two older and would be more acceptable.

So he stayed away in the evening and went instead to the Bad Face part of camp in the morning and watched until she went to the creek for water. When he called softly from the bushes, she came quickly, all smiles and little touches. As it turned out, she had a place already picked out where they could be alone. After she told her mothers some story, she met Curly there. They spent the afternoon talking a little and coupling a lot. With Black Buffalo Woman he even liked the talking.

In English what he said would have been something like, "With this ring I make my pledge to you."

She watched him hesitate and was touched. "Among the Sahiyela," he said, "young men and women who love each other say it by exchanging rings. The ring is a circle like a lodge, and it promises they will share one lodge for their lives. They wear their pledge on their fingers for everyone to see."

He handed it to her, rubbed and oiled to a high gleam now. They were stretched out on the grass side by side, his clothes off, hers in disarray, her hide chastity belt flung into a bush.

She turned the ring around and around, her heart big. She focused at last on Hawk carved on the round, flat top. "Hawk perches in my heart always," he said.

She shot her eyes up at him, full of surprise. She knew he was telling her that Hawk was his familiar spirit, his guide. He was also hinting that he had seen beyond. In that place, he was saying, Spirit had appeared to him in the form of a hawk.

She embraced him and made her body speak understanding. It was part of her woman's wisdom to understand that gestures said more than words. She knew this seeing beyond was a big step for him toward being a man. She knew he hadn't yet spoken of it to anyone but her. She knew the loneliness of his silence.

He loved her beyond imagination.

She sat up, and her skirt fell far enough to cover most of her thighs. He was sorry. She tried the ring on three fingers of her left hand, and it fit the index finger perfectly.

"It is a custom among the Sahiyela?" she said softly. "The man gives a pledge, and the woman gives a pledge?"

She spread the fingers of both hands and looked at them. She had two rings of her own. One was hammered copper in the style of the Indians to the far west who always ate big fish from the salt sea, and one was silver, from the Indians to the south and west who lived in stone houses. The silver ring had small inlays of turquoise and onyx. Both of these rings had come to the Lakota country across long trade routes, probably brought here by the *wasicu* who went everywhere to hunt the beaver. The rings were so costly that only the daughter of a successful father could have afforded them.

She slipped the silver ring off and put it in Curly's hand. "Turquoise for an unclouded mountain sky for Hawk to fly in," she said, "and black for the *wakinyan* that bring the rain. One side of life and the other."

He held his breath in. She did not know he was a *wakinyan* dreamer.

Curly looked at the ring in his palm. His heart thumped in his chest, and his pulse thumped at him what he should have known all along.

He raised his eyes into Black Buffalo Woman's. He could not wear any ornamentation. The *wakinyan* would bolt disaster at him. No, she hadn't guessed why he dressed shabbily.

He accused himself: why hadn't he thought of this before he carved the ring?

He whipped himself: This was what came of doing things in strange ways, getting a vision when you weren't ready. This was what came of keeping your vision a secret.

He nearly stuttered the words: "I cannot wear your ring. Not yet. I saw something. . . ." She would understand he meant he saw beyond.

Maybe she did, but her face hardened. She took his ring off and closed it into the palm of her hand. "Light Curly Hair," she said, "the people say you are Our Strange Man." She glanced down and back up. "You are."

She stood up, and her skirt fell below her knees. She held her hand out flat, offering him his ring back.

Curly shook his head. He didn't offer her ring back. "I will . . . I will keep your ring and treasure it." He looked up at her. He had no idea when he might be able to wear her ring. Never, probably. His eyes pleaded with her. "Will you keep mine?"

She looked into his face for a moment, then made a motion that wasn't quite a shrug. "Yes," she said. "A *secret* pledge." Her lips trembled with scorn.

She turned away, picked up her chastity belt, and walked away stiffly.

TWO PATHS DIVIDE

In the huge council lodge the leaders said they'd been giving in to the whites far too easily. To the east they were taking everything, putting the Indians onto little squares of ground and saying, "Stay put while we grab everything else." The Indians couldn't even leave their allotment to go hunting or visit relatives without begging permission, and many times the agent of The One They Used for Father didn't say yes.

One of the traders' sons said the white talk about The One They Used for Father was silly. They used the English words "Great White Father," which was one of their ways of making themselves important and treating Indians like children.

Other Lakota said the whites usually promised to teach the Indians a new way, a better way. Despite these offers, the result always looked the same. Before long the people were poor and dispirited. Half of them stayed drunk. No one paid much attention to the ceremonies anymore. People even sold their sacred objects for a little powder and lead, or some food, or even a bottle of poison drink.

In return the Indians gave their land, their way of life, their spirits, their connection to Power, everything.

Regardless of what the whites promised and whether they meant well or not, declared the leaders, these were the actual results.

One man made up a song about the way the whites were coming, coming, coming and bringing destruction:

"In the half of the sky
where the sun lives
clouds are gathering.
In the half of the sky
where the sun lives
dark clouds are gathering.
In the half of the sky
where the sun lives
dark clouds are gathering,
and white men storm upon us."

Curly wondered whether the new *wakinyan*, the new destructive powers, were the *wasicu*.

Some of the chiefs had traveled all the way to the big white town St. Louis and witnessed these things with their own eyes. Others had seen them on the far side of the Muddy Water. Everyone had heard about them. All the leaders agreed, but they noticed Spotted Tail didn't speak. He'd just been among the whites for a whole year. They heard he had some strong opinions. But he sat quiet.

Well, the whites had caused the Sahiyela, brother people to the Lakota, a lot of trouble. And the Wasp had stung Little Thunder's band on the Blue Water. But the Sahiyela were few. Little Thunder's people had been caught alone. If the Lakota stuck together, if they watched the soldiers and opposed them everywhere, the whites could do nothing. For they were not the Sahiyela, with a few hundred fighting men. They were the Lakota, with ten lances for every Sahiyela spear.

Now, finally, Spotted Tail stood up and spoke.

"Brother-in-law," said Tasunke Witko, "will you eat with us?" It was the next night. He handed Spotted Tail a bowl of stew and a horn spoon. The two of them sat behind the center fire in the lodge of Tasunke Witko, honored guest and considerate host.

"Is it mud soup?" asked Spotted Tail with a big grin. Though the two were host and guest, they were also brothers-in-law, which meant that teasing was in order. With Spotted Tail, often rough teasing and practical joking.

Uncertain, Tasunke Witko answered that he would serve his honored brother-in-law only the best mud, from Paha Sapa.

Curly's mothers smiled at each other. They loved it when their brother came to visit. They sat at the back of the lodge. Curly and his younger brother, Little Hawk, watched from one side of the fire.

"I have mud soup for my special medicine," said Spotted Tail. "At least the white men think so. I'm afraid I practiced deceit at Fort Leavenworth."

"Your sisters are always embarrassed to hear about your exploits," said Tasunke Witko.

"Hai!" exclaimed one of his wives from the back of the lodge, meaning she was surprised her husband would say such a thing.

Spotted Tail grinned. "I told one young officer—Blue was his name—that I can live on mud soup and mud soup alone." More scoffing sounds from the rear, as if the women didn't know who was more wayward, their husband or their brother. " 'Plenty of stuff in mud soup that's good for you,' I said. This Blue acted skeptical, so I showed him. I mixed up some mud soup and drank it down."

Tasunke Witko rolled his eyes. Grunts from the rear spoke mock disgust.

"I mixed it weak," Spotted Tail went on, "because mud's so good I don't need much of it. 'Earth,' I said to Blue. But you know, he wouldn't eat any.

"So I said I'd show I could live on nothing but mud soup for a month. Every day I got mud from a special place on the riverbank known only to me and this officer. I took Blue over to the well and made a ceremony of mixing up a big bowl of soup. I told Blue that my prayers added greatly to the richness of this life from Earth, so I didn't need much of the mud in the soup. Just a little."

He smiled sideways at his brother-in-law. "I figured that, with just a little mud in it, this soup was no worse than drinking the water of the Muddy Water River, which the whites and the Two Circle People and their dogs drink every day.

"Then I spoke a few genuine words to *mitakuye oyasin* and drank the soup. Every day, of course, I also swore to Blue that I would eat nothing but mud soup that day."

His sisters tittered. Spotted Tail was the biggest eater they'd ever known.

"Then I would go home to the cabin where the soldiers made us live and have a good meal of prairie-turnip and pemmican stew. What good is a white man if you can't have a little fun with him?

"At the end of the month Blue admitted that I still looked really good. To him I looked just as fat as when I started the diet, maybe even fatter.

"On that last day I got Blue to eat a bowl of the soup. I told the officer that since he didn't know the prayers, he would need stronger soup to get the benefit." Everyone's eyes were big now. "So I put plenty of riverbank mud into the officer's water. Ah, how the fellow slurped up the goop.

"But I liked him," ended Spotted Tail, laughing. "I really did. He was a good white man."

Tasunke Witko enjoyed his brother-in-law and did not turn him toward the evening's business. Spotted Tail knew without being told that Tasunke Witko wanted something urgently, and what it was—he could read his wives' brother that well. Later Spotted Tail would get around to it. So they traded stories, teased each other, talked about family and friends, and told the news of the two years since they'd last seen each other.

When it was fully dark and the fire was dying, the Sicangu himself said quietly, "Some Lakota say the white men have made Spotted Tail a coward."

Tasunke Witko made a demurring sound that was not a denial and then said, "Those who know you would never say that." Yet some Lakota did. Even Tashunke Witko himself saw something impossible, his brother-in-law, a renowned Lakota warrior, a shirtman, talking conciliation toward these arrogant and very aggressive enemies, the *wasicu*. Talking it now, when confrontation was on the way and all the people were beating like one heart and the drum of the heart said, "Fight, fight, fight."

This was why, after yesterday's long council, when Spotted Tail finally spoke, Tasunke Witko asked him to come for dinner tonight.

It was like the man to bring it up so directly, Curly thought admiringly. Whatever it was, Spotted Tail would always take on it straight ahead, in a frontal assault.

Then why did he speak of compromise and retreat? The camp was a hubbub of gossip about Spotted Tail. No one could understand. This was the man, afoot and armed only with a sword, who had knocked thirteen of the

Wasp's charging soldiers off their horses. Why did he suddenly want to bend his knee to the *wasicu*? And want all the Lakota to kneel with him?

How could he talk such talk and be the same man?

Curly wondered if imprisonment could really have frightened him—everyone said so. Unspeakable. It should have been unthinkable. But everyone agreed. The thought felt awful to Curly, like a rash. He itched to get rid of it.

Spotted Tail said it again: "Some Lakota say the white men have made Spotted Tail a coward." Then he let it sit there in front of everyone, ugly as spilled intestines—in front of his brother-in-law, who was a respected *wicasa wakan*, his two nephews, his beloved sisters, especially himself. He was not being subtle or oblique—he wanted everyone to feel the ugliness. He wanted it to hurt. It hurt him. Maybe if they could see, maybe if they realized he would be the last Lakota of all to turn tail, maybe then they would begin to understand.

"I am a shirtman," he began. He met the eyes of his host. He felt his sisters' eyes and ears from the dark in the rear of the lodge. He knew his nephews were eating up not only his words, but every gesture and every nuance. None of them wanted to think ill of their relative. He must accept the fact that his nephews probably would think ill, especially his favorite, the gifted and hot-blooded Curly.

This was a responsibility life should not have brought Spotted Tail. It was his nature to live heartily, without second thoughts, relishing battle and the hunt. It was not his way to analyze, to try to see deeply, to peer into the future. He hated the winter he had spent among the whites. He hated being the only one to know.

"My responsibility is to everyone," he said. If he stated the obvious, they would see how loud he meant them to hear his words. "I do not like what I see, but I will tell you what it is.

"The white men are ants that feed on a carcass and in

tiny pieces carry it away. You wonder what happened—it's almost gone—it was here yesterday—it's too big to carry—then it *is* gone.

"They are flies. They buzz around you, more of them than you can imagine, and soon you have the sickness they bring and are dying. They are the wind. It seems slight, niggling, but it parches the hungry wandering coyote, fells it, and shrivels its body until only bones are left.

"You cannot imagine how many of them there are. On the Muddy Water River are several villages with as many as all the Sahiyela people. Where that river flows into the River of Canoes, Mississippi, there is a village as big as all the circle of Lakota lodges. They have a hundred such villages on this side of the big salt water and a thousand on the other side."

He paused for effect. "I have seen some of this. They showed me more in pictures in the talking papers. They told me still more. They said they have villages as many as all the Indian people, all put together, and these villages are only part of one nation, and they have many nations." After a moment he went on, "I looked with the *cante ista,* the eye of my heart, and listened with the ear of my heart, and I know this to be true."

Spotted Tail listened to the silence around him and felt it and considered. He could sense that they didn't understand.

Well, he had said almost this much in the council lodge. Everyone knew this. He had decided that tonight, among his relatives, he would say what more he knew, as far as he could see it.

"The worst is, they have a terrible blindness, these *wasicu*. They do not understand choice."

He was referring to a most sacred subject, and none of his hearers needed any explanation—no Lakota who had even started on the path to adulthood did. A human being had *skan,* something-that-moves, spiritual vitality. The force of life itself gave the person *skan* when he or she was born. It also gave him choice, and through choice he or she grew into the man or woman he or she became. *Skan* was the motive power, choice the direction.

A Lakota had a choice between good and evil, the red road and the black road, between what made life beautiful and what made it ugly. He or she had help in making choices—the quiet voice that is in everyone, the spirit helper (usually in the form of an animal), what he or she saw when crying for a vision, personal medicine, prayer, ceremonies performed alone or with others. Still, choice remained, inviolate.

Whether your way was to paint yourself in a certain manner, to wear something of iron or never touch iron, or whether you should charge the enemy first or simply swell the ranks, that was your nature, your vision, the route of your spirit on the earth. Other Lakota would respect it. None would try to coerce it or even influence it. None would mock it. Your understanding was the essence of you, and to follow it your sacred choice.

All this was so fundamental as to not need saying. So what could it mean that an entire people did not understand choice? It was almost unthinkable. Were they human beings?

"Among the whites some think they can see and choose for others." It was so stunning that Spotted Tail just let the words hang in the lodge, heavy and oppressive. "Then comes what you would expect. They quarrel with one another not only about small things, but about the biggest. They fight and kill each other. Instead of respecting another man's way, they stop at nothing to get him to adopt their way. Like the Mormons."

The Lakota knew the U.S. government this very summer was sending an army against the Mormons at the big salty lake to make the Mormons live like the other *wasicu*, especially not to take more than one wife. Incomprehensible.

"They hate our way," said Spotted Tail. His voice was weary now and faint. "Their deepest desire—believe me about this—is to change our way of living. Their deepest desire is to make us like them. I swear it."

Tasunke Witko coughed. Spotted Tail understood that he was voicing everyone's horror.

Why would anyone do such a thing? No Lakota would commit this sort of murder of spirit.

"I was as shocked as you are," Spotted Tail said, "and also found this difficult to believe. Eventually, I believed it. Then I began to see that they have power to inflict their will upon us."

He paused.

"So I went to the mountain near the fort and saw a little," he said. "They would not let me go far, but I sat on the bluff above the river and cried for a little vision. Something came to me, but not to my eyes. It came to my whole body. A trembling. A rumbling. A great shaking. A shuddering, a quaking, a violent upheaval, as of *Maka,* Earth, herself."

He let a long moment go by, so they could absorb his meaning. "The old stories tell of upheavals like that. *Maka* shakes, and even her ancient face is changed. Trees are uprooted. Rocks that were high fall low. Cracks open in the earth. Mountains become plains, and plains erupt into mountains.

"It is all swift beyond imagining, violent beyond imagining, terrible beyond imagining.

"I hope my words make you afraid.

"I have a sense, my relatives, that what is coming from the white men is swift beyond imagining, violent beyond imagining, terrible beyond imagining, like an upheaval of the earth."

Spotted Tail let this claim sit. Maybe now they would see.

"When the entire surface of the earth is changed, there is nothing to do but live on it as it is. We cannot camp by the shore of a lake if it is now a creek. We cannot follow a trail the earth has swallowed up. We cannot eat buffalo that died in the time of our grandfathers."

He would sum it up now. He felt his words were not enough.

"I am a shirtman. I must help take care of everyone. I have a little foresight. What I see is terrible, and I hate it. I wish I could live as an ordinary man, and hunt and fight and couple with my wives and teach my sons to do the same. I wish it . . ." He did not add "more than you can imagine."

"But I will use what little I see to guide the people to the new lakes, new mountains, new trails of the earth, the new red road. Though I cannot make out the path, I will set my foot on it, trusting in the powers." He listened to himself. Somehow he felt that only now had he himself accepted this truth. Yes, that was just what he would do. "I will seek to keep the sacred hoop whole and the sacred tree flowering. Whatever it takes.

"I have asked myself why I am the one to see. I am a man to fight, not to invent a new life. I want to fight. But I won't. Maybe if the people see that Spotted Tail, of all men, is changing his ways, they will change, too.

"I don't know where the change will lead. "I don't see that. I only know that we must start walking the path."

Curly's heart was a cold rock. Regardless of the truth in what Spotted Tail said, Curly's ears heard a spirit of defeat—no, worse, of surrender. His uncle surrendering. One of the shirtmen of the people giving up.

Curly's blood screamed rejection.

Tasunke Witko waited a long while. It was not just politeness. He was thinking about what Spotted Tail had said. Not especially the claims of incredible numbers of *wasicu*, an old tale raised once more. That didn't matter as much to him as Spotted Tail's assertion that the *wasicu* were spirit killers.

A-i-i-i, surely they were impossible to understand. You might fight your enemy—that had respect in it. You might even kill him—respect again. But to do what the *wasicu* did: afflict your enemy with disease, pen him up, starve him, and then rescue his body on the condition that he surrender his spirit . . . Incomprehensible. Not the way of men.

But he believed Spotted Tail. Everything about his brother-in-law sang conviction.

What a peculiar people, the *wasicu*. They had a certain genius. They could make things—wagons, wheels, guns, knives, watches, far-seeing glasses, and much more. But these were only things. In return for them the *wasicu* wanted you to relinquish your own genius, which was not of things but of the spirit.

From the beginning, said the oldest men, what the *wasicu* wanted was your spirit. From the beginning, their real desire was for the blackrobes to gouge spirit out of you, like a man scraping the seeds out of a gourd. Then they would fill the empty gourd with their religion.

Tasunke Witko understood the life of the spirit. He knew it was the only real life.

So he knew what he would do. It was simple. He would oppose his brother-in-law with all his power.

To be defeated by superior numbers, that was only physical.

To give up your spirit, that truly would be death.

He looked at his sons sitting in the near dark. Truly death. He thought of the loaf-around-the-fort women, offering themselves to any man for the price of whiskey, then spirit-killed until the effects of the *mni wakan* wore off, then offering themselves again, endlessly, turning from human beings into wandering carcasses. And this wasn't the worst of it. Men without spirit would rape their daughters, murder their brothers. The hoop of the people would be broken, smashed beyond recognition or repair. The tree of the people would no longer flower. Its branches would hang brittle and dead.

For his sons Tasunke Witko would fight. For the reasons Spotted Tail gave to yield, he would fight.

Fortunately, now the mood of all the Lakota was to fight. He wondered how it would be in ten or twenty or thirty winters, when the *wasicu* came in hordes.

Inside himself he shrugged. It didn't matter.

"Would you like to smoke?" he asked Spotted Tail.

His guest nodded.

Tasunke Witko filled the *canupa* reflectively, used sticks to pick up a live ember from the ashes, and lit the *cansasa*. Smoke rose toward the top of the lodge. *The breath of earth,* he whispered in his mind ritually. He wondered whether he would be able to send breath to the sky for the rest of his life.

He handed Spotted Tail the *canupa*. His relative smoked.

Soon Tasunke Witko would walk Spotted Tail back to his lodge. Maybe the boys would walk along—the company would be good.

Spotted Tail had chosen. He was a good man.

Tasunke Witko had also chosen. He was implacable.

The three walked back from Spotted Tail's lodge slowly. Tasunke Witko was taking in the night smells and the night sounds and even the night sights. They could see reasonably well, for it was Wimakatanhan, the moon coming toward full. Their eyes had had plenty of time to adjust.

Many times he had walked with his two sons, or stood or sat quietly with them, to show them life at night. It was so different it was like another garden of life, a gesture by Maka, Earth, to show she could make many different worlds: the one in the air, the one in water, the one under the surface of the earth, one in the sun, one in the night sun. Maka was a virtuoso.

Tasunke Witko smiled to himself. He was poised for a terrible fight. Now was a good time to remind himself of what a life maker Earth was, what a show-off in fecundity. He liked to tell his sons about part of that, the abundant life of birds at night. Sundown was heralded by the bird that comes at dusk and splashes in the air, the nighthawk. Night was the dominion of the hushed-wings, the owls— there were so many of them! A person who sat against a tree and watched and listened would observe many—the grows-a-horn, the shivery bird, the big ears and the small ears, the little one whose call heralds spring, the gray owl, the black one, the one that lives with prairie dogs, the owl who trumpets winter in. All this life would be sent to its other world at sunup by the red-dawn-coming bird.

Tasunke Witko did not think being aware of these birds as you walked through the night was especially the skill of the hunter. For him it was one gesture of an awareness that was holy, the awareness of the myriad forms of life, of which human beings were one and cousins to the others.

He noticed his sons without looking directly at them. He was glad that they were habitually attentive to the night and all the world around them, attuned. They could notice while thinking of other things, which was what they were doing now. Each of them was disturbed.

It was Little Hawk, naturally, who burst out. He was only eleven winters old.

Little Hawk spaced out the words, like deliberate slashes of a knife. "My uncle has been gelded by the *wasicu*."

Curly felt a gush of relief, and then embarrassment. He was glad his brother had said it. The same thought had boiled in Curly, but no allowance would have been made for such an outburst from a man of eighteen winters.

Their father walked for a moment and did not speak. No reprimand was necessary, for Little Hawk knew as well as anyone that his outcry was unacceptable.

After a moment Tasunke Witko spoke gently. "I admire and respect my brother-in-law. He is a worthy man and a worthy shirt wearer. He is trying to think of all the people."

It was a statement admirable in its eloquence and its restraint.

Curly tasted bile in his throat. Sometimes respect for the sovereignty of each human being tasted foul and bitter.

Curly was awash in shame at himself and fury at his uncle. Obviously he had not mastered himself sufficiently to have true respect for others' right to choose.

Shame again. If his uncle would no longer stand up for the people, all the more urgent that Curly should contribute his power, large or small, for the common good.

All right. He said to himself, Han, *yes, yes, absolutely yes,* in rhythm with each of his steps.

"Father," he said softly. "I need to talk to you." He hesitated one last time. "I have . . . seen something."

By the moon he saw his father's face light with understanding, kindness, gladness. Curly felt his hardness and his fear thaw a little and trickle icily through his heart.

INTERPRETING THE VISION

Curly finished smoking the *canupa* and gave it back to his father. Tasunke Witko scraped the bowl out and put it back in his pipe bag. Curly looked at the bag, and odd feelings tugged at him. It had fringes of sorrel-colored hair. This hair came from the mare sacrificed at the scaffold of the woman who gave him birth. The sorrel horse was one Tasunke Witko had seen when he looked beyond, when he started walking the path of the *wicasa wakan*.

Curly took a deep breath. He had asked for this talk, but it was still hard. He looked Tasunke Witko in the eyes and breathed deep again.

"I have seen something," he said.

Even now he could hardly get the words out. After three long years it had begun to turn sour, as any power will when it is not used.

If his uncle would withdraw his strength from the people in their time of need, Light Curly Hair would lend a new power, from a new vision, a new experience of Spirit.

The council had broken up this morning, and the bands had started scattering to the four winds. Tasunke Witko had taken Curly aside for this talk. They bent willow branches into a low hut and covered it with buffalo robes. They built the sacred fire, heated the rocks red as dawn suns, and put them in the pit. Inside Tasunke Witko splashed the water on the rocks, and they purified themselves in the breath of rocks four times. They smoked and prayed and contemplated. Now, back outside, Curly murmured again, "I have seen something."

"Yes," said Tasunke Witko, looking kindly at his son. "You have seen beyond, and felt reluctant to talk about it."

He meant to make it easy for Curly. He had known for a long time. He had suspected when he saw how the boy was suddenly terrified of the *wakinyan*. He had known for sure when he realized why the boy dressed shabbily.

Tasunke Witko worried about his older son. He had no idea what the boy might have seen, a big vision or a small one, or whether he might continue to see more throughout his life and have to learn to cope with Power. Often waking dreams that came without the dreamer's seeking were big and life-changing. Maybe Curly had seen something very *wakan*. Maybe he would be a *wicasa wakan* like his father. Maybe he would be one of the great *wicasa wakan*. Tasunke Witko thought maybe the boy was picked out by Spirit for something special. He had always thought the boy's light hair was a sign.

What was for sure was that dreaming of *wakinyan* without speaking about it was dangerous, to the people and especially to the dreamer. But Tasunke Witko had forbidden himself to interfere with his son's chosen way. The boy knew what was right, and he was a Lakota. You couldn't help another person with some things.

Curly couldn't seem to find the next words.

Tasunke Witko helped out. "It's hard to see beyond when you're young," he said. "It seems overwhelming."

"Yes," said Curly. He felt a little softening inside. Hawk was still, neither at ease nor agitated, just waiting.

"You may speak now or whenever you're ready," said Tasunke Witko gently. "Or not at all."

"Pila maya," Curly said. Thanks. Gratitude flowed into his heart like a warm spring.

So, sitting in front of the sweat lodge, Curly at last began. He had in mind to tell everything just as he had seen it, or almost everything. He would hold a little back, what he felt Rider wouldn't tell. You always kept a little for yourself alone.

"I was upset. I saw Bear-Scattering dying, his flesh rotting while he was still breathing. Also, I was feeling miserable about not having any coups, or a vision, or any power at all."

Tasunke Witko looked at his son, and his heart felt tender.

"So I rode out along the river to be alone. Then I just saw this place and felt . . . something strange. On the spur of the moment I decided to cry for a vision." Curly glanced sidelong at his father, and his eyes fell. "It was impulsive." The father wished his son didn't feel apologetic.

"I knew I wasn't ready. I hadn't prepared at all." Now he mumbled. "It was a stupid thing to do."

"Just tell me," said Tasunke Witko kindly.

"If it seemed stupid," Curly plunged on, now sounding defiant, "it also felt like me."

Tasunke Witko smiled and nodded sympathetically.

"The first day I cried for a vision all day. I cried to the west, the north, the east, the south. I cried but heard no answer." The boy paused. Even now he had trouble telling what had happened. In a way Tasunke Witko was glad— it gave him something to help his son with.

"Then I noticed that I was not getting an answer. All the creatures of the earth had disappeared. The sky was empty of winged people. The dirt showed no crawling people. No four-legged people could be seen." Curly looked savagely at his father. "Then I knew. My answer was a curse. In response to my cry, all living things died."

The ferocity of Curly's voice actually hurt. There was plenty to help him with.

Curly's head dropped again. *Oh, my son,* Tasunke Witko's heart sang, *your only misstep is shame.*

"I fell asleep that night," Curly muttered. "The next night I didn't even try to stay awake."

He looked up at his father angrily. *I'm rotten,* his eyes said, *but this is me.* "The answer of Spirit never changed." Meaning silence, emptiness, nothingness, the void. His eyes held Tasunke Witko's in a dare. "On the third afternoon I quit."

Curly fell silent. Sometimes there was nothing to do but wait. Tasunke Witko had never had a more painful wait than this black stillness.

Curly finally went on, "When I tried to get back on my horse to come back to the village, I was weak and dizzy. I was afraid of falling off. I sat against the sunpole tree to rest, and that was when it happened."

Curly felt mesmerized again as he told it. "I saw a horse trotting lightly. It pranced beautifully, floating without touching the ground. . . ."

Tasunke Witko felt pitched around, like a skin boat on a rough river.

His son had seen beyond, and *what* he had seen— Tasunke Witko had scarcely heard of a waking dream so sustained, so vivid, so powerful.

Powerful, yes. Curly had been endowed with one of the great gifts: invulnerability from enemy fire. He had come to know his spirit helper, Hawk. He had . . .

He had dreamed of Inyan, an ancient power, very great.

He had also dreamed of *wakinyan,* a difficult medicine. And he had been shown his way, the path of the warrior, not the *wicasa wakan.* In the dream Rider did nothing but ride into war.

The waves of joy and sorrow and fear and exultation tossed Tasunke Witko up and down roughly.

Fool, he accused himself. *I have been a fool. My son was struggling with a vision. When I should have helped him, I rode up and accused him of alarming me and his mothers. He was lying there fresh from seeing beyond, and I noticed nothing. Fool!*

Three years of pain because . . .

Tasunke Witko sat staring at the ground.

That was past. What was important now was to give solace and understanding to his son. Often they couldn't cross the unseen barriers between them. Tasunke Witko now had to do so and offer to his son what he gave to other dreamers. The two of them must discover what the waking dream meant to Curly, what meanings he already knew, what meanings he might discover now or soon. Some meanings would be clouded, probably for a long time.

What the *wicasa wakan* or any other person saw meant nothing. The object was for Curly to see. As a guide Tasunke Witko might stimulate, or elaborate a very little, no more.

"Let's go back into the sweat lodge," said Tasunke Witko.

Four more rounds of sweating, of praying, of asking for wisdom. Between rounds, they sat with the lodge cover lifted. Bathed in sunlight and in cooling air, they did not talk. Nor did Tasunke Witko think. He turned the pictures of Curly's vision over and over in his mind, getting to know them.

He burned a little sweetgrass to invite the presence of the spirits. Then the work started.

"You realized it was your pony. It had gotten rid of its hobbles and was running free and trotting toward you. Its legs danced, and its neck was held high."

Tasunke Witko had the knack of repeating dreams back to the dreamers, either sleeping dreamers or waking dreamers, almost word for word. It came from his trance-like concentration while they told what they saw. He found that it made them feel affirmed in the dream and in its power. It also made them believe in his ability to see into the dream. This was his calling, *wicasa wakan.*

"On its back sat a rider leaning forward, perfectly motionless on the prancing pony, except that the fringe on the heels of his moccasins trembled."

"Yes," Curly put in. "Everything was clearer than life ever is, sharp and gleaming, like quartz crystals in a rock."

"So you knew: you were seeing beyond."

Tasunke Witko could see in Curly's face that he was seeing it again now, and seeing more, realizing more than he had the first time.

"The moment you knew, the pony changed colors—it became a bay, then an appaloosa, then a grulla, a strawberry roan, and other colors in succession." He flicked a smile at Curly and was pleased to see his son's face rapt.

"The pony was saying," the boy plunged ahead, " 'I am not just *a* horse. I am Horse.' Rider was like a bright stone I'd found. I turned him in my sight to study every facet of him."

Curly's voice was thrumming with excitement now. "Now I know what I only glimpsed then. The rider was me. That was clear because he never spoke to me, yet I knew his every thought. His thoughts were my thoughts."

Said Tasunke Witko, "So who was Rider?"

"Myself, grown up."

"Yourself as a possibility," prompted Tasunke Witko.

Curly nodded happily, almost dreamily. Tasunke Witko wondered if the boy saw that this vision was a mountain to climb.

"Do you see how to dress yourself for war, and paint yourself?"

"Yes," Curly said in acceptance, "like Rider exactly. Hair long and loose. In it only a few beads and one eagle feather. The feather upside down, like a war eagle when it is about to kill. Very plain clothing."

"Paint?"

Curly's voice had the hypnotic throb of the drum now. "Rider wore no paint at first. Later lightning streaks and hail spots." Curly leapt forward: "Am I intended for a life of war? In the dream Rider was a warrior only." The light in Curly's eyes spoke his enthusiasm for being called as a warrior.

"A warrior especially," Tasunke Witko agreed. He barely felt his disappointment that his son was not called to be a *wicasa wakan,* at least not yet. "But the dream hints of other ways, ways that might be revealed now or later."

His son fell silent for a moment. He was evidently seeing again, fully seeing, far from this sweat lodge, far from his father and from the ordinary earth.

"We'll talk about dreaming of *wakinyan* after a while," Tasunke Witko said gently. In the tone of a quotation, he went on, "Beneath his left shoulder, slung over a thong from the opposite shoulder, one eagle feather adorned an Inyan creature. Also Inyan was tied behind the ear."

"Inyan medicine," said Curly.

"Yes." This was a delicate point. Inyan represented a power that might change everything Curly had seen. It might lead to new visions later, to a completely different path. Not everything was revealed at the beginning.

"You must tell Horn Chips about Inyan," Tasunke Witko said.

Curly nodded soberly. Tasunke Witko wondered how much he had heard about Inyan medicine. It was very ancient, very strange—most Lakota were leery of it.

Tasunke Witko made a little *humph* to himself. The blessing and hazard of a vision was, when you started walking its path, you could sense its promise but not see its further course or its end. If you could, you might not start.

Tasunke Witko went on quietly. "From the obscuring, velvety blue-gray of these shadows came the enemy fire, streaks flashing toward the rider, fast and dangerous, maybe arrows, maybe bullets. They flashed toward you, ominous in the air. But before touching your flesh they disappeared. Like raindrops from a high thundercloud over desert, they evaporated coming to the earth's flesh. None tore your skin, none broke your bones, none shed your blood."

Tasunke Witko stopped. This was where he sensed that Curly had left something out. That was good—a dreamer must always keep something for himself alone.

Curly felt his silence like a clot in his throat. He didn't want to talk about the hands of his own people grasping at him from behind, clutching, holding him back. Or his sense that he could be hurt only by the hands of his own or when the hands were holding him.

He swallowed hard. He would trust himself. His impulse was to keep silent, and he would. There was no need to bring grief before its time. Hawk was still quiet.

"I am promised invulnerability," said the boy. His tone struck even him as queer. "But the Sahiyela were promised that at the Creek of Turkeys." He looked at his father pleadingly.

"Power is always mysterious," Tasunke Witko said.

Curly contemplated. Goose bumps rose on his skin. What if invulnerability was an illusion? He shook his head. Maybe later he would understand and in understanding find his courage. Hawk stirred.

Tasunke Witko took a deep breath. This part of the dream frightened both of them. "Do you understand? You must go first, in front. You must overcome fear. So you must keep your life and your medicine in such order that you will always feel the power of your dream within you."

Curly looked his father straight in the eye. "Yes," he said hesitantly. Even this was a good start.

"It will be hard to go always in front, always feel bold. You have to." The father eyed his son hard. "Always lead the charge, as Rider did, knowing that the enemy arrows and bullets cannot hurt you.

"I must tell you this next part carefully, and you must listen well." The father's chest wanted to expand with pride, but his bowels were trying to turn watery. This was difficult advice to give a beloved son, whose bumps and bruises you'd kissed. "When you are riding forth dangerously, as in your dream, you are protected. If you try to hang back for safety, not only will you be vulnerable, Spirit may paint you a lesson in your own blood."

Curly felt his father's fear, felt him quail as he emphasized the words. Then Tasunke Witko took a deep breath and went on. "Now Rider was stripped to nothing but a breechcloth, and rode harder, faster, in a martial vigor. Behind him a thunderstorm erupted. Dark clouds roiled, lightning flashed and gave birth to sound. A zigzag of lightning rose on Rider's cheek like a wound. Hail spots welted his body."

Curly felt his own power in his father's telling and thrilled to it. He intoned the words himself:

"Into clouds and shadows rode the rider, forever and forever into clouds and shadows." The rhythmic energy was softening now. "The storm cleared, the hail spots faded, the day shone bright as polished metal. Horse and Rider flew forward." He hesitated, thinking of the Lakota hands pulling at him, the picture he was passing over. "Over his head flew a red-tailed hawk."

The father looked at the son. Curly said meekly, "I have dreamed of *wakinyan*." He was thinking of the three years of danger because he'd kept silent.

"You will talk to Porcupine," said Tasunke Witko evenly. His father seemed unperturbed by Curly's failure.

"Do you think I will have to do things backward?" blurted Curly. A clown, even if a sacred clown.

Tasunke Witko shook his head. "Rider is a warrior."

The boy felt a warm gush of relief.

Tasunke Witko went back to the telling. "On you flew, Horse and Rider, into the shadows, hooves floating above the earth, forever and ever on."

Curly took over again, his voice singing. "Hawk rode the wind over my head, and I knew Hawk. She has lived my whole life imprisoned in here." Looking his father in the eye, he put a flat hand to his chest. "Her flight, her soaring through the air, liberated my heart."

Curly fell silent.

Tasunke Witko spoke softly. "In your dream you received a spirit guide. That is a blessing. You must keep Hawk in your mind at all times, and seek her guidance."

"Father," Curly burst out, "Hawk has always been with me. She's trapped. . . ." His throat constricted. "I have lived my whole life like a prisoner. I love my family, I love my people, but . . . I'm never comfortable." He hesitated, then looked into his father's eye. "Not around anyone." Black Buffalo Woman might be an exception, but he wasn't sure yet. "Hawk beats in my chest, wanting out. She is only calm when I'm alone. I believe that when I fight as I am instructed, riding in front, she will fly. She will soar. I will be liberated."

Tasunke Witko looked at him fondly. He said softly, "My warrior son."

They talked briefly about the medicine bundle Curly would make. Tasunke Witko would ask Curly's mothers to tan a deer hide to special softness and whiteness for it. Inside Curly would wrap the skin of a hawk and . . . He should not discuss the exact contents, not even with his father. As more power was revealed to him, he would add items that came to him as power.

Tasunke Witko had something more to say about seeing beyond. "The hard part," explained the father, "is acting by your vision when it seems wrong. Sometimes it will seem to you that your vision will get you killed. Then you must picture Rider vividly in your mind and act like him.

What would be suicide for another man is safety for you."

Tasunke Witko. This next part was hard, partly because it involved him. In thinking about his son's vision he had understood why the youth held himself apart from everyone. "I must warn you," he said, "this is a great vision, and a difficult one. I think you will have to be alone much of the time. People will think you strange, but you will have to go your own way."

"I like it that way," put in Curly. "Already."

Tasunke Witko thought, *You do it, my son, but you are lonely.* "It seems to be your nature," he agreed. "I think you will be lonely. I think that women, family, and children will not keep you warm, as they keep most of us."

Like a cold hand on Curly's guts came the thought of Black Buffalo Woman. Would he never have her, then?

Curly looked his father full in the face. Yes, that was what his father meant. Yes, he saw that his father also meant that he himself might not have lots of grandchildren, and that was a sorrow. That his son would not be a close companion, amiable by the lodge fire.

Curly could think of nothing but Black Buffalo Woman, and she was not a thought but a light, prickly touch against his chest. Would he lose Black Buffalo Woman?

Then what do I care about this vision? he thought angrily. *It costs too much.*

A long silence passed. Sometimes Curly thought he wasn't breathing. Finally he said, "It will be hard."

Tasunke Witko now gave the advice he had given many times, but this time each word clanged in his mind. "Living by what you see is always difficult, and your vision is especially difficult, yes." The father refused to let his own sadness affect his counsel. "Remember this," he went on. "Sometimes your vision will seem intolerable. Not only dangerous, but miserable. Too much privation, too much responsibility, too much solitude, too much danger." He hesitated. "It is true that other paths might avoid hardships, might even let you live longer. For you they would be spiritual death. Your vision may or may not be the road of physical death. It is spiritual triumph."

Tasunke Witko waited and watched his son's face. It was impassive. Then he went on with the familiar concluding words. "Only from the end, from the pinnacle of death, will you be able to see how the river of your vision led in the true way to the salt sea."

They took a final sweat. The father prayed for his son to have the strength to live his vision.

Tasunke Witko tried to keep his personal feelings out of his voice. His fear, his sorrow, his excitement should not become obstacles for Curly. He did for his son what a *wicasa wakan* did, not a father.

He thought what he would tell his wives later. Something like: "Our son has seen something. Something big. It is a cup of goodness and a cup of sorrow at once."

They would rejoice. Any full measure of life was a cup of goodness and a cup of sorrow at once.

When father and son woke in the morning, they bundled up the hides, left the willow framework of the hut, and set out after the band. They were one day behind.

"How do you feel?" the father asked the son.

Curly noticed his heart. It was rocking from awe to eagerness to panic. The dream gonged in his mind, the memory of Rider larger and more vivid than anything merely real.

What will I do with my vision?

Heroic pictures ran pell-mell in his head. The sounds of hooves, the war cries—"It is a good day to die!"—the yells of effort, of surprise, of death or triumph.

"You can fight to live," his uncle Spotted Tail had said. "You cannot fight against death—you fight to live."

Curly forced his mind away from his uncle, the relative who now seemed a weakling. He summoned up the smell of dust and blood. He imagined the feel of the ceremonial entry into camp and the joyous trilling of the women in tribute to his courage, to his spirit, to the power of his dream.

In his mind he led the way, riding headlong into arrows and bullets.

His flesh puckered at the thought.

"I feel every which way," he answered. "Every emotion I can imagine."

Tasunke Witko smiled at him. "Fine," said the *wicasa wakan*. "You should."

HEYOKA

"I saw Rider gallop through the velvety blue-gray of these shadows," Curly said. Porcupine, the *heyoka* man, listened somberly. Many times criers for visions had come to him to tell about the *wakinyan* they saw in their waking dreams. The thunderbirds were always a power demanding the most careful treatment.

"Enemy fire streaked toward the rider, maybe arrows, maybe bullets. They flashed toward him, ominous in the air. But before touching his flesh, they disappeared. Like raindrops from a high thundercloud over desert, they evaporated before striking the earth's flesh. None tore his skin, none broke his bones, none shed his blood."

Curly made no comment on Rider seeming bullet-proof or on this lack of adornment. He was here to learn to cope with the destructive power of the *wakinyan*.

He also left out the part about the people's hands pulling at him from behind. "Behind Rider a thunderstorm erupted. Dark clouds roiled, lightning flashed and gave birth to sound. A zigzag of lightning marred Rider's cheek like a wound. Hail spots welted his body." This was what mattered.

"Into clouds and shadows rode the rider, forever and forever into clouds and shadows.

"The storm cleared, the hail spots faded, the day shone bright as polished metal. Horse and man flew forward." He omitted the appearance of Hawk above his head.

When Porcupine was satisfied that the young man had finished, he raised a mirror to Curly's nose. There, Curly knew, the *heyoka* would see the entire dream in his breath, and perhaps other medicine that might belong to the young warrior. Curly waited patiently, breath in and out, pulse beating, the earth beating.

At length Porcupine nodded two or three times. "We will have a *heyoka* ceremony for you," he said simply.

The people acted joyful—they welcomed *heyoka* ceremonies enthusiastically. The children found these ceremonies a lot of fun, with the sacred clowns acting silly, and the adults acted like it was all in fun, nothing but fun.

Porcupine took Curly into the *heyoka* tipi, shaved his head, and suggested some meanings of the pictures he had seen in the misted mirror. He added that he had seen the gopher and described the medicine of that creature.

Then the two went out into the village. The ceremony was serious play, a joking spirit thrown into the teeth of the west wind, the lightning, and lightning-gives-birth-to-sound.

Helpers killed a dog quickly and singed the hair off. When the dog was boiled, everyone would have a piece. Holy flesh—thunder dreamers would put medicine paste on their hands and arms and pluck meat out of the boiling water without burning themselves.

Porcupine sang the words of the traditional *heyoka* song over and over:

> "*These are sacred.*
> *They have spoken.*"

Curly sang these words to the four quarters while the dog was boiling:

> *"In a sacred manner I send a voice to you.*
> *In a sacred manner I send a voice to you.*
> *To half of the sky I send my voice in a sacred manner.*
> *In a sacred manner I send a voice to you."*

Porcupine painted Curly's entire body red and drew black lightning flashes and daubed on blue spots of hail on top of the red.

Finally the clowning got started, and the people loved that. Two of the *heyoka* pretended that a small mud puddle was a big lake and they had to cross it. They mimed building a boat and paddled to the middle and got overturned by a wave—the two *heyoka* dived into the puddle, which was thumb-deep, and got all muddy. Then one of them became a muskrat and dived to the bottom and brought up some mud. The other turned into a goose and chased the muskrat, squawking. Everyone thought they were very funny.

It was lunatic humor, of course. Nothing was as unpredictable or as dangerous or as overwhelming as lightning. Crazily, this destruction brought the rain and made Earth green.

After the clowning and dancing, Porcupine and Curly went again to the sacred tipi. There Porcupine explained about dreamers of *wakinyan* far more deeply than Curly had understood them before.

"There is no dream more powerful, more to be feared, more to be obeyed, or one that consecrates the dreamer more earnestly," began Porcupine. "If you dream of *wakinyan,* you are *heyoka* all your life, before anything else, before guardian, scout, holy man, healer, leader, husband, or father."

He let this challenge sit in Curly's mind a moment.

"*Heyoka* walk one of two paths. Some become clowns and do things backward." At the ceremonies they walked in reverse, said "yes" when they meant "no," and vice versa, and sat on their backs or their heads instead of their bottoms.

"The form of *heyoka* for others is more spiritual," said Porcupine, "and so it will be for you. You may be seen as eccentric, but you will not be a clown. You will be attentive to the spirit of the west, Yata, and his powers the *wakinyan*. You will watch for all winged creatures that may fly to you, especially the animal aides of Yata, hawks and bats."

Curly said nothing to Porcupine about Hawk.

"You will pattern yourself after Rider in appearance," said Porcupine, "for Rider was a *wakinyan* dreamer. You will wear the buffalo beard as a fringe on the heels of your moccasins. You will paint your face with streaks of lightning, and your body and your horse with spots of hail. You will wear plain clothing, nothing that makes a show, just as Rider did."

Porcupine said the next words in a matter-of-fact way, but with subtle stress. "You will keep to yourself, separated by your devotion to your dream. You will not marry until later in life, or not at all. You will live in a lodge at the end of the circle. Though you may be sociable in your own lodge, outside it you will say what is necessary briefly and with dignity and return to your solitude."

Tumult churned in Curly. He felt the rightness of all the interpretation—it was he. But to marry late or never!

"You will ride into battle ahead of everyone else. Even riding a trail, you will keep your horse to the side of others, not directly in front or in back of them."

Now Porcupine emphasized the conclusion. "If you keep your vision of the *wakinyan* in your mind ceaselessly, and regard them always with the *cante ista,* more will be revealed to you in time. New paths will open."

Porcupine sent him off on this path with a half-shaven head and streak of black lightning on his left cheek.

MAKA SICA

Curly walked nervously through the camp circle of the Bad Faces. He bore their ambivalent eyes upon him in silence. He wondered for the thousandth time why Bad Face Oglala must resent Hunkpatila Oglala. Hawk perched uneasily.

The young men were lounging and talking on this fine autumn evening. Curly half-smiled at He Dog and his brothers, who smiled back. With a nod Curly acknowledged his rivals: Pretty Fellow and his brother, Standing Bear, No Water nearby with his brothers the twins. They regarded Curly without expression. He deliberately kept the left side of his head to them, the side with hair. He was sure they noticed the streak of black lightning painted on that side of his face.

They would mark carefully everything that he did in the village. But they would not have to mark what he did with Black Buffalo Woman. He was on a mission more important even than seeing her.

He was here on instruction from his father to consult Horn Chips. Two winters had passed since the *wicasa wakan* had instructed the boy to tell his father what he had seen beyond. For two winters Curly had ignored this advice. He was embarrassed. He wondered if Horn Chips would talk to him.

He was also uneasy about the shaven right side of his head. His scalp gleamed in the sun. On the other side his light hair still hung to his hips. He was wearing it loose, in the manner of a supplicant.

He could imagine the jokes his rivals would make about his half-shaved head—now he was trying to hide his telltale hair, they would say, but was too dumb to hide all of it. But they would know now that he had dreamed of *wakinyan,* and somewhere in their hearts they would be respectful, or intimidated, or envious.

Envy. Was that the meaning of the hands of his own people grasping at him from behind?

Curly hated his bare scalp. His hair would take years to grow to full length. He wanted to wear it long and loose into battle, a brassy flag leading the way.

Curly saw by the expression on Chips' face that the old man was not surprised to see him and that he understood the meaning of Curly's shaven head.

After the proper amenities and a smoke, Curly described to Chips the Inyan creatures he saw Rider wearing under his left arm and behind his ear in his vision. He didn't tell the rest of what he saw beyond. He had an uncanny feeling, though, that the *wicasa wakan* knew, or knew the gist of it.

Curly suspected this man knew too much. Not that he was old—Chips was still in his twenties. But he had the air of an ancient, silent, withdrawn, enigmatic, not open to fun. He spent his time conjuring with Inyan and saw things no one else saw. Old in spirit. Which was why Curly was reluctant to be here.

He made himself sit still. He noticed that Hawk was easy enough. *So you belong here,* he told himself. He wondered whether the hide-wrapped bundle in front of Chips held the Inyan the *wicasa wakan* used for seeing beyond.

The *wicasa wakan* nodded. All the *wicasa wakan*'s manners seemed a little abrupt. He was impatient of mere politeness and of behavior not rooted in reality, meaning spiritual reality, the only reality. He acted as though there wasn't time enough under the sun to spend with people who were unwilling to be rooted. "Tell me everything about your *heyoka* ceremony," said Chips.

Curly told it all without comment or expression. He said nothing about his sadness. He had decided his vision truly meant he couldn't marry for years, or be sociable, or have much of the satisfaction of companionship.

When Curly finished, Chips was silent for a while. Then he said simply, "Tomorrow we will go to the Maka Sica." The badlands, the place where the earth itself was misshapen, where the gods had destroyed the ancient animals and hurled their bones into the earth. A place all the Lakota were afraid of.

Curly rode behind and to one side. He couldn't keep his eyes off Horn Chips. The *wicasa wakan* was incommunicative. He acted like his mind was on other things or in another world, and Curly should know what world and be paying attention to that. He hoped cultivating solitude, keeping to yourself, didn't mean becoming a Chips. Curly thought everyone should be calling Chips "Our Strange Man," not Light Curly Hair, son of Tasunke Witko. He didn't want to become like this *wicasa wakan*. He wondered if communicating with Inyan, which he'd heard was always done in secret, would make him clandestine, cryptic, and enigmatic, like Chips.

They were riding down the valley of Earth-Smoke River, which the *wasicu* called White River, near Sage Creek. Horn Chips looked constantly into the Maka Sica, searching for something. Curly couldn't guess what he was looking for at such a distance, unless it was the color of the earth itself.

The Maka Sica was the earth gone strange, phantasmagorical shapes rising from the broken plain, shapes like the monster animals people made with the shadows of their fingers on the walls of the lodge. The monsters were in violent earth colors in great layers, yellow, red, black at the bottom, with splashes of blue-green here, silver there. The people said these monsters looked like they were made of soil, but they were so ancient they had turned to Inyan.

Curly thought it was like the face of a very old man or woman, crevassed and scarred and wrinkled, but dried out far beyond what could happen to a person. Soil and grass and other rooted people had been scoured away, like hair and supple flesh, exposing the bone beneath. Actually, it seemed to him more like a battered skeleton than an old face. The bones of the skeleton stuck up in strange, phantasmagorical shapes, points, spires, horns, contours of the monsters of the dream world.

The people were afraid of this place. Huge bones could be seen here, the leg bones and backbones and skulls of animals that walked the earth before two-legged people did, mammoth creatures with terrible teeth and claws. These creatures were so violent that the gods themselves destroyed them, the tale went, and with lightning bolts speared them deep into the earth, so that only edges showed.

Curly was a little afraid, too. But if Chips said that the way of spirit for Curly lay here, that his power stemmed from this place, he was willing to go and meet it. Power was always frightening.

Chips stopped abruptly and dismounted. He waited without a word for Curly to do the same. Then they started walking from the river valley toward the ogre shapes and the monster bones.

As far as Curly could tell, they walked idly, here and there. Chips kept his eyes on the ground, moving around aimlessly, seeming to study the earth at the feet of the walls that looked like mud and felt like stone. Curly followed in a curiously listless mood. He didn't know what they were doing and didn't care. They must have walked around for a quarter-day. Curly felt torporous in the hot September sun.

Then Chips said softly, *"Wanh!,"* an exclamation of delight. He fingered some dirt away, picked something up, and handed it to Curly.

It was a shell, no, what used to be a shell turned to stone, shaped like a very small pinecone. It was whorled like the shell of a snail, but sharpened to a point at the center of the whorl.

"You will keep it," said Chips flatly, "just as a reminder. Before long you will come back to the Maka Sica and walk aimlessly among the Inyan creatures of this kind until one speaks to you, or you feel it may speak to you. You will take that one and wear it behind your left ear always."

Curly said nothing.

"We'll find another Inyan creature for under your arm," said Chips. "Now let's smoke."

They sat next to a boulder. Silently, as they smoked, Chips pointed to stone shells embedded in the boulder, part of the fabric of the rock itself. When he put the *canupa* away, the *wicasa wakan* said simply, "Inyan are the most ancient people."

He paused. "This stone was once alive as we are, able to breathe, to move, to seek food, to make others of its kind. Yes, even the Inyan people were once alive. All is connected by being alive. This stone speaks to us of our bond even with Inyan. *Mitakuye oyasin.*" We are all related.

The *wicasa wakan* looked about. The horizon was blocked in all directions by the ogre shapes of the Maka Sica. "Another teaching," said Chips. "The earth owns two good days, one for the sight, one for the vision. The earth owns two good days, one for the body, one for the spirit. The earth owns two good days, one for the mind, one for the *cante ista.*"

Chips looked about a while. Curly couldn't imagine what he was thinking. This talking made Curly uncomfortable. Why did Chips constantly act like he was seeing things Curly didn't see, talking to spirits Curly didn't hear?

"Your way in youth seems to be war," said Chips.

Curly was pleased. He hadn't told the *wicasa wakan* about Hawk in his chest.

"You will drill the other Inyan creature we find and wear it under your arm as Rider does. It will be a protector.

"An Inyan like this one," he said, nodding toward the shell, "you will wear behind your ear. When your winters of war are past, when you want to see further into things,

Inyan will speak to you, will act as your guide. Though that is for a later time, do not forget it.

"Remember always that Inyan are the most ancient of all peoples, and the wisest. They are your way. Come to me when they begin to speak, or to another who talks to Inyan, and I will help you start on the path. Until then you wear this Inyan behind your ear as a promise."

This time Horn Chips fell silent for a long while. Curly sat equally silent, patient, his mind on Chips' words. He wished he didn't have the urge to squirm.

"For now I will give you a word that will help you stay in touch with Inyan. *Wanisugna.*" It meant "living seed within the shell." "Say this word prayerfully to Inyan sometimes. *Wanisugna.*"

Suddenly Chips smiled, and his expression was truly enigmatic. "Now," said the *wicasa wakan,* "we will have a true surprise. We go to visit the *wasicu.*"

Chips set out toward the horses. Curly fell in behind him and to one side. Why, of all times, why would Horn Chips want to visit *wasicu* now?

MAN-WHO-PICKS-UP-STONES-WHILE-RUNNING

Curly had heard about the camp but had not seen it. The *wasicu* had come to the Maka Sica several times now, in the warm moons when traveling was easy, staying even past the moon when the Wasp hit Little Thunder's village on the Blue Water. The Lakota did not disturb these *wasicu.* The tale was, the giant bones in the Maka Sica were great medicine for them. The Lakota respected any man attending to his medicine. And to them the bones were like an area of raised scaffolds lifting bodies away from scavengers, a haunted field, possessed of unpredictable powers, to be avoided.

The camp was in a grove of trees in a little canyon where a stream trickled, even in this Moon When Leaves Turn Brown.

What did Horn Chips want with them? Curly had begun to think of them as like the Wakinyan Tanka, except from the east, and wanted to stay away from all of them.

The interpreter walked out to meet them where they tied their horses, along with a tall, lanky, bearded *wasicu* so eager he was almost pushing around the interpreter. The man walked a little awkwardly on stick legs, like a crane.

"Benoit," said Chips politely.

"Horn Chips," said the interpreter. Curly remembered this man now from Fort Laramie. His father was a Frenchman, an interpreter and guide before him, his mother a Mniconjou.

"Light Curly Hair," said Chips.

The interpreter nodded to Curly.

"The Man with Crazy Feet," said Curly, smiling. The Oglala youths had played kicking the ball with this fellow, and he could do the trickiest things with his feet to tap the ball around you.

The interpreter grinned. Curly could smell whiskey on him.

"Dr. Hayden," Benoit launched forth in English, "this is my friend Horn Chips, of the Bad Face Oglala Lakota." The tall *wasicu* stuck out his hand, and Chips touched it softly. "Light Curly Hair of the Hunkpatila Oglala Lakota." Curly looked at the hand before touching it very quickly and tentatively. It was the first time he'd touched a *wasicu*.

"This is Dr. Ferdinand Hayden," Benoit said in Lakota, "Man-Who-Picks-Up-Stones-While-Running. He is a *pezuta wicasa*," a healer, "and a man who studies the ancient bones." All around them, laid out on big canvases, were bones and pieces of bones of animals from the time before, some of them still partly encased in mudstone. They made Hawk fidgety.

This fellow Dr. Ferdinand Hayden had a peculiar and very impolite gaze. He looked straight into your eyes, but he didn't just look. He directed an intense scrutiny at you and projected his spirit along it, so you wanted to bat it away with your hands. Yet he smiled like he meant to be friendly.

"Will you eat with us?" said Dr. Ferdinand Hayden. Benoit translated.

The invitation treated them as honored guests and could not be refused.

Besides, Chips was looking like the snake who had just caught the frog.

"He talks so fast because he's always in a hurry, *paguduh, paguduh.*" Benoit beat a rhythm of horses' hooves on his thighs. "Always a gallop, never a walk or trot." Then Benoit rolled his eyes—he talked as much with his body as with words. "That's why we call him Man-Who-Picks-Up-Stones-While-Running. He dashes around collecting old stones, *fossils,* he calls them," Benoit used the English word, "like a hungry bird hopping from seed to seed." Benoit drank whiskey out of his tin cup. "A starving bird."

The interpreter ripped rabbit flesh off a leg bone with his teeth. "Watch for this fellow, though. He's going to be an *impo-o-ortant* man."

"Why?" asked Chips. The *wicasa wakan* actually seemed gleeful. Curly couldn't imagine why.

"He's obsessed with this medicine of the old bones. You should see him go after them. A couple of years ago when he couldn't get the *wasicu* to make a group of men to come for the bones, he came up the Big Muddy on his own and walked all over the upper Missouri country alone. A whole year, winter too, all alone." Benoit started in on another leg. "He's like a child about it. I don't know why."

They knew Benoit had been to one of what the *wasicu* called schools and learned to read and write. And they knew that *doctor* meant a man of learning. Strange that Benoit couldn't understand him.

"The other one's weird, too," said Benoit, sipping at the whiskey again. "The soldier leader. Lieutenant Gouverneur Kemple Warren." The guide pronounced the name very clearly, with a hint of mockery. "He fought with the Wasp against Little Thunder." Benoit looked at Chips and Curly sideways, knowing what this would mean to them. "He collects flowers like a madman. Goes everywhere looking for flowers, plucks them out of Earth, puts them in paper envelopes, writes down all sorts of things about them." Benoit chuckled. "He doesn't notice much about his relatives the living things, except flowers. Sees everything about flowers. One day a bear's going to stick its nose up his ass while he's bending over a flower."

Benoit used the English word *ass* and made a gesture of goosing himself.

When they'd eaten, Man-Who-Picks-Up-Stones-While-Running and the lieutenant joined them. When the lieutenant was introduced, Curly didn't shake his hand but acted like he didn't know what was expected. He wondered whether he should kill the soldier. He could slip back into camp tonight and do it. For the killing at the Blue Water the man deserved it. But Curly felt no rage toward him personally.

Benoit started right in having fun with the translating. He'd go like this: "Doctor wants to know the *truth* about why you've come to the Maka Sica. The way he says it, he wants *passionately* to know." Benoit's tone was teasing. "He thinks you're very, *very* interesting."

Chips and Curly looked at each other skeptically. This *wasicu* was very strange, not being politely distant but jumping right in, and inquiring far too closely about personal matters.

"We came here to find Inyan," said Chips. "Show him the Inyan creature, Curly," the *wicasa wakan* went on mildly.

Curly just looked at his mentor aghast. Why would he show his Inyan to a *wasicu*? Even if it was just an example? He wondered, *Does Man-Who-Picks-Up-Stones-While-Running know something about Inyan that might speak of its power?* Chips gave Curly a jerk of the head that meant, "Do it."

He unfolded Inyan from a hide wrap and revealed it. Shockingly, Man-Who-Picks-Up-Stones-While-Running reached out and grabbed it.

Chips shot Curly a look of warning. Otherwise Curly would have ripped Inyan out of the *wasicu*'s hand.

"This is an ammonite," he said, "the most common of fossils in the Maka Sica."

Benoit added with amusement that the fellow's tone was saying, "Why do you want a stone as ordinary as this?"

"It's a marine shell," went on Man-Who-Picks-Up-Stones-While-Running, "from the sea. An octopus or squid."

"He's not saying out loud that he doesn't even bother to stoop down for ones like this," added Benoit. "He has some manners. Sort of."

"It's the oldest of all fossils in this area," said Man-Who-Picks-Up-Stones-While-Running. "Comes from the bottom stratum there." Dr. Hayden pointed at the hills around them. "The black layer."

"He's struggling to find something nice to say," put in Benoit.

"It's the oldest relic of the history of life around here," concluded Man-Who-Picks-Up-Stones-While-Running.

When Benoit translated these words, Chips gave Curly a look of triumph.

"Dr. Hayden," said Benoit, "Horn Chips is a holy man and diviner." The guide was good and drunk now. "Tell them about your dreams. Maybe he can help you."

Man-Who-Picks-Up-Stones-While-Running brushed this idea away with a hand. "No, no, I wouldn't impose."

"He has nightmares every night," said Benoit in Lakota, "about the ancient animals." He switched back to English. "Tell them. Horn Chips is very wise about dreams."

Dr. Hayden flicked the idea away again. His hand was thrashing around nervously, like a horse's tail at flies. "No, no," he murmured. Curly thought it was embarrassment splashed all over his face, embarrassment at the thought of asking a "savage" for help. That and contempt.

Chips handed Man-Who-Picks-Up-Stones-While-Running a mirror of polished metal. "If you will breathe on this glass," said Chips, "I will look at your dream and help you with it."

Now the hand slashed wildly, fending the mirror off. To control the hand, Hayden stood. "The dreams don't bother me at all," he said fiercely. Then, in a calmer voice, "You're welcome to stay the night in camp." And he stilted off on his crane legs.

Benoit chuckled. "If you stay," he said, "you'll hear Doctor braying and mewling in the middle of the night. All day long he digs up bones. All night long the animals take their revenge by trampling him, over and over and over. In his sleep he rants his protests."

Chips looked significantly at Curly. "We'll go," he said to Benoit. "Thank you." His tone suggested, "I mean it." He said aloud, "How do you stand being around them?"

"Strong drink," said Benoit, chuckling. "I'd better not walk you to the horses—my legs are wobbly."

Curly was glad to get away from the smell of Benoit's whiskey. As they were untying the reins, Chips said, "They are pitiful, the *wasicu*. They don't know enough to make peace with their own dreams. So the dreams torment them."

Curly wondered whether Chips was hinting. *Yes*, he thought, *my vision would have tormented me, had I not told it. Will torment me, if I don't live it*.

They got mounted. "How can anyone be afraid of *wasicu*?" asked Chips rhetorically. "I feel sorry for them."

BETROTHAL

During the Winter When Many Children Died, in the Moon When the Chokecherries Are Ripe, he took Grandmother Plum gently by the elbow and led her to the creek near a small waterfall. They sat on a boulder on the bank.

The village was camped in the Shining Mountains in this, his favorite moon. Father Sun shone almost until night-middle-made in this moon, but they couldn't see him. All evening he was behind the peaks to the west.

Here the two could be alone, the falling water would keep them from being overheard, and Hawk would be at peace.

"Unci," he began, "I am a coward. I get ready to live as I saw beyond, and get ready more, and more. I went to the Maka Sica and got this Inyan creature." He touched the seashell tied behind his ear to indicate which one. "I trapped a red-tailed hawk and made a hat from its skin and feathers, a hat I will wear into war. I made a medicine bundle." Grandmother Plum had seen him making these preparations. "Ready, ready, ready. But I never go to war."

Her listless gaze went toward the waist-high waterfall. He wondered what she was thinking. Whether she was thinking.

"It's like a stutter. I start and I get stopped. *Kuh-kuh-kuh-kuh* and I never get to say 'coup.' "

His foolish mimicry made him dejected. He thought of his other foolishness, talking to an old woman with deaf ears and a blank mind. He looked at her face. She sat patiently, his hand on her elbow, her eyes cast down in the direction of his knees. He had the sense that if she could make any gesture at all, she would slide closer to him, or put an arm around him. Probably more foolishness.

He slipped his arm around her waist and drew her close.

"Maybe Power deliberately gets in my way." He held this awful idea in his mind a moment. "Last summer, after the sun dance, you remember I got hurt with the arrow?" He fingered the scar just below his knee. One of the boys, playing at shooting arrows, had wounded him by accident.

"Red Cloud led some young men against the Psatoka. Young Man-Whose-Enemies-Are-Afraid-of-His-Horses, He Dog, Pretty Fellow's brother Standing Bear. And because of my vision Red Cloud asked me."

Because of the paper the tribe had signed promising not to fight the Psatoka, it was the first war party to go out openly in a long time. It made people feel as though the good days were back.

"Because of the accident, though, I didn't get to go." If she was hearing him at all, she remembered that he had spent the whole moon after the sun dance on a crutch. His friend Lone Bear had gone in his place.

"I didn't understand. One part of what I saw beyond seemed true. I could only be hurt by my own people. But the other part? Frustrated."

He drew a deep breath, in and out. "The next time Red Cloud took young men, he didn't ask me." He fretted about it, too. "Maybe his medicine said he shouldn't." In fact, Red Cloud hadn't invited any Hunkpatila, just Bad Face youths.

"I can't get st-st-started," he repeated. "I st-st-st-stutter."

He gave a madcap cackle.

When the villages came together for the sun dance, at the fullness of the same moon, Black Buffalo Woman at first would have nothing to do with him. When he came near, she turned her back or started talking animatedly to a girl-friend or even thought of some reason to disappear into her parents' lodge.

Then she was shut away in the *isna tipi*. This was essential. The natural power of her flow might be greater than the hundreds of objects made powerful by prayer and conjuring and might destroy their medicine.

After the sun dance she came to him immediately and led him to the willows. Her manner didn't allow any choice on his part, any hesitation, even any talk. She wanted to be loved in the bushes now, in silence and in a kind of fury. In her urgency he felt somehow an edge of tears.

When she was worn out, she lay spooned along his front side naked, resting, soft, peaceful. He felt like he had tamed her spirit as his father tamed the wildness of the moose birds. But like them, she could not be grabbed and and she might fly off at any moment.

She even slept a little. Curly couldn't sleep—he was much too excited. He and Black Buffalo Woman together like this, it was his most vivid dream, almost like his vision. It felt like a place and time not of the everyday world. He wanted to be aware of every instant of it, aware in the heightened way he wanted in battle.

She woke and lay sweetly in his arms for a while. Then she turned toward him and looked into his eyes mischievously. Finally she got up and put on her chastity belt and slipped her dress on.

She looked at him for a long moment. Then she held something out, a thong that must have lain inside the bodice of her dress. On the thong hung the ring he had made for her, with Hawk carved on the top.

Holding his eyes, she took it from the thong and slipped it onto the middle finger of her right hand, where it fit best. She held it up into the late-afternoon sun, and they both looked at the way Sun, Wi, glinted off its polished surfaces. He waited.

"I will wear your ring," she said.

Then she flew off.

By nightfall it was the talk of the Oglala villages. Everyone knew that Black Buffalo Woman was wearing a ring made for her by Curly. A Sahiyela ring maker had helped him with it, they said, and he had offered it as the young Sahiyela men did, as a promise of marriage.

The Oglala women babbled and cackled about this. Their people had no long engagements to be married. Once marriage was agreed on by the families, the nuptials were done within a day. But they did have love matches. Curly's uncle, his mothers' brother, Spotted Tail, himself had made a love match. They all remembered that. Love matches didn't necessarily make the best marriages—they put the tumultuous urges of the young above the wisdom of the families. But everyone was charmed by the idea of a love match and hoped it would work.

They knew about the ring Black Buffalo Woman gave Curly, too. He refused to wear her ring, people said—he claimed his vision prohibited it. "Well, well," they babbled, and speculated about other reasons he might refuse.

Curly felt embarrassed about this. Did Black Buffalo Woman have to tell everything? Yet he was proud. She had made her commitment.

"We'll test these young couples, naturally," the families said. "They won't be allowed to marry for a long time."

"As long as his vision keeps him from wearing her ring," her father and brother agreed, "it keeps him from marrying, too."

"That's good," the women said. "Black Buffalo Woman will have to let other young men come courting, too. A love match has to prove itself. If their commitment won't stand up to years of waiting, it isn't enough."

"Then our wisdom will prevail," said her father and brother.

Curly felt all the eyes on him but he said nothing to anyone, not even to Hump. He hung around the lodge of Black Buffalo Woman's family, hoping to see her, hoping especially to see his ring on her finger in front of everyone.

She didn't come out. The family wouldn't let the two of them be together right now, certainly not together alone. A certain cooling down was required. Curly watched the faces of her father and her mother and brother and thought they were not displeased. Maybe they were on the verge of smiling. At the least they would wait and see. That was enough.

He didn't care if they saw what was on his face. For once he didn't keep it neutral. He was happy. He was delirious. He had what meant most to him.

Which was something more than her promise of marriage. It was Black Buffalo Woman's other statement. In her way this creature of his, impulsive, over-intense, ready to fly, was saying as clearly as she was capable of saying, was saying by wearing his ring, one treasured word, *iy-otancila*. "I love you."

If he could be alone with her now, he would look directly into her eyes and say the same word.

Yet something niggled at the back of his mind. Could he have Black Buffalo Woman *and* follow his vision?

HAWK RISES

"They have good horses," said Buffalo Hump mischievously to his *hunka*. He was making a joke of trying to tempt Curly to come along on a raid he was leading the next morning. He knew very well no tempting was necessary. "They live in grass lodges, so they'll fight like women."

Curly gave Hump a dirty look. With that scowl and his hair, light as a *wakan* buffalo and chopped short on one side, Curly could probably scare these strange people to death, Hump thought.

The *hunka* turned over to pretend to sleep in their brush lodge. Hump hoped he had a good report of these people. Relatives of the Snakes, they were said to be, just not speaking the same language. Not tipi Indians, so maybe more ready to flee than fight. Why, then, did they have good horses? Would they really be poor fighters? Hump wriggled in his blankets. That was why you fought, to find out.

Tasunke Witko had been here recently, counseling Curly. Hump hoped the father wasn't trying to make the son cautious as an old man. Yes, Curly would be anxious about proving himself. Fine. That's how young men got to be warriors. And Hump would keep an eye on his *hunka* to keep him from acting crazy. But Hump knew his *hunka* needed to burst free.

Curly felt his stutter again against the people of the strange tongue. They turned out to be good fighters. Well out from their camp the enemy warriors opened fire on the young Lakota. They had a good position on a hill, with plenty of rocks to hide behind and a gully to slip into. Plenty of guns, too, more than the Lakota.

Maybe today would be another day when Curly was stuck and Hawk wouldn't soar. Before the fighting started, he unbraided his hair on the left side and let it flow long, the traditional sign of willingness to take risks, even desperate risks. He owned a pistol now, a weapon useful only at close range.

"Under the necks of our horses!" shouted Hump. They circled the strangers fast, shooting from beneath the necks of their running mounts, but it didn't work. When you shot under your pony's neck, it was hard to be accurate. The enemies had good cover. Since the Lakota offered elusive targets, they hardly fired back. The Lakota lost a couple of horses.

"We'll crawl up there!" boomed Hump. Curly almost smiled at the looks of dismay on the faces of He Dog and Black Elk at the idea of creeping uphill on foot under fire. He Dog was the only Bad Face along, and he was still living mostly with Curly's band. Curly and Hump felt better when the resentful Pretty Fellow and the imperious twins were not around.

Everyone dismounted and tried to get within bow range

on foot, but the cover was too thin and the gunfire uncomfortably close. They backed off.

As they were riding in a circle again, Curly's pony went down hard. Curly catapulted across the ground like a log going end over end and sat hard. He was dizzy and disoriented. After a moment he realized he was unprotected against fire. His pony was down to stay.

Suddenly he felt it. Hawk turned into the wind and rose. Without using his hands he could feel the emblematic hawk hat still pinned into his hair. He looked around and saw a loose enemy horse. Yes, it suited.

When Curly was mounted, the horse took its own head and charged up the hill, going home. Curly's heart quailed for an instant. Then he realized, *This is what I do in my vision.*

Straight at the enemy they galloped. Gunfire made a wind past his naked arms. It kicked up gravel. It ricocheted off rocks. But it left his flesh untouched.

A warrior rose out of the gully ahead, his rifle lifted. Curly leaned around the pony's neck and drove an arrow into him.

Curly's horse jumped the fallen man, nearly landed on another, shied sideways, and skittered down the hill.

The young Lakota whooped.

I did it. I rode into fire invulnerable.

Hawk was soaring up the sky of his heart.

Hump rode out to meet Curly, but the youth felt it strong in his soul now. He turned the pony and kicked it back uphill hard.

He saw a warrior lower down the gully ready to shoot. He guided the pony straight at the man, fierce in his courage. Curly sat up high, ignored the enemy's shot, raised his pistol, and killed the man.

The air was more exhilarating, his body more alive, and music sang in his spirit. Light Curly Hair knew he was in his native home.

Giddy with joy, he jumped off the horse and ran to the

fallen stranger. He seized the topknot, made two quick arcs with his knife, jerked, and held the scalp high.

His comrades roared.

He cared nothing for the enemy fire, so he did the same to the first man he had slain. And just as he finished, he felt the lightning strike his leg.

He stopped. Thoughtless, he dropped the reins, and the pony ran off.

Suddenly he knew, and his heart fell.

He had taken something for himself, these scalps. He looked at them in his hand.

He had violated his vision. Now he was vulnerable. He was lucky this bullet hadn't killed him. He wanted to vomit his guts onto the earth.

Curly ran in a funny hop, bounding from rock to rock, bush to bush, while his comrades fired to keep the strangers' heads down. His skin puckered and itched. He had no power. Anything might shed his blood.

Hump ran to Curly and clapped his shoulders proudly, exclaiming something.

Curly looked at the scalps in his hand. Disgusted with himself, he threw them on the ground.

In respect the other warriors kept a little distance.

Hump checked the wound, a hole in the flesh. He looked his *hunka* oddly in the eye, walked away, cut a piece of moist skin from a dead horse, and tied it tightly over the wound.

Curly said nothing at all. He couldn't feel Hawk at all. His heart felt dead.

"Let's get out of here," said Hump. The leader had a big grin. From his point of view, Curly realized, they had done well: no one hurt seriously, a couple of horses dead, new ones captured, four enemies killed, eight first coups, some scalps, and a great show of medicine.

Curly's guts wrenched.

He looked inside himself and felt Hawk, calm enough, but dull, listless.

"Let's go," he said tersely.

They started toward where a couple of boys were holding the traveling horses. Curly noticed that Hump went back, picked up the scalps, and hung them from his belt.

Curly wouldn't touch them, ever.

He rode back toward camp with the others. Hump and Black Elk and He Dog were full of smiles for Curly. When others kept their distance, it seemed more like respect than aversion.

Curly no longer felt like he was stuttering. He had launched forth on the wind. Hawk inside him felt wounded and exhilarated at once. She had soared high, gloriously high, and hurt a wing.

INTIMIDATION

No Water waited. He had been waiting for a long time. He had patience and patience and more patience, he told himself. He could wait a very long time.

He was watching Black Buffalo Woman and her mother in that field digging prairie turnips. From these trees he couldn't see the digging tool go into the ground and the root come to the hand and the sack, but he knew the bending and levering motions. Black Buffalo Woman had been digging roots a long time, longer than No Water expected. She would make a good wife—she was diligent.

No Water wanted her for other reasons, though. He touched the hide wrap under his arm protectively. It had been long enough. Now he would have her.

No Water knew men wanted women in different ways, to make love to, naturally, to talk to, to bear children, to play with, to share life with. His particular desires toward Black Buffalo Woman were clear to him. He wanted to own her. He wanted to possess her, to make her go here and there, to tell her quietly to lie under him and have her do his bidding without hesitation, to train and use her as he would a horse. He knew that these desires were ugly. But the desires of many men toward attractive women were ugly.

In fact, this ugliness was remembered in one of the most holy of all Lakota stories. When White Buffalo Woman brought the sacred *canupa* to the people, many, many generations ago, she came walking in a mysterious way toward two young men. She was very beautiful, with long hair hanging down and dressed in white, shining buckskin. One of the young men immediately had ugly thoughts about her. The other said, "This is a sacred woman. Throw all ugly thoughts aside."

White Buffalo Woman put down what she was carrying, which was the sacred *canupa*, and covered it with sage. She knew their minds. She told the young men that they did not know her but invited them, "If you want to do what you're thinking, come."

The young man with ugly thoughts said to his friend, "I told you, but you wouldn't listen." Then he went to her.

A cloud came and covered them. The beautiful woman stepped out of the cloud and stood. When the cloud blew away, the man with ugly thoughts was reduced to a skeleton being eaten by worms.

White Buffalo Woman told the other man to go to the people and instruct them to prepare a big lodge for her. Then she would come to them. Frightened by the skeleton, the young man did what he was told.

A skeleton being eaten by worms!

From the first time he could remember hearing that story, No Water thought he would have been like the young man who had bad thoughts. Later, when he knew what it felt like to want a woman, he identified himself with this wretch completely. Yes, he felt the ugliness of it.

So he was pleased that the woman of his desires was named the opposite of the sacred *canupa* bearer—*Black* Buffalo Woman. Yet in the story Black Buffalo Woman was one of the forms of White Buffalo Woman. When she walked away after making the people the gift of the *canupa,* White Buffalo Woman turned first into a red buffalo cow, then white once more, and finally black.

Black he associated with the west, the home of the *wakinyan,* an immense, destructive power, and with the black road, the way of difficulty and strife, the opposite of the good, red road.

He felt blackness in himself and relished it.

He had wanted Black Buffalo Woman for a long, long time. When he was first a man, but she was not yet a woman, he used to watch her playing with the other girls. He liked the coltish way she walked and ran and walked and skipped. She was small but seemed more graceful than the other girls. She liked silly tricks and surprises and trinkets like beads and bells. Mostly she liked cavorting around, sprinting, jumping, tumbling, even doing cartwheels. The way she moved reminded No Water of a creek running downstream fast, bubbling and leaping on its way.

When he gave her little things, she squealed with delight. She never seemed to notice him much, though. No one gave any thought to the overgrown boy with the big, thick, clumsy body. Not so clumsy now—his muscles had caught up with his bulk—but still thick, heavy, rocklike. He wanted to possess her. She would submit.

He touched the hide bundle again. He had waited patiently for five winters, since the day of her buffalo ceremony, or at least since he had stolen this bundle. Everyone knew she was fully a woman now, with many suitors. She was ready for marriage. It was time. Even if that ring said she was waiting for Light Curly Hair. No Water sniffed his amusement at that.

He thought of what he would do when Black Buffalo Woman was his, all his. He would plant himself in her like a tree trunk. The two of them would put deep roots into the soil of the band, roots made of children, family ties, village cooperation, leading and following, and many other good things. He would grow big in the tribe, a man everyone admired, a chief, finally a chief of chiefs. Under him the Bad Faces would be a great people, the troubles of the past forgotten. In the end Black Buffalo Woman wouldn't even wonder about her wispy pretender to glory. He would be insignificant and No Water great.

At midafternoon the two women picked up their sacks full of turnips and headed back toward the circle of lodges. As they passed, Black Buffalo Woman spoke softly. Her mother nodded and went on. Black Buffalo Woman turned into the bushes, as though to relieve herself, and then stepped straight toward No Water.

He rose, uncertain, from behind the dead tree. Had she known all along that he was watching her? Today and other days? She came on challengingly, swaggering a little, perhaps intending to upbraid him for . . . she would call it spying on her. But he had the answer. When she got close enough to see perfectly, he simply held out the bundle.

She snatched the hide and threw it open. The cloth was in pieces, the middle area that held her blood missing. She glared at him.

"Red Rock made it into a potion," he told her simply.

It took a moment to register. No Water had dared to take her bundle out of the plum tree, risking the wrath of the *tonwan* that guarded it. He had taken it to the bone keeper, who must have purged him later of the evil influences. The bone keeper had made her first flow into a love potion, an instrument of seduction. People said no woman could resist such a potion.

She slapped him with the hide. It made a satisfying *whap!*

He grabbed her wrist. She felt how easily his massive

hand could break her bones. She dropped the bundle. It was powerless now.

No Water's big face was impassive. He didn't care what she thought. She liked that about him, always had. He went forward like a buffalo bull, too strong to care. "I put it into the stew last night. You ate it."

Her heart quailed. She knew some powers were stronger than she was. Still, the words shot out. "I will never be your—"

He stopped her mouth with a hand. "Your brother wants me for your husband." Her brother had the right to give her in marriage. Of course, she could object. "Your father wants me," No Water went on relentlessly. "Your mothers want me. Your uncles want me."

All this might be true. No Water was a rising man.

"I will possess you."

He put his arms around her and pulled her close. For a long moment they just looked into each other's eyes. She felt his big hand on her left breast and nipped in her breath a little. Was he going to force her? Right there?

"No," No Water said with a little smile, taking his hand away, relaxing his arms. "You will ask me to possess you. Because of the medicine. And because of your nature. It is a bad nature, perverse. You will want me."

He lifted her up easily, her head higher than his. He put his mouth to her breast through the thin antelope skin and sucked her nipple. She saw from the glint in his eyes that he knew she was aroused.

He set her down. She felt weak-kneed and almost grabbed him for support.

He took her face in both hands and spoke the words slowly and forcefully. "Stay away from Light Curly Hair. I know everything about the two of you. Everything. I have watched you. If you go with him again, I will kill you."

He stared at her balefully. "Not him. You."

She looked into his eyes and believed him.

He let her go. She slipped to the ground like limp cloth.

"Take off his ring. Don't wear it again," he commanded. He walked off without looking back.

She picked up the hide of the bundle and watched his back disappear into the trees. She took the ring off.

A NAME

They prepared to march into the village formally, in the old way, as in the days before they had promised the *wasicu* to stop fighting other Indians. One man went ahead to alert the village of the procession of triumph.

The others painted themselves. They tied their horses and sat on rocks and trees and adorned themselves with the utmost care. A warrior marching into the village after a victorious raid on an enemy told the story of his personal battle, and of his entire life as a warrior, on his body. Though all these men were young and none yet had a full eagle-feather warbonnet, they would make a fine show. These were the moments Lakota men lived for.

Only Curly sat apart, observing quietly.

He Dog mounted the white, black-tipped tail feather of an eagle upright in his scalp lock, meaning that he had killed an enemy. Since he did not paint it red, he had not been wounded. He Dog was the one Bad Face Curly liked a lot, a simple man of few words, big-chested and thick-bodied, quick to laugh, confident and courageous in war.

Black Elk dangled a similar feather from the armlet at his biceps, a simple indication that he had fought with an enemy. Young Man-Whose-Enemies did the same.

The two who had stolen horses suspended from their scalp locks eagle tail feathers colored green—the green symbolized Wakan Tanka in the aspect of Earth, mother of life.

One man put yellow paint on his body, symbolic of God the Rock, the spirit of revenge, destruction, and violence. Another painted outside his left eye a half-circle of red with forked ends, symbols of spirits of lightning, a claim of being irresistible in war.

The men who had struck first coups put miniature red bows into their scalp locks. They would now be entitled to carry coup sticks.

The two wounded by arrows fastened small red arrows into their hair.

Some indicated old wounds—red dabs on the right forearm for knife cuts, red dots on the left forearms for wounds from arrows or spears.

Those who had danced the sun dance painted themselves red on the thighs, calves, and feet.

Curly watched carefully as Hump decorated himself, the most elaborately painted and feathered of all the warriors. As the leader of a war party, he painted his hands red. Because the party had been successful, he wore the blue-painted tail feather of an eagle upright in his scalp lock. The blue symbolized Wakan Tanka as wind motion, for He had lent the party swift and elusive movement. As one who had taken scalps in the past, Hump carried a chokecherry staff. The war club suspended from his right hand meant he was willing to go to battle whenever called upon. The black paint around his mouth and on his chin said he had returned bearing the scalp of an enemy killed in battle. He donned a scalp shirt with fringes of human hair at sides and arms. From now on Hump was entitled to wear it at will.

Buffalo Hump was a man much decorated in war. Now everyone would recognize him as a leader. He fought fiercely, happily, a little recklessly. He led sensibly. Curly was proud to be his friend.

But Curly sat apart, alone, feeling alien. He could not deck himself out with all this finery. He could not tell his exploits in paint and feather. Because of his vision.

He was entitled to lots of decoration. He had earned the right to wear two white tail feathers with black tips upright in his scalp lock for killing two enemies. He could have hung a piece of lead on a thong around his neck, the sign of being wounded by a bullet. Since his horse had been shot out from under him, he could have worn another eagle feather painted yellow with red stripes, symbolizing Wakan Tanka in His aspect as the sun, who had given Curly strength to escape. He could have carried a chokecherry staff like Hump's. He was also entitled to paint a black horizontal line on his cheek for having killed an enemy who was not a Lakota, plus black crosses for being in battle on foot and a diagonal black slash for being in battle on horseback. He could have donned a collar with streamers for each battle he'd taken part in. Most impressive, he might have worn his hair unbraided but bound, the sign of a man who has done desperate deeds and was willing to do them again.

Instead he sat quietly and braided his only hair long enough to braid, the left side. He pretended not to notice the pitying glances of his comrades.

His plainness was good, surely, even if it was hard. He reminded himself: In his martial exhilaration, his throbbing excitement about achieving the invulnerability promised in his vision, he had forgotten the obligations that went with his powers. He had taken the two scalps. For this breach Power had sent a bullet into his calf. He had no intention of making such a mistake again, ever.

Curly marched into the village behind the others. Keeping his face down, he watched in the corners of his eyes for the face of Black Buffalo Woman. What would she think, seeing that he walked at the back, apparently the one member of the party who had done nothing or even disgraced himself? Would she blush, humiliated? Would she even care?

What would his mothers think? His married sister, his brother, Little Hawk? His friends. Some would know of his vision from Tasunke Witko, but . . .

The women raised their trilling sounds to the skies for the victorious warriors.

Two shield men led. The others came four abreast, their

weapons glittering in the afternoon sun, feathers aflutter, their paint strong and virile. Behind them all stepped Curly.

The crowd murmured. He kept his eyes down and his face expressionless. He felt humiliated. The only thing worse would be to let his sense of humiliation show. He heard muttered fragments of the words he knew too well. "Our Strange Man."

He wanted only to disappear.

Dark was falling, and Black Buffalo Woman didn't want to miss a moment of the dance. She looked one more time at the red part in her hair. She put the mirror into a parfleche, took out a tied bunch of sweetgrass, cut off just a little, and popped it into her mouth. She took some spruce gum in one hand. Before the first dance she would chew it to sweeten her breath. Then she put all her rush aside, stepped through the door, and followed her mother demurely to the big circle where the whole village was gathered.

Oh, yes, she would have to remember to tell Curly that she had lost his ring. The word was already around the camp, and some did not believe it.

The Hunkpatila and Bad Faces came together for this big dance. Victory dances had parts where sweethearts danced together—you told the *winkte* who you wanted your sweetheart to be, and he matched you. She wouldn't dance with Curly, because he wouldn't dance. True, he had a wounded leg now, but he never participated in dances anyway. He would stand away from the big center fire in the shadows with the others who didn't dance, the old, the infirm, and the sour-spirited. It was what she liked about him least, the way he stood off from other people.

To Black Buffalo Woman the drum was something larger and stronger than you. It throbbed through you, it took you over, it sent its pulse through your body and made you move as it willed. She loved it. Why would

Curly disdain it? The word *strange* came up for him too often.

She took a place in the big circle next to her mother. The singers and drummers grouped near the fire, the women on the opposite side. The *winkte,* the men who lived as women, stood in the middle. They directed the victory dance. *Winkte* understood matters of love and could give young men songs of seduction their sweethearts would find irresistible. But not as irresistible as the seduction songs of bone keepers. She shivered.

The drum started its pulse.

Across the circle she saw Curly watching her covertly. A lot of good it would do him tonight. Though he'd done something good, so they said, he'd marched into camp in that weird way, like a beggar to be pitied. And tonight he would act aloof. So her eyes were for her potential dancing partners. Who would she say would be her sweethearts for tonight? Probably one or two of the Bad Face young men who had been courting her, standing near her lodge with a blanket to wrap her in and hold her close and talk. Maybe Black Twin, who had an interestingly devious mind. Or White Twin, who was odd but just as good-looking. Maybe Pretty Fellow, who was beautiful, broken nose or not. Maybe He Dog, who might turn out to be a chief. Surely No Water.

The singers lifted their voices in a victory song. She watched the dancers, her body moving to the beat.

Maybe she should choose Young Man-Whose-Enemies, who would one day be leader of the Hunkpatila. That would cause talk.

Who would ask for her? When the *winkte* had two requesting each other, that was a real match. No Water would ask for her, for sure.

She thought she would speak his name at least once. She was strangely excited about dancing with No Water. She couldn't deny that he was attractive. He was so big and strong. Until a few days ago she had thought he was a little dull. But he had done so much to get her—that was intriguing. He had risked being possessed by the *tonwan*. And the way he had told her she would be his, so masterful, that still made her heart squeeze when she remembered it.

He'd called her perverse. Intriguing.

The potion? She didn't know yet. Potions didn't always work. But she couldn't deny that she was fascinated.

Curly made her heart squeeze, too, always had. She was eighteen winters old now, and she had been in love with Curly probably for half her life. She had made love only to him. She wondered if he had her ring somewhere on his person.

A woman changed, though. She didn't always take her girlish loves seriously. Sometimes she married another because it was wise or just because she felt like it. A young woman needed plenty of suitors. This was Black Buffalo Woman's time before the responsibilities of a husband and children. She intended to take advantage of it.

And tonight, as she danced with every man she could, her every movement would be flaunted in Curly's face. And No Water's face.

It was time, the drums said. She stepped forward with the other women. When the *winkte* came near, she whispered, "No Water."

When the time came for the fighters to tell of their exploits, He Dog tried to push Curly into the big circle first. Curly refused wordlessly, standing his ground at the back of the crowd, next to his father. So He Dog chuckled low and shrugged and went out to show how he had killed one of the men of the unknown tongue. Others followed, gladly. They danced and mimed and chanted how they had killed or struck coup or stolen horses, and the women made their excited trilling. Strength and unity throbbed in the people. Then the young men and women would dance again, never touching, but their attraction tangible as the rays of the sun on a hot day.

Curly watched Black Buffalo Woman. She was dancing opposite He Dog. Earlier, when she had danced with No Water, Curly realized they had spoken for each other. His skin prickled like he was poisoned.

"Brother," said Hump softly next to Curly's ear, "you must dance your deeds."

Curly had not heard his *hunka* coming. Most of the others had strutted their bravery by now. Curly looked up into Hump's eyes and shook his head no.

"You showed great medicine," said Hump. "The people need to feel your strength among them."

Curly shook his head again.

"It is not his way," said Tasunke Witko quietly.

Curly felt a twist of pain. Difficult, in a world where the respect a man earned was almost entirely based on coups, very difficult not to be able to declare your deeds, to have to hide your accomplishments always. Yet he noted that Hawk was quiet on her perch, content.

"It is not his way," repeated Tasunke Witko.

Hump padded off silently.

Curly's one moment came when the women danced in a circle with the scalps. His mother Red Grass led the way, the only woman with two scalps hanging from the top of her stick. She strode with pride, all the more fierce because her son had kept silent. The crowd murmured. He heard the words "Strange Man" for the thousandth time. Yes, strange—two scalps dancing at the end of the pole and nothing said about them.

His medicine of invincibility would be an open secret, he knew that. The other warriors would tell their families, and tomorrow the tale would be all over the camp. They would say he was one of those rare ones, meant for desperate deeds.

He was glad. Maybe that was weakness, but he was proud. Even if he didn't get to dance his power before the world, he was a warrior, a true warrior.

Without seeming to, he looked around the crowd. Black

Buffalo Woman's eyes gleamed hot, and maybe they were fixed on Curly's mother. The Black Elk family, the Man-Whose-Enemies-Are-Afraid-of-His-Horses family, and other Oglala families looked exultant. They didn't embarrass any of the fighters by looking directly at them, even their own.

"They are proud of you," said Tasunke Witko. He put a hand on his son's shoulder lightly, and took it back. "Two scalps. I am proud of you. Not accepting praise is hard, I know."

Curly nodded without looking at his father.

The women raised the trilling to a new intensity as the mothers brought the dance to a finish. Curly looked at the Bad Faces and knew they were not pleased. Only one Bad Face had been invited on the raid—they would remember that slight. The twins would remember, and Pretty Fellow of the smashed nose, and No Water the clumsy.

A flash from his vision came to him, Lakota hands pulling from behind.

He promised himself he would remember every bit of his vision every day and never again violate it. He would go to war at every chance. He would ride ahead of his comrades, unafraid. He would know his own invincibility. He would take nothing for himself, not property, not glory, and especially not scalps.

Black Buffalo Woman watched Curly without seeming to. Two scalps. Two scalps! And two enemies killed. Her lover was strange, very strange, but he was bold, and blessed in war.

She wanted him. It made her tremble with want, looking at him and seeing those scalps dance on the end of pole.

It would only take a little time—they would do it fast and hard, the way she wanted it. It would only take the time of one dance. No one would notice. Her flow was just finished, and she would not take on life within her. She wanted it.

Just as she started to slip out, she glanced at No Water. He was glaring at her. Openly and antagonistically.

The memory made her shiver. "I will kill you," No Water had said. "Not him. You."

Her loins went cold. She cast her eyes down and did not let herself look at either man. Though the drum still beat, she was frozen still.

Curly lay sleepless on his blankets in his parents' lodge. It wasn't his leg keeping him awake, for the wound felt good enough under his father's poultice. It wasn't even the loud, raspy breathing of Little Hawk next to him, though that was irksome. He did fret more about forgetting his vision and taking the scalps. And about Black Buffalo Woman—tonight of all nights he would have liked to sneak away into the willows with her—his body sometimes raged with wanting.

But even that didn't seem right, he told himself. Why should he and his woman have to sneak into the bushes? He was a man of twenty-one winters now and much respected, even if neither he nor anyone else could say so out loud. Black Buffalo Woman was the right age for marriage. Why didn't they go ahead?

A thousand reasons, he reminded himself. As a *heyoka* he was called to a life of silence and contemplation, not to family life or conviviality. As a warrior he was pledged to do desperate deeds. Surely his medicine would protect him, but if he made a mistake, or misunderstood his medicine . . . Family life did not seem right as long as his spirit was flung completely into the maw of war. Also, he had promised to become an Inyan dreamer, as revealed in his vision. He didn't know what hardships that might mean. And he was committed to gaining nothing for himself, not horses, not good clothes, not an abundance of food, not a lodge with fine furnishings. Could he ask a woman to share such a life with him?

Could he *not* ask Black Buffalo Woman?

He would talk to Hump about all this. Tasunke Witko,

too. Now that he thought about it, Horn Chips, too.

He turned over, restless.

He fingered Inyan underneath his left arm, next to his heart. He and Chips would pray over it sometimes and ask for its aid and guidance. Inyan creatures were the oldest people on earth. From time to time in Curly's life he would beg Inyan to speak, to advise him at crossroads. He would wear it next to his heart, always, so that he might hear what it said.

He turned over, restless and more restless.

Why hadn't he been able to speak to Black Buffalo Woman tonight? He had stayed up all through the dance, until the sky began to get light. She was always dancing or standing close to her mother, very close, as though under her mother's protection. When he tried to catch her eye, she wouldn't look—he was sure that was deliberate. At dawn she and her mother skipped back to their lodge hand in hand, like children without a care. He watched them sullenly from afar.

His father and mothers and brother got up and started on their day. Curly pretended to be asleep. He'd had no rest at all. Now he couldn't even fidget or flop from side to side. Finally they all went out, and he drifted off.

He ate a little, feeling better. He didn't know why he'd fretted so all night. Cooking in your own juices, Tasunke Witko called it. He put his horn out and accepted a little more soup from Red Grass. He would sit for a while, waiting. Hawk was easy within him. He would sit and think and ponder his vision. This afternoon he would go into the sweat lodge and pledge himself to it anew. He would go forth into the world as a warrior, trusting his feet to find the path, trusting Hawk to guide him. Trust was all.

His father came in without a word and got something out of a parfleche. His beaded ceremonial blanket, Curly saw. The one Curly's birth mother had made him, showing what this *wicasa wakan* beheld when he looked beyond. Tasunke Witko put the blanket around his shoulders and went out. Curly pondered—what was his father doing?

Curly was putting his mind back to his own concerns, his own duties on his own way, when he heard his father begin an honor song:

"My son rode forth
against the people of the unknown tongue.
Against the people of the unknown tongue
my son rode forth."

The voice of His Crazy Horse rose bold and quavering at once toward Wi, Father Sun, on the opening words, "My son." Through the rest of the line it fell in a caress. The second time Tasunke Witko made the words "my son rode forth" clamor heroically.

"My son rode forth
against the people of the unknown tongue.
Against the people of the unknown tongue.
my son rode forth."

Curly got up and stepped outside in nothing but his breechcloth. His father was making a circle within the lodges, intoning this honor song. People were falling in behind him in a double line to show their esteem for Curly.

"For his courage
I give him a new name,
the name of his father."

Tears rose in Curly's eyes.

"For his courage
I give him a new name,
the name of many fathers before him."

The line behind the man known until now as Tasunke Witko was long. The people were smiling broadly, the old men and women and the leaders and the young warriors and the children. They walked in a stately manner, ceremonially, but the children were laughing.

> *"I give my son a great name.*
> *I call him Tasunke Witko."*

The tears were flowing freely now. Curly could see his mothers immediately behind his father—what would be his father's name now?—and his brother and sister behind them, and Buffalo Hump. He noticed that all the great ones were there: Man-Whose-Enemies-Are-Afraid-of-His-Horses, Bad Face, Red Cloud, and most of the young warriors. He looked briefly for No Water and Pretty Fellow but didn't see them. Maybe they were in the column—what did it matter today?

> *"I give my son a great name.*
> *I call him Tasunke Witko.*
> *I give my son a great name.*
> *I call him Tasunke Witko."*

Curly's father made the circle of the lodges again, singing the song in honor of his son, and this time the people joined their voices to his, a mighty chorus of praise, the people as one spirit.

> *"My son rode forth*
> *against the people of the unknown tongue.*
> *Against the people of the unknown tongue*
> *my son rode forth.*

> *"For his courage I give him a new name,*
> *the name of his father.*
> *For his courage I give him a new name,*
> *the name of many fathers before him.*

> *"I give my son a great name.*
> *I call him Tasunke Witko.*
> *I give my son a great name.*
> *I call him Tasunke Witko."*

They finished the circle the second time, all the people raising up the naming song mightily together.

When Curly's father stopped singing, he left the head of the line and walked ceremonially toward Curly. His face full of feeling, he said, "I greet you by the name Tasunke Witko."

Curly hesitated and started to stammer.

His father smiled lightly. "From today the people will know me as Worm," he said.

PART **THREE**

Loss

*In the center of the sundance
ground
he sits beside a small fire.
He picks up some needles of the cedar
tree
and throws them onto the fire.
Then he makes gestures of washing
himself with the smoke.
When he has finished the ceremonial
cleansing, he slaps the ground
with an open hand.
"I, His Crazy Horse," he says,
"from the Hunkpatila Oglala of the
Titunwan Lakota,
I look, and I tell you truly what I
see."*

The drum throbs.

It was driving him mad.

He waited near the three other young men, his blanket wrapped up to his eyes. As though anyone would not know who he was, with his hair the color of a sage hen chick sticking out at the top. At least the right side, once shaven, had grown out until he could braid it now. Or let it hang long and flash the color of the sun when he and Hawk rode into battle.

The four young men did not look at each other, for this was a kind of fakery. Each was apparently waiting for a chance to stand wrapped close with Black Buffalo Woman for a short while. His Crazy Horse, once called Light Curly Hair, now honored with his father's name, stood farthest from the lodge and so by convention claimed the most time with her. Since he had more war honors than almost any man twice his age, no one would deny him this privilege. Not even He Dog, who stood next to him. She would come to him first and stay with him longest.

Actually, she would spend almost no time with anyone else, for they had no interest in courting her. He Dog was here because Crazy Horse had asked him. Next to He Dog was Lone Bear, up to his chin in a good blanket. Next to He Dog was Hump. If all four stood in line, they knew, no other men would come courting tonight. Crazy Horse was sick of seeing others lined up to court his woman, especially Bad Faces.

Not that this trick would cure anything. He couldn't figure out what was wrong. Black Buffalo Woman wasn't wearing his ring, again using the excuse that he didn't wear hers. He also thought she was avoiding him. All this made him feel like a lunatic.

Half of him was saying, *How foolish! How silly to imagine such things!* And reminded him of the signs of preference Black Buffalo Woman had given him. She had slipped away with him exactly seven times. He remembered them all in detail that was exquisite and excruciating all at once.

He drove himself mad with remembering them. Also, and most important, she sometimes wore his ring openly. Sometimes.

He also tortured himself with thoughts of the signs of preference she didn't give him. She hadn't gone into the willows with him since he got his new name. And she could be stubborn. He imagined the dialogue.

She: "You don't wear my ring."

He: "But I *can't*—you should understand that!"

She, mockingly: "But I *can't*—you should understand that!"

He: "You dance with others and not me."

She: "You won't dance."

He: "You don't slip away with me anymore."

She: "An invitation to disgrace."

He: "You let others court you."

She: "I'm obliged to."

He: "But *No Water*!"

She: "No Water is a fine young Lakota. And he doesn't dress like a beggar."

He: "You pretend we aren't betrothed."

She, with a shrug: "You have tied no horses at my lodge."

It wore him out just to think so many words in a row. And thinking was as futile as saying them would be.

His father and mothers hinted often that Crazy Horse should send a relative with horses. No Water was the favorite of Black Buffalo Woman's family, they said, and he commanded more and more respect these days. Her father and mothers were inclined to No Water. The brother who owned the right to give her away in marriage also preferred the Bad Face. The Bad Face people wanted her to marry within the village, it was said, to tighten the bonds of kinship and give the band new children. They reminded everyone that a youthful betrothal didn't mean much. They said Crazy Horse no longer seemed interested and would be relieved to see her marry another.

Crazy Horse snorted at this foolishness. Black Buffalo Woman knew better.

On other evenings his family would hint that it was all political. Red Cloud was making himself the first man of the Bad Faces, they said. They traded dark looks, not needing to say that most people thought Red Cloud was the one who had actually struck the fatal blow against Bull Bear twenty years ago, put up to it by Smoke. This was why he had never been made a shirtman. *A-i-i-i,* even though he was strong in war.

Now he was drawing all the strong young Bad Face men to him, they said. He Dog mostly lived back with the Bad Faces now, probably to be near Red Cloud. Pretty Fellow was the war leader's friend, always loitering around his lodge. Red Cloud was also drawing the promising three young brothers to him, the twins and No Water—he was maneuvering to get the family to give his niece Black Buffalo Woman to No Water in marriage.

"Hunhunhe," would mutter Crazy Horse's father, Worm, in apprehension. Worm sought for himself the great Lakota virtue of being common as grass—that was what his new name suggested, for the worm was common. But Red Cloud was self-glorifying, seeking to make himself separate from others and above them. Or so many people said.

Crazy Horse listened to all this talk and said nothing. He could be as he was, he could follow his vision, but he could do no more.

He was all mixed up. Did he have the right to marry at all? Sometimes he didn't think so. But wasn't his path pure and clean, dangerous but glorious? And didn't Black Buffalo Woman love that?

She would belong to him, surely.

She felt giddy. These days, torn between two men, she seemed to feel giddy all the time and even dizzy. This was a familiar giddiness, though. She eased closer to Crazy Horse, her shoulder and hips touching his.

She felt his arms stiffen unpleasantly.

She glimpsed No Water's back going into her lodge.

She smiled to herself. Oh, yes, that would make Crazy Horse angry, as it did every other young man interested in her. No Water walked straight into her lodge these days and courted her by the center of fire of her own home, with the blessings of her family. If No Water weren't a rising man, important, this rudeness, this bypassing of other young men, would cause not only anger but fights.

It was time for her to begin to speak nothings. "Where will your people camp this winter? Is your sister well? And her husband? How is your brother?"

She felt Crazy Horse relent when asked about Little Hawk. "My brother will be the most daring of us all," he said with naked pride. It touched her—his voice seldom showed nakedness, or his face. She felt a pang of regret. She loved him sometimes, maybe all the time, she truly did.

Other than the words about his brother he said almost nothing. He held an arm around her shoulders, and his face and body said it all. No Water had disappeared from his mind. She filled his thinking, his feeling, his being. She felt it, and she knew it. He seemed unwilling to contaminate this feeling of his entire self with the commonplace currency of words.

Regret. Unfortunately, she knew too much about the way he loved her. And she had made up her mind to speak tonight. To resolve something. Now. It would shock him.

"You don't really want me," she said. The words came out like a cough, and she repeated them. "You don't really want me." She looked at him hard, wondering what he would do.

"What do you mean?" he said. The words came out flat, slowly, one at a time, like pebbles tossed onto ice. He felt relieved that he was able to talk at all.

"Your mind is really somewhere else, all the time."

He shook his head gently. Some things he was sure of.

He let himself be aware of her warm body against him. "Not at all."

She lay her cheek against his chest, and he felt her head nod. "It's always on . . . whatever you see in your head. People talk about it, you know. You walk around camp, but you don't see us. You're looking at . . . something you think is better."

He had nothing to say.

She raised her face to him, and now he saw the tears. "You don't want a woman, you don't want a family, you don't want a warm lodge and lots of children. You want to be out with your friends, testing yourself against some . . ." She hesitated, and then threw the word away. "Ideal."

His throat almost strangled on the words. "Is that so bad?"

Now her face got more serious, challenging. "I won't be a second wife. Not to anything. Me second, the family third . . ."

"Not second and third," he protested.

"You won't even be alive to see them grow up," she said softly. She bit her lip and shook her head no. "Very young men are in love with fantasies of battle," she said. "Grown men take care of those they love first."

"I would always take care of you."

She nodded, and her tears flowed again. She hid her face in his chest. "I know," she mewled.

After a long moment she looked back up. "Why haven't you staked horses at my lodge?"

He hesitated. He couldn't say why, it was complicated. He decided. "Tomorrow I go raiding," he said. "I will bring lots of horses back."

She knew he meant it. He looked at her, his eyes burning, and she knew. She took a deep breath, in and out. She didn't know what to say. He didn't realize that to her his crucial words were, "Tomorrow I go raiding." She said, "I should move on."

He didn't respond. She lowered her head. She'd slipped into the woods with Crazy Horse just once since No Water threatened her. She remembered his words very well—"I will kill you. Not him." Her woozy belly and weak knees said he meant it.

Now she often felt relieved that she could resist Crazy Horse. Deep breath, in and out.

He held her tighter.

Originally, she had scoffed at the idea of marrying No Water. *Acch,* no, all heavy and stiff and rigid as a tree trunk. No Water should marry an old woman, because he was like an old man.

But when he had stolen the stains of her first flow . . . When he had a spell cast on her . . .

She was as much fascinated as horrified. She toyed with pictures of his boldness in her mind, stealing the bundle, getting purified of the contamination of touching it, conjuring over it. She felt a little thrill.

Power. It lay before most men openly, and they were afraid to pick it up. They wanted it, but they lacked will.

No Water picked it up, seized it, even stole it. He used it however he pleased, ruthlessly. She felt this spine of will in him. He would take whatever he wanted.

No Water made her breath come short, when she thought about his brazenness. He frightened her and made her knees watery.

"You must decide," she told Crazy Horse.

In fact, she had to decide. Her family was pressing her politely. If she said firmly, "I will not marry the Strange Man," it would be over. If she said something as oblique as, "He is attractive, that No Water," her brother would say a quiet word and the next day horses would be staked at her lodge. So far she had said only, "I don't know about that fellow." Had said it over and over.

He squeezed her, and she turned her breasts against his chest and moved her hips gently against him. A reminder. *Oh, how I love you,* he thought.

She would move on to the next blanket soon, He Dog's. She sometimes said she was glad for forms, which gave necessary shapes to human behavior. Crazy Horse hated forms, which forced people into their shape. He must say something more before she left or repeat his promise of horses. He tried words in his mind: *My heart decided years ago . . .* He drew in the scent of her deeply and prepared to speak.

Suddenly He Dog bellowed, "Let's rescue that captive in His Crazy Horse's blanket!" His voice was teasing, playful.

"His Crazy Horse is stealing all our time," said Lone Bear in the same spirit.

Black Buffalo Woman cocked her head back and looked into his eyes, her body pressed against him. "I always stand too long in your blanket," she said. He saw her sucking at her cheeks to keep from smiling too broadly. She took the teasing better than he did.

The lodge door swished behind her. He looked into her grandmother's face. The old woman rushed at them in a small fury. "Get away from my granddaughter!" she shouted, her voice cracking.

Crazy Horse tried to turn Black Buffalo Woman away from her. Old, bony fingers tore at his blanket.

Black Buffalo Woman lurched backward and almost took both of them down.

Humiliation flashed in him like gunpowder. He opened his blanket quickly to let Black Buffalo Woman out and closed it back up to his eyes.

"You think you're better than our Bad Face young men." The old woman spat the words contemptuously. "You're not fooling anybody."

She shambled off into the trees, perhaps to relieve herself. He felt as if he'd been attacked by a little, wrinkled, empty bearskin. And whipped.

As Black Buffalo Woman slipped into Lone Bear's blanket, Crazy Horse caught his friend's merry eyes. "If you're going to steal a woman, you have to be able to fight off her grandmother," said Lone Bear.

"At least," agreed He Dog.

Crazy Horse walked off, chest tight with frustration.

THEFT

Crazy Horse rode into the clearing at the rear and a little to one side of the line of riders, as was his way. He let his eyes roam around the group of Bad Faces without appearing to inspect them. Red Cloud, No Water, the twins, He Dog, and half a dozen others.

Hump grinned back past Little Hawk and winked. "They invited us Hunkpatila to be the lunatic point of the spear," he said. "Let's show them." And the five of them goaded their ponies into the circle of warriors and cut in and out and curlicued and curveted and kicked up the dust in their friends' faces.

Little Hawk dismounted laughing, which pleased Crazy Horse's heart. It was his first time to go to war with his little brother. At fifteen winters, Little Hawk was thicker-bodied than Crazy Horse, and just as tall. His hair had darkened more than his older brother's, to dark brown, so he was less conspicuous. Already Little Hawk had a reputation for daring, even recklessness. He and Hump together would make a fine spear point. Even Crazy Horse, pledged to desperate deeds, was more cautious than these two. And compared to the first three, Young Man-Whose-Enemies and Black Elk were sedate. "No hanging back this time," Hump said to them. "We are the Hunkpatila."

So they lounged with the Bad Face young men and munched on pemmican from the bags and talked about what they would do. Red Cloud had sent the *canupa* to Hump, inviting him to pick some young men to come with him. All the Hunkpatila were glad to come. After all, the leader was Red Cloud, Mahpiya Luta himself.

Of all the Oglala men, this Bad Face was the best known in war. Among the Sicangu, Spotted Tail might have rivaled Red Cloud. But Curly's uncle had fought seldom since his year of imprisonment. Some people still murmured that he was a lackey of the *wasicu*.

Red Cloud said they would go against the Psatoka. That was always good, and the young men called out, *"Hoye!"* in approval. The leader said nothing about what his medicine had revealed to him, how they should fight, how many horses and scalps they might bring back. He had no need. The young men were like ponies just turned out, eager to run with the stallion.

Except for one. "My tooth hurts," No Water complained. He held his jaw while Red Cloud was talking, and even moaned once or twice. The young men looked at each other. No Water's medicine was two teeth of the grizzly.

Little Hawk smiled, but Crazy Horse scowled at him. It wasn't funny, a man's medicine warning him against going into battle. If Hawk ever warned Crazy Horse, he would not go. Just a few years ago a man had gone into battle with his hand hurting. His medicine was the paw of the raccoon. He came back dead.

Red Cloud squatted and spoke softly with No Water for a while. Finally No Water got up and mounted and headed back for the Bad Face village. Even slumped in dejection, his body looked too big for the pony.

"That pony should ride him," said Hump. He grabbed a front tooth and pulled at it crazily.

"Ow—oo-oo-ooh," Little Hawk howled, imitating a sick wolf, flopping his body around in mock pain.

Crazy Horse waggled his head foolishly. It was kind of funny. But half his mind was on the danger in front of him and half on the woman he would be returning to. With horses.

"Besides," Hump said, "any way to get rid of that lunkhead is a good way."

Little Hawk was avid, so Crazy Horse showed him his own ways. They found a village of Psatoka hunting and surprised them. The brothers and *hunka* rode in front, charging hard, and the Psatoka broke and ran. Far into their own country the Oglala chased them, past Shifting Sands River, which the *wasicu* called Powder River, and the Buffalo Tongue River, the *wasicu's* Tongue River, and almost to the river the *wasicu* called Bighorn. They even killed one of the Psatoka old-man chiefs.

Crazy Horse talked to Little Hawk about dash and courage and good sense. He showed his brother how he always dismounted to get a steadier shot and never took a wild shot from horseback. You took a pledge, Crazy Horse said, and the most dangerous act would be to violate it. Crazy Horse would always ride in front, would abide by his oath to leave no comrade fallen on the field of battle, and would give his fellow warriors cover while they retreated. But that did not mean taking needless chances. Not using good sense was throwing your life away, and an insult to your own medicine.

Crazy Horse talked, and Little Hawk said how glad he was to fight with his brother and see how to do things and learn lessons, but he didn't seem actually to listen.

When the two of them sneaked in and ran the pony herd off, though, Little Hawk acted sensible enough.

So they rode home with no one badly hurt, plenty of coups and scalps, the strength of the sun on their faces, the feel of good horseflesh between their legs, comradeship, and the ponies Crazy Horse needed. For once he felt good to be with others, his brother and his *hunka,* yes, but all the others, too, the Bad Faces and Red Cloud, this man he'd scarcely known but now admired, now that they shared the fellowship of warriors. For once Crazy Horse didn't wish he was out riding across endless countryside by himself, or in the sweat lodge alone, or on the solitary mountain crying for more vision. He was comfortable in company.

In the fighting Hawk rode close over his head every moment. At night and at all other times Hawk rested peaceful in his heart. Crazy Horse, who offered advice so freely to his little brother, thought maybe after twenty-two winters, approaching twenty-three, his own life was coming together. Because he was about to marry and because in battle he was following what he saw beyond with the help of his spirit guide, asking no questions.

Crazy Horse didn't recognize the voice the first time. Everyone was getting painted and dressed and decorated for the victory procession into the Bad Face camp, and he was hardly listening. This dressing up was something he didn't like, another something he was left out of, not even included with his brother and his *hunka*.

The second time he knew the voice of Pretty Fellow but didn't catch all the words, or didn't admit to himself he caught them. Pretty Fellow and some other Bad Face youths had ridden out to greet their returning comrades.

Crazy Horse would never have asked Pretty Fellow what he said, but he couldn't help looking in that direction. This time Pretty Fellow added an impudent tone. "Someone has been walking under the blanket." Though he didn't raise his eyes in that direction, he thumped his hips straight at Crazy Horse. Then he worked all the mocking melody he could into the next words. "Black Buffalo Woman and No Water."

All the Bad Faces approved raucously—*"Hoye!"* they cried.

Black Buffalo Woman married to No Water!

Crazy Horse's mind strained toward the idea, as lungs labor and struggle for breath when a man's fallen hard. But it strained futilely.

He did see that none of the Bad Faces would look at

him, not even the wounded one Crazy Horse had dragged to safety a few days ago. Red Cloud stared into space, his face neutral.

Crazy Horse swore to himself that he would remember this moment about Red Cloud. Like a politician, the man had three reasons for everything. He might lead you on a raid and to a kind of glory. It would be in order to make his plan to marry his niece to your enemy come off without a hitch.

Crazy Horse glanced at Little Hawk and Hump and saw the quick sympathy in their stricken faces. But sympathy only sharpened his humiliation. He gathered his belongings, mounted, and rode off alone. He called back to Little Hawk and Hump to give the ponies to anyone who needed them.

PURGING THE HEART

He went back against the Psatoka. He launched himself against these enemies crazily. He hated his life and acted like it.

One night he sneaked up on the horse guard and deliberately made noise so the fellow would hear him. He wanted to fight hand to hand. When the guard just yawned, Crazy Horse cut the fellow's throat in anger.

Hawk did not go into battle with him. She didn't flap her wings in protest against the walls of his heart, either. She was quiet, as though numb. He muttered that losing Black Buffalo Woman had killed his soul, his spirit guide, and his self.

Another time he spotted a rifle he wanted in the hands of a young Psatoka and decided to take an outrageous chance. He crept into camp that night. Silently he slit the lodge cover and slipped under it. In the blackness, between the breathing bodies, he cut the gun down from where he knew it would hang from the poles at the back center of the lodge. No one stirred. Someone rasped lightly as the breath came in and out.

It made him so mad he swung the heavy barrel of the gun into the pallet, not caring who or what he hit. In the moment of confused ranting that followed, he slit the lodge hide so high he could step through upright and walked calmly out of camp, giving the Psatoka their chance.

The Psatoka gave him a fine chase that night, and he enjoyed it. When he had lead balls to fit this new gun, he would shoot their own rifle at them. He would kill the former owner for being stupid enough to let him come into the lodge at night.

One day he lay in wait for a pair of Psatoka wolves. He had seen the men out looking for buffalo. Since Crazy Horse knew where the herd was, he laid an ambush. He came out of it with one pair of far-seeing glasses, like the ones the *wasicu* soldier chiefs wore, and two Psatoka scalps.

He didn't know why he took the scalps, in violation of his medicine. Maybe because Hawk was not with him. Something muddled and sick had congealed in his heart and lay there, foul and putrid. Hawk could not live in such a heart.

He went back to war. It felt like scoring his heart with the point of a knife. He had seen *wasicu* scratch their writing deep into the bark of trees with their knives. On his own heart he wanted to write the sign meaning "dead man."

When he came back, a long moon later, he hardly knew himself where he had been. He was exhausted and gaunt, wasted, like a man who'd had a long illness. He knew he certainly would not tell anyone else about these days, ever.

He sat his pony on the edge of camp, uncertain. He looked at the two scalps hanging from his lance, the evidence that he had trampled his own medicine into the dust. What would do he do with them?

People took no notice of him. Since he'd gone away without saying where he was going and had come back without notice to anyone, they probably supposed he wanted his privacy. They were respecting that. Only the dogs seemed to know he was there.

He threw the Psatoka scalps to the dogs. *Let them worry at them until they fall apart,* he thought. They meant nothing to him. Maybe he could throw his bad moon to the dogs, too. The people would never ask about the scalps, and he was grateful for that.

He would have to get Chips to help him bring his medicine back to life. When he had the energy, and when he cared.

He gave the rifle to Little Hawk and the horses to his brother-in-law. He kept the far-seeing glasses. He would need them in war. If his spirits didn't lift soon, suicidal war.

At sunset two days later Horn Chips appeared at Crazy Horse's brush shelter. Crazy Horse was on his blankets, where he'd been since returning to the village. He wasn't getting a good sleep, just dozing sometimes and thinking he'd never get up again and feeling sorry for himself. Besides, if he lay on his blankets, he wouldn't have to talk to anyone, not even Hump and Little Hawk.

A cold shadow fell on him. Chips stood there, blocking the sun. The *wicasa wakan* sat down without being invited, lit his *canupa,* and handed it to Crazy Horse. The warrior had to sit up to take it. As he puffed the smoke from his mouth, he thought mechanically that he was offering breath to Father Sky. Even such a familiar thought felt good.

Without introduction Chips said, "I hear Black Buffalo Woman has ruined your life. I hear No Water connived and ruined your life. I hear Red Cloud schemed and ruined your life."

Crazy Horse hung his head.

Chips let anger put an edge on his voice. "So you are a weakling. Other people can ruin your life."

Crazy Horse looked sharply at Chips, anger against anger. Chips ignored him.

"I don't want to hear any more of this pathetic talk, or see you mope around anymore. You want to live?"

Crazy Horse didn't answer. He was simmering. They sat and smoked for a while. Chips said nothing to ease the hurt he'd inflicted.

"Go to the Split Rock on the Sweetwater River. There you will see moss stones like this one." He held an Inyan creature out to Crazy Horse. It was a stone of many colors, and in places you could see all the way through it. In some of those places were bits of flaky stuff, like moss.

"This Inyan creature doesn't speak. Some of them do. Make a sweat lodge and ask for help. Walk around among the stones, your eyes not focused on anything in particular, your ears open for all kinds of sounds, not any special one. You may feel something about one Inyan creature. If you aren't busy feeling sorry for yourself, you may even hear something from one. Bring it back.

"Sometimes, but seldom, the Inyan people speak. A man who spends his whole life paying attention may hear their words, may get a song from them. If his ears aren't full of his own moaning about some woman, or about what others do to him."

Crazy Horse sat there with his head between his knees.

"What are you waiting for?" asked Chips. "Get up. Go!"

Crazy Horse started to look around at the falling dark. Instead he took thought and got up.

"Remember you probably won't hear anything. If you feel something toward one Inyan creature," repeated Chips, "if you think it might speak one day, bring it back."

Crazy Horse bobbed his head and got gone.

Riding back from the Split Rock with his moss Inyan creature in a pouch, he thought of why Black Buffalo Woman had married No Water instead of himself. He hadn't given this careful consideration until now. He hadn't even been able to get himself to form the words: "Black Buffalo Woman married No Water instead of Crazy Horse."

The reasons seemed clear to him. All that he had heard he rejected. It wasn't because she couldn't wait. When you love truly, you will wait forever. It wasn't because Red Cloud manipulated it. Love is like the compass of the *wasicu* and points always to the one true direction. It wasn't because she was pressed by her family. It wasn't because she preferred No Water. It wasn't because she was afraid and confused. None of those things mattered to her. He knew, because he looked into his own heart and saw they meant nothing. His and Black Buffalo Woman's hearts were the same.

Another reason altogether came, came with luminous clarity. His medicine had arranged that Black Buffalo Woman should not marry him. He didn't know why—perhaps that was yet to be discovered. He felt no doubt about it, though. He knew that medicine worked mysteriously and with power men could scarcely imagine. Medicine made water flow downhill, moved the air, raised the sun each morning, sent the moon through her every-month changes. Medicine could keep one man from marrying one woman, easily.

Idly, he wondered what his medicine might have in mind for him. Maybe he was one of those meant to be a shirtman, like his uncle Spotted Tail. Owners of the people, these young men were also called. A strange figure of speech, for it truly meant "those responsible for the people." These young men were chosen by the society of White Horse Riders, and they alone were obligated to put the good of all people ahead of everything. It was better if they weren't married.

Since the winters of loafing around the forts had begun, the custom of putting the people in the hands of shirtmen had mostly died out. Crazy Horse pondered the case of his uncle Spotted Tail. Because he was a shirtman, because he had to consider all the people ahead even of his own family, Spotted Tail had thrown his life at the soldiers' feet.

That had turned out strangely for everyone. The *wasicu* did not take the life offered, but in Crazy Horse's view they gave the people back half a man.

He wondered if . . .

Oh, he must stop speculating like this.

His medicine took Black Buffalo Woman away from him. That was enough to know.

Black Buffalo Woman stooped to gather more white sage. No Water must be planning to make a sweat lodge—he had told her to pick a big armload. He wasn't much interested in ceremonies, her husband, but Red Cloud had come and talked to him a long time last night. Maybe Red Cloud wanted them to make the sweating sacrifice together.

She sniffed at the sweet-smelling plant. It was one of her favorite fragrances. She didn't understand people who didn't notice all the smells of the earth. They made her giddy sometimes. She pulled the plant gently out of the ground.

She'd been giddy with fear of encountering Crazy Horse. Now she was just waiting for cold weather to set in for good. The villages would separate for the winter, and she would not have to worry about seeing him.

Before Crazy Horse had left—more of his weird solitary wandering—No Water had commanded her not to go anywhere by herself, anywhere at all. The order made Black Buffalo Woman catch her breath, she was so glad. She was terrified of a confrontation. Sometimes she felt Crazy Horse's gaze on her. His eyes felt hot enough to burn her back.

Oh, didn't he understand? She just got so . . . She didn't know what to do and she couldn't stand it and it was driving her crazy and everyone wanted her to . . . And it was true, she was perverse.

Now she was with No Water and things were simple. He was masterful. Life ran smoothly.

She was taking on life within her. When she saw Crazy Horse again next summer, she would have a child. Surely that would close his eyes to her. Forever, she hoped.

When she heard the clops, she raised her blanket over her head. The hoof sounds came right up to her. It must be what she feared—Crazy Horse, returned from wherever he had gone on whatever eccentric errand. She knew him. He would wait forever. Besides . . . She felt it as a tingle all over. She *wanted* to bare her face to him.

She lowered the blanket.

She couldn't help it, she just started babbling. "I had duties," she said rapidly, "a duty to my brother, who had the right to give me away, a duty to my father, and fathers are wise in these matters, and my mother, mothers know best for their daughters, and everyone said—"

"Shhh!" He was interrupting her. "Shhh!" again.

They looked at each other, just looked for a long moment.

At first her mind raced. He was wearing Inyan tied under his arm, one of the Inyan that men got from the Split Rock. People said those Inyan creatures gave men songs sometimes. Crazy Horse was wearing it next to his heart.

Her mind was buzzing like bees. Well, maybe Crazy Horse would start listening to that Inyan creature and stop looking at her. She hoped so.

He said softly, "Everything will be good between us. I have sworn that it will be good." He hesitated for so long she thought he was finished. Then he added, "In my heart I have no anger anymore. Not even against myself."

He touched his heels to his pony gently and reined it toward the village at a walk. He felt self-conscious about Inyan next to his heart. He didn't know whether or not the Inyan creature had spoken to him, but since he started wearing it, those sentences had kept coming to his mind, over and over. No anger, not even toward himself.

He had another thought. On the Sweetwater River he sat by a still pool and looked at a star, luminous on the surface of water. The gentlest breeze rose, the water riffled, and the thought came to him. Black Buffalo Woman was like a star seen in water, brilliant and beautiful, and gone with the first rising of the wind.

THE BATTLE OF PLATTE BRIDGE

Bad Heart Bull kept for the Oglala people a buffalo robe with paintings on it. At the end of each winter, he made a painting to help the people remember what happened that winter. This document of tribal history the people called a winter count.

He marked down this particular winter as When Three Men Were Hanged at the Soldier Fort.

If the whites had counted their winters with names instead of numbers, they would have called it the Year of the End of the War between the States. Or, if Bad Heart Bull had been looking back from ten years later, he might have called it the Winter When Everything Changed.

What it meant, in both cases, was that two peoples who had been doing a martial dance, circling around each other, testing, feeling each other out, were finally ready to fight to the death.

Crazy Horse was ready and gladdened by the prospect. He had turned twenty-seven in the autumn. Since Black Buffalo Woman had married No Water, he had devoted himself entirely to living up to his vision of Rider. He did not court, did not loaf with his friends, did not take his ease in his parents' lodge, did not learn the old stories, did not participate in village life. He made arrows and bullets and other weapons, trained his horses for war, worked with Chips to strengthen his war medicine after the mistake with the two scalps, stole better horses and better weapons, and looked for the enemy and fought. The result was that he had more war honors than all but the rarest of men would accumulate in a lifetime. He was ready in body, in training, in experience, in spirit, in medicine.

If his people still thought his ways strange, they now recognized that the pursuit of war was in some way a sacrament for him. It was as much understanding as he could hope for.

He immediately sensed the truth about this new fighting. It would last until the *wasicu* either left or took over. Too much had gone wrong—everything had gone wrong, in fact, everywhere Lakota lived. There were the many small offenses of the *wasicu*. There were the big troubles of the Dakota relatives in the lake country the *wasicu* called Minnesota. There was the continuing corruption of the Lakota who hung around the forts. There was the attempt to stake a trail through the heart of the Oglala hunting ground, the Shifting Sands River country, where the warriors threw the soldiers out contemptuously. There was the offense just this spring of hanging the three Lakota who did as the *wasicu* asked and turned a captive white woman over. Mostly, there was the arrogance of the entire white attitude toward the Lakota and all Indian peoples.

Only the War between the States had kept the hostilities to a skittish dance so far. Now that their war had ended, the soldiers were coming.

Crazy Horse thought more strongly that they were like *wakinyan* of the east, except that they had the destroying power of lightning without the blessing of rain.

He was impatient now: Though the Lakota had sworn at the big council at Bear Butte eight winters ago to stand firm against the *wasicu,* matters had never come to a decisive contest. Now the gods of the *wasicu* and the spirits the Lakota knew would commit themselves to the combat would rise in the bodies of the two peoples and contend one with the other, and on the face of Maka, Earth, under the eye of Wi, Sun, blood would flow, and one people would thrive, and the other would die.

The call to arms arrived in a form recognized by everyone, a *canupa* sent by thousands of people. The Sahiyela and the Mahpiyato and the Lakota who lived south of the Shell River came traveling in the Moon of Frost in the Lodge bearing this *canupa* and a terrible tale. One moon ago the village of the peace chief Black Kettle had been smashed brutally at Sand Creek. Though the people had wanted peace so much that they camped where the agent told them to camp, the soldiers had made a sneak attack on Black Kettle's sleeping village. Several hundred Sahiyela were killed, mostly women and children. The rest escaped on foot over the snowcovered plains, weeping and starving and freezing, while everything they owned went up in flames back at Sand Creek.

Afterward the soldiers took the scalps to the city where they dug the gold, Denver, and waved them like flags from the stages of their theatres, waved even scalps taken from between women's legs, bragging about their great victory.

So the Sahiyela and their brother peoples of the south country wanted revenge.

Crazy Horse wanted revenge more hotly than most. Among the women and children killed were Yellow Woman and her son, the ones he had rescued in the storm ten winters ago, and the new child, a daughter.

This *canupa* galvanized all the Lakota. Warriors who usually loafed around Fort Laramie came to the camps of those the whites called "wild" Indians to join the fight. Spotted Tail himself wanted to fight. Though he thought he would never feel quite as close to the man again, Crazy Horse was pleased with this rousal of martial spirit in his mothers' brother. Now and forever, everyone said, the Sahiyela peace chiefs surely wouldn't be peace chiefs anymore.

An Oglala named Drum-on-His-Back was able to tell them what the whites were thinking—he had learned to read the white-man newspapers. Crazy Horse thought nothing good could come of learning English, much less learning to read it, but he was glad to know what the *wasicu* were thinking. Some of them said what happened at

Sand Creek was an outrage, said Drum-on-His-Back. They were even talking about punishing the officers who had led the fight against Black Kettle. But most of them, especially the newspapers of the whites in this country, said the Indians had to be rubbed out, whatever it took.

So Crazy Horse prepared himself in wordless joy. He had ridden across a desert of spirit to fight the Psatoka after he lost Black Buffalo Woman. War was not meant to be cold rage but exhilaration.

Now he could feel Hawk buoyant in his heart. War was his way and this was his time, the risking of flesh, the clash of medicines, the test of spirit, the ride along the narrow edge of life and death.

His people deserved to win. He did not know whether they would. He thought a warrior's duty was not to know the outcome but to fight the battle well, even beautifully. Now he would do what it was his calling on earth to do, perform the blood sacrament. Whether he lived or died, Hawk would soar over his head, and he would truly live.

They raided. All along the Holy Road, wherever the whites looked vulnerable, they raided—Sahiyela here, Mahpiyato there, the numerous Lakota everywhere, the young men of each tribe alone, two together, all three at once. Burning, scalping, killing, stealing, laughing all the while. Crazy Horse regretted only that it did not seem decisive—you could cut the talking wires, run off horses, kill some soldiers, and chase the rest into the forts, but that solved nothing, not for good.

He was troubled about something else: The young men treated this like most war, less as a cause than as a kind of rough play. Those who loafed around the forts had had little opportunity for war honors for a decade. They were less interested in inflicting lasting defeat on the *wasicu* than in counting coups and collecting scalps. For them war was mostly the old style, individual heroics, the display of courage and medicine. For this reason they did not maintain discipline, did not fight together, but simply sought personal glory.

Crazy Horse understood their feelings very well. It was the right kind of war. It was his kind.

He also understood that for the sake of the people the traditional ways were not enough. Which was why he and some of the other war leaders campaigned to get all the fighting men of all three peoples together for a big fight at the crossing of the Shell River near the mouth of the Sweetwater, what the *wasicu* called Platte Bridge. The *akicita* would be revived to enforce discipline, and the soldiers be lured out of the fort with decoys, all the warriors waiting for the signal to attack together, they said.

The first idea was to burn the bridge. Many white people got up the Holy Road by crossing the river here. They would find fording the wagons much harder. Or ferrying them. The second purpose was to kill a few soldiers.

Everyone cried, *"Hoye!"* in rousing assent.

They were going to decoy the soldiers away from the fort and across the bridge into some rough country to the north. They could overwhelm the soldiers, they were sure of that. The stockade at this Platte crossing had about 120 troopers. Red Cloud, Hump, and Big Road led the Lakota, Roman Nose and High Back Wolf the Sahiyela—together they had more than a thousand fighting men.

The warriors marched close to the fort very slowly, so the horses wouldn't raise a cloud of dust. They were going to try a decoy, and the soldiers mustn't know how many Indians were waiting. Near the bridge the leaders deployed their men out of sight of the fort, behind that ridge and on this gully. Only those with long-seeing glasses crept to the ridge tops and studied the fort, far across the river, southeast of the bridge.

Crazy Horse led the decoys down a gully, about twenty of them. To most of them he indicated places to hide themselves along the retreat route, so they could help if the pursuit was too hot. Then he led Little Hawk, one of the sons of the trader Bent, and an Arapaho into plain view of the fort, where the soldiers could see them with the telescopes.

"Point at those pony herds," Crazy Horse said to Little Hawk.

Little Hawk did, saying, "They got a new herd shipped in."

"Make them worry about their property, property, property," said Bent, making the word sound like beating hooves. He pointed, too.

"Let's stop," said Crazy Horse. "Make it look like we can't decide."

While they were stopped, Bent said, "Did you hear what our old-man chiefs did when we made the last treaty? The toy soldiers offered us beef and bacon and flour and all their *things* for signing. The old-man chiefs said, 'Yes, and some white women, too, for our lodges.' "

The Arapaho barked laughter.

"The toy soldiers were shocked," said Bent, "shocked. The soldiers prong our women, but *the very idea* . . ." He rolled his eyes.

Everyone laughed and they moved on. Crazy Horse unfolded his blanket and snapped it in the air as though scaring the ponies to make them run. They all laughed. In this mad way they proceeded toward the fort until the gate swung open and the pony soldiers rode out fast and clattered across the bridge. The wagon guns followed.

Crazy Horse pointed and shouted to the others and, when the soldiers were still out of range, lifted some foolish arrows into the sky. Then he said a few soft words to the gopher, which lives by trickery, and to the wind, whose power is to confuse the enemy. The four decoys began their retreat.

Bent and Crazy Horse made little stands, until too many bullets began to churn up the dirt around them. Little Hawk and the Arapaho pretended to whip furiously at their horses to get them up the hills and out of there.

When the soldiers fired their wagon guns, Crazy Horse was sure it was going to work. The pony soldiers' blood was boiling.

He quirted his pony down the side of a hill and up the far side. He turned to look. The pony soldiers were charging hard. A little closer, a few arrow flights, would do it. Then he heard something odd and looked at the top of the next ridge.

Lakota jostling each other for position to see. Hundreds of Lakota looking down at the soldiers and bristling to fight.

So he stopped his pony and sat and watched the soldiers stop and point and turn around and head back.

When he got to the ridge, Big Road was yelling at the warriors who had broken by the *akicita* men and spoiled the ambush, "Idiots! Fools!"

Red Cloud was staring at everyone in his haughty way.

Hump trotted toward his *hunka* wearing a forlorn expression.

Crazy Horse was too furious even to look at him. They rode off by themselves. Crazy Horse wanted to think and throw rocks at the empty prairie.

They did run off the herd of new ponies the soldiers had gotten. High Back Wolf, a Sahiyela fighter of repute, got killed doing it.

The next day about twenty-five soldiers tried to make their way to the west along the Holy Road, led by Caspar Collins. Collins was a young officer the Lakota liked. He'd spent time in the camps and learned their language. So when he rode into an ambush, Lakota on one side and Sahiyela on the other, Red Cloud and others yelled at him to go back.

Collins ordered a retreat. Then he came back alone to help a soldier who was down. Admiring him for this act of courage, most of the Indians held their fire. But Collins's horse, a fine-looking gray, took the bit in its mouth and ran off into the Sahiyela. Still angry about High Back Wolf, the Sahiyela swarmed on him.

As they rode back to their villages, Little Hawk said what a shame it was Caspar Collins had gotten killed.

Crazy Horse didn't have his mind on that. He was thinking that the three brother tribes, Lakota, Sahiyela, and Mahpiyato, had sworn to avenge the outrage against Black Kettle's village at Sand Creek. They had gotten together over a thousand warriors and marched against an important white station, Platte Bridge. And accomplished absolutely nothing.

POLITICKING

The Society of White Horse Riders asked all the villages of the Oglala people to come together in late summer, at the fullness of the Moon When All Things Ripen. They did not need to say that they would name four shirtmen, four owners of the people. Nor did they need to say that the shirtmen would help provide what the warriors had lacked at the Platte Bridge, discipline.

When the Bad Faces and the Hunkpatila got to the camping place, two bands were not yet in: the True Oglala and the Oyukhpe. But the politicking about who would get the shirts was at full boil. The men of the society had the choice—establishing the bands' young leaders was their duty—but they would be influenced by their families and friends. The talk was that the Bad Faces were insisting on the selection of one of their own. Four bands, four shirtmen, one from each band, said the Bad Faces. If this was not to be, the Bad Faces would take down their lodges and leave.

It was awkward. Not only was there the old enmity between the Hunkpatila and the Bad Faces because of the Bull Bear killing, there was the dispersion: Some Oglala lived below the Shell River, some around Fort Laramie, and some in the northern hunting grounds. Earlier this year the soldiers had moved the *wasiyuta el unpi,* literally "those who live among the whites," whom the interpreters called the loaf-around-the-fort Oglala, downriver to Fort Kearny, those who would go. The Oglala seemed hardly to know each other anymore.

The awkwardness came most of all from wondering who would be the new shirtmen. But that, Crazy Horse told himself, was something he didn't care about.

He scratched at the door flap, bent low, and slipped into his parents' lodge. With Little Hawk behind him, he circled sunwise behind the seated men to his place. He had been surprised when his father asked him to come to the lodge to share supper with Red Cloud and was more surprised to see Horn Chips here.

The five men ate in companionable silence and then smoked over good talk. Not talk of matters of substance, but smaller things—whether winter would come early, where the buffalo would be this autumn, where the whites might be vulnerable to a man who saw in his medicine that he must lead a raid.

The closest they got to matters of controversy was to tell a few funny stories about the soldiers led by the foolish Connor, who that year had come into Shifting Sands River country, which the white people called Powder River country. Connor was clearly afraid. Afraid of Indians? Afraid of the country? Afraid of being out on his own? Whichever, his campaign had been a joke, and they had driven him out easily. Still, that was the untouched hunting grounds of the Oglala. Regardless of how much the whites wanted a road through to the goldfields in what they called Montana, the Oglala would not have Shifting Sands River country violated, all were agreed on that.

Red Cloud was an observer of people. He noticed everything. Divining their true thoughts and feelings from the expressions on their faces and the small movements of their hands and especially the way they held their bodies—all this seemed to him a straightforward matter, if you were observant. For many winters it had struck him as odd that other people did not practice this habit faithfully, as he did. It was advantageous.

He noticed, for instance, that Little Hawk joined the talk easily and even spiritedly. Though he was the man of least repute here, he was in his parents' lodge, and his way was to be impulsive and speak his mind simply. A naked and naive way to behave. Maybe it would change when Little Hawk got older, maybe not.

Worm played the host impeccably. What might be truly on his mind—what he might say to his elder son after everyone had left—Red Cloud could not see on his face. But he was sure that Worm would not advance Red Cloud's cause. Worm still resented the Bad Faces and had taught his sons to do the same. What a waste. An impediment to Red Cloud's goal: To bring the Hunkpatila and Bad Face bands closer and closer until they were as one. Under his own leadership.

Horn Chips simply kept silent. A complicated man, Horn Chips, dark and obscure even to Red Cloud. Some of these men of strong medicine . . . No matter. All you had to do was assure yourself where Horn Chips stood. Which Red Cloud had done.

Which left Crazy Horse, Our Strange Man indeed. Red Cloud was intrigued by the young man. He wore shabby clothes, accumulated no belongings, did not marry, seldom fraternized, collected no scalps, performed prodigious deeds in war, and refused credit for them. . . . What could a wise man make of such behavior?

Red Cloud did not believe what it suggested, that Crazy Horse was without ambition. Nor did he believe that this behavior had been dictated to the young man in a vision and that the revelation was being followed unswervingly. Red Cloud did believe that people had visions—he knew it for a fact. But he also knew that interpretation was everything, and interpretation often suited the ambitions of the dreamer.

He had a peculiar notion about Crazy Horse. He thought the young man was trying to take the subtlest and most audacious route to the leadership of the Oglala. He thought the warrior, in forswearing all honor, was making a covert bid for the highest honor. For who could claim to be nobler, truer, purer, than a man who sought nothing for himself, nothing at all? Who more likely to become the grandest of heroes?

It all gave Red Cloud a chuckle. It was clever. But it was unnecessary, roundabout, painful, and perhaps misguided. A pretense, like the father's choosing the name Worm to signify commonness, a humble station. Others knew, as Red Cloud did, that human nature was not so ideal as all that. Which would enable the people to see through the ploy. Red Cloud intended to help them see through it.

Now Crazy Horse was in his mode of false humility, contributing nothing to this conversation. Red Cloud knew he made the young man uneasy. And he would take whatever advantage was available. This was just good sense.

The Bad Face war leader was an orator, a man given to words that were each as beautiful as one of the many eagle feathers in a full-length warbonnet. The words made a fine sound, there was no denying that. But Crazy Horse was distrustful of words and of men who relied on them. Besides, Red Cloud wore a ponderous dignity, like a buffalo robe that covered him all the way to the eyes. Crazy Horse would never rip the dignity away and felt he couldn't talk through it.

It was an odd conversation, propped up by a voluble youth, a deferentially quiet host, a man who spoke only oratorically, and two men of no words, Horn Chips and Crazy Horse.

So it was Red Cloud who finally spoke to Crazy Horse.

"Who will the White Horse Riders choose?" He looked straight at Crazy Horse as he spoke.

Crazy Horse shrugged lightly, saying it was a matter of indifference to him. Until right now he hadn't thought of wanting the shirt. "There are many candidates," he said.

"What do you think?" Red Cloud looked at his host, then Horn Chips, and both shook their heads. Then he turned to Little Hawk.

"The fathers will choose the sons," put in Little Hawk bluntly.

That was what everyone was saying. Man-Whose-Enemies-Are-Afraid-of-His-Horses would use his influence to see that Young Man-Whose-Enemies was nominated. Brave Bear of the Oyukhpe would do the same for his son Sword, and Sitting Bear of the True Oglala for his son American Horse.

Most people thought that was good. Though chieftainship was not hereditary, the sons of chiefs would have inherited good qualities and would have learned at their fathers' knees. The only son who caused any doubts was Pretty Fellow, the son of Bad Face. People didn't want him as a shirtman and probably not as a Big Belly. He was too vain and self-absorbed. But not even Little Hawk would say that in front of Red Cloud of the Bad Faces.

"What do you think, His Crazy Horse?"

It was almost rude, asking a second time. Crazy Horse kept his eyes down, so Red Cloud wouldn't see the offense.

Sore points stuck up everywhere here. Red Cloud himself had never been a shirtman. Maybe that was because he was suspected of having killed Bull Bear or because his father had been a loaf-around-the-fort drunkard. Red Cloud had everyone's admiration now. He was probably the most admired war leader among the Oglala. But he was not a shirtman.

He was a politician, Crazy Horse remembered. He had helped maneuver Black Buffalo Woman toward No Water.

Crazy Horse raised his eyes to Red Cloud.

"I think the fathers will choose the sons," he murmured.

"They say you are being considered," Red Cloud pushed on. "Will you accept?"

So now it was in the open. Horn Chips hated all this. He despised Red Cloud's incessant maneuvering, his obsession with things of the world rather than things of spirit. He did not like coming here and lending silent support to Red Cloud's request. But Red Cloud was his relative. He could not refuse Red Cloud this favor. And regardless of this odious politicking, he wanted his protegé to know what he thought: A man who listened to the wisdom of Inyan had no time to involve himself deeply in the daily affairs of the people.

Crazy Horse knew what Chips thought. They were waiting for his answer: Would he accept?

Finally Crazy Horse said in his soft way, "A man who owns nothing and has no status. A man who has his own calling, apart. I do not think this responsibility would come to such a man."

Such a self-effacing answer. And one that would drive Red Cloud mad. Horn Chips felt proud of his protegé.

Crazy Horse kept his face still. He refused to let Red Cloud see his tumult. Here it was, the conflict he was afraid of. The warrior fought, an exercise of spirit, and was a guardian of the people. A beautiful and useful way to live, and his calling. The shirtman was a warrior with heavier responsibilities to the people and less latitude for seeking his own way—his life belonged to the people. Later he would probably become a Big Belly, with still more responsibilities and the duty of maneuvering through talk. A Big Belly spent his time dickering instead of doing—anathema to Crazy Horse.

Yet. Yet. He felt the honor of it, the recognition. It was like some ice in a cave on even the hottest day and the sweet trickle of cold water on a parched throat. Besides, now that he didn't have Black Buffalo Woman, maybe being a shirtman lay on his path. A shirtman did not have to become a Big Belly. And with the decisive conflicts with the *wasicu* approaching, this was a time for a warrior to think of all the people.

What twisted his gut was that it was Red Cloud who was asking him to step aside, to decline another honor. Red Cloud, who had maneuvered to help Black Buffalo Woman from his arms into No Water's.

It was intolerable to be asked, and he intended to give only this ambiguous answer.

He stilled himself and tried to pay attention to Hawk. Right now he couldn't feel her.

"Perhaps my younger brother is right," said Red Cloud politely. "Perhaps the fathers will choose the sons. The names in the wind are Young Man-Whose-Enemies-Are-Afraid-of-His-Horses, Sword, American Horse, Pretty Fellow, and His Crazy Horse. Four sons of Big Bellies, one from each band, plus His Crazy Horse."

He let the words sit, letting everyone see the asymmetry of the five names suggested.

"Some people say He Dog is being considered, too." Another Bad Face. "I think that of those choices," Red Cloud went on, "the man of the most individual excellence is you." He looked directly into the eyes of Crazy Horse. "Your war medicine is the strongest. You must have over a hundred war honors."

He turned with a smile to Worm. "How many war honors does your older son have?"

Crazy Horse saw that his father could not resist. "Over two hundred and forty," blurted Worm.

"Staggering." Red Cloud smiled broadly at Crazy Horse. "Yes, you deserve all the respect the people give you." Red Cloud lingered here, letting everyone feel this compliment. Even Crazy Horse had to admire his performance.

"What is on my mind about the shirtmen, though, is not

a matter of individual excellence. All the candidates are worthy in different ways. All have much to contribute." He was glossing over the fact that most people did not think Pretty Fellow had much to contribute. "What is on my mind is healing."

Crazy Horse watched Red Cloud like an enemy knife, flashing in the sun as it moved. He had to be careful not to be lulled by its beauty.

"For nearly twenty-five winters the Oglala have been divided against themselves." Crazy Horse was surprised that Red Cloud came so close to mentioning the cause of this division. "I will go so far as to say the other bands have slighted my own, the people of Smoke and Bad Face."

He let them all ponder the nakedness of his declaration.

"To name the four sons of the four chiefs of the four bands would heal our wounds," said Red Cloud.

You want me to set my enemy above me, thought Crazy Horse. *Maybe. More likely if you didn't push at me, but maybe.*

He waited to see if the Bad Face war leader would suggest that his band would pull out of the ceremony if Pretty Fellow was not selected. But Red Cloud only said, "Shall we smoke a little more?"

Crazy Horse wanted to speak, but Red Cloud had brought the discussion to a kind of end. "Why must I make sacrifices for the sake of my enemies?" Crazy Horse wanted to ask. "Why are honor and the good of the people set against each other? Where lies my path, my honor? Why do you inflict your noise on the silence I need to consider these questions?"

Before Worm lit the *canupa*, Chips broke Red Cloud's carefully crafted silence. "Perhaps you and your father would like to sweat with me, and we will ask the powers for guidance," said Chips.

It was a peace offering, a suggestion that Crazy Horse should ignore Red Cloud's suggestion, and even Chips' support of it, and surrender the matter to his medicine.

Crazy Horse smiled at Chips with his eyes. "Thank you," he said. "We will."

For a moment he looked into his heart. What would that single eye tell him that his two eyes, analytical, could not see? He didn't know.

Crazy Horse could not see the heat of Red's Cloud displeasure in his face, but he felt it. It was like sitting too near a fire.

Crazy Horse was thinking that it was paradoxical that the phrase for shirtman, *wicasa yatapika,* literally "owner of the tribe," was a way of saying "owned by the tribe," responsible for the people.

The great council lodge stood, handsomely painted, with the sides rolled up high as a man's head so all the people would be able to see and hear the initiation. Now they congregated inside the big circle of lodges to see who would be chosen, and Crazy Horse could feel the anticipation. It was thick in the air as the tension before lightning strikes.

He had not put out the word that he did not wish to be considered as *wicasa yatapika.* It would have been simple. He could have said to his father, Hump, or both that his path lay in another direction. They would have relayed the message to the right people, and the members of the society would have honored his choice.

Horsemen rode ceremonially around the camp, the helpers of the Big Bellies. They would make four circuits and on each would pick out one young man to wear the shirt. Crazy Horse had no idea whether he would be one of those chosen or even whether he wanted to be.

He did not know clearly why he had not put the word out. During his prayers in the sweat lodge he had tried to ignore the wants of other people, the opposition of Red Cloud and Horn Chips and his family's yearning to see him honored. He had tried likewise to set aside his unworthy desires. *Beyond my longing to appear grand,* he had asked himself, *beyond my wish to impress Black Buffalo Woman, beyond my dislike of Pretty Fellow, beyond my yen to thwart Red*

Cloud and my rivalry with Bad Face young men, what do I want?

He asked Hawk in his heart, but he felt no answer. He thought he was too roiled to get it.

So here he stood, uncertain.

The women raised their trills to the skies. Crazy Horse craned his neck to see. The first young man selected was Young Man-Whose-Enemies. Everyone murmured. Confidently, Young Man-Whose-Enemies mounted the big American horse offered him, a member of a great family taking in stride another honor.

All the way around the circle the horsemen walked their ponies. The second man picked out was American Horse, son of Sitting Bear. He sat his big mount self-consciously, aware that every eye was on him, drunk on his own glory.

All the way around the circle once more, and then into the crowd. Again the trilling. Sword, son of Brave Bear. His face was flushed with boyish gratitude.

Crazy Horse let his breath out. So far three shirtmen, sons of chiefs of three bands. The fourth would be the son of the chief of the fourth band, Pretty Fellow. Crazy Horse was relieved and nettled at the same time.

His eyes searched out Pretty Fellow. The Bad Face stood next to his father, just a few steps in front of Crazy Horse, outfitted in new buckskins showily beaded and quilled. *Ah, he does deserve it,* thought Crazy Horse.

Around the circle at a slow strut came the horsemen leading the fourth riderless horse. They stopped in front of Pretty Fellow. Then guided their horses through the crowd to the rear, where stood the son of Worm.

Crazy Horse allowed himself to be led forward. Now not only the women trilled but the young warriors. Whispers skittered through the crowd:

"Our Strange Man!"

"Three sons of chiefs and a true warrior!"

"Our best man!"

"Three for their fathers, one for his deeds!"

* * *

Red Cloud heard different words make their way through the Bad Faces, mutterings:

"No one from our band."

"They will never forgive us."

"Two Hunkpatila and no Bad Face."

Red Cloud looked at Chief Bad Face. They had already agreed on what they would do—go away from this place immediately and name their own shirtmen, as was their right.

Red Cloud and Bad Face turned away and walked toward their own lodges. They would not stay a moment longer. The war leader noted with disappointment that some Bad Faces gravitated toward the big council lodge to see the ceremony. Including No Water and his wife, Black Buffalo Woman, and their two children.

The four shirtmen sat on new robes at the center of the lodge. Beautiful robes, Black Buffalo Woman noticed, luxuriously thick and tanned very soft.

Two old men spoke of the duties of the shirtmen. The first named the traditional duties that everyone knew—leading the warriors responsible for order in the camp and on the march and helping to protect every person's rights. This fellow stressed that a man who agreed to live with others was not entirely his own. That consent obligated him to take note of the good of all. For a shirtman the common good became paramount. Shirtmen were called to a higher standard than ordinary people.

The second old man urged them even further. "Think of the welfare of the poor, the weak, the widows and orphans!" he cried. In fact, he declared, the Society of White Horse Riders had decided upon new and greater duties for these initiates, the first shirtmen in a long time. "When you meet enemies," he said, "advance toward them boldly—death is better than corruption. Think no ill of others," he beseeched them, "and repay not ill with ill. Many dogs will lift their legs at a leader's lodge. An ordinary man might respond with anger, but a shirtman has a higher duty. He must be above disputation, above retaliation, above envy, above greed. If this sounds difficult," implored the counselor, "remember that we call you to be great-hearted."

Black Buffalo Woman thrilled to the nobility of these words and to the thought that her lover, Crazy Horse, would rise to fulfill them. She knew perfectly well that her husband wouldn't.

When they brought the shirts to the new servants of the people, she was stunned by their beauty. The older shirt-men themselves had made them, each from two skins of bighorn sheep, dewclaws left dangling. Bands of quillwork decorated the shoulders and arms, and the shirts were painted in upper and lower halves, two red over yellow, two blue over yellow. The sleeves of each shirt were fringed with hair, a lock for every war honor—a coup, a wound given or received, a horse stolen, an enemy killed, a comrade rescued.

Crazy Horse stood to put his shirt on, and the crowd gasped. Hair hung from his sleeves thick as needles on a pine tree. "Over two hundred and forty locks," people whispered.

Black Buffalo Woman looked sideways at her husband. She looked back at Crazy Horse. Suddenly the child in her belly felt heavy, and the one holding her hand seemed a nuisance.

In his ceremonial shirt Crazy Horse felt vulnerable, naked. He took a moment to look deeply at these hundreds of people, people he was responsible for now, and responsible to. He felt their admiration, which was also expectation, and obligation. He let his eyes circle slowly, for he needed to see them.

The feeling welled up in him unexpectedly. As his eyes traveled around the circle, his spirit rose. He never had many words for his feelings, but one now was *pride,* great pride. Emotion surged through him, and for once he did not mind if people saw. *Thanks, thanksgiving,* other words. He wanted people's acceptance and their praise and was indescribably grateful to have them for this moment.

He held back a chuckle. Maybe his life path forbade him honors because he would get drunk on them.

He let his eyes move on around the circle, giving acknowledgment and receiving it.

His eyes met Black Buffalo Woman's. The glow of emotion there gave him a stab. But now he could no longer feel jealous of No Water, or rivalrous. Just today he had been called to nobler feelings. Now he must be Black Buffalo Woman's brother only. He promised himself that he would be.

And now he felt . . . a flutter of apprehension.

SOLDIERS INTRUDE

Morning Star watched the Oglala warrior come up at a gallop. He knew who it was. Our Strange Man, his people called him, and Morning Star smiled, thinking *strange* was too mild a word for him. Morning Star was wary of getting seared by the man's intensity. He was one of those men who seemed to look for edges to live on. He was lean and hungry and dedicated and impassioned. He should marry, Morning Star thought, learn the solace of a woman and a permanent lodge fire, and get a little extra fat on him. Morning Star knew his advice would be dust in the wind, so he would never give it. That tickled him.

Morning Star had an amiable outlook on life. He thought some men were too dedicated to what you could not eat, get warm by, make love to, or go for a fine canter on . . . Well, such fellows were getting too serious.

Crazy Horse galloped right in among the Sahiyela men and nodded at the four chiefs in greeting. Morning Star, Two Moons, Red Arm, and Black Horse said, *"Hau!"* to him. Morning Star noted with some satisfaction that the warrior's pony was half-gaunt from hard riding. This fellow was known far and wide never to have owned a first-class horse and to destroy the half-decent ones he got. Any number had been shot out from under him.

Morning Star motioned for Crazy Horse to ride along-side him. He would tell the warrior a few good stories and have the pleasure of keeping the news the fellow wanted from him until tonight, by the fire.

Morning Star told it badly, Crazy Horse saw, not slanting the story for the people like himself, a Sahiyela leader who preferred peace. Morning Star and the three other Sahiyela leaders had told the silver eagle chief, Carrington, that the Lakota, Sahiyela, and Mahpiyato of the Shifting Sands River country would tolerate no further white intrusion. The soldiers might keep the one outpost on Shifting Sands River they'd already built, Fort Reno. They could not build farther north. There was to be no traffic through this country, especially no wagon trains along what the whites called the Bozeman Trail. But most of all, they repeated, no forts.

Morning Star smiled ironically. Crazy Horse liked the man's spirit. "The silver eagle chief knows how to give an eloquent answer," the Sahiyela leader allowed. "While we were talking, his men were unloading the big naked tree trunks for the main posts of the fort."

He let that sit. "His answer in words was that he had in-structions to make a fort there on Piney Creek. He must carry out his orders." Morning Star underlined these words with sardonic humor. To the warriors nothing was more peculiar about the whites than the way they were al-ways refusing responsibility by saying they were follow-ing orders. No Lakota or Sahiyela took orders from another in that way. "As he spoke, I looked into his eyes, and saw that he understood nothing we had told him."

Morning Star looked at the other chiefs. Every face spoke mocking amusement. "You tell a man to stop or you will hang his hair on your lance. He smiles at you like you

are a child. You have ten warriors for every one of his."
Morning Star shrugged. "What do you say next?"

Crazy Horse sat his pony on a knoll and watched the soldiers build the fort. Standing there was an act of warning,
even of provocation. He didn't leave the pony below the
hilltop and watch from the grasses because he wanted to
be seen. He would have liked for them to chase him. He
felt like killing a soldier, or a dozen.

Now he could tell his comrades that, yes, he had seen
it with his own eyes.

His warrior's eyes told him the fort was very vulnerable. It sat in a low place between enclosing hills, so the
Lakota and Sahiyela would have the high ground. It was
too far from the timber the *wasicu* needed for building, and
the *wasicu* had to leave the enclosure even to get water. A
poor site, it seemed, but maybe the *wasicu* had their peculiar reasons. In any case, he thought, the young men of the
Lakota, Sahiyela, and Mahpiyato would come and kill the
soldiers, however many hundreds there were, and burn
the fort to the ground.

Everyone had heard the story, for it showed what the
wasicu were like. In the last moon the *wasicu* had called one
of their big talks. Since the massacre at Sand Creek the
prairies had been aflame with Indian anger. The white
peace talkers wanted to make things right, they said, to
help everyone forget Sand Creek. And they wanted to talk
about Shifting Sands River country, although they called
it Powder River.

The Lakota who went to the talk were mostly loaf-
around-the-forts or people who didn't live in Shifting Sands
River country. But since this country was theirs, Man-
Whose-Enemies-Are-Afraid-of-His-Horses went for the
Hunkpatila and Red Cloud for the Bad Faces.

They kept themselves busy saying no. No road along
Shifting Sands River, no wagons along Shifting Sands
River, no forts along Shifting Sands River. Part of their old
country, along the Shell River, had been spoiled by Fort

Laramie and the Holy Road. They would not let the same thing happen to Shifting Sands River. If they did, how would they feed their children?

During the talk soldiers they'd never seen came in from the east. Their leader, the silver eagle chief, came to the talk to meet the chiefs. With a few questions Red Cloud had found out what his mission was—to build forts straight through Shifting Sands River country and offer protection to wagons traveling that road. The silver eagle chief thought he was coming to the council to meet the Indians who would be his neighbors!

Crazy Horse had seen Red Cloud's face when he told what he said next, alive with delight at the stupidity of the whites. "See?" the war chief asked rhetorically. "While they sit here asking us for Shifting Sands River country, they send soldiers right past the council, heading north to take it!"

He and Man-Whose-Enemies-Are-Afraid-of-His-Horses warned the silver eagle chief and walked out. Whatever the other chiefs might say or sign, those chiefs of people who didn't live along Shifting Sands River, that was of no concern to Red Cloud or Man-Whose-Enemies-Are-Afraid-of-His-Horses.

Now the silver eagle chief was building his fort anyway. Every blow of a hammer smacked his declaration of will over the rolling hills.

Very well, this place, Piney Fork, would be where it was decided.

Crazy Horse turned his pony away.

So Red Cloud sent around a *canupa* for war, and the rest of the summer the warriors harassed the whites. When the soldiers sent wagons to the mountain foothills for timber, the Indians attacked the trains. Every man who built, went for water, or cut wood or hauled it needed another man guard him.

Crazy Horse supposed Red Cloud was devising his stratagems or consulting his medicine. Red Cloud was accepted as the war leader—everyone was willing to follow him. The six shirtmen were also leaders—six because the Bad Faces had held their own ceremony of the Society of White Horse Riders and named two more owners of the people from their own band, He Dog and Big Road. Crazy Horse was glad, because these were good men.

Several hundred warriors came and went from around Piney Fork. Red Cloud thought they could put together 1,500 men, or even 2,000. Crazy Horse said he thought they could enforce discipline this time, and hurt the whites badly.

Crazy Horse wondered why they didn't go ahead and do it. The moons went by, the Moon When All Things Ripen and the Moon of Ten Colds. Yes, they harassed the whites during these moons, killing soldiers when they could, annoying when they could. During those two months the 700 soldiers were reduced by about 50. But Crazy Horse was impatient with Red Cloud's tight rein.

In the Moon When the Leaves Fall the people hunted buffalo instead of white men—they had to make meat for the winter. But the Winter Moon also slipped by, and it wasn't until the beginning of the Midwinter Moon that Red Cloud got all the Lakota and Sahiyela and Mahpi-yato together.

As at the Platte Bridge, they tried to decoy the soldiers into a trap. This time the young men kept their discipline, but the whites were wary and hung back.

So the warriors schemed again. This time Hump would be the leader on the field. This time the decoy must work. To make sure of it, Hump chose a man he knew would take any risk needed: Crazy Horse.

Near the end of the Midwinter Moon they once more crafted the trap.

Crazy Horse purified himself in the sweat lodge. Outside the lodge, naked in the bitter winter night, he sat as in a trance and watched his vision of Rider once more, galloping into battle, the bullets flying toward him but evaporating into the air, galloping forward untouched.

He was preparing for the venture into that place of spirit between life and death. Tomorrow morning he needed to enter that arena of clarity. There he would know what to do with a knowing in all of his body and spirit. He would feel what was to happen before it happened. And Hawk would soar.

When he had finished picturing Rider, he made some decoy medicine from the dirt of a gopher hole. Tomorrow morning he would sprinkle it on his horse and on himself. He had to make the decoy work. He would think of the power of the gopher to deceive, and he would invoke his wind medicine, which led enemies into confusion. He would risk himself.

Fortunately, Hump had given him a job he could do in his individualistic spirit, decoy the soldiers over the hill.

The Mniconjou had sent a *winkte,* one of the men who lived as a woman, out into the hills north of the fort. This *winkte* had a way of seeing the future when she rode her horse in a zigzag pattern she had seen in a dream. She came back to camp and said she had caught a few soldiers. The Mniconjou sent her back out to dream more. She came back saying she had caught more than she could hold in both hands. "A hundred in the hands!" she said.

"Hoye!" cried the Mniconjou fighting men. Good!

Yes, it was good, thought Crazy Horse. Maybe this time he could make the decoy work and dance the dream into reality.

Tomorrow morning he would tie the Inyan creature behind his ear more securely, check Inyan on the thong next to his heart, and retie his third stone, the one in the tail of his bay warhorse, so that it would not be shot beneath him like the others. While he attended to this medicine, he would give thought to the age of Inyan, the ancientness of life they spoke of, and would remember his willingness to hear whatever they had to say. He would paint the streak of lightning and the hail spots on himself, pondering the lightning he had seen in his vision, the thunderstorm he had survived after the killing on the Blue Water, and the Wakinyan he had seen during snow, and the power of the West, the Wakinyan, which flowed through him. He would put the skin of the red-tailed hawk on his head and think of Hawk flying above him into battle.

He would let the strength of his arms and legs, the keenness of his eyes and ears, the figurings of his mind be gathered into these larger powers he participated in, be gathered into Spirit, and find voice in the point of his lance.

Finished, he sat a while longer, silent, thoughtless, attending to Hawk. She was at peace.

"Cold as the cellar of the colonel's heart," Paddy the sentry sang, "and dark as the cell of his skull." He sang it over and over to a stupid little tune someone had made up, or whispered it when his voice got tired, or hummed it, keeping time by tapping his feet in the stirrups. Sometimes he even waved his arms like he was directing the fort band. No telling what his horse thought. Or what the German thought. Paddy and the German always seemed to draw this duty together, and the German never said a bloody word, or smiled at Paddy's jokes, or did anything but glower. Paddy couldn't swear he spoke English.

The sentries had been singing this foolishness for months, for Colonel Carrington was a soldier who talked constantly about rules and regulations and procedures and orders, and cast scarcely an eye to the welfare of his men. They sang it here on Pilot Butte because not a man was within a mile to hear them, at least no *wasicu*. They sang it on the catwalks inside the fort, sometimes with the real words and to the devil with the colonel if he heard, or to doggerel they improvised, every man jack of them knowing what the real words were.

The words about it being dark didn't apply now, of course, today being sunny and bright and clear as any colleen's eye, and cold as her nay-saying lips. Bitter, freezing, ball-breaking cold it was, a cold that his native Ireland couldn't match, a cold for more than itinerant Irishmen and taciturn Germans, a cold worthy of epic heroes and great deeds at arms.

Four days before Christmas it was, when his ma would be making holiday pudding back in Galway, and here he was in a wasteland eyeballing a bunch of savages for the village idiot.

Except for the dimness in the colonel's skull, they wouldn't have to stand watch out on this butte. Colonel Carrington had put the fort in a hole, so you couldn't see out and the enemy could look in from every angle. Ah, lads, an officer's brain is made from what they mucked out of the stalls.

As it was, though, sentries stood on this hill a mile south of the fort from dawn to dusk every day, to provide intelligence of the enemy. *Actually,* thought Paddy, *any Injun what killed me now would be doing me a favor.* He wiggled his toes and banged his hands together. At least hell would be warm.

Sounds of . . . yes, by God, gunfire.

He put the telescope to his eye and brought the wood train into focus. The fort was so far from wood for buildings, the lads had to make expeditions for it nigh every day. With the woodcutters protected by soldiers.

Aye, he saw them now, the bloody savages. Aye, charging the wood train, the soldiers shucking their axes for their rifles.

Paddy looked ironically at the German. The fellow was off his mount and squatted there, as usual, like he was blocked of bowel. He'd paid no attention to Paddy using the glass. So Paddy ignored him and raised his semaphore flag. In big motions he signaled the fort: WOOD TRAIN UNDER ATTACK. It warmed him a bit to flail his arms about.

"Sir, I respectfully request command of this mission!" snapped Lt. Col. William Judd Fetterman.

Carrington thought, *There's nothing respectful about almost roaring at your superior officer.* But he didn't say so. He looked at Capt. James Powell. Carrington had sent for Powell, but Fetterman had pounded in practically on the captain's heels. Carrington had calmly started telling Powell that the wood train was under attack again and forty-nine infantrymen and twenty-seven cavalrymen were mustering for the rescue. These rescues had gotten to be nuisances. Though the Indians couldn't do any real damage, they swooped down on the woodcutters a couple of times a week.

"Sir, I respectfully request this command!" Fetterman looked apoplectic, but then he always did.

"We've had this discussion, Colonel."

"Sir, I joined the army to fight."

Yes, to whet your sword, to win glory and rank and the moist eyes of maidens, thought Carrington. *Such soft eyes moisten only for fighters, men afflicted with the boyish yearning to be heroes and short of common sense. Like you.*

He looked at Powell, who also wanted a chance and showed more good sense than his senior officer.

Carrington turned away from Fetterman. "Colonel," he said, "they tell me you have a favorite boast, one you make when you think your fellow officers won't hear. They say it's: 'Give me eighty men and I'll ride through the entire Sioux nation.'"

Fetterman was visibly taken aback. He hesitated and blurted, "By God, sir, I would."

Carrington looked wryly at Powell. So Fetterman didn't even have sense enough to pretend to be prudent.

Carrington let his breath out in a rush. Well, he supposed so. He didn't even want to look at Fetterman when he said it. "All right, Colonel, go rescue the wood train. The Eighteenth and Second," the infantry and cavalry units, "must be nearly ready. I've assigned you two other officers, Captain Brown and Lieutenant Grummond, and the two scouts." He reviewed the strategy briefly for the younger officer, still with his back to Fetterman. Carrington was thinking surely the scouts, former officers, would help him stay out of trouble.

Now he turned to Fetterman. The man looked so gleeful that Carrington wondered whether he'd heard a word of the instructions. "Colonel, your job is to rescue the wood train, not to engage the Indians unnecessarily." Carrington was mindful of the possibility of ambush. "You may run them back a little, but not beyond Lodge Trail Ridge."

From the look of him Fetterman was off rambling in his boyish fantasies of soldiering.

"Do you hear me, Fetterman? In no case beyond Lodge Trail Ridge."

Fetterman nodded.

"Dismissed."

Fetterman had trouble keeping his legs to a walk as he left the room.

"Colonel," said Powell, "do you realize? Forty-nine men of the Eighteenth, twenty-seven of the Second, two officers, and two civilians. You've given him eighty men exactly." Powell chuckled at the irony.

Carrington didn't think it was funny.

THE BATTLE OF THE HUNDRED IN THE HANDS

Crazy Horse rode for his life, his quirt popping, the pony digging hard up the hill.

When Crazy Horse started, the others did the same. "We will be like a flock of birds scared up," he had explained to them, "flying for our lives."

He thought they were brave men with good sense. His brother, Little Hawk, and his friend Lone Bear, fellow Hunkpatila. Three Bad Faces, two Mniconjou, one each of the visiting Itazipicola and Sicangu.

He looked over his shoulder. The pony soldiers were coming at a gallop, whooping and hollering. They paid no attention to the wood train behind them, headed back. So maybe it was working. *Yes, yes, we are like wounded animals!* cried Crazy Horse in his mind. *Come shoot at us and laugh.*

He gave a moment's thought to his medicine of the wind, asking it to confuse these enemies.

The pony soldiers stopped. Maybe they were waiting for the walking soldiers to catch up.

Crazy Horse rode back toward them, shouting, calling English-word insults he'd picked up. Spurts of snow burst up from the ground, but the fire was short of him. He rode closer and yelled louder and more mockingly.

The other decoys did the same. Some of them exposed themselves. Others yelled taunts. Others stood on their horses to offer conspicuous targets.

Now the pony soldiers came on at a canter. The decoys retreated to the top of the hill, circled around waving blankets, and trotted toward the next hill.

The pony soldiers stopped on the crest.

Now Crazy Horse rode badly, his weight too far forward and fighting the mouth of his pony a little, so that the pony slipped and squirreled its way down the hill. He was falling behind the others.

The pony soldiers came on. The pounding of the hooves of the big American horses sounded like one of the rolls of their drums.

Crazy Horse quirted his warhorse to the crest of the hill. He judged he was too far ahead of the soldiers. The other decoys were out of their sight. From the next hill they would follow Lodge Trail Ridge into . . .

He charged the soldiers. The picture of Rider sustained him. Closer and closer he got. He heard bullets kicking dirt and rock and snow all around him. He pictured them evaporating into the air.

The soldiers charged him. He spun his pony and scrambled up the hill.

Fetterman stopped on the crest of Lodge Trail Ridge. The Indians were scooting around below like spooked sage hens, birds without brains.

That nervy one came back once more, not as far this time. The bugger was pushing his luck. The U.S. Army was going to put an end to all that luck in just a few minutes.

Fetterman thought of his orders. He was at the limit. But there were command decisions in the field. Even a strutting cock of a constipated colonel had heard of command decisions in the field.

"Lo, the poor Indian!" Fetterman shouted. It was his battle cry. The scout Wheatley and Captain Brown grinned at Fetterman. Fetterman wondered if that was fear hiding behind their flashing teeth. He couldn't tell and he didn't care.

Orders were for followers. In the War between the States he had learned that if nothing else. A soldier saw his destiny and he seized it. See and seize. That was it.

Over and over he shouted it as the other cavalrymen came up. "Lo, the poor Indian!" he would roar, and stand up in his stirrups and wave his pistol like a flag. He had heard the ridiculous and sentimental phrase all his life. Today he would make some Indians poor, very damned poor.

He would show that coward Carrington. And put something on his record that would mark him down for the future, yes. Now he felt the wind in his face, he smelled burnt powder, he saw his quarry, and his blood was up.

The head of the infantry column, his particular command, was getting close now.

He wanted to get that Lo who was strutting about showing off, thumbing his nose at the whites. He would make that son of a bitch pay.

"Is that him, Wheatley?"

"Yessir." The scout claimed that Lo was the one named Crazy Horse, a man who stood tall among them.

Well, Lt. Col. William Judd Fetterman was about to make that Injun stand shorter by the height of his scalp.

Orders were for cowards.

He put his spurs to the horse. His heart quickened to

the rhythm of horseflesh between his legs. Oh, Lord JesusGodAlmighty, wasn't it all fine, so fine!

Crazy Horse looked back at the soldiers. Over the ridge they swarmed and down toward the forks of Peno Creek, the pony soldiers first and finally the walking soldiers in their column like ants. His decoys were riding straightaway along the creek now, a file on either side, as he had instructed.

He looked back and he looked around. Soldiers back, snow and sagebrush to the side. Snow and sagebrush and death.

He put his eagle-bone whistle to his mouth and blew the call. With his breath he cried out to his decoys, "We have done it."

The two lines of the decoys simply crossed, making an *X*.

That was the signal. Fifteen or twenty hundreds of Lakota and Sahiyela and Mahpiyato warriors rose as one, twenty warriors against each soldier. Feathered arrows made the whistle of eternity in the air.

The decoys turned and sprinted back into the thick of the fight. The walking soldiers were firing their long guns to little effect. Quickly the warriors would be among them, and they wouldn't even have to use their little powder and lead. Arrows would be enough. And then clubs and tomahawks and spears and knives.

The fighting looked fiercest in the midst of the pony soldiers crouched behind their horses or behind rocks, where the two *wasicu* who weren't soldiers were shooting with their many-times-firing rifles. As Crazy Horse came up, he saw the Mniconjou Eats Meat gallop straight into the white line. As he tried to bolt out the other side, he went down.

Crazy Horse felt his medicine rise in his chest again and quirted his warhorse straight at the *wasicu*. Hawk's wings thrummed in his chest to the beat of the hooves of Rider's horse, and he felt his invulnerability. Over his head Hawk screamed primally, "KEE-ur-r-r, KEE-ur-r-r!" He sailed straight over one kneeling soldier and through the line and out the other side.

As some of the Sahiyela tried to ride through the line, Crazy Horse used two of the only four shells he had and sent one trooper rolling down the icy slope.

He saw that the soldiers were starting to use their guns as clubs. He smiled grimly to himself. The warriors would have plenty of firearms after today, but no ammunition.

He turned his horse and cantered over the battlefield, surveying. He felt that he flew like Hawk over the snowy plain far below. He saw everything. He swooped down where he pleased. When he liked, he wheeled high and watched.

They had done it.

He flew down to earth.

He looked at bodies, mere corpses now, no longer men. They were ugly. The positions of arms and legs were ugly. The wounds were ugly. The expressions on the faces were ugly.

He murmured, "Human beings without spirit are ugly."

He dismounted. He wanted to walk the killing field, smell the blood-letting, stroll among the deaths.

We did it, he thought.

Next to the body of an infantryman he bent down. Blood was dribbling down from a gut wound. He touched the liquid on the uniform, still warm. He touched it on the snow, congealed, icy. He shook his head regretfully.

Yes, we did it.

THE WAGON BOX FIGHT

After they killed the hundred in the hands, the Lakota kept the big camp together. The Midwinter Moon, when the days are shortest and the snow deepest, was no time to be moving the villages. The hunters went out every day, but there was not enough game in one area to feed so many people. This was one of the hungry winters.

In the Snow-Blind Moon the camp split into smaller villages. The village of Crazy Horse, which people now called the Long Face camp after Worm's brother, went up to the headwaters of Shifting Sands River. The living there was hard, but Crazy Horse told his uncle Long Face he wanted to keep an eye on the soldiers in Fort Reno, which was nearby. Maybe the *wasicu* would fill their Shifting Sands River forts with many more soldiers. Maybe they would get out of the country. He wanted to know which.

He and Little Hawk rode long and cold every day, hunting for meat. They wore moccasins with the hair on and thick blanket coats and as always rubbed soot mixed with fat on their cheeks to prevent snow blindness. Crazy Horse had the joy of the hundred in the hands to keep him warm.

These were his days. Hardship, yes, that was a warrior's life. The fighting wasn't the worst for him, or the hunger, the bitter cold, the exhaustion. The loss of friends and relatives was painful. Lone Bear had died at the fight of the hundred in the hands, and that death hurt him. All deaths hurt him, Lakota, Sahiyela, even *wasicu*. But this was a warrior's time, and he chose to glory in it.

One day when they were going up toward Crazy Woman Fork, their ponies played out. The brothers put on pine-bough snowshoes and kept going. Finally, in some broken country, Crazy Horse spotted a herd of about a hundred elk in a little canyon. They got downwind and crept as close as they could. When the elk finally smelled them, the beasts thrashed through deep drifts toward higher ground. Before they got away, the brothers killed eight stragglers.

When the fire was built and some meat roasted, Crazy Horse cut off a piece and held it out. "To the west," he said, "where the *wakinyan* live. To the north, home of the white giant. To the east, home of the sun. To the south, where we are always looking." He made this gesture not only in thanks for the eight elk that would feed his family and some of the village's poor ones, but for the herd that would feed the village. "Father Sky, Mother Earth," he said, *"pila maya."*

He had other reasons in his heart for gratitude. Now he wouldn't have to hunt food anymore this spring. He could turn his mind to war.

He also had a thought he didn't dwell on. He would give the teeth of these eight elk to Black Buffalo Woman. Nothing decorated a ceremonial dress more beautifully than elk teeth. It would cause talk, but he didn't care—he had a right to make a woman a gift, even another man's wife.

He thought of her every day. The Hunkpatila and the Bad Face camps had been together this winter, and she had always been in his eye. She had teased him about being so old and such an important man, yet having no wife. No Water even kidded him about living with Grandmother Plum. "Hey," he gibed, "why isn't the woman in your lodge young and eager? Why aren't you making sons who have your courage?"

They were acting like cousins, sort of. Black Buffalo Woman meant him well and seemed still to feel guilty about the way she'd acted. No Water would probably sleep better if he felt sure Crazy Horse was dreaming about another woman. But he wasn't dreaming of another, and never would.

Yes, he would give her the elk teeth.

He spent his days watching Fort Reno and his nights in cold, lonely bivouacs. Now that his family was fed, he acted homeless. He built no fires and ate only pemmican. He watched for the couriers, the men who went out hunting, those who made trips for water or wood. He approached them as silently and as fiercely as Hawk attacking from the air. Swiftly and mercilessly, he killed them.

He left their bodies to the ravens. He didn't scalp them. He didn't leave any kind of signature. His people would know well enough who slew without scalping. And it didn't matter if anyone knew. To their companions the dead men simply disappeared.

These killings were for Lone Bear, who had died because *wasicu* came into his country, where they had no business being. It didn't matter that the hundred in the hands died. They offended, so they died. Lone Bear had been defending his home and deserved to live.

Crazy Horse didn't count his kills, because it didn't matter. The days of watching in silence, waiting with meditative patience, approaching in a warrior's way, and attacking with Hawk soaring—these mattered.

At the sun dance, in the fullness of the Moon When the Chokecherries Ripen, the talk was of the forts in Shifting Sands River country.

Man-Whose-Enemies-Are-Afraid-of-His-Horses had gone in to talk to the whites at their request. He told them the Oglala didn't want peace—they just wanted the Shifting Sands River road closed. Plus guns and ammunition. When could they trade for more guns, he asked, and more ammunition?

The warriors smiled as they told it. It was good to see the whites' faces when their headmen stood up to them.

And that, thought Crazy Horse, *is what comes of giving the* wasicu *a good whipping*.

The whites said a hundred weren't killed on Peno Creek, but only eighty-one. Crazy Horse and others answered that the soldiers were a gift from Spirit, a realization of the dream of the *winkte,* and when Spirit gives you something, you don't count the number.

Red Cloud went in to the talk also, but he kept his mouth shut. People nodded approvingly. This was good. Though the whites were treating him like an important man, Red Cloud was not a chief but just a war leader and should have nothing to say in council with the whites. But some people muttered that he was working to make himself a big man with the officers and Indian agents. Maybe he wasn't thinking of kicking them out of Shifting Sands River country, these people said, but only of seeing how much he could get for giving the country away.

Crazy Horse held his tongue. No one could give the Shifting Sands River country away.

He heard that some headmen agreed with whatever the whites said about this or anything else. His uncle Spotted Tail seemed to be one of these. Last summer Little Thunder had given up leadership of his band of Sicangu to Spotted Tail. He was a big man now and all for living on a reservation, hunting where the whites told him to, trading only at the agency, and in general acting obedient. He was willing to sign away the hunting grounds of Shifting Sands River, where he didn't live anyway.

Crazy Horse wondered if Spotted Tail would even sign away Paha Sapa, the special hunting country of the people, which the whites called the Black Hills. No, he decided, that place belonged to all the Lakota. More than any other place, it was where Lakota men and women went to seek visions and to raise their dead on scaffolds. It was sacred.

Crazy Horse tried not to think about it. Spotted Tail was his mothers' brother. The teenage Curly had loved the man. He had taught Curly hunting and war and much about life. A shirtman, he had shown himself willing to throw down his life for the people. He had seemed to vibrate with aliveness. Yet since he had come back from captivity, he had acted like a dog hanging around the whites' camp hoping to be thrown scraps.

The rest of the talk among the warriors was of how they would run the whites out of Shifting Sands River country this summer. No whites from Paha Sapa to the Shining Mountains, from the Elk River, which the whites called the Yellowstone, to the Shell River! Lots of warriors had a plan, and the war leaders consulted closely. The warriors wanted to know what Crazy Horse was going to do—many of them wanted to follow him, whatever he did. The war leaders kept talking, but no one decided anything.

* * *

Worm watched his elder son light the *canupa* and accepted it from his hands. He drew deep, puffed the smoke out, and watched it rise toward the center hole of the tipi and Father Sky beyond. He handed the *canupa* to his younger son.

He was honoring his sons by coming to their lodge, making them hosts, and they knew it. He looked at each of them and their friend Buffalo Hump obliquely, not directly in the eyes unless they invited it. The ropy, slender Crazy Horse with his light hair always had his eyes on something no one else could see. The bigger, huskier Little Hawk, a contrast to his older brother, was impulsive, impatient of nuances. The handsome Buffalo Hump, tall, beautifully muscled, was quick to laugh, quick to flirt, quick to fight.

Worm had encouraged the setting up of this lodge, where his two sons lived with their grandmother Plum. Neither of them was married, the younger twenty-one winters old, the elder nearly thirty and a shirtman. Men of that age didn't belong in their parents' lodge. For an old woman to take care of their lodge, that was the best way. By good luck their grandmother needed a home and had always had a special connection with Crazy Horse.

Worm glanced at her in the shadows of the lodge, her hands working slowly at making moccasins. For a moment he thought she was looking straight at him and smiling impudently. True, old Plum was far past the age when she needed to deflect her glance downward, away from men, and mostly she was expressionless. But she had been improving recently. Maybe he hadn't imagined that smile. He knew her well—she'd lived with him for twenty years. He wondered whether she could speak if she wanted to. He suspected she could. What would she say? Since people talked as though she wasn't there, she knew everything.

He had a funny thought. How nice to have a woman in the lodge who never said a word. His wives, who were sisters, were magpies.

The *canupa* had made its circle and came back to him.

He took a moment to puff and watch the breath of Maka, Earth, rise ethereally. Then he said, "Little Big Man and two other Bad Faces came visiting today."

Crazy Horse nodded.

Worm wondered if his son knew the trouble simmering. "Many of the Bad Face young men are among us," he said.

Since the sun dance a dozen young warriors of other bands had made their wickiups with the Long Face band of Hunkpatila. Or, as most of the young men called it, the Crazy Horse band. They were waiting to see where Crazy Horse wanted to fight and when. Evidently they'd rather follow him than their own war leader, Red Cloud.

"It will cause hard feelings," said Worm.

"Red Cloud is still the first war leader of the Oglala," said Crazy Horse. "Or Buffalo Hump." He glanced deferentially at his *hunka*.

Crazy Horse never liked to talk about what people would think or how they would feel. Politics, he called it. He just wanted to do what seemed right, without considering what other people would think of his actions. Worm thought this was the young man's nature and to be respected. It was also naive. Naivete had cost his son the woman he wanted.

Little Hawk spoke sarcastically. "Red Cloud isn't thinking about how to run the soldiers out of the country."

Worm interrupted his younger son with a look. The youngster was about to blurt out what many of the people were thinking but shouldn't be said. Maybe Red Cloud wasn't looking to kick the whites out but to get a good deal for giving in. Little Hawk's way, in war and in council, was to rush in first and think later. Even now he went on a little. "The warriors know that my brother will fight forever," he said less noisily.

"Red Cloud will remember this," said Worm. "Like the elk teeth."

Crazy Horse looked away fast at that one, and Worm saw Hump suppress a smile. So his eldest son had thought

Worm didn't know about the elk teeth. Worm knew Hump disapproved—Hump had always thought his *hunka*'s attachment to the woman was excessive.

Yes, it was foolish, making presents to another man's wife, even stupid. Which Worm had said as clearly as was polite.

He sighed. This business of the warriors coming to follow Crazy Horse was troublesome, and Worm foresaw more of it. It was his son's vision to be a warrior and his medicine to be a powerful one. Yet Worm's son's destiny seemed to be always to look to his own medicine and his solitary glory. Which wasn't the way of a leader.

Worm addressed Buffalo Hump. "What do you think should be done against the forts?"

Hump shrugged lightly. "We'll make them think their hair is on fire," he said. Despite his easy tone, Hump meant it and would do it. But he evidently didn't want to say what he thought the strategy should be. He would save his thoughts for the council, with the other war leaders.

"What do you think?" Worm asked his elder son.

Crazy Horse scraped the ashes out of the *canupa*, thinking. Finally he said, "I don't know. I don't decide such things." He did not add, "And I seldom go to council and never speak." "For myself," he said, "I will go against the Psatoka tomorrow."

Little Hawk smiled broadly. "Me too."

Hump said nothing. His job was to stay and help with the planning.

Worm looked at his elder son. Crazy Horse had as much as said, "I'm going to fight the Psatoka. When the chiefs make up their minds where and when to fight the soldiers, they can let me know." Which would have been rude.

He saw a difficult course for his elder son. Then he looked into Little Hawk's face. Yes, it was easier just to act and not think.

* * *

Soon the Lakota went against the woodcutting detail at Fort Phil Kearny again. It didn't go the way Crazy Horse wanted.

Everyone wanted to free-lance. Hump did lead some decoys, but the young warriors from the north, the Miniconjou and the Hunkpapa, rushed down and ran off the horses near the wagon boxes. Some of the soldiers fled into the timber, but most of them forted up behind the fourteen wagon boxes set on the ground. The warriors circled the boxes and fired arrows from under their ponies' necks, but the soldiers were well shielded by the boxes and answered with the many-shooting rifles. Hump and Crazy Horse didn't want to get good men killed attacking such a position. There had to be a way to make the whites use up all their ammunition.

The Lakota tried a charge up a ravine on foot, but the white fire made them pull back again. Two more foot charges, another mounted charge, and still the lead came flying. When more soldiers came out from the fort with wagon guns, the Lakota gathered up their wounded and one of their dead and galloped off fast, like buffalo with their tails up.

Crazy Horse's mind was on five bodies, bodies left on the battlefield, five of the six Lakota killed today. They lay so close to the whites that not even he could get to them and drag them away. One of them was Jipala, who had walked slowly straight toward the wagon boxes singing his war song and shot arrows into the wagon-box circle faster than a many-times-shooting rifle would fire. It hurt Crazy Horse deeply to have to leave a brave Lakota on the field where he died.

When Crazy Horse and his brother started eating the stew Plum had made, Little Hawk said that Yellow Shield had counted his first coup today, on one of the soldiers guarding the horses.

Crazy Horse thought bitterly, *Coups!* Sounds and pictures jumbled through his mind. *Yes, strike an enemy with your*

*hand. Strike him with your coup stick or your lance. Take his scalp.
Kill him. Strike his woman before his eyes. The list went on and on.
Coups! Do it for honor, for glory, to look big in the people's eyes, to
get big between some woman's legs, but it is all . . .*

Finally, he said softly to his brother, "Everything's so
different now."

Little Hawk didn't see—none of the young men did.
The whites didn't beat you by whipping you on the battlefield. They simply changed everything. Trade goods.
Firearms, which your enemies had. Emigrants across the
country, every summer more than all the Lakota added
together. The game killed or driven off. Now war was ruined—it was ignominious. A challenge of spirit turned into
a slaughterhouse. A man felt ashamed to fight.

"What should we do?" asked Little Hawk.

"Get guns," said Crazy Horse. "Lots of guns and lots of
ammunition. Nothing else will work."

When Little Hawk went out to stand in the blanket
with some girl, Crazy Horse sat with Plum. He helped her
pit the berries for the pemmican. He thought maybe it
made her feel good to get more done, however it got done.
He felt sure she liked the company, even if she couldn't
say so.

Sitting there, he discovered he didn't want to talk
tonight. They were communicating without talking, the
two of them, feeling the slickness of the fruit and hardness
of the pits. It was real, unlike words, and he liked it.

He looked straight into her eyes, which he hadn't done
in years. When he looked right at her, the eyes were
glazed, indifferent. But when she thought he wasn't looking, they had intelligence in them, sometimes. *Will you ever
speak again?* he wondered silently.

He had something to say, so he said it. Not just to
Grandmother Plum, but to the lodge walls and the spaces
in the village beyond them and the four-legged and rooted
and winged people in the night and the vast prairie and
the sky still more vast. "Arrows and lances and clubs won't
do it," he said distinctly. "Big hearts won't do it. Clever

strategies won't do it." He imagined his words rising into the sky like steam from the rocks of the sweat lodge. "If we don't get enough guns, the hoop of the people will be broken for seven generations. Or twice times seven."

He thought something he didn't say aloud: *It is broken anyway.*

INTRANSIGENCE

The rest of the summer and autumn the Oglala had no big fight against the soldiers. No whites traveled the Bozeman Trail except soldiers, and they moved only in large numbers. When another invitation came to visit Fort Laramie and talk peace, the Oglala made their excuses and stayed home.

To Crazy Horse it was another sign of how peculiar the whites were. They knew the Oglala didn't want peace. They wanted the whites out of Shifting Sands River country for good. So the whites did something funny in their minds and pretended they didn't know what they knew and smiled in an odd way and said, "Want to come in and talk about peace?"

Some Lakota would always talk, of course, for presents. Especially the ones who didn't live in Shifting Sands River country to begin with and didn't need it. Which was funny.

Crazy Horse wanted presents, too, if they were guns and powder and lead, or cartridges for the new kinds of rifles.

Visitors came from the Spotted Tail people and the southern bands and told about the iron road. They brought white-man newspapers to show pictures of it and told how hundreds of men prepared the way, smoothing the road and laying the twin tracks. Drum-on-His-Back puzzled out the marks that were words and told everyone how excited the whites were about their railroad.

It was astonishing, the visitors said, the way all the white men worked together and set up the road so quickly, each man like a limb of a hundred-legged bug, each doing just what was needed at the right moment. A small thing for each man, but when it was done right, the bug scooted fast.

Crazy Horse wondered if this was why the whites always drove the Indians off their land. For a Lakota living was individual and private. You strove to keep your mind walking in a beautiful way.

The white men, though, seemed to focus more on group goals, and they were good at achieving them. Their soldiers could make hundreds of men bring off a tricky maneuver together. Their iron-road laborers could work together so that the twin tracks got laid down from salt-water-everywhere in the east to salt-water-everywhere in the west, and very fast.

The way they walked was ugly. He had never met one except maybe Caspar Collins that was likable, or honest, or full of love for other whites, or who lived in awareness of Spirit. Yet they could build a fireboat and travel four sleeps in a day.

Strange, strange, strange people.

The southern visitors also said the whites were killing hundreds and hundreds of buffalo to feed the iron-road workers, so meat was almost impossible to find in that country. The Spotted Tail people were worried about starvation this winter.

Hump and others talked hard at the visitors about this point. If they kept making peace papers and giving the whites permission to have more and more roads, trading for presents so they could survive this one winter, the buffalo would be fewer and fewer. Next year and the year after that what would the people eat? In a generation? In seven generations?

The visitors didn't answer.

Someone else had been north to visit the Hunkpapa and said the Sitting Bull people, who stayed far away from the whites and took nothing at all from them, were rich in robes and meat.

"But we can't see the future," said the southerners. "We're just trying to stay alive to see the grass green once more."

Ah, Uncle, said Crazy Horse to Spotted Tail in his mind, *what are you doing? You go to the Indian agent and he issues you rations to live, or half-starve. Or he gives you what he doesn't steal, or gives you back what he stole to begin with. Your people become beggars.*

Life for the body, death for the spirit. And next year or the next, death for the body, too. To Crazy Horse this was no choice at all. You lived for the spirit, the Hawk inside you, or your life would turn to ashes.

Crazy Horse promised himself he would never let his people have to beg for food. He and Hawk would fight until not even the whites could tell where the wagon ruts of the Bozeman Trail used to be. From the Elk River to the Shell River, from the Shining Mountains to Paha Sapa, the Shifting Sands River country would belong to the Oglala.

Otherwise, he and Hawk did not care to live.

FLIRTATION

It was a sunny day, warm for the Moon When the Wind Shakes Off Leaves. The women were outside cooking or tanning buffalo hides from the hunt, or pounding meat for pemmican, or sewing and trading gossip. Children were playing everywhere, and the dogs were underfoot.

Crazy Horse, Little Hawk, and Little Big Man walked across the camp circle, laughing. Little Big Man could make Crazy Horse laugh out loud, a rare thing. It was his weird face and his weird body. When he told jokes, which were no better or worse than anyone else's, he made his eyebrows wiggle like worms, or jabbered his lips insanely, or did a dance with his hips. Little Big Man had a short, squat body and a face that looked stiff as a wood carving until he started acting like that, so it was doubly funny.

Crazy Horse liked this young Bad Face. He was a true warrior who understood that every day was a good day to die, and that made him a good companion. He visited in the Hunkpatila camp often now, and the two sons of Worm returned the visits. If that meant having to see No Water and the twins and Pretty Fellow and Red Cloud, it also meant getting to see Little Big Man, and Black Buffalo Woman.

Black Buffalo Woman stirred her stew, seeming not to watch out of the corner of her eye the Strange Man walking with Little Hawk and Little Big Man.

Suddenly Yellow Shield walked between lodges leading two young horses.

The camp circle hushed. Even the children seemed to stop yelling, and the dogs didn't yip. Though no one looked directly at Yellow Shield, everyone was watching.

Eagle Foot was sitting in front of his lodge, smoking and enjoying the sun. Five or six sleeps ago Yellow Shield had disappeared with Eagle Foot's woman. They hadn't been seen since. No one knew whether they would come back to camp or go visiting with another band for the winter. However amiable he looked sitting there absorbing the sunlight, Eagle Foot was a violent man. He got into fights with other men, quarreled loudly with the woman who used to be his wife, and probably even hit her. Once Black Buffalo Woman saw him trip over a dog and angrily beat it to death with a limb and not even take the meat. Maybe he would beat his rival now.

Yellow Shield walked straight up to the lodge without a word to Eagle Foot. The former husband appeared to take no notice.

Black Buffalo Woman held her breath. Evidently Yellow Shield was making a gift of the horses to show good-heartedness toward Eagle Foot.

She stirred the stew and tasted it. Rabbit, the way the Strange Man liked it, with plenty of wild onions. She'd made rabbit because it was meat she snared herself, something of her own. She realized she was still holding her breath and let it out.

Yes, everyone said it was a woman's right to choose her man, especially when she was no longer a maiden but a mature woman. If she put his belongings outside the tipi, that was an end of it, so they said. If she went off with another man, her first husband would be too proud to complain.

That was theory. Husbands weren't always so benevolent.

Yellow Shield staked the horses behind the lodge. He walked away. Eagle Foot gave no sign at all, unless drawing deep on the *canupa* was a sign, and letting the smoke out like a big sigh.

She glanced up at Crazy Horse. He had been watching Eagle Foot and Yellow Shield, too. With the same thoughts she had, she was sure.

She stirred hard. *It would not be the same with me,* she thought wretchedly. Not the same for a woman who has been made into a symbol. With her three children she was a sign of the resurgence of the Bad Face band. She was married to an important Bad Face leader. She was the niece of Red Cloud, the war leader of all the Oglala. She wasn't just any woman.

She felt a squeezing in her chest and wondered if she was glad or sorry.

"Cousin, what are you cooking?" cried Little Big Man.

"Rabbit stew!" she called. "Come and taste it, all of you!" It was generous of Little Big Man to understand and find an excuse to bring Crazy Horse to her.

She watched the Strange Man's face as he sipped the stew out of the spoon. He murmured his appreciation, which sounded bigger than the words.

"I bet a younger woman would cook better for you than Plum," Black Buffalo Woman said, pretending to tease. But she didn't know who she was teasing, him or herself.

Crazy Horse looked wounded.

Yes, she thought, *it isn't funny—it hurts.*

And knowing he still loved her—that hurt, too.

Sometimes she really did wish he would marry. Sometimes.

Other times she wished she dared slip away with him into the willows again.

No Water watched from the trees. She handed the Strange Man the spoon with a special grace in her arm and waited his response expectantly.

No Water had his rifle in his hands. Somehow he felt self-conscious about coming back without meat this time. His hands squeezed the stock, but he knew better than to raise it.

The Hunkpatila has been lifting my lodge flap when I was gone hunting.

Lifting it this hunting trip, probably earlier trips. *How long?* he screamed inside himself. He didn't even let himself think the bigger question: Are my children his children?

He watched the four of them talking, smiling like innocents, cousins and friends enjoying each other and the day. She looked at the other two directly but cast her eyes down from the Strange Man's glance, as a woman does from a lover's gaze.

They are deceivers.

He remembered the day he had watched them as teenagers, Light Curly hair topping her over and over. The memory crawled on his skin.

They are deceivers.

Who knew that better than No Water?

He wanted to bite something in half.

No Water hated her. She had married him because she thought he would be a big man in the tribe. He *was* a big man. But Crazy Horse became a shirtman, and big in war, and the younger warriors idolized him, the fools. They didn't see how weak he was. She didn't see it. Now she thought she'd chosen wrong.

His wife was intrigued by this . . . thing, like watching

the sun glint off glass, seeming powerful when there was really nothing there, only mirages.

I'll show you. You never had any choice. I made the choice. I'll show you.

They wouldn't even make a lodge together. They wanted her to stay with No Water so they could make a fool of him in his own home. She would laugh and moan and cry out when he topped her, and everyone would know and laugh at the deceived husband.

They are mocking me.

He would make her tell, *make* her tell. Then he would kill that skinny, pretentious, woman-slinky, and very Strange Man. He would catch him atop Black Buffalo Woman and bash his head in. Then he would strangle her and watch her eyes bulge as she died.

But then No Water thought of Red Cloud, her uncle, her family, her connections. They would not stand for even a little force used on Black Buffalo Woman. They would tell her to put his moccasins outside the tipi. They would ruin No Water in the band.

Besides, many people would avenge the Strange Man. They were fascinated by his softness, which they did not recognize as weakness, like birds watching a snake.

Fine, he thought. *I'll be more subtle. Somehow.*

Little Big Man's laugh caromed around the lodge circle. Little Hawk pounded Crazy Horse on the back.

No Water raged to kill all of them.

INCIDENT AT HORSESHOE RANCH

Some of the warriors, the ones who hung around American Horse, said they were friendly with the white people at Horseshoe Ranch and maybe they could trade for some powder there. Too many men had guns but no powder.

Crazy Horse just nodded his head. As was his way, he didn't even speak to agree. Everyone understood.

Little Big Man admired Crazy Horse extravagantly. When the sandy-haired man had asked quietly for volunteers to do a little raiding, seventy men volunteered. Even loaf-around-the-forts who hadn't fought in a long time wanted to ride with this leader.

So Little Big Man, Crazy Horse, Little Hawk, and the American Horse warriors left the others behind and rode to the ranch.

Horseshoe Ranch was built around an old stage station and stockade. They rode in with their faces unpainted, crying out *"Hau, kola!"*—Hello, friends! Little Big Man noticed that Crazy Horse hung back, but he himself cantered rowdily right on into the yard with the American Horse warriors—he wasn't a man to act suspicious. When the door slammed, they just yelled louder, "Hello, friends!"

The first bullet knocked Blue Stone right off his horse.

Ponies and riders almost ran over each other getting out of there.

Blue Stone and another man down crawled out of the line of fire and came running.

Little Big Man looked at Crazy Horse for leadership. Crazy Horse was ready. "Don't forget," he said ironically, "even if they're friends, they're *white.*" His eyes were wicked.

Three or four American Horse warriors said, "Let's go!" at the same time. Little Big Man was galloping ahead of them.

Shooting did no good—the whites were holed up in the main house firing back through slots cut in the logs. So the Lakota set fire to the stables and the stockade. Then, since it was getting dark, they decided to pick up their warrior friends and ride to the place of Mousseau nearby. His woman, who was Sicangu, would give them something to eat.

Later, in the full dark of night-middle-made, the smoldering stable and stockade logs still glowed. Little Big Man had an idea. He sat on his haunches and howled like a coyote. He had a little fun with it, sticking his flat nose into the air and forming a snout with his fingers to make the other warriors laugh, even Crazy Horse. Well, if the whites were still in there, they apparently weren't interested in any coyote. So the warriors slept.

In the morning the whites passed up a chance to leave with a detachment of soldiers.

"They must want to fight," said Little Hawk. So the warriors gave them good sport.

By dark the Lakota knew where all the holes in the logs were for shooting. If there was a risk to be taken, Little Big Man and Little Hawk wanted to take it. They calculated the firing angles and sneaked up and set the main house on fire.

On the hill the Lakota watched it burn. Little Big Man improvised a dance and a song:

> *"We came visiting—*
> *You said hello with your rifles.*
> *We came visiting—*
> *You said hello with gunfire.*

> *"We asked for food—*
> *You gave us lead.*
> *We asked for coffee—*
> *You gave us bullets.*

> *"We asked to be friends—*
> *You gave us hatred.*
> *We asked to be friends—*
> *You gave us hatred.*

> *"From hatred we made bones.*
> *From hatred we made you into bones."*

He didn't sing it in a melancholy way—he made it grisly and mocking. After the first time through, he got some of the other warriors to join in, which made him feel good. He noticed that Crazy Horse still kept apart, didn't join in singing or dancing or cheering on. He wondered why the Strange Man never sang or danced.

In the morning, though, they found no bones or bodies in the ruins of the house. A tunnel led to a little fort made of sod. The whites had slipped away in the darkness toward Mousseau's place. By the time the Lakota got there, the Frenchman and his wife had hightailed it. The Horseshoe Ranch whites had grabbed some horses and headed for Laramie.

Little Big Man and Little Hawk quirted their ponies after the whites, and the others followed, whooping. Little Big Man looked back and saw that Crazy Horse was coming, though he wasn't hurrying.

In some little hills they caught up with the Horseshoe Ranch whites and ran their horses off. After a while the white men thought better of their cover and ran for a hilltop with a little timber. But the Lakota chased them out again and now started herding them across the plains like wild horses. Every once in a while a white would fall and a Lakota would dismount to scalp him.

Little Big Man and Little Hawk were having a fine time, making the whites run like prairie chickens. Little Hawk yelled, "Scalps today!"

Little Big Man looked back and saw Crazy Horse ride toward an old, hairy-faced white man who had fallen behind and tried to hide. To Little Big Man's surprise the leader didn't shoot him. He stood off and watched the man scurry into a gully.

Little Big Man cantered back to Crazy Horse. "*I* had a place to hang that scalp," said Little Big Man edgily, nodding toward his lance.

The leader said nothing. He pushed his pony forward fast, but Little Big Man came up alongside and looked at him, waiting.

"Maybe we've done enough killing today," said Crazy Horse.

Little Big Man felt like he'd been slapped.

Crazy Horse wiped off his face paint and took the war-eagle feather out of his hair. He felt melancholy. These white men had been friends of some Lakota here, and they had fought spiritedly. True, they had acted dumb—so scared by the troubles all around, probably, that they shot at friends riding up just to trade for food. So if half of them were lying along the trail dead and scalped and only four were left alive, they deserved it. But Crazy Horse felt melancholy at all of this.

He saw that Little Big Man was still seething at the stopping of the fight. The blood ran hot in Little Big Man. That was part of what made him a good companion, and a good comrade in war.

Crazy Horse said to Little Hawk, "Make sure all the warriors stay back." He nodded at Little Big Man. "Especially that one."

"They'll kill you," said Little Big Man with a snarl. It seemed as though he was mad at his friend for taking this risk. Crazy Horse looked at him, learning something.

"They will kill you," echoed Little Hawk.

Crazy Horse smiled easily. Yes, it was a risk, and that was all right. He shrugged as though to say, "It is a good day to die." He handed Little Hawk his repeating rifle and said, "If they do, this belongs to you." He set his knife down and picked up his *canupa* in its otter-skin case and held it out before him. Slowly and deliberately, he walked toward the white men. Every few steps he made the sign that meant "friends."

When he walked, his legs felt all right. When he stopped to sign, he felt them shake. If anyone noticed his nervousness, white or Lakota, he did not mind.

The whites kept their guns pointed at him. He was so close now that none of the four would be able to miss. He walked right in among them, sat down cross-legged, and took his *canupa* out of its case. Taking his time, looking politely toward the ground and not into the whites' eyes, he filled the *canupa* with *cansasa,* lit it, sent the first smoke to the four directions, Father Sky, and Mother Earth, and handed the *canupa* to the oldest white man.

The fellow took it and smoked.

After they had all smoked and all the weapons were set down, Crazy Horse signed, "Enough good men have died today."

The oldest white man said, "We cached some goods at Mousseau's place. If you let us go, we will give them to you."

Crazy Horse smiled. Telling where the goods were was like giving them away already. He wondered if there was any powder in the cache. He looked into the white men's faces. They were exhausted. They had run a long way across the hot plains. They had no water and must be parched. They had some small wounds. But they had been brave, and now they faced him and spoke up like men and neither whined nor begged.

Crazy Horse made the sign for "yes."

After the long trip back to Mousseau's place, the Lakota left with *cansasa,* beans, coffee, sugar, whiskey, clothes, beads, and other things, but no powder. They took the goods and left the white men alone.

That night Little Hawk cut the seat out of his first pair of white-man pants and wore them saucily. He found some rolled paper in a pocket.

"Money," said Crazy Horse. "Maybe it will buy some powder."

"It better," said Little Big Man irritably.

BURN! BURN! BURN!

In the spring of the next winter, the year known as Wears-a-Spotted-Warbonnet Was Killed, the whites quit. So they said. In this year of 1868 they would abandon the forts on the Bozeman Trail forever. For as long as the grass should grow and water flow, all the country between the Muddy Water River and the Shining Mountains, from the Shell River to the Elk River, and in the center of it Paha Sapa would belong to the Lakota, to hunt in and live as they pleased. Thus the peace paper this time said: The Indians won.

So the southern bands went in and signed the paper and got plenty of presents, including guns and ammunition. "Now that we are all friends," said the agent, "why should we not give you guns?" When he said this, the soldiers turned their backs and the people pretended not to see their scowls. Most northern bands also signed, even the hostiles—even Man-Whose-Enemies-Are-Afraid-of-His-Horses of the Hunkpatila. "The Shifting Sands River War is over," said the whites.

But the Oyukhpe Oglala did not go in, or the Bad Faces. Crazy Horse felt like cheering when he heard what Red Cloud was reported to have said: As long as soldiers stayed in the forts of Shifting Sands River country, he would touch a pen to no peace paper.

The word was out. The Sahiyela were invited in, not the Lakota, so Crazy Horse rode to the fort as the invited guest of Little Wolf's band of Sahiyela. Hump, Little Big Man, Little Hawk, and He Dog came along. The smiles flashed like knives, with a dangerous edge.

The silver eagle chief had sent word to Little Wolf that on this day the soldiers would walk and ride out of Fort Phil Kearny, their wagons and wagon guns rolling behind them. And they would never come back.

Most of the goods would roll off in the wagons, the silver eagle chief said, but Little Wolf's people were welcome to the rest.

The Sahiyela were talking about all the things they might get: horseshoes to use for spear points, surely, or steel to shape into knives, maybe beans, maybe coffeepots, maybe the cloth of the curtains the white women had put up, maybe flour, probably empty flour sacks.

Crazy Horse had in mind something else altogether.

The five Lakota watched from Pilot Butte, where the sentry had stood and signaled so many times that the wood train was under attack. With his eyes Crazy Horse followed the columns filing away to the south in great clouds of dust—hundreds of men, hundreds of horses, and dozens of wagons make a lot of dust. He wished he couldn't see them for the dust and would never be able to remember anything here on Piney Fork but the dust of the soldiers taking the back trail.

His mind went back to that winter day he had decoyed the hundred in the hands past Lodge Trail Ridge and into the ambush. He felt pride in it, but not much pleasure. War was of the spirit. Only slaughter was of the body.

Even as the last soldiers went out the gate, the Sahiyela ran over the forts like ants after sugar. The Lakota smiled at each other.

When the last soldier was beyond the Pilot Butte, they cantered down to the fort and through the gate. No one to report their approach now, no one to turn them away now, no one to tempt them with whiskey, no one to tell them only one Indian at a time in the trading room.

Sahiyela women were scurrying about everywhere, their arms full of white-man belongings. Flour sacks for dresses, awls, lemon crystals for making lemonade, hatchets, a couple of tools to make round lead balls with, tins of oysters, Iroquois shells, odd ends of wool and of calico, a spool of glossy ribbon, an iron for pressing clothes (they didn't know what to make of that), combs, mirrors, a pair of blacksmith's tongs, horehound candy, a tattered quilt, and a real prize—a bronze medal with the image of a man named Millard Fillmore on it.

One old woman stood in a doorway, her arms crossed, legs spread defensively. "This is my lodge!" she hollered.

"This is my lodge!" She glared at everyone, booming out her claim over and over, like a crazy person. "This is my lodge!"

Then Crazy Horse noticed a half-dozen women setting up housekeeping in various rooms. Little Wolf gave him a tilted smile to say he'd noticed, too. The chief spoke softly to one of the *akicita* men, and he gently started moving the women out of the fort. "None of us will live in the white-man lodge," the *akicita* man said to one of them. "We do not live in one place. We follow the buffalo."

Crazy Horse and Little Big Man grinned at each other. When they were finished, neither the Sahiyela nor anyone else would be living in this fort.

They staked their ponies for a quick getaway.

"This is your privilege," Little Wolf said to Crazy Horse. "You earned it the day of the hundred in the hands.

"I tried to get the silver eagle chief to give me what was in there," said Little Wolf, pointing to where the powder magazine had stood. He traded mad grins with Little Big Man. "But he was too smart for that. He gave me these." He tapped one of four round metal containers. It made a dead, thunking sound—it was full.

Little Big Man opened it and sniffed. He was proud of knowing how to work the gadgets of the whites and knowing how to take care of his rifle expertly. He looked up at Crazy Horse and winked and said, "Coal oil." Crazy Horse smelled it. It stank like a tar seep.

Little Wolf got the Sahiyela out of the fort while the five Oglala splashed coal oil around the bottoms of all the buildings and the stockade. Crazy Horse watched them carefully, making sure the coal oil stretched far enough. "I want *everything* gone."

Little Big Man worked the fastest. Crazy Horse thought he was like a kid playing with fire.

When they were finished, a quarter can of oil was left.

"Let's keep it," said Little Big Man enthusiastically.

Crazy Horse shook his head no.

"Let's burn the gate twice," said Little Hawk. "Close the door flap on them."

He Dog exclaimed assent—*"Hoye!"*

"Let's burn the trading room double," said Crazy Horse, "where they thought they could buy us."

"Hoye!" cried Hump.

Everyone agreed, though Little Big Man was disappointed.

Crazy Horse held his torch up. They had dipped heavy limbs in coal oil and lit them with lucifers left by the soldiers. He looked toward Hump at the far corner to his left, He Dog at the corner to his right. Little Big Man and Little Hawk had volunteered for corners out of sight. They would act when Crazy Horse yelled.

Crazy Horse pitched the torch against the bottom of the wall.

WHUMP! went the flames.

WHUMP! WHUMP! Hump and He Dog ignited their corners.

His pony shied so hard Crazy Horse almost lost his seat. He called out to the skies, a primal bellow. *"He-ya, he-ya, he-ya, he!"*

WHUMP! WHUMP! on the far side of the structure. Crazy Horse quirted his pony hard away. The heat almost blistered his bare back.

A huge stench came up his nostrils, acrid and burning.

He heard hoofbeats of the other riders behind him.

They sprinted to the top of Pilot Butte and turned to watch.

The fire was mammoth. It stank. It roared like rapids. It was a great red maw devouring everything, like the sunset at the end of the world.

"Burn, burn, burn!" yelled Little Big Man.

Crazy Horse thought, *They're like Wakinyan, but they burn.*

"Unci," Crazy Horse began. He took his grandmother's elbow in his fingers and said no more for a while. She moved her upper body a little where she sat. Yes, she heard. Yes, she knew he wanted to talk. As usual she kept her eyes averted, acknowledging nothing.

"Unci, the soldiers left the fort today. We burned it. The Sahiyela took everything that was left. Little Hawk, Hump, Little Big Man, He Dog, and I burned it."

She turned her head toward him. In the light of the center fire he could see how vacant her eyes looked. *It's not natural. She makes them look vacant on purpose,* he told himself. Sometimes it frustrated him. *I pour out the words,* he complained in his mind, *and her bucket doesn't catch them.* Sometimes the fear came back: She no longer had a bucket. Maybe she just liked to be touched the way he always took her elbow. Maybe she just liked to hear his voice, or anyone's voice, and have the sense of companionship, but understood nothing.

He knew better. He thought he knew better.

He let his eyes wander around the tipi. Nothing there but shadows. Little Hawk was out there dancing. The people of the village were dancing their triumph over the soldiers tonight. He was grateful that their lodge was apart, and he couldn't hear the music.

He waited a little, and as always the awareness came to him. He felt it, not enough to call another being, a shade, a soul, even a presence. It was not even so much as a picture. He only had a faceless memory, a sense of warmth, the comfort of her arms around him and more of her flesh, chest or breasts or crook of neck, and beneath that her pulsing heart, her heart beating with the same blood that ran through him, the drumbeat beneath every day he lived, ever-going, the muted, ceaseless thump of life, life,

life, the single song of this world: *Mitakuye oyasin.* We are all related.

Sometimes he loved the beat of her pulse in his fleshly memory, and sometimes it made him want to scream.

Tonight, as often, after he started a talk with his grandmother, he sat for a while cross-legged, the *canupa* extinguished in his lap, the glow of the fire on their faces, just sitting next to her, and the awareness coming to him. To both of them, he thought. At times like this, they were together, the three of them.

He enjoyed just sitting there companionably, himself, his mother, and her mother. But there was a bargain always kept. It was that he spoke his mind, spoke it when the words were hard to find, spoke the words that hurt, spoke them when they tried to clot in his throat, spoke words when only tears would do. It was something he offered to his grandmother, and to himself, and to the one he never named.

"They are dancing tonight, and proclaiming their deeds. The women make the trilling for them. They say we won the war. But, Unci, we are losing." He looked into the flat, slate blackness of her eyes. "They counted coups and they killed and the soldiers ran away. But we're losing." He thought for a moment, groping for the words. "When it rains on a gentle slope, you can't see the water run into the valley, or only a trickle of it here and there. The whites are trickling into our country, each drop as nothing. Today there are none here on Shifting Sands River. Tomorrow we will be knee-deep in them. The next day or the next moon or the next winter, we will be drowning in them.

"The worst is, Red Cloud is going to see The One They Use for Father in the east. That one will make Red Cloud chief of an agency." Crazy Horse snorted at the word *chief.* He went on, "Then the Bad Faces will be loaf-around-the-forts."

He threw his head back and looked into the blackness of the center hole, where the tied lodge poles blocked out the sky. He heard his grandmother's soft breathing and looked back at her. Suddenly, forcibly, he saw his face in hers. It was odd: For twenty-five winters he had felt keenly that he looked only like himself, an individual, a solitary, even an aberration. Now, these last several winters, he had seen that they looked alike, he and she. Maybe he and his grandmother and the one he could not name. People said that, except for his light skin and hair, he looked just like that one. That idea always pleased him and hurt him, the feelings twisted together.

"In a way it has been a good time to be a warrior, Unci. Battles to fight, many battles, endless battles. Many honors to win. Times to feel like a warrior."

He tried to hold her eyes with his, tried to penetrate all the barriers she had put up over all the twenty-five winters. He said slowly, each word like a drumbeat, "Of course, we must lose the war."

He smiled a little. "To a warrior the war is not all. He lives for a moment in battle, a . . ." He pondered. "His life is the sharp edge of a tomahawk whirling in the sun. Like life, one day it flies suddenly out of the hand and is gone forever. Yes, suddenly."

He shrugged. He looked into his grandmother's face and considered her life. She was not simply *witko,* as everyone else thought. She chose her silence. He felt sure of it.

In that silence, he imagined, she saw and understood. Maybe from there she knew a wisdom beyond his, and the words he was about to say. He wondered what it might be.

At last he went on.

"A warrior, a warrior like me, does not think of sitting in the sun and watching his grandchildren play and maybe letting someone's young wife bring him a little soup. In the summers of the arrow and spear, that does not feel like living."

He let the feeling rise in his chest, the elation of riding into enemy fire, the spirit growing to become Rider, and then suddenly the sense of living forever within that instant. He thought of telling her all this, but the words felt weary even before he spoke them. So he didn't trouble the ears of his grandmother, or of the unseen one, with false words. Instead he said, "But maybe things have changed."

So he told Grandmother Plum about the fight with the whites running from Horseshoe Ranch. Before long he came to the part where he saw the hairy-faced old man running away helpless. "I remembered Hairy Face," said Crazy Horse. "He used to come to camp trading for the Hudson's Bay Company. I didn't know him well, or especially like him, but he did something curious. He trained a beaver to be his pet. Truly. This beaver would follow him wherever he went. Sometimes he put a rope around its neck and led it like a horse. Sometimes he tied it to a tree so it could chew on the trunk.

"Little Hawk and I used to wait for the part that was fun. He'd sit down on a rock and wave his hands and sing, or usually he whistled. When he'd wave his hands hard enough, the beaver would slap its tail on the earth, like a drum. Do it over and over. On they'd go, whistle and drum, whistle and drum. And Little Hawk and I would start giggling."

He sighed. "If he saw us, he would run us off or pick the beaver up. But I can still see him making music with the beaver."

Crazy Horse squirmed to get his legs more comfortable. "A little thing. So I saw him trying to hide because he couldn't keep up anymore, because the others were running too fast. He hadn't had a drink all day, his face was bright red with trying to go fast enough, and for sure his scalp was itching. . . ."

Crazy Horse smiled to himself at that and then sobered. "I felt a little sick. We were chasing these helpless men across the plains. Yes, they shot at us. They were more scared than smart. They wounded two of our men. So we were going to spill their lives into the dust."

He took a deep breath and let it out. "I let him go. He looked pitiful running, crazy with panic. Later I made peace with the others and let them go, too." He felt no need to talk about the danger of that. "I told Little Big Man we'd done enough killing for one day." He looked sideways at his grandmother. "He had no idea what I was talking about."

He saw light in her eyes. He didn't know whether it was the reflection of the fire alone or understanding.

"Things have changed," he repeated. "Red Cloud has quit. I'm weary of fighting. There's not much left to fight for."

The thought of Black Buffalo Woman rose in him. At times like this he felt as though she were inside him and they were communicating without the need of words or even touch. He hadn't touched her since she married No Water.

"Maybe I should take her as my wife," he said, not mentioning the name. He held his grandmother's eyes and breathed in and out. He felt sure she was looking at him. "I have loved her a long time, more than ten winters. The way she looks at me, I know she has the same thoughts." Now Plum was looking at him as if she knew. "Maybe . . ." Maybe that would change dust to honey in his mouth.

But he didn't say the words. He didn't have to. His grandmother knew.

They sat together and watched the fire. It seemed to glow and dim, almost in a rhythm, like breathing. He slid his hand down from her elbow to her hand and held it.

He felt for Hawk in his heart, but she was still, silent.

He asked himself, *What happens to a man following the vision of a warrior when the war ends?*

RED ROAD OR BLACK ROAD?

When his father's voice called, "Come in," Crazy Horse lifted the door flap, bent, entered, and disbelieved his eyes.

Pretty Fellow and his brother Standing Bear sat behind the center fire next to Worm. Closest to Worm sat White

Twin, the one the people often called Holy Buffalo now, No Water's brother. *Oh,* Crazy Horse reminded himself, *Pretty Fellow is called Woman Dress now. I must remember that.*

He looked at them flatly. What did these Bad Faces want in his father's lodge? Had White Twin come to say something for his brother No Water? Pretty Fellow—Woman Dress—and Standing Bear to speak for their cousin Red Cloud?

He felt himself sucked into a world he disliked and distrusted, Red Cloud's world, persuading other people to do things, moving his fingers through other people's lives, making weaves of his own design . . .

"Join my guests and me," said Worm. Crazy Horse heard his father gently pointing out his impoliteness. He saw the bowls the men had eaten from and the *canupa* that were now out. Politely, he sat.

"We must go," said White Twin. "We want to be in our own lodges tonight." Which was not so far that they needed to leave now, at midday. "We're sorry we can't stay and talk with you," he said to Crazy Horse. To Worm, "Thank you for your hospitality." The three visitors rose, White Twin imposingly tall. Crazy Horse looked at Pretty Fellow's—Woman Dress's—nose, the one broken by that kick many winters ago. To him the nose looked as straight as ever. But not to Woman Dress, naturally, or his family. Worm followed them out the lodge flap.

Crazy Horse sat alone, angry at himself for his suspicion and hostility. He couldn't even remember why he had come to his father's lodge. Part of a ribbon of *cansasa* lay on the cutting board, probably a gift from the visitors. Once it had been cut, the gift could not be refused. Crazy Horse wondered whether they were trying to bribe his father, and why.

Worm was back in a moment. "Are you all right?" he asked his son. Crazy Horse nodded. "You don't have to say it, you know. They see your feelings." This was an indirect reprimand, the old habit of a father telling a son to behave. Crazy Horse didn't like it any more than he had as a teenager.

"What did they want?" he asked impatiently.

"They brought news from the southern bands," Worm said slowly, "and the loaf-around-the-fort people. It seems that the soldiers haven't killed anybody recently." Worm flashed his ironic smile. "They had some other gossip, and a message. The message was delicately put but not delicately meant: They will not let you have Black Buffalo Woman."

Crazy Horse lashed out. "They will not *let* me, they will not *let* her."

Worm interrupted him softly. "The woman herself does not matter. They cannot allow the offense." He paused. "No Water thinks maybe he should cut off her nose."

Crazy Horse burst out, "If he touches her, I'll kill him!" His mind was wild with pictures of Black Buffalo Woman mutilated.

A Lakota had the right to cut off the tip of the nose of an adulterous wife, and some did.

Worm went on, "If you lift the lodge flap again when he is away, he will do it."

Worm waited. Crazy Horse let the guilt and fury subside. He hated the violation of his privacy. What lodge flap he lifted was not his father's business. He had never mentioned his love for Black Buffalo Woman to Worm, and never would have.

Yet the harmony of the peoples was at stake here, and he, the shirtman, had to act well.

"They will not let her go," Worm said firmly.

"Hah!" Crazy Horse still could not stop himself. "They have turned into white men, telling other people what to do. She is a Lakota woman. Of all people the Bad Faces know this."

He meant that the trouble that had split the people nearly thirty winters ago had been over a woman, a relative of Bull Bear. She had run off with Bad Face, his people had stood up for her right to choose, and Bull Bear had ended up dead on the ground.

"They know it," Crazy Horse repeated.

"It will cause a fight," said Worm imperturbably. As before, he meant it. A generation of hostility had come from that, and it was only now healed, after the bands had whipped the whites over the issue of the forts.

Crazy Horse felt his flood of anger ebbing again. Many a dog lifts its leg, but a shirtman must take no notice.

He needed to make a conciliatory gesture to his father. He got out his *canupa* and his own *cansasa* and started filling the bowl. He gave the *cansasa* to Worm. At last he said, "Only fools would split the people over a woman."

"They are telling us they're fools," said Worm. "I know Red Cloud, and Black Twin and White Twin, and No Water, and I think in this matter they are. I think you are not."

Crazy Horse let his breath out all at once. "I will say this to you and no one else. Since she married No Water, I have not touched her."

"I am glad to hear it," Worm said. "The question is, Will you?"

Crazy Horse puffed and sent the smoke up to Father Sky. He thought of all the pain the last split of the people had caused, thirty winters of pain. "I hate the way they act," he said, "bending other people to their will." The Lakota as a people professed to despise that kind of domination, but many still used it.

Worm nodded. "I understand," he said. "And you are a shirtman."

Now the words rose from his innards, but they clotted in his throat and stuck there. "I will not divide the people," he should have said. "I will put the people's needs above my own. I am not just any man with natural desires. I am a shirt wearer, pledged to put the welfare of all the people ahead of my own wants, even wants that all men share."

He should have said more: My vision commands me to the solitude and danger of a warrior, not to home, center fire, and the comfort of women and children.

He knew no words against all that and had no thoughts that would defeat it. He had only feelings. Ten winters and more of longing. And the sense that only a woman could solace him now.

He would say nothing to his father. It was nothing firm anyway, just a sense, a feeling, shapeless, seductive.

The words lurched into his mouth like bile, but he did not speak them: I will not take her. No, the words offended him, they stuck in his throat. He would say nothing.

It was Red Cloud the whites wanted in Washington, D.C. They insisted.

"He's not even a chief," many Oglala complained. "He can't sign a paper."

"The whites want *his* mark," said others.

"It's their newspapers," some said mockingly. "Their newspapers make Red Cloud a big man, so he's the one who has to go."

People gave each other unhappy looks. Really, it wasn't funny that the whites understood so little. It made them worse to deal with. Man-Whose-Enemies-Are-Afraid-of-His-Horses, Sitting Bear, Brave Bear, yes—these were the headmen of the Oglala. They could probably persuade the people to do what they had promised when they signed the paper. Even then, each man had choice, and the chiefs would work by leadership, not command. No Lakota could speak for another.

Then the true word came. Red Cloud had stalled, pretending not to decide whether to go see the Great White Father, until they promised to make him head chief of all the Oglala.

That's what people whispered, snickering, but their smiles were pained. The whites were unbelievable. There could be no head chief of all the Oglala—the Big Bellies were several. Everyone remembered what had happened when the whites tried to make Bear-Scattering head of all the Lakota. When the chief accepted, forced by the whites, he had predicted his own death. And the whites had killed him.

But what was most outrageous was that your enemies tried to choose your people's leader. Passing over the men the people respected, those who had demonstrated they thought of the welfare of all the people, the whites wanted to put their own man in. One who had split the people nearly thirty winters ago with a violent act.

The whites were arrogant beyond belief. Or stupid. People wondered why the powers made them so many and gave them guns. It was like putting everyone's welfare in the hands of youths. Except that Lakota youths were not as wild and insolent and destructive as white people.

Crazy Horse, though, approved of Red Cloud going to see The One They Use for Father. Maybe recognizing these Bad Faces, giving them status, would ease their spirits, he told Worm. Maybe it would keep them from scheming for power all the time. And maybe they would not be so quick to take offense because a woman of their band and a shirtman of the Hunkpatila loved each other.

Crazy Horse went to his *hunka*. "Let's go check out the Pani horses," he said.

Hump took his meaning, all of it, the suggestion of adventure, the anger, frustration, the blocked fury.

He shook his head. "Come with me north," he said, "where people still act like Lakota." He hesitated and then added the angry words he meant. "And not dogs groveling near white campfires hoping for scraps."

Crazy Horse thought for a moment. It was attractive. He was related to the Mniconjou—Grandmother Plum was a Mniconjou and might be happier there. Maybe she would even start talking again.

Then, suddenly, Hump named it. "I wish I knew the words to get you away from her," he said regretfully.

Black Buffalo Woman's name sat between the *hunka*, unspoken. Crazy Horse saw how strongly Hump felt—otherwise he would have never dared say even this little. It was an old sorrow between them. This was the closest they'd ever come to talking about it.

Crazy Horse only shrugged.

So they went against the Pani together. When they got back, bringing ponies, the news came. At the last Man-Whose-Enemies-Are-Afraid-of-His-Horses had decided not to go to Washington. But Red Cloud had gone, and several other Oglala, including Drum-on-His-Back, who had learned to read the whites' writing.

"Your mothers' brother, too," said Worm, "and some other Sicangu." Crazy Horse thought of his uncle Spotted Tail and Red Cloud negotiating with the whites, probably from their knees. Worm chose his words carefully. "They're asking the 'Great White Father' to take pity on them."

Worm smiled sardonically.

He Dog came to Crazy Horse and asked him to lead an old-time party for hunting and raiding, with several lodges along and women to do the cooking, the way the big parties had gone out before things changed. The young warriors wanted it, said He Dog. They would go against the Psatoka, as in the old days.

Crazy Horse was touched by the request. While Red Cloud and the other politicians tried to find honor at the house of The One They Use for Father, he and the young men would look for it at the frontier of life and death. *"Hoye!"* he said with grim enthusiasm. "Let's go."

Before they left, the leaders of Kangi Yuha, the Raven Owners Society, invited everyone to a big ceremony to make He Dog and Crazy Horse bearers of the short lances.

The duties of these two men were strict. In battle, they had to drive their otter-wrapped lances into the ground and not leave that spot. Their companions charged and tried not to retreat. If they were driven back, the other warriors could pull up the lances and release the bearers from their obligation—if that was possible and if the lance bearers served courageously. Then they could retreat and later retire honorably as bearers of the short lances.

Normally the new lance bearers went immediately to war. But this time Crazy Horse and He Dog got a surprise—the Big Bellies wanted to perform another ceremony.

Two Big Bellies brought out the ceremonial weapons known as the lances of the Oglala. They were said to be hundreds of years old, older than two or three times seven generations. They were given to the people originally as a promise that the strength of the Oglala would always rise again, like grass in the spring.

Everyone had heard of these lances, but they had gone unused for as long as any but the oldest could remember.

Now the Big Bellies sang songs entrusting these ancient lances of the Oglala to Crazy Horse and He Dog, and with them the promise of strength and renewal for the people.

The two warriors led their big war party away toward Psatoka country carrying these emblems. The people walked them out of camp raising resounding cheers, once-in-a-lifetime cheers.

Worm worked his way to the front. He wanted to see his son's face. His elder son had walked a difficult road, refusing to take scalps, to count coups, to wear the insignia of success in battle. Until now the Oglala with the most war honors had looked like a poor man of no accomplishment. But today Crazy Horse was achieving something his heart had yearned for, the zenith of honors, the highest war rank the Oglala could offer. His face was solemn, but Worm saw a rare lightness in the young man's eyes.

Tears ran down Worm's cheeks.

Black Buffalo Woman cut the moccasin carefully, more carefully than she usually did. She was not fond of sewing or cooking or other domestic tasks. In fact, she wanted No Water to take a second wife so that as sits-beside-him wife, she could supervise the domestic chores instead of doing them and focus on helping her husband make his way. There was plenty a clever wife could do.

She was cutting this moccasin carefully because it was for her Strange Man. Yes, he would always be "My Strange Man" to her. Now the Strange Man was one of the two most honored warriors of many generations of the Lakota.

She handed the two pieces of leather to Plum, the ancient one who was the woman of the sandy-haired man's lodge. Plum was deaf and dumb and dull of mind, but she could sew if you cut the pieces for her and put the awl and sinew in her hand. And talked to her to keep her from drifting off into the daze she usually lived in.

Black Buffalo Woman's eyes twinkled when she looked at Plum. She couldn't help feeling that Plum was the great sign of her victory. The Strange Man wanted no other wife but Black Buffalo Woman. Having lost her, he lived with his grandmother, and a grandmother who could do almost nothing for him. All but the simplest tasks fell on him. That made Black Buffalo Woman smile.

That's why the women of the village sat with Plum and helped her sew moccasins and the like. That's why Black Buffalo Woman, while her band was camped with the Long Face people of Crazy Horse, could seem to be helping Plum while waiting for her Strange Man.

He would be back soon, probably with lots of Psatoka horses. Though not any scalps. She sighed. Well, he would find her making his moccasins.

When she thought of the elk teeth and the other gifts, and his face when he handed them to her, her heart ached.

Turmoil. Black Buffalo Woman always put him into turmoil. She had come to him the first time on the day of Spotted Tail's supposed hanging and helped him learn love and death together. Whenever he saw her after that, his only awareness was of her. When a smell is that sweet and strong in your nostrils, you suck it in deep and maybe start dreaming, or live as though you're in a dream.

Crazy Horse touched Grandmother Plum on the shoulder. Though she didn't seem to recognize him, he was sure she did. He stood there awkwardly before the two women.

"Thank you for helping our *unci*," Little Hawk said politely.

Crazy Horse was glad his brother had remembered decorum. His heart beat fast—was she making moccasins for him?

"Plum needs to rest now," said Black Buffalo Woman. "I'll help her." She assisted the old woman to her feet and led her toward the lodge.

Was Black Buffalo Woman arranging for them to be alone in the lodge together? Then he took thought. It wouldn't do for them to be seen entering at the same time. "I'll be back," he murmured, head down. "I have something for you."

The beads were in the parfleche he was carrying, but he needed time.

He walked away from the tipi as though he had a task. He turned his attention inward to Hawk. He felt nothing.

Strange, always strange: When he was around Black Buffalo Woman, he never could feel Hawk. He never knew whether Hawk was comfortable or agitated in her presence. He didn't know why.

He came back without his brother, as she knew he would. She had built a center fire.

They talked idly for a while:

"How are your children?"

"Very well. Yourself? Your brother? What is the news from the Holy Road?"

"Nothing ever changes."

This was an intimate remark, coming from him. They traded news and gossip a little, as though they talked to each other often and comfortably. She slipped in the information that No Water was away just now.

Her Strange Man mostly kept his head down, as though he were the one obligated to avoid a meeting of the eyes. She smiled to herself—even smiled openly—and looked him straight in the face, telling him something.

At last he came out with it. "I have something for you. From one of the posts on the Holy Road." He handed her four strands of beads. White, always useful. The color called chief blue. Sahiyela rose, a muted version of the hue of wild roses. The yellow called fatty yellow. She held them up in the light shafting down from the center hole. "They're beautiful together," she said truthfully. "I will make something and wear it in your honor."

This was brazen. He offered no response. Finally, he glanced sideways at the old woman and said, "I miss you."

She touched his forearm. He sucked in his breath and drew it back.

She smiled at him, not quite certain. Did he think the old woman saw? Or heard? Everyone knew better. She had a moment's misgiving. Maybe he was too strange, lived too much in a private world. Maybe he would end up like his grandmother.

No, she told herself, *no danger*. Her presence gave him strong feelings, she knew, nearly made him intoxicated. He was one of the most honored men among the Oglala. He was a hero, a naive and foolish hero, perhaps, but a hero. And she could make him feel intoxicated.

So she plunged in. "I must tell you something."

Crazy Horse was horrified. He could scarcely believe it, even of No Water. To steal the bag of her first flow, her offering to the powers of fecundity. To follow her to the plum tree, defy all the spirits, and steal it.

Then the truly incredible part: To use it to have a spell cast upon her. Use it to alter her mind, though not her affections. Use it to manipulate her, control her, dominate her, take over her will.

He had given No Water credit falsely. He thought No Water loved her. But no Lakota usurped the will of a loved person.

And he thought he had lost her. Not so. She had loved him all along, helplessly. He thought she had betrayed him. Not so. No Water had victimized them both.

A picture came to his mind: Black Buffalo Woman being topped by the man she despised, being dominated, being coerced. He obliterated it. Unbearable.

He looked into her eyes. They shone back at him, open, vulnerable. She was telling the entire truth.

He felt shattered.

"I want to show you something," she said. Now she was taking the big risk. Her breath came tight, but she went ahead. She pulled on a buckskin thong around her neck. Slowly she drew out the ring of carved bone he had given her nearly ten winters ago. It glowed from the time she had spent rubbing it with fat.

"I wear it always between my breasts," she said. "No one knows but No Water. I never take it off. Ever."

She held his eyes.

She got up. "Tonight I will send the children to my sister's lodge," she said softly. She glanced up at him and back down, feeling shy now. She left the lodge quickly.

Walking home, she felt giddy. She thought she had done it. Yes, he would come to her tonight. Surely. She knew his heart. Didn't she?

He told himself it didn't matter. Red Cloud was taking many of the Oglala to live at an agency, where they would need no warriors.

He told himself that after thirty-one winters his real life was over and he should take whatever comfort he could find.

He told himself that No Water would not mind, that it would cause no trouble.

He didn't truly believe any of this.

He admitted to himself that he had never wanted anything or anyone as he wanted Black Buffalo Woman. His body, his guts, his bones, even his skin yearned for her. If he walked across a desert without water for half a moon, this was how his body would ache for water.

Uncertain, he stepped outside the lodge. The night sun was approaching night-middle-made. He looked at the vast sky of stars, some making clouds of misty light, some separate, isolated, brilliant, cold. It was as though he heard a drum. The plunk of the drum lifted his feet and set them down, lifted them and set them down. The throb of the drum put his hand on her door flap. He himself lifted it.

She slept with her head on his shoulder and a bare leg thrown across his. He did not see how she could sleep. He wanted to hold every moment of their being together, to feel every touch and hear every whisper again in memory, to kiss her for a week, to be inside her forever.

She stirred, moved her body against the length of his, then kept napping. Twice already she had taken short naps, then waked to rouse him again.

He put a finger on her cheek and felt her warm breath on his chest. Out and in, very slowly, out and in, warm and moist. That breath, her life, touched his skin and grew in him an awareness, a presence. In his mind were no words for that presence, but in his body and in his memory he recognized the solace, the comfort, the succor.

He felt whole.

In the morning light Black Buffalo Woman looked into his eyes, and they were different. She wasn't sure what had changed. His face was unpainted and wasn't so grave that it made him look forty winters instead of thirty-one. But that wasn't it. His mouth, maybe—it was sober, but for once had an edge of humor. The twin vertical lines between his eyes were gone, a difference for sure. He had wrapped his braids in strips of beaver she had given him last night, the fur a little darker than his hair.

The eyes were it. She had seen Crazy Horse in every light, every time of day, every circumstance, every mood, but she had never seen him playful, truly playful, as his eyes looked now. They were lovely.

She was sorry this was the Moon When the Chokecherries Are Ripe, which had the shortest nights of any moon.

He was taking food in her lodge at dawn. When he left, everyone would see. They would also see No Water's moccasins, which she had set outside the door. She was happy.

When they woke this morning, Crazy Horse said the fateful words: "We are taking women on the raiding party tomorrow. Will you come with me?"

She heard what he left unsaid: *I want you for my wife.* She answered, "Yes."

No Water was gone to the Rawhide Buttes to trade. So she would tell the children they were to stay with relatives until she got back, in no more than a quarter- or half-moon from now. Someone would pick up No Water's moccasins where she had left them, and tell him.

Crazy Horse finished eating and set the bowl aside. "Come outside." He led the way out of the lodge, where the whole village would see them, and sat on the side of the door away from the moccasins. "Put your back to me," he said gently, and patted the earth in front of his crossed legs.

She lowered herself to the ground and felt his strong hands take hold of her hair. She dared not look up at all the eyes on them. "I want to braid your hair," he said. "Then if you have some vermilion," and he knew she did, "I will paint a red circle on your cheek."

She felt a pang in her heart. This circle was the sign of a woman greatly beloved.

She looked back at the many inquisitive eyes. She felt triumphant.

They rode out of the village together ceremonially, in everyone's view. She had the right to choice, like every mature Lakota woman. She was making her choice for all to see.

She knew what the women were saying. Some said that when Crazy Horse turned out to be the bigger man, she simply switched. Others talked about what No Water and Red Cloud might do when they found out. Some, though, were smiling at her. They knew she was marrying for love.

Actually, she herself wasn't sure much of the time. She felt giddy, topsy-turvy, her emotions thrown every which way. She couldn't explain it. Her mother accused her one morning of being enamored of the drama of throwing off one man and taking another and all the attention, even the furor. She wasn't sure about that. But she knew the fledgling woman of all those winters ago still wanted Crazy Horse. She had discovered that last night. No Water made her want to be taken, which was exciting and frightening. Crazy Horse made her want to give, which was fulfilling.

She looked sideways at her Strange Man as they went over a rise and out of sight of the village. She was committed now. She studied his face—slender, and for once in his life, the face of a truly young man. He looked at her and smiled, and she felt his passion. For this moment she was sure. She loved him.

HIS PEOPLE'S HANDS

Standing Bear wrist-whipped his pony into camp, not caring where the pony stepped or what droppings it made or what dust it whirled up. If it was about to collapse, so was he, and he didn't mean to slow down for the sake of politeness now.

A woman glared at him.

"No Water," he growled at her. She look alarmed—his ferocity would frighten any woman, he thought—and ducked into a lodge to tell someone.

He'd been sickened by the spectacle. He'd watched them flirting with each other outrageously. Standing Bear knew it wasn't simply that the woman fascinated the Strange Man. Their flirtation had ended nine winters ago when the woman had made a good marriage. That infatuation was meaningless anyway—every fool felt that way for a little while as a teenager. No, it was more. The Strange Man cared only moderately for the woman. Anyone could see that.

Strange Man, Standing Bear thought. What he and Pretty Fellow called the Strange Man in private was "the misfit." The other name was making something obnoxious into something glamorous.

The Strange Man didn't want the woman—he wanted to insult No Water and the Bad Face people.

A man he didn't know came out of the lodge. "I am Standing Bear," he said to the fellow, "and I want No Water."

The Strange Man despised the Bad Face people. Pretending to advocate peace and goodwill between these factions of the northern Oglala, he had in fact taken every opportunity to oppose them. Now he was throwing dust in the faces of No Water and Red Cloud.

Standing Bear had never forgotten the day Crazy Horse had kicked his brother in the face—the face!—and broken his nose. That day Standing Bear held poor Woman Dress's head in his lap and swore to get even with the misfit.

This was his chance.

No Water came running.

"My friend," said Standing Bear, "His Crazy Horse . . ." He'd intended to tease and mock No Water, to inflame him about this betrayal. From No Water's expression, he saw that wouldn't be necessary. "His Crazy Horse has run off with your wife."

No Water slipped into camp. He had come at a hard run, nearly killing the mule. Now he needed some discretion. The last thing he wanted was for Crazy Horse to find out too soon that he was here. He needed a gun. He meant to leave nothing to chance. Where could he get one? Where, where, where?

A dog growled at him. He kicked at it and it slinked off. He looked around the lodge circle. Who was here? Who had come on this war party? Who were all their hosts?

Bad Heart Bull's lodge—he knew it from the painting on the hides. Bad Heart Bull was the man who painted the winter counts. He was related to both sides, No Water's and the misfit's—a problem.

He had an idea. He would say he wanted to leave on a hunt before sunrise. He smiled. Bad Heart Bull had a pistol. Perfect.

He walked gently toward the lodge. He would speak sweetly. Then he would walk softly to whatever lodge Crazy Horse was in. He could be delicate when he needed to.

And he could slaughter when he needed to. Which was now.

Little Big Man was surprised at how good the feeling among the warriors was. When he'd seen Crazy Horse bringing the woman, he'd been afraid. The warriors would be worried about what the No Water and Red Cloud families might do. But everyone rode cheerfully and talked with good humor. He guessed the feeling was that these two should have been together years ago.

The second day out from camp they came on some other Oglala camped on a little creek. Friends invited the new couple, Little Big Man, and others to a feast. Lots of food, coffee with plenty of sugar, good talk, comradeship—it was a fine time. Their host told a wild hunting story to the men around the center fire. In the back the women were speaking softly and laughing often. Crazy Horse started a story about a grizzly he had seen fall off a boulder. It was a funny story, and Little Big Man had never heard the leader act so silly—

The lodge flap ripped open. No warning, no sound, no scratch for permission to come in.

No Water bounded toward the center fire. His shout crashed at them, and Little Big Man didn't understand the words.

Crazy Horse reached for his knife. He started to jump to his feet, but Little Big Man held him back by one arm. Crazy Horse pulled at the arm.

"No, no!" shouted Little Big Man.

No Water's hand jabbed at Crazy Horse's face with a revolver. Little Big Man saw the flash of powder, heard the roar, and caught his leader's limp body in his arms.

REVENGE

Blood everywhere. Crazy Horse's clothes soaked, Little Big Man soaked.

Little Big Man got his friend and leader stretched out and tried to check the wound. Crazy Horse wasn't dead yet. He was jerking his head from side to side violently. His pain must be terrible. His silence was terrible.

The rip in Crazy Horse's flesh was directly under the left nostril. Little Shield sent someone for a healer. Blood washed all over Crazy Horse's face, so Little Big Man couldn't see whether the bullet had come out or was in his brain.

Black Buffalo Woman ran. She ran blindly, she ran frantically. She couldn't get the picture out of her head—her Strange Man with his face shot off, the gun smoking in her husband's hand.

She was next.

Her mind was in a thousand pieces. She had some memory of ducking under the lodge skirt, wondering if No Water saw her, running crookedly among the twilit lodges, falling headlong over some earflap poles, dodging a dog, and skidding to the ground, sobbing. And running again.

Then she remembered her cousin. The picture of her cousin's lodge and the center fire and the family came to her like a rope to a drowning woman. She held onto it desperately, and somehow she found herself at the lodge flap. She scratched frantically and went in before they said a word.

The family looked at her gape-mouthed, dinner bowls in their hands.

She blurted out all run together, "NoWater haskilled HisCrazyHorse and he'llkill *me* next!"

"A pony!" No Water shouted to the men, any of them, all of them. "Give me a pony!" He was frantic. He wanted to bellow, to roar, to command, but his voice sounded like a shriek, even to himself.

"What's the matter?" said Left Hand. "Come sit down and smoke."

No Water could see Left Hand's friends weren't so eager to offer hospitality. His face scared them.

Yes, I'm crazy, he thought. He did roar now. "Cousin," he shouted at Left Hand, "give me a pony! I've killed His Crazy Horse." The words shocked even No Water, so he threw each one again, like rocks. "I've killed His Crazy Horse. Give me a pony!"

Everyone got right up.

Babble: "His Crazy Horse, killed in an Oglala camp?"

"His Crazy Horse, killed over a woman?"

"Our Strange Man murdered by another Oglala?"

"Two of our best men destroyed? So suddenly?"

"Yes, you idiots, it's terrible!" No Water screamed in their faces. "Now get me out of here!"

He waved the pistol in the air. Nervous, Left Hand took it from him.

Left Hand heard someone rumble low, "Let's turn him over to the His Crazy Horse family." So he grabbed his cousin's elbow and hurried him away. "Isn't this Bad Heart Bull's pistol?" said Left Hand. "Don't tell me anything. Just go." They sprinted to the pony herd and No Water went.

Bad Heart Bull put the pistol away. It was warm from No Water's hands, and from what it had done. He walked slowly to the lodge where the dead man lay. He thought he might vomit. He had helped kill his cousin. Worse, he had helped bring tragedy on the Oglala. Again one Oglala leader had killed another. Again the hoop of the people was broken by one of their own.

The healer was blowing his eagle-bone whistle, so Bad Heart Bull knew Crazy Horse wasn't dead yet. Spotted Crow, one of Worm's brothers, squatted near the downed man. A healer mixed a medicine and put it on Crazy Horse's face. The healer sang. He implored the grandfathers. He shook his rattle and sang again.

Crazy Horse was pale as buffalo fat, and his eyelids didn't even flutter.

After a while Spotted Crow slipped away. Bad Heart Bull caught up with him. "It was my pistol," he said.

Spotted Crow looked at him, his expression unreadable. "He told me he was going hunting early in the morning," Bad Heart Bull added.

Spotted Crow studied his eyes for the truth. Finally, he said, "I want to avoid a feud. Do you?"

Bad Heart Bull said simply, "Yes."

"Then come with me."

Spotted Crow and Bad Heart Bull could do nothing but watch. The young men had a lead rope on No Water's mule, the fast one he had worn out getting here. They were beating it with clubs, stabbing it with their knives, destroying the poor animal. Finally one young man stepped up and cut its throat. Blood gushed all over him, the mule pitched to the earth, and he shouted vengeance at the sky. Spotted Crow saw with disgust that the fellow wasn't even a relative of Crazy Horse. He was a fort loafer come north for the summer, probably wanting to go on a lark of war with the man everyone talked about.

None of the youths could think of what to do next. They looked at each other, stumped, their lust for revenge momentarily slack.

In that instant Spotted Crow said, "He's alive. So far he's alive."

"The healer is singing for him," Bad Heart Bull added.

The warriors looked at each other and broke into some foolish babble.

"Let's wait," said Spotted Crow. "There's plenty of time to settle this."

They started arguing among themselves.

Spotted Crow turned on his heel and went back to the wounded man. "They won't follow No Water tonight," he said to Bad Heart Bull.

Black Twin led his brother No Water toward Horn Chips' lodge. No Water seemed undone by what had happened. Black Twin thought that was strange. If you were going to kill a man, why turn fool hen about it later?

Like other Bad Faces, Black Twin thought maybe Crazy Horse did need killing. The man pretended simplicity, humility, and devotion to the sacred. But he wanted glory and power as much as any of them. These so-called virtues were just a way of making himself into a hero, of playing to the crowd, and a remarkably devious way. Black Twin despised him.

Horn Chips was sitting in front of his lodge waiting for them.

"You turned Black Buffalo Woman's head with a love potion," Black Twin accused Chips bluntly. He said it loud enough for the whole camp to hear.

The *wicasa wakan* just shook his head no.

Warriors started gathering, and women behind them. Everyone had heard.

"You made Black Buffalo Woman crazy with some medicine!" Black Twin boomed even louder. "You made her leave her husband and follow that other man, like she was drunk," Black Twin said.

Chips shook his head again, but people babbled Black Twin's words. Black Twin didn't let himself look pleased. His brother needed a defense, no question. Chips' contempt was visible on his face.

"Answer me!" Black Twin shouted. "How do you expect me to keep my relatives away from you if you don't answer?"

Chips looked up at Black Twin in surprise. *Subtle,* he thought, *to put a thought in their minds that way. To pretend to want to stop them from doing something while you're egging them on.* He supposed he would have to say something.

"I saw you make that medicine!" bellowed Black Twin.

Chips wasn't afraid of this rabble. Black Twin was only making a show, trying to put a defense of his brother in people's minds. If Chips had been afraid, he wouldn't have let them see it. Right now he felt contempt for them.

"You saw me make two medicines for him," Chips said. "A pebble to tie into his warhorse's tail." Everyone knew Crazy Horse kept having ponies shot out from under him. "And a bundle for protection against enemies' bullets." Everyone knew he had that kind of medicine.

People nodded. "I saw him wear the bundle at the fight When They Chased the Psatoka Back to Camp," someone said.

Black Twin nodded gravely.

"It's the truth," said Chips. He didn't add, "And you know it." Black Twin had also seen Crazy Horse with these two medicines.

Chips looked hard at Black Twin. What was interesting here was something else: The twin was putting himself in charge, taking over in place of his own brother, No Water. Maneuvering for position, always.

Black Twin said, "Get gone, you and your family. I don't want to see you in this circle again."

Chips nearly jumped in surprise. He controlled himself and looked up at Black Twin flatly. He supposed he shouldn't be surprised. He would have to go, for he had been Crazy Horse's teacher.

He felt a pang. Today he had lost a man he cared for, and the people he lived with.

Chips shrugged. He much preferred his Inyan creatures, even when they were silent, to a world like this.

The relatives of Crazy Horse said it was the old Bad Face jealousy. The Hunkpatila got to camp at the horns, they got a martyr in Bull Bear, they had a great warrior like Crazy Horse, their men got to be shirt wearers, grumble, grumble, grumble.

Well, some of these relatives intended to shed blood, No Water's blood, the blood of both his brothers, and the blood of anyone who defended the killer. They would have left already except that their Strange Man had asked them not to.

Crazy Horse came back from a bizarre and ugly land. He knew where he was. He remembered the healer's songs. He remembered No Water's hand and the gun. He remembered a hand on his arm, holding him back. He didn't remember the shot, but his face told him. He would never be able to move his face again. He wanted to cry out, "Let go of my arm! Let go of my arm!"

He also had moments that were nearly lucid. Then he wanted to tell everyone, "No trouble, no trouble. No more Lakota blood on the ground. Especially no punishment for Black Buffalo Woman, who has done no wrong."

Guilt washed him up like huge waves and dropped him into the troughs between. He had betrayed his vision. He had abandoned the difficult road for the comfortable one. The Powers had punished him hard. As he deserved.

Sometimes when the healer tended to him or his relatives visited, he said this much with his fingers—no trouble. They said they understood. Some of them acted resentful, but his uncle Spotted Crow came and said he understood the signs.

One day—it might have been the third or the tenth—Worm came. With his brothers Long Face, Spotted Crow, Bull Head, and Ashes. Maybe they had visited before, he wasn't sure.

"Someone held my arm," he signed to his father.

"Yes, the people know," Worm said. "I told Little Big Man never to hold you back again."

Crazy Horse rested a little. Over and over in his dreams he felt the hand on his arm. Little Big Man's hand, he knew now, a friend's hand. Terrible.

He made more signs. Worm said out loud, "You are right. I favor peace."

Crazy Horse signed that Black Buffalo Woman should go back to No Water if he promised not to punish her. She had done nothing wrong.

Worm said, "Yes, I will tell everyone."

Crazy Horse signed: "No one else hurt yet?"

"No," said Worm, "just a lot of nasty words. People are divided three ways. Your young men want to kill No Water. Black Twin, White Twin, and the rest of that family are ready to fight, expecting to fight. And we here, my brothers and I, we are working for peace. So are He Dog and Bad Heart Bull," two men with relatives on both sides, men of high reputation. "We will persuade them, maybe."

Crazy Horse rolled over to sleep and to ride the big waves of guilt and sorrow and loss. He had not signed to his father the worst. Hawk felt dead in his heart. Since he was shot, she had not stirred. His chest was just a scaffold for a corpse.

* * *

Worm stayed and kept watch. Looking at his son hurt his heart. The face was very swollen, like a melon. Just imagining the pain hurt. A ragged red wound, like a sword cut, slashed the upper lip. Powder burns rimmed the wound, like a kiss of black lips. A red crater opened in front of the ear and below it. Worm could hardly think his son would ever look normal again.

As Crazy Horse slept, he shook one elbow over and over and moaned, "Let go-o-o, let go-o-o."

This morning Crazy Horse was willing to try it. He mumbled aloud for the first time since he had been shot. It felt awful and sounded worse. "Where's Little Hawk?" he asked. His brother should have been here all along.

"Gone raiding," said Worm.

Crazy Horse remembered. Little Hawk hadn't wanted to go on the old-time war party against the Psatoka. He'd wanted to go along the front of the Shining Mountains, where white men were hunting for gold and stirring up trouble. Stirring it up deliberately, some said, when they knew the soldiers had given that country to the Lakota.

"News," he prompted. His voice sounded very nasal, and his tongue was thick as a frog in his mouth.

"No Water brought me three horses," said Worm evenly, "very good horses. I didn't send them back."

Crazy Horse would have nodded if he'd felt up to moving his head. This was a world of news. The No Water faction was willing to take the route of conciliation instead of killing, thus the offer. So were Worm and his brothers—thus the acceptance.

He saw his father studying his face. "Good," he said.

"Bad Heart Bull took the woman to No Water," Worm went on. It hurt Crazy Horse to hear that even now his father wouldn't speak the name of the woman he loved. "She was willing." He let that sit. "No Water gave the promise and accepted her."

So it was done. He felt a little quivery.

"Good," he said softly. He turned away from his father's eyes. He wanted to be alone.

He wondered why Hawk lay like a dead thing within him. *Yes, yes,* he thought bitterly, *it feels good to be healing when you're already dead.*

LOSSES

He couldn't get up for the gazing-at-the-sun-pole dance. His head reeled when he tried to stand. But when he could ride a little, the Long Face band followed the other villages from the big ceremony to the mouth of the Big Horn River, where they were hunting buffalo brazenly in the country of the Psatoka.

That was when Little Hawk's raiding party came in, without Little Hawk.

Crazy Horse knew the moment the two young warriors stepped into the lodge at night with mud streaked on their faces. Their story was simple enough. They were coming back from raiding in the Snake country, where the party had been too small to do much. At the southern end of the Shining Mountains some whites had fired on them without any reason, the miners who were always going in there looking for gold. Crazy Horse said nothing, but he thought, *In the country promised us forever by the peace paper.*

Since they were few, the Lakota broke and ran, laughing at the way the whites were wasting their bullets with long shots. Later the Lakota saw that Little Hawk wasn't with them. These two went back to see what had happened to him. The tracks showed that Little Hawk, always sure of his medicine, always reckless, had charged the whites alone. Now his body lay too close for the warriors even to bring it away. Little Hawk lay on the ground, where the scavengers would get him.

Crazy Horse felt his guts writhing. They wanted to pitch themselves out.

Worm listened patiently to the story and then got up from his fire and went out into the night. Crazy Horse thought how much the two of them were alike, always wanting to be alone with any strong feelings, not sharing, not grieving together or rejoicing together, but far apart, like icy stars. Crazy Horse hated that about himself, and about Worm.

When the warriors left, Crazy Horse sat quietly in front of the fire with Grandmother Plum. He thought. He remembered. He listened to a sad music in his heart.

He wondered what his grandmother was thinking. She had lost a grandchild. He looked at her face, red and brown, seamed, still as a rock. *Inyan,* he thought, *the oldest of creatures.*

He studied her face in the faint light from the embers. She did not look up at him, or acknowledge his gaze in any way, but simply sat, unmoving.

He edged close to her and took her old hand in his. It was bony, like a claw. Yet it was warm, and her blood, which was his blood, pumped through it.

He sat, heavy in his grief, but not quite so heavy, for he was holding her hand. In the motion of her arm he felt her chest rise and fall. Soon, perhaps with the single eye of his heart, he became aware of the life, the spirit, within her. He breathed it in, and breathed his spirit out to her.

Before long he sensed the dance of emotions within her. He felt them and their natures as the body feels sunshine and rain. Loss, now, because of Little Hawk. Loneliness, the loneliness of more than twenty-five winters of silence. These were the strong emotions, those that gave shape to the dance. And he sensed something deeper, further down, a rightness, a wellness. Was his grandmother healed in her way? Loneliness, though, that was the strongest.

Will she ever speak again? he wondered. *Will she talk to me?* He stared into the embers.

This thought returned him to the memory of the brother who would never speak again. Crazy Horse heard his voice, telling a joke. He could not hear the words, but he remembered that it was a joke, and he recognized the antic tone.

He could not smile. A tear ran down each cheek. He clasped his grandmother's hand a little tighter, and together they faced the dying center fire.

The next day he hunted buffalo. Slowly, carefully, like an old man, but he hunted. It felt awful, but it was his duty to his family. He told himself that duty and family were more important than they'd ever been.

Riding back to camp loaded with meat, he saw a rider on a friend's pony hurrying away, galloping. Then he came upon the friend. Surprised, he asked who was riding his horse. "No Water," was the answer. "He's afraid of you."

Crazy Horse was like a pony that breaks its stake rope. He cut the meat loose, let it fall onto the ground, and rode like a madman. He was dizzy, he was weak, he was about to topple off, but he rode. Yes, his father had accepted the gift ponies from No Water. Yes, they had sent Black Buffalo Woman back willingly. Yes, the peace was made, the rift smoothed over. Yes, Crazy Horse knew all this was for the best. He didn't care.

At this moment he loathed No Water. This man had cast a spell on the woman he loved. This man treated people like ponies, to be bought, sold, traded, trained, used, killed. Crazy Horse saw a gun coming up in his face, flinched at a flash in his eyes, and felt day after day of pain.

When No Water jumped the borrowed pony into the water and swam the flooding Elk River, Crazy Horse reeled. He caught the pony's mane and let himself down to the ground.

He watched his enemy flee.

The sense of wrongness, the wrongness of everything,

sat in his gut like a foulness. He hated No Water, and he hated himself.

"Now the Big Bellies have their excuse," said Worm.

Nevertheless, Crazy Horse would not go to the council. He knew he could ask to speak to the Big Bellies on his own behalf, and they would hear him out. He knew, if he did not, what the result of the council would be. And he would not go.

They met in a big lodge, circled around the fire, the chiefs of the Oglala, two young men who not long ago had started wearing the chief's blanket of their fathers, Young Man-Whose-Enemies of the Hunkpatila and Sword of the Oyukhpe, plus their fathers. Sitting Bear for the True Oglala and Bad Face for his band. They paid no attention to the fact that eight or ten young Bad Faces stood outside, clamoring for the Big Bellies to take the shirt signifying an owner of the people away from Crazy Horse.

Bad Face stated the case against the Hunkpatila warrior. He had chosen a course of action that disrupted the people gravely. (Black Buffalo Woman was not mentioned by name.) Since he had known it would cause division, he clearly had acted with flagrant disregard of the common welfare. And after the rift was sewn together by the efforts of many good men, Crazy Horse had done ill again. Though his father had accepted the horses from No Water, ending the matter, the Strange Man had chased No Water and tried to kill him.

No one needed to say that No Water and his family had gone south with their lodges, permanently away from the trouble.

One by one, the other chiefs said the same. No one mentioned Crazy Horse's heroism in war. That was not at issue here. The only question was, Had he lived up to his responsibility as a shirtman?

No one mentioned, either, that this council was taking place because the enemies of Crazy Horse had agitated for it. No one mentioned that neither the young warrior nor any of his relatives was here to speak for him, yet the opposition was well represented. It didn't matter. The chiefs were less concerned with justice to one man than with keeping the peace among the people.

Crazy Horse knew they were coming. He was waiting in Worm's lodge, the case holding the shirt in his lap. He didn't take it out and look at it. He pictured it lovingly, the two bighorn sheep skins, the dewclaws, the many pieces of hair, the multicolored quills representing Hawk. Since his spirit guide Hawk had died, he cared nothing about the shirt.

One of his mothers, Red Grass, slipped under the lodge cover. "They're on the way. Eight or ten Bad Faces are with them," she said. "Including Black Twin, White Twin, and Standing Bear," Woman Dress's brother. "Armed."

"They won't dare come into this lodge with their weapons," said Worm.

Crazy Horse smiled at his parents gently but kept silent. Since he had acted foolishly against No Water, he felt oddly meek, like a man who had been sick in spirit and was now convalescing.

A scratch on the door flap. Worm bade them enter. As Sitting Bear led the way in, Crazy Horse heard Young Man-Whose-Enemies tell the young Bad Faces, "We won't have any trouble here. And we aren't going to have any 'accidents' either." The young warriors made no attempt to come in.

The chiefs sat in a half-circle around the center fire, next to their host, Worm, honored guests. None of them would meet the eyes of Crazy Horse. They smoked a little. Finally Worm scraped the ashes out of his *canupa*. Then Crazy Horse rose and handed the case bearing the shirt to his war comrade and fellow shirtman, Young Man-Whose-Enemies.

Everyone sat in melancholy. No one had anything to say, except the one who seldom spoke. "I am not angry," he said. "I am at peace with what has been done. I regret the trouble I caused among the people."

Everyone sat in stupefied silence. Worm actually smiled—smiled lovingly at his son. After a while the Big Bellies filed out silently.

Young Man-Whose-Enemies walked last, behind the other Big Bellies, carrying the shirt.

"Our great man deserves the shirt," said Black Twin from behind the chiefs, his voice low and squeezed.

"That shirt should go to Red Cloud." Standing Bear's voice sounded belligerent. "As soon as he gets back from Washington."

The Big Bellies just walked on.

Young Man-Whose-Enemies knew perfectly well that the Bad Faces were sensitive because the Oglala had never entrusted Red Cloud with high leadership. In theory he himself wanted to heal whatever wounds were hurting the people. He almost walked on in silence, back to the council lodge. But he turned back, holding the shirt. He fixed Black Twin with his eyes angrily and said, "I have seen enough bad work tonight."

"Your man has been stripped of honor," said Standing Bear mockingly.

Young Man-Whose-Enemies thought a moment. Then he said, "No, a man can lose honor, but no one else can take it away from him."

He stared at the Bad Face until the man dropped his eyes and the young warriors backed away.

Worm looked at his son's face in the light of the center fire. Crazy Horse had filled an old *canupa*, a short one, the sign of a man with few honors. He sucked in the smoke from this *canupa* and blew it out several times, like a slow pulse.

Things were a little better now. The sounds had stopped from the robes where Worm's wives slept, the sounds of soft crying.

Crazy Horse blew out the smoke once more. Finally he

said, "It's all right, Father. I deserved it. I was false to my vision."

Worm regarded his son.

"I'm not angry, Father."

Worm touched his son gently on the arm. He would not say all that was on his mind now. He knew Crazy Horse wasn't angry. He knew his son felt he deserved humiliation.

Worm thought anger would have been better than what he envisioned in the landscape of his son's spirit now. A cold, bitter wind whistling through a parched desert of the heart.

PART **FOUR**

SOLDIERS
FALLING
INTO
CAMP

THE WINTER RED CLOUD'S
HORSES WERE TAKEN AWAY
(1876)

*The spirit of His Crazy Horse
sits in the center of the sundance
    circle
at a small fire.
With his knife he cuts a hank
from a braided strand of
    sweetgrass.
He lays the piece carefully
on the blaze
and watches its smoke
ascend to the sky,
ritually inviting the spirits
to attend him in this place.*

Worm nodded briefly at He Dog, meaning, "Go ahead and speak for us all."

He Dog started so softly that Crazy Horse couldn't understand the words. Rubbing the new scar below his nostril, he said so.

His friend He Dog spoke again, softly but not hesitantly: "We suggest that you marry. An excellent choice would be Black Shawl, of Big Road's band."

The Strange Man smiled a little at what he saw. His best friend among the Bad Face people, his father, and his father's brothers had put their heads together for the welfare of the two main divisions of the northern Oglala and his personal welfare. Without asking him, they had spoken to this woman and her family and gotten consent. She belonged to the other division, the Bad Faces. They were still trying to mend the hoop of the people.

Yes, probably it would be good for him, besides.

He drew on the short *canupa* he now smoked because he had lost high status. His family said that was unnecessary—it was no disgrace to be brought low by your enemies, they said—but he himself had made the choice. He was accustomed to losses.

He knew Black Shawl by sight. A good woman, to all appearances, of great dignity in her bearing, though no special beauty. It had never occurred to him to wonder why, but she had never married, and she looked older than twenty-five winters.

He looked around at these men, the ones who had acted more wisely than he in the affair of the woman he'd thrown himself away for. Their wisdom had saved the people another rupture. He looked around his lodge, a lodge kept by an old woman generally thought deaf and dumb, a woman who did not have many years stretching before her. He knew she would like a younger woman to do most of the work.

He thought of himself. He would like a woman companion. His brother was dead now. His brother by choice lived with his family in his own lodge. Yes, he would like a companion. He didn't think his heart could be healed, but it could be eased. If he were not feeling so much like a man just getting his health, he might have thought of this himself.

"I thank you for being so considerate of me." He let that sit. "Is the woman willing?"

Worm nodded yes.

"I want to say yes, I will share my life with her, such as it is. If she understands how I am. My medicine may make me a poor husband. I will give you an answer in the morning."

He took the old woman's elbow, and they turned together to the fire for its warmth, her shoulder pressing against his this time. He stared into the embers for a long while, until they began to seem to glow and darken, glow and darken, like the pulse of a person, or of the earth. "Unci," he murmured, "should I marry?"

He thought of what he had wanted from the people. Not position, no, or influence or wealth or even glory. Yet even while he shunned honors, he had wanted honor. He had wanted the people to see him in a certain way, a special way. "Even strangeness can be thought of as special," he said into the darkness.

He looked at his grandmother. He thought of what he should have been keeping his mind on. Seeking to be Rider in a pure way, without wondering how people thought of him. Listening for wisdom from Inyan. Attending to the guidance of Hawk. Walking his path simply, without wondering whether he cut an impressive figure in the walk. Pursuing a sacred way without asking whether people noticed, respected, admired.

"So much is vanity," he said.

He thought of all he had wanted with Black Buffalo Woman. Passion, romance, mystery. All that was gone now, and so was the desire for it. "Foolishness," he said.

He thought of marrying, having a companion. He thought of loving, not as a big feeling but as a continuous attention, and the deeds that came from that attention. He thought of sharing food, staying warm by the same fire, sleeping in the same robes, moving the lodge together, hunting and skinning and tanning and cooking, all together.

"Am I fit to be married?" he asked his grandmother.

He thought of life being born and dying, every day, a relentless churn of births and deaths, the biggest circle of all the circles on the earth. He felt within himself the lust of flesh to be born, the surge of its will to live on Maka, Earth. He felt within himself the desperate clutch of flesh to hold on, live longer, never let go.

Once he had seen a wheel on a white's wagon come off and squirt downhill, headed nowhere. It had finally rolled out of sight. Maybe it was still going somewhere, just rolling and rolling, pointlessly, the way he was living.

He started to speak, hesitated, then spoke. "Sometimes I'm . . ." The words he thought of were "weary of it."

He sighed instead of uttering the words. They weren't enough for the feeling.

"Should I marry, Unci?"

His grandmother just looked blankly into the darkness.

It was very late, but Red Grass said to come in. She knew his footstep.

"Don't get up," he said. The center fire was only a few coals. She came to him in the darkness and led him outside by the hand. "Mother," he said, "I have a request for you."

She squeezed the hand.

"In the morning will you go to Black Shawl in Big Road's camp? Tell her I want her very much."

His mother slipped her arms around him. It was hard for her to be near him these days without weeping, hard to see the powder-blackened scar under his nose, see the melancholy in his eyes.

"Tell her, though, that it will be marrying a man who

is half-dead. I have no joy in life anymore. I don't want to live. Maybe I will seek death."

He hesitated, and finally decided those words were enough.

"Ask her if she will have me, now that she knows."

Red Grass embraced him.

Red Grass saw that Black Shawl recognized her before she told her name and the name of her son. She sat with Black Shawl in front of the lodge and busied her hands with helping cut the prairie-turnips. She found it hard to start talking. She didn't know what to explain, whether to offer any comment.

"My son says to tell you he wants very much for you to be his wife."

Red Grass saw the tremulous . . . something . . . pass across Black Shawl's face. But the woman kept her head down, not showing her emotion nakedly to her future mother-in-law.

"He says, though, that you would be marrying a man who is half-dead. He says to tell you he has no joy in life anymore." Red Grass waited and watched. No, she didn't think she would put in a mother's explanation about her son's heart. If the woman couldn't surmise the truth, she would make a poor wife anyway. Red Grass studied her face.

The next words cost Red Grass a lot. "He says to tell you he doesn't want to live," she said, her voice gravelly. "Maybe he will seek death, he says."

Black Shawl looked up into Red Grass' face, and Red Grass cast her eyes down. She had been impolite, she realized, scrutinizing Black Shawl like that. But what she saw in those eyes in the moment Black Shawl raised them made her heart flutter with hope. It was pride and awareness and determination.

So the family of Crazy Horse didn't know, thought Black Shawl. Didn't know that she too knew what it was like to love someone and lose. She too knew what it was like to grieve. And unlike Crazy Horse, she knew how the spirit could survive anguish and emerge stronger.

She was excited to come into the Strange Man's life in this way, so much to help him with, so much to give.

She looked at Red Grass for a long moment and got up and went into the lodge. She reached into the shadow of the lodge skirt for a pair of moccasins, took them out, and set them in front of Red Grass. Red Grass would not be surprised that the beadwork was meticulous and beautiful. Black Shawl saw the surprise on her face when she saw what Black Shawl had pictured there: the lightning from Crazy Horse's vision.

"Tell him I have watched him from afar," she said. "I believe I know his heart, and I admire him. Tell him that if he wants me, I consider myself the luckiest woman among the Oglala."

BEGINNING AGAIN

She glanced at his face from time to time as he ate. She was sure of what was on his mind. As soon as he felt his full strength again, he would go to the Shining Mountains to get the bones of his brother. Any day now, she thought.

She imagined it over and over. He would carry a leather sack to put them in and a blanket to wrap the filled sack in on the scaffold. The bones would be picked clean by scavengers, dried by the wind, whitened by the sun. She saw her husband squatting beside them, washed with feelings.

Abruptly she banished the picture from her mind. It was hard sometimes to know him and look into his eyes and see the melancholy and the world-weariness and endure the way he kept it all to himself.

She filled his bowl again. He rubbed his scar and looked into the shadows of the lodge, his mind seeing . . . she had no idea what. She turned to fill Grandmother Plum's bowl, but it looked full. Sometimes she wondered if the old woman ever ate anything.

He was extraordinarily considerate, this husband of hers. He treated her with great respect. Often he was tender, especially in the robes. She knew that sometimes he took real solace from her, especially from the warmth of her body and the generosity of her robe loving. But his one true mate seemed to be his melancholy. She did not have to compete with Black Buffalo Woman but with despair. She saw, she was not afraid, she wanted them to share whatever came. She didn't think he would let her, not fully.

Sometimes she thought what would change everything would be their son. A son would draw him out of the recesses where he lived. He would want to teach a son everything he knew. Then, even if they had to struggle as a family, because the buffalo were getting few or because the white men wouldn't leave them alone, that would be grand. The shirt, the other woman, the humiliations, the loneliness—none of them would matter. Their struggle would bind them.

She would give him a son. Then, surely . . .

She sat beside him and ate, looking at him surreptitiously. She had thought to make a marriage of admiration, respect, and affection. She hadn't expected to feel such a gush when he held her, when he told stories, when they walked together. Nor had she expected to feel so frustrated when he hid in the corners of his mind.

He put his bowl down empty. When she reached to pick it up, he covered her hand with his. He looked into her eyes and smiled. When he smiled, he was beautiful. He said, "Will you come to the Shining Mountains with me?"

He had painted his face and his pony. He had left his sandy hair unbraided, flowing below his waist. He was going into a fight, and he wanted the people to know it. Your Strange Man is going into a fight, and taking his wife.

He looked at Black Shawl tying belongings onto a pack mule behind him, her fingers fumbling. He smiled at her with his eyes only. She would be fine. He looked at the pony he was leading, one of Little Hawk's warhorses, bearing an empty rawhide sack and a handsome blanket, red, a warrior's color. The back of that pony still looked empty to him. He hoped he would feel his brother along, sooner or later.

The warriors stood well off, some of them affecting not to notice. They didn't yet know how to treat him, a stranger man than ever, first honored above all, now humiliated before all. Idiots, Black Shawl had called them angrily, but they weren't. Just men, just uncertain. *I will rise from my failures,* he said in his mind. *I will trust my vision and thus rise from my failures.*

The words felt empty to him. So far. Since No Water had shot him, he still had not felt Hawk move in his breast. He felt her presence, but she seemed numbed. That was how close No Water had come to killing him.

He saw Black Shawl rise into her woman's saddle. He knew she didn't understand why he was remote much of the time. She didn't understand what he had lost. Hawk, his animal spirit, his lifetime companion, closer than his brother, than his father, than his brother by choice, even than his blood mother. He wondered whether he would ever feel Hawk again. Bleakness. Emptiness beyond emptiness.

At least Black Shawl would understand when he put his vision before everything.

The women stood closer and made keening sounds for his lost brother.

He touched his pony with his heel. He felt chilled by the keening sounds. He understood the sentiment, but . . .

Some woman, he didn't know who, began to call his name as was done starting a strong-heart song. Other women joined in—"Crazy Horse, Crazy Horse." Today, for a reason he didn't know, this chant warmed his heart a little. *Women understand better than men,* he thought.

They lifted up the song, one voice leading, the other repeating:

> *"A-i-i-i! A-i-i-i!*
> *A warrior rides out,*
> *a warrior, strong.*
> *Others sit in the lodges and are jealous.*
> *Others sit in the lodges and whisper jealously.*
> *A warrior rides out, strong.*
> *A-i-i-i! A-i-i-i!"*

He made no acknowledgment. He was surprised, though, how much the song touched him. He paid attention to his heart. No, he didn't sense Hawk stirring, not yet. But she didn't feel utterly dead. Maybe his heart was a place where Hawk would spread her wings again one day.

They found Little Hawk's bones where his comrades said he had fallen. Crazy Horse sat down, Black Shawl next to him. He made himself look at the bones directly. He permitted himself no aversion of eyes, or of attention, or of feeling.

His brother had been so different from him. Little Hawk was an impulsive fellow, full of fun, not given to weighty thoughts or worries about the future. When his spirits were high, he played or hunted or found a woman or went out to fight. It was simple for him, and he always brimmed with confidence. Sometimes Hump or Crazy Horse, like others, urged him to be more cautious, but that wasn't Little Hawk's way. He never saw difficulties, only possibilities. He was a fine warrior and would have become a great war leader.

Now his easy courage had killed him.

Crazy Horse lost himself for a while. Later he realized he'd been seeing pictures of Little Hawk at different times. The little boy who'd slip into his brother's robes sometimes for warmth. The kid who'd steal his brother's favorite piece of meat and get really angry if Curly snatched it back. The boy who'd get frustrated trying to make an arrow shaft straight. The youngster who couldn't find the patience to watch an elk a quarter-day.

Pictures, sounds, feelings: His brother's arm around his shoulder. The funny quack of his laughter. His eyes rolling in mockery. The comical way he bragged and told every detail about the first woman he had. When they wrestled, the contagion of his excitement and the ferocity of his effort. The way he sneaked blueberries while their mothers were pounding them for pemmican and got his hands slapped and stuck out his tongue merrily and stole more and ran off.

Finally Crazy Horse put the bones into the sack, tied the sack on his brother's fine warhorse, and covered it with the red blanket. They rode back to the lodge like a procession.

It was not over.

He made it as easy for Black Shawl as he could. They moved the lodge constantly so no one would find it. He came back every night. He ate and slept with her, even if he wasn't really there in his mind. All day long, every day, he hunted the Big Horners, as they called themselves, the white miners who came into the Shining Mountains, which they called the Bighorns. They came regardless of the peace paper. He killed them regardless of whether they had hurt his brother. Implacably, silently, he killed them.

He didn't know how many he would have to kill. When the rage in his heart eased, when Hawk came back to life, he would quit.

He found them alone and in pairs, scooping up the creek water with their pans and hammering at rock. He used arrows when he could, to avoid warning their companions, so he could kill them, too. He littered the mountains with bodies like a man throwing away corn husks.

Whether he killed with arrow, bullet, spear, or knife, he drove an additional arrow through the body and into the earth beneath, the earth of his people and not theirs. He left them unscalped. The whites might not know who had punished the Big Horners, but the Lakota would know.

After about one moon he and Black Shawl went back to camp. Crazy Horse said nothing about what he had done, and the people danced no victory. He held a dance to give away Little Hawk's horses. His uncle Long Face ceremonially took a new name. Originally known as Little Hawk, he had given that name to his nephew. Now, in honor of the dead youth, he would call himself Little Hawk again.

All this changed the people in one way. They saw that whatever had happened to Crazy Horse as a leader of the people, his war medicine was strong. They wanted to follow him into some fights.

Crazy Horse's spirit did not lift. His war medicine was only his skill, because he couldn't sense Hawk living in his heart. Days sometimes seemed as black as nights. Black Shawl kept the nights from being truly intolerable.

Before long Black Shawl told him she was making life within her.

He held her and murmured into her ear how happy he was. They held each other in their robes, awake and occasionally talking, for half the night. They talked about their coming son, about his being born near the time of the sun dance, an auspicious time, about who they would choose to name him. Crazy Horse told Black Shawl that he would be as glad for a daughter as a son, though they both knew that wasn't quite true. They did not make love, of course, because a decent Lakota man didn't come to his wife when she was growing life within her or when she was giving suck.

After Black Shawl fell asleep next to him, dark thoughts seeped into his mind. Was he fit to be a father? He had made plenty of mistakes. His son would bear the burden of the loss of the shirt. Was it right to bring a Lakota child into a world where Lakota had no way to live? Or merely selfish? The shadow of Black Buffalo Woman's complaint flitted across his mind. Yes, he would not live long enough to raise his son to manhood.

By long habit he fell still within himself—no words or thoughts—and waited. Waited for Hawk.

He felt a hot flush of shame. He didn't have his companion, his guide, anymore. And if he had lost that gift, he was truly unfit to be a father.

DESOLATION

"Brother," said Hump, "let's go fight the Snakes."

Crazy Horse smiled at his *hunka,* feeling shy and pleased. So much was hidden in the simple words: "Your spirits are sour—let's do something that's fun." Or, "You've been sitting around too much—you need some action." Or, "Stop moping and do something." Or, "Sure, a lot has happened, but you've got your strength back—let's go." Or, "I've missed you—let's do something."

In fact, Hump surely had in mind a pack-mule load of other things he meant and didn't have to say. When Red Cloud got back from Washington a moon ago, he said everyone should go onto a reservation and this Shifting Sands River country, which the whites called Powder River country, wasn't in it. This so outraged the young men that one of them dropped his breechcloth in Red Cloud's face, right in council. Still, some people went in to get presents—they were hungry and needed rations, even bad white-man food, and needed powder. Later the whites claimed that Red Cloud had promised them an agency far to the north of the Holy Road, right in the heart of Lakota country. But no one would stand for this.

So Hump was saying, "Let's forget all this political foolishness and do what warriors do: fight."

Crazy Horse thought so, too.

Something nibbled at his mind that Hump didn't know. Maybe Hawk would come fight with him.

The Wind River country was miserable. The sky crowded in low and drizzled on them for several days. The ground froze at night, and during the day it turned into a greasy mess. The horses slipped around in it, or it stuck to their hooves and they stumbled. If a man so much as dismounted to make water, he felt like he was skating on river ice and was lucky not to sit down in his own urine.

The wolves pushed ahead and came back with report of a huge camp of Snakes in a country of clay soil, at least as bad as this. The Snakes had repeating rifles, plenty of them.

Some of the men muttered. Their bowstrings were soaked. The powder for the only three guns was wet just from the rain sitting on the outside of their horns. Everyone's spirits were soggy.

Hump said flatly, "We're going on."

Crazy Horse wondered why his *hunka* was so determined about this raid that had started out as a lark. But he would say nothing to disagree with his *hunka* in front of the others.

The two leaders split their men and approached the Snakes from far left and right. Soon the horses were slipping and sliding and their hooves were gobbed with clay. They would be worthless in a fight. Crazy Horse sent his wife's younger brother, Red Feather, to tell Hump this.

Hump came back riding fast to answer in person, maybe meaning the way he rode as an answer. He glared at Crazy Horse. "We turned back here once before." Crazy Horse remembered. They had come out for Snake horses and gone back empty-handed. Afterward Hump thought the people were laughing at them.

"I came to fight," said Hump. "You go on home. I'm going to fight."

Crazy Horse couldn't remember when either of them had spoken so sharply to the other. He wasn't going anywhere, of course, not if Hump needed him. *"Hoye,"* he said, "let's fight. There are worse things than getting whipped." He needed Hawk now, but he felt alone.

It went badly. Before long the Oglala were quirting their horses to get away. Hump and Crazy Horse took turns charging back toward the pursuing Snakes with their rifles, to keep the enemy slowed down. Crazy Horse was half-sick with worry. He didn't feel Hawk at all. And the horses were skating all over the place. If either man ended up dismounted, he was dead.

Hump hollered out in alarm. His pony limped hard and went down, probably shot in the leg.

The Snakes were hard upon him.

Crazy Horse dismounted and tried to keep them off. But the Snakes were eager now, blood in their nostrils. After a few moments he couldn't even see Hump among the ponies' legs and heads and rumps, and the arms lifting spears and clubs.

Rage spewed up.

Crazy Horse mounted and charged, not like his old charges, protected by Rider, but a ride of mere fury. Clumsy, too, his pony slipping and sliding.

He got close enough to see Hump on the ground, but the fire drove him off. Then he turned back hard, the pony like a clown slipping and sliding around while his *hunka* died. He whipped the pony furiously.

Suddenly Red Feather had hold of his reins. "Isn't one enough?" shouted the young warrior. Meaning one good man dead. "If we don't go now, the others will have to come for us." Meaning the other warriors would die, too, trying to get bodies away.

So Crazy Horse let his pony be pulled the wrong direction and keep going all night. Snow fell on him.

His heart lay still under cold grief and an icy guilt. He kept thinking that he and his *hunka* had never spoken to each other roughly until that. This was a miserable way to die, with a sour spirit. And it was all his fault. When No

Water shot him, he lost Hawk. When he lost Hawk, he killed Buffalo Hump.

After a few days Crazy Horse and Red Feather went back for Hump's body. For some reason, only the skull and a few bones were left to put on a scaffold. Crazy Horse held the skull in his hands. His head ran dizzy, but he refused to let himself remember. Not now, not yet. He wasn't angry. He was desolate, desolate, desolate.

LULLABY

"Go to the river and bathe," said Worm in a kindly way. Crazy Horse knew what his father meant: "Get some soapweed, wash yourself, and pray—purify yourself ceremonially in the flowing water of Mother Earth. Your child is being born."

He could barely keep his mind on what he was doing. His mind was in the birthing lodge, with Black Shawl. He stood thigh-deep in the turbulent runoff and scarcely noticed the cold. He washed himself carefully, especially his genitals, trying to devote every motion to Wakan Tanka and failing. When he prayed aloud, he concentrated better: He asked for blessings on his new child and on his wife, health for them both.

"Let's smoke," said Worm.

They smoked Crazy Horse's short *canupa* without talking, maybe for a day, maybe for a moment.

Crazy Horse pictured what was going on in the birthing lodge. Two women relatives chosen for their good temperaments were there to help. Black Shawl would be on her knees in front of two tall crossed sticks, stretched as high as she could get and holding on. One woman would be in front of the mother to receive the child, the other behind, maybe with her legs against the small of Black Shawl's back. They would make her swallow warm root water to ease the passage. If she hurt terribly, one of the women would tickle her throat with a magpie feather to make her gag and spew the pain out.

When the child came, the woman in front would wipe its mouth out and start the breathing. In this caring act she would give the child her temperament and character, so they had chosen a good woman for that task. Then she would tie and cut the cord, which would fall off in four days, and give Black Shawl a taste of the afterbirth, so she would have many children.

The second woman would wash and wipe the baby with the inner bark of the chokecherry soaked in water. As she washed, she would tell the child how she had lived her life well and advise the baby to follow that example. Then she would rub the baby with a mixture of fat and red earth. Finally she would put powdered buffalo chips into a blanket to absorb the baby's wetting, wrap the child well, and give Crazy Horse's son to the mother.

Maybe Black Shawl would hold their son then, and maybe sing him a lullaby.

> *"Your father makes meat,*
> *so you make sleep."*

Then, finally, she would come out of the birthing lodge and show him their son.

Finally.

"Let's take a sweat," said Worm with a hint of smile. "Suck the juices out of you and calm you down."

They sweated all through the afternoon. At mealtime they found a little soup at Worm's lodge. Worm started making small talk of this and that.

After a while, he said, "Did you hear Black Buffalo Woman has borne a child?"

"Yes," said the son, naming what his father was afraid to say, "a sandy-haired child."

"Did you hear No Water has a new wife and Black Buffalo Woman lives in a small lodge by herself?"

"I heard," he said definitely, eyeing his father. Did the

man think he was going to claim the child? Or the woman? And cleave the people in two again?

Worm passed on to other things. "They moved the agency to Horse Creek."

Crazy Horse snorted and murmured, "Yes." A good place for it, Horse Creek, where the first lying peace paper had been signed twenty winters ago.

"Still, the people are hungry."

Not only hungry, but coming to the wild camps to join in the hunts, thought Crazy Horse. The wild Oglala had no more to eat than the agency Lakota—there were not enough buffalo.

"They say that if the white men will give them powder, the loaf-around-the-forts will let them move the agency to the White Earth River," said Worm. Far into Lakota country, where the whites had promised they'd never go.

Crazy Horse resisted flashing his father a look of exasperation. Did the man think he wanted to talk about such things while his son was being born?

When, oh, when would his son be born?

"Let's sweat again," he said.

It would take a long time to get the fire going and the rocks hot, until past dark, even here in the longest days of the year. He was glad for something to do.

He was sound asleep in his own robes when he felt Black Shawl's feet padding beside him. She slipped in and touched his side. "Black Shawl?" he said.

"We have a daughter," she said.

He took the warm little bundle from her. *"Hau!"* he said softly. "She will be a great mother of the people."

Black Shawl started building up the fire. She knew he was a little disappointed. Every man wanted a son to teach the ways of a warrior, this man especially. But this man had a big spirit—he didn't know how big—and would love his daughter hugely.

The flames were bright now. He brought the bundle close to the fire. Black Shawl watched his eyes devouring the tiny face of his daughter. She was profoundly satisfied.

He handed her back to Black Shawl and walked on his knees toward Grandmother Plum's robes. After a moment her face materialized out of the darkness. His hand was under her arm. She put her ancient face above the face in the bundle—or did he move her there? The two faces mirrored each other, both wrinkled, both wizened, both looking timeless and wise and ignorant and implacable and blank as rock. Both unseeing, probably. Both silent, inarticulate. Great-grandmother and great-granddaughter.

Black Shawl was sure she saw a gleam of understanding in Plum's eye. Well, almost sure.

He held the old woman. His wife squatted close with the child, her knee against his. They were all together.

His eyes went from Black Shawl to Grandmother Plum to the child and back, over and over. Finally, he said, "When this child is grown, everyone will stand in wonder at her sacred ways. We will call her by the name They-Are-Afraid-of-Her."

Suddenly Plum raised a hand, stuck out a finger, touched the infant cheek.

Suddenly Crazy Horse heard it. Or did he? Black Shawl swiveled her head toward his immediately. Yes, he heard it.

Grandmother Plum was humming. Humming an old, old lullaby to the child. He and Black Shawl grinned at each other.

He let his mind sink into the rocking, wavelike motion of the music. Yes, an old lullaby.

He laughed silently. It bubbled out of him, soundless as a spring.

He put one arm around his grandmother and the other around his wife and child.

The music rocked them gently.

When they were all asleep, he slipped out. He told himself he wanted to see Morning Star, the one that promises more light to those who desire it, and to offer a prayer of thanksgiving for his new daughter.

He gave all his attention to Morning Star, sending the words across the dark sky, "My relative." He did say a prayer of thanksgiving, silently, not wanting to disturb something in himself.

Then he knew why he wanted to be peaceful, undisturbed. Hawk was stirring inside him. Perhaps not fully alive, but awakening.

He just sat and noticed Hawk. There, always there. There forever.

The feeling gushed up in him: *Thank you, my daughter*.

PAHA SAPA

In early summer of the Winter Many Pani Were Killed, the wild Titunwan Lakota gathered for a great council at Bear Butte. The people seldom came together for a big talk. Crazy Horse remembered the last one, sixteen winters earlier, after the Wasp, Harney, hit Little Thunder's village on the Blue Water and killed women and children.

Then Crazy Horse had been a youth, and in a private way that council had been one of the turning points of life. When he had seen that the people needed whatever power he had to give, he'd told his father his vision. That was how he had started discovering his powers.

Now he was a leader. True, he'd been disgraced by the Big Bellies. But they were mostly at the agencies now, and the young men were following Crazy Horse, they and all the families that wanted to stay out and live the old way. He was a leader by default. By choice, however, and according to his custom, he would not speak in council.

How different things were now. He stopped his pony and looked across the valley at Bear Butte. It never changed. The sacred mountain of the people, the peak most chosen for seeking visions, that would never change. Only Inyan endures.

The people in the camp were different, though. He was different. He looked sideways at his wife and pictured grandmother and child on the pony drag behind. Yes, he was different, a man with a family.

The biggest difference in the Lakota was simply numbers. Sixteen winters ago he had seen the lodges stretching in every direction and felt certain that the Lakota would whip the whites if they only stuck together.

Today his band was the last to come in, and he saw maybe one lodge for every ten back then.

Much else had changed for the worse. Fifteen or twenty winters ago the buffalo seemed few sometimes, but all the Lakota lived where they wanted, following the herds. Now most of them lived on agencies. That was the real result of the war they'd fought for Shifting Sands River country and the peace paper signed by Red Cloud, who was no chief at all, and Spotted Tail, who was the whites' creature. But even Man-Whose-Enemies-Are-Afraid-of-His-Horses, head of Crazy Horse's band and a man respected by everyone, had signed the peace paper. And now his son, Young Man-Whose-Enemies, was a peace chief.

However it had happened, only a few Oglala and Sicangu still roamed free, plus some of the Muddy Water River people, like Sitting Bull's, come west. They lived near their Oglala relatives now because the buffalo were completely gone from the land of the Muddy Water River.

Crazy Horse remembered the song.

"In the half of the sky
where the sun lives
clouds are gathering.
In the half of the sky
where the sun lives
dark clouds are gathering.

In the half of the sky
where the sun lives
dark clouds are gathering,
and white people storm upon us."

He resisted looking at his family. He wondered whether he would be able to feed them this winter. He was one of the most admired hunters and warriors of his people. He should have abundance, so that he could help the poor of his people. If the most able wondered about feeding their families, what was it like for others?

White people storm upon us.

He told himself for the thousandth time to spend his life on matters of the spirit, living forth the power of his medicine in war, listening for whatever Inyan might say, following the guidance of Hawk. Then Maka, Earth, and the Powers would take care of him.

That was getting hard to believe. He thought maybe something was changing, something fundamental and permanent. He thought of the four ages of life on this earth, which are also the four ages of the life of a single man—rock, bow, fire, and *canupa*. He remembered the buffalo that stands at the west, holding back the waters that will flood the world and end this age of mortal life on earth. Even when he was a youth, the grandfathers of the tribe had taught that the buffalo was almost bald now and stood on only one leg, holding back the waters of the final destruction. He wondered.

Often now he sat alone and sang to Inyan. Often he sweated for half a night, preparing himself for communication. Sometimes he sought a vision again, enacted the great rite *hanbleceyapi*, asking the Powers to give him insight.

Nothing yet from Inyan except the pulse of the earth. Horn Chips had told Crazy Horse that they seldom talked, only when a man was ready, perhaps beyond his warring years. Crazy Horse felt that he would never be beyond those years. When he was fighting, he felt himself, and he felt Hawk with him. Maybe the beat of the earth was the single wisdom of Inyan. Yet he needed their wisdom. He didn't see how he or his family or his people could live much longer.

In council at this place, at least, no one spoke aloud for moving to the agencies. Little Big Man said they had gone in to see how the agency people were doing and maybe get some food for themselves. The good part was that the agent gave out rations every five days. The bad part was not just the dependence—the flour was wormy and the salt pork moldy, unfit for anyone but white people to eat.

Worse, there was never enough to go around. Each chief competed with the others to act most like a white's lackey, so his people would get the most food. The people knew that everyone was stealing their rations, not only the agents but the freighters and the first sellers and every other handler along the way. Some of the whites said that if you could get to be an Indian agent for four or five winters, you could make yourself rich.

So everyone had the same thought: *Out here we go hungry sometimes. There we would beg, humiliate ourselves, get robbed, and then starve.*

Now the leading men fell into disagreement. Some said the buffalo had disappeared because they were killed or driven off by the white men. Others said the people had abandoned the power that brought the buffalo to them. "If we go back to doing as White Buffalo Cow Woman taught us," some said, "the buffalo will come back."

Crazy Horse didn't know who was right. He agreed with the man who said, "We cannot know everything or control everything. Let us do what is right, stay on the side of the spirits, and see what happens."

Drum-on-His-Back told a story that was funny and poignant and bitter all at once. The newspapers he read were always talking about the white people's great man, Abraham Lincoln. The people had heard of this man. The whites were so foolish they split in half and killed each other by the thousands for four winters, *a-i-i-i,* split worse than any Indians ever were. At the end they killed their own leader, this Lincoln. Well, one of the newspapers said that Lincoln had defined an Indian reservation as "where Indians live surrounded by thieves."

Everybody laughed at that.

That evening Crazy Horse smoked his short *canupa* in front of his lodge with Little Big Man. Crazy Horse liked to be with this Bad Face, who was impetuous and lively and reckless and passionate, all like his brother, whose name Crazy Horse would never speak again. In the relaxation of friendship, Crazy Horse often said what he didn't want to say in council. When the younger warrior spoke in council, people knew that he was often giving voice to the thoughts of their Strange Man.

"It's not just that we're hungry either way, here in our hunting grounds or there at the agency," said Crazy Horse. "It's not even mostly the whiskey. Here we're alive. There they're dead. Here we will remember our power, and it will be enough or not. Here we'll struggle, and we'll thrive or not. We will feel pain, and happiness, too, and we'll live or not."

He puffed and watched the smoke rise toward the sky. "There they are living death, not just death from whiskey or boredom or sitting around. Spiritual death. They die from losing connections to the spirits." He actually raised his voice a little. "Worse than dead—numb."

The cold moons were another hungry time, for the wild tribes and the agency bands. Part of the whites' story was that the freighters couldn't get their wagons through to the agencies from the railroad—the snow was too deep. "Funny," said the Lakota, "they're getting wagons through to the Montana gold camps. Maybe they just need a good reason."

Red Cloud got so angry about it that he was muttering about another big Lakota war when the grass turned green. Some of his warriors said, *"Hoye!"* Others said he was just bargaining, using the threat to negotiate more rewards for his band. The only way he could be a big man now, they said, was by outmaneuvering Young Man-Whose-Enemies, Spotted Tail, and the other peace chiefs for a bigger share of the scraps the white man threw out.

The people of Crazy Horse—everyone now called that village Crazy Horse's band—were hungry, like everyone else. Something worse was worrying the Strange Man. They-Are-Afraid-of-Her had the coughing sickness. Sometimes she seemed all right, but sometimes she coughed all night in her robes and seemed weak and pale. Watching her cough gave him still, silent, black rages.

One night in the dead of winter, a Mniconjou climbed the wall at the White Earth River agency and killed the agent's nephew. No one knew what was between them, but the peace chiefs saw this would mean big trouble. Sure enough, the whites used it as an excuse to do what they had promised never to do—send soldiers to the agency.

When they heard the news, Crazy Horse, He Dog, and Little Big Man just sucked on their *canupa* regretfully. Now soldiers were stationed right at the foot of Paha Sapa. Those hills were the first hunting grounds of the people and where many, many Lakota went to see beyond and to raise their dead on scaffolds.

Worse, this had divided the people again. United, the agency warriors could have driven the soldiers off. Instead the peace Indians and wild Indians fought each other, and the wild bands ran back to the northern hunting grounds.

Now the soldiers were in the middle of Lakota country. Once they got there, or anywhere, when had they ever left?

Crazy Horse rode out alone to Medicine Lake, where the leaders of his people had often received visions. He purified himself in the sweat lodge. He fasted and thirsted and cried to see beyond.

Drum-on-His-Back had told Crazy Horse a funny story

about the whites and the powers. They were always talking the One Big Spirit, and you never knew exactly what they meant. They had a strange attitude about this Spirit—they thought they knew all about Him, and no one else knew anything. As if no man who wasn't white had ever put himself in harmony with Power and lived from the center of that harmony. Anyway, the whites prayed to this Spirit to be on their side. If they had a fight, for instance, they would pray to the Spirit to help them win, to align Himself with them.

Drum-on-His-Back and Crazy Horse had never heard anything like it. Instead of putting themselves on the side of the great powers, the whites asked the powers to be on their side. Odd people, you could never understand them.

Crazy Horse listened to the beat of life upon the earth. He watched the doings of all his relatives, from the rooted and four-legged people to the star people. He sat at the center of the circle of the universe and felt its power within himself. And at the end of three days, he saw nothing new. Yes, he must act as a human being should act. Yes, the people must walk the good, red road, letting Power flow through them. No, it would not save any lives.

When the warm wind came and took the snow off the plains, word came from the Muddy Water River agencies that Custer, the yellow-haired killer of women and children at the Washita, was coming to the sacred Paha Sapa. He was coming with a thousand soldiers, big wagons like travelers used on the Holy Road, and plenty of wagon guns.

Little Big Man told Crazy Horse this story in a tone of outrage. "They call us friendlies and hostiles," he said, "the Lakota who live at the agencies and the ones who follow the old way. Now maybe they will find out that we are all hostiles."

Crazy Horse smiled a bitter smile, thinking maybe for once his fiery young friend was right. Even the agency chiefs . . .

At a big council of the headmen of the wild camps, the

whole story came out. It seemed that the whites were hungry, too, back in all their towns. They needed money, lots of money. So Custer was going to look for gold in Paha Sapa and tell everyone, and then the whites would come to the Lakota and beg to buy the Hills. The peace paper said that Paha Sapa belonged to the Lakota as long as the grass grew and water flowed. Or until three out of every four grown Lakota men signed a selling paper.

"Even the cowards on the agencies won't give them three out of four," said He Dog.

"So they will steal what they want," said Little Big Man. Then, with a sardonic laugh, "Or they will kill the three and let the fourth sign."

The Strange Man sat quiet and let his friend speak for him.

Could they keep Custer out?

The headmen shook their heads. Everyone was willing, but the men had only one or two shells each. Every soldier would be carrying dozens of shells, with more in the wagons, plus the wagon guns. Against that many bullets you needed more than a big heart.

Maybe they could get enough shells from their relatives at the agencies, they said. Maybe the agency warriors would come to fight against this killer of women and children. Maybe even Red Cloud would stop maneuvering for more pay and say no.

No one knew. Right now they could do nothing against Custer.

The wolves had a worse story to tell. Ahead of Custer lots of white men with pans and shovels were already on the way. Hundreds of them, in small groups, moving fast and going wherever they wanted, not caring a bit that the land was promised to the Lakota.

These miners were the real problem, everyone knew. What did it matter if the Lakota refused to sell the Hills and the white government relented? If thousands of miners streamed in, what could you do? A man can't catch every drop of rain in a cup. Soon the miners would be cutting big holes in the ground and the deer and elk would be gone from the Hills. Someone said a man seeking a vision would have to find a place to stand among the white people's droppings.

The two friends laughed with their eyes and bit their tongues. Crazy Horse jerked his head sideways, and they left the council. When friends understand each other, they don't have to say much. Little Big Man could have said the words for Crazy Horse: "This council isn't going to lead to anything. Councils usually don't. Besides, a warrior does not sit and calculate the odds, or figure how to make a show and dishearten the enemy. A warrior fights. That is his honor."

What Crazy Horse actually said was, "Let's go discourage some miners."

In the Moon When All Things Ripen, messengers came from the white men or from Red Cloud, which some of the people said was the same thing.

Some of the young Mniconjou went out to meet the messengers ahead of Crazy Horse, and he heard them egging each other on. "Let's count coup on them," one young man said, and two or three yelled, *"Hoye!"*

"Lash them with bowstrings," said someone, and Crazy Horse hurried to the front. Some wild young Lakota had deliberately insulted some Sahiyela leaders by acting like this, treating them like enemies.

Crazy Horse was glad to see Big Road and Touch-the-Sky hurrying out, too. His uncle Touch-the-Sky had brought his Mniconjou to the Crazy Horse camp recently, wanting to live free. They greeted their agency relatives and led them to the big council lodge. The three headmen understood that whatever happened, Lakota must not fight Lakota.

Crazy Horse was pleased with his people. The loaf-around-the-forts laid presents out on the ground. No one except the headmen touched them, and the headmen took only *cansasa*—they called it "tobacco" now—to show a willingness to talk.

When amenities had been exchanged and it was time, the loafers said they had come to get Crazy Horse and the other headmen to come to Red Cloud Agency to talk about the sale of Paha Sapa.

The outcry shook the lodge hides. Some of the young men shouted, "Traitors!" One young warrior yelled that they would talk with bullets, not words.

It was all impolite, but Crazy Horse kept his face neutral and rebuffed no one. Out of turn or not, his young men were right. He felt proud of them.

The loafers could be impolite, too. "Fools!" said one. "Don't you see Paha Sapa is already lost? The whites took it—stole it!"

"We may as well get something for it!" snapped another.

Their voices were not wise and patient and thoughtful, as council voices should be, but roiled and contemptuous.

Crazy Horse raised a hand slightly. He looked into the eyes of the loafers, one by one. He knew what they expected. They thought they would hear from Big Road or Black Twin or Touch-the-Sky or Little Big Man, but not Crazy Horse. The Strange Man spoke only in privacy, and let others express his thoughts in public.

So maybe his words were worth something. Maybe because he had never spoken in council, he could make his words remembered. He looked at their eyes, pair by pair, slowly, letting them see that the words were welling up in him.

Then, quietly, almost inaudibly, he said to them, "A man does not sell the earth the people walk on."

That was all.

No one else had anything to say.

They looked at each other. One by one and two by two, they got up and left.

After a while Crazy Horse was sitting there alone.

He was pondering a fact: Lakota people had come to him with a suggestion to sell Paha Sapa.

THEY-ARE-AFRAID-OF-HER

The first thing he saw was dried blood on the legs of Stick and her sisters. They were not even his relatives, but he knew then. And blood on their arms, and their hair cut above the shoulders. Yes, he knew.

They-Are-Afraid-of-Her.

Worm and Little Hawk came out to take his lead rope and his weapons and lead him to the lodge. As he walked behind them, his feet made hollow thumps on the earth.

Black Shawl was sitting on their robes hugging herself, swaying, moaning, her clothes torn, and her face smeared with mud.

Yes, They-Are-Afraid-of-Her, three winters old, was dead.

Her cradle board was gone. The place where they had spread her robes was empty.

"How long?" he mumbled.

"Four days," said Worm.

So while he was out killing miners, his daughter had died. He was stunned that he hadn't known, hadn't felt the change in the air itself.

Crazy Horse looked at Worm and Little Hawk and saw that Worm's lips moved, but he could not make out the words. He felt he was somewhere very odd, maybe underwater, and they were far away.

Crazy Horse knelt beside Black Shawl and put an arm around her waist. As far as Worm could tell, she did not respond.

Amazingly, the old woman did respond. Grandmother Plum got up off her robes and came and sat on the other side of Black Shawl and held her hand. *A-i-i-i.* Crazy Horse put his hand on both of theirs. He did not act as though Grandmother Plum had done anything unusual. Worm glanced at his brother, Little Hawk. His eyes were wide.

"Be strong, Son," murmured Worm. Little Hawk said the same words.

"It was the coughing sickness," said Worm.

Crazy Horse sat there unaware. He looked downward into nothingness, as though into a lake infinitely deep, and he was sinking slowly in the dark water, slowly, inexorably sinking, and the water was blacker every moment.

A quarter-day or several days later—he didn't know how long he, his wife, and his grandmother sat with their arms around each other—his father came in bringing food and Crazy Horse asked, "Where is she?"

Worm gave no emotional reaction. He simply told his son how to find the scaffold.

He knew it was the right one from a distance. He saw her red blanket. From closer he saw the cradle board Black Shawl's sister had beaded, hanging from one of the poles. He imagined the toys they would have folded into the blanket with her small form, a rattle, a rawhide doll.

He tied his pony to a sapling, pulled himself onto the scaffold, and wrapped his arms around the lump in the blanket. "It is my fault," he said. "I was not meant to have children." He sank into oblivion.

The buzzard perched on top of the vertical pole. It looked at the pile spread out below, red cloth and bare flesh. This was a puzzle. It watched flies land on the flesh and crawl around. It watched ants crawl from the ground up the pole and under the blanket. But something was wrong. The buzzard saw all the indications of death and smelled death, a certain sign. But it saw the flesh above the ribs moving slowly but unmistakably, up and down, up and down.

How could something be alive and dead at the same time? How could this conflict of pictures and smells be? It knew rotting, and it knew what was not yet rotting.

It heard sobbing noises. But death was silent. It saw movement. But death was still. It smelled decay. Everything was confusing.

The sobbing noises got louder, very loud. A scream came from the pile. Part of the pile sat up.

The buzzard pushed into the air and flapped upward. It winged away. It could wait.

"I HAVE COME TO KILL!"

Crazy Horse did not come back from their daughter's scaffold for nearly half a moon. When he did, he looked more gaunt, more dispirited, more distracted than Black Shawl had ever seen him. She tried to get him to stay and eat and rest and take the comfort of her body, but he would have none of it. He gathered together some warriors, including Little Big Man and her brother Red Feather, and went back out against the miners. Custer was come and gone now—his survey was completed and gold officially discovered. The miners infested Paha Sapa. Crazy Horse acted as though he intended to kill each one, like a man savoring his favorite fruit, bite by slow bite.

When he got back, he had little to say. He sat around indifferently, in a world of his own. A sad world, she supposed, a melancholy world. A bitter world? She didn't know.

It was the feeling of helplessness that drove her wild. They had not made love for four years, since she knew she was making life within. Good husbands did not approach wives when they were with child or nursing. Now she was ready for him, but he would not come to her. It was as though she had nothing that could please him, nurture him, ease his heart.

And if she could not give him solace, neither could she take it from him. She was helpless and lonely.

She heard the talk of the camp. Little Big Man said

Crazy Horse had acted brash and reckless against the miners. "Ah," the people murmured, "recklessness killed his brother."

Until now Crazy Horse had been known as bold but judicious. He never shot his rifle from horseback, for instance, but always dismounted to make sure of the shot. He would charge the enemy head on, but only when he felt his bullet-proof medicine rising him. He never led others into unnecessary risks.

Now all that was changing, said Little Big Man.

Black Shawl could hardly sleep for fear.

In the Winter Seven Loafers Were Killed by the Enemy, which the whites called 1875, Red Cloud and many other chiefs went back to Washington. Most of the agency chiefs went this time, all but Young Man-Whose-Enemies. When they got back, they said Red Cloud insisted on a new agent and someone to keep him from stealing from them. They were tired of cattle being driven around the mountain and counted twice. They were tired of sacks of food that didn't weigh what they should. They were tired of being hungry.

"And what else did he say?" the people in the wild camps wanted to know.

"The whites asked us to sell Paha Sapa," said the chiefs, acting surprised.

"Of course, you're surprised," said the hostiles. "Who would think the whites would ask for Paha Sapa?"

"We said we'd have to talk to the people," the chiefs went on.

"Of course. And do you want to listen, or are you just telling the One You Use for Father that as a tactic to get a few more dollars?"

Young Man-Whose-Enemies came to Crazy Horse and they talked a long time. The agency chiefs and the whites had agreed on a big talk in the Moon When Leaves Turn Brown. They were going to talk about selling Paha Sapa.

Young Man-Whose-Enemies, the peace chief, had come to ask Crazy Horse, the war leader, to join in the talk.

The chief said what direction he was leading the people. The world was changing, like it or not. He was not living in the past. He was trying to make a future for the people. The Lakota were going to have to live a new way. They would farm, because there were no more buffalo. They would come to terms with the white man. They would make a transition into a new order of existence.

All this was not unprecedented, said Young Man-Whose-Enemies. Twice seven generations ago, before the memories of the oldest men now living, the Lakota had lived by growing corn and other crops along the Muddy Water River. Then they had learned to follow the buffalo herds. That seemed a better way at the time—Young Man-Whose-Enemies himself loved it. But it was over now.

A wise leader thought of the children, the aged, those who could not fend for themselves. He did not make a life only for the strongest hunter-warriors but for everyone. That was what Young Man-Whose-Enemies was doing. Now the old life was too hard. The Lakota had to find a new way. He asked his friend Crazy Horse to join him in the search.

Crazy Horse puffed on his short pipe a long time, to let his friend know that his words were heard. He rubbed the scar below his nostril. He turned all the words over in his mind once more. He thought of what he would say. He thought how much Young Man-Whose-Enemies's words were like his uncle Spotted Tail's. And how treacherous the words seemed to him, and how hard it was for him to remember that he was dealing with honorable Lakota leaders, men who were looking out for the best interests of all the people.

Finally he answered.

"Yes, life changes, sometimes changes in big ways. There was once a time when only Inyan was, Stone, and then a time when Inyan helped make Earth and the waters and Sky. There was the time when the *pte,* two-legged creatures, were created and multiplied. There was the time when the four directions were created, and the thirteen moons. I am sure that other great ages will exist, but I don't know whether two-legged people will be part of them. It is not my place to think about the great ages, but to live within this time of *pte.*

"It is our spirits that must live," he said. He paused awhile. "Live in awareness of mystery. Live according to what knowledge of Spirit we have, through our visions, by the guidance of our spirit animals, and in time with the pulse of the earth, which is the pulse of our blood."

He set the pipe down, cut a chunk of sweetgrass off a braid, set it on the fire, and watched the smoke rise to the spirits. "I cannot go against my vision, or what I see with the *cante ista.* The only life is the path they open."

He paused a long moment. "Even if life at the agencies looked good to me, I would only walk the path revealed to me. But everyone sees that the agency life is bad. People become lazy, inept, dependent, helpless. Instead of hunting they beg. They demean themselves. The women become pay women for the whites. Men and women alike become drunkards.

"Worst, the people get so greedy for handouts, a little more beef, a little more cloth, a bit of flour, whiskey, sure, even coffee, so greedy they are willing to sell Paha Sapa. The people's best hunting grounds, where the bones of our ancestors lay, where we receive visions from Spirit.

"It doesn't take sharp eyes to see that this is no life at all."

He made no big rhetorical climax. The words themselves were enough. The two friends sat and smoked in silence for a long time. Both knew there was nothing more to say, nothing more to do. Two Lakota had truly looked, and what they saw was different. Young Man-Whose-Enemies would work to get the best terms possible with the whites for the people's new life. Crazy Horse would fight against that life, which was really death.

So they gave each other the handshake of respect, with arms crossed, and went their separate ways forever.

To open the council the white treaty talkers asked not only for Paha Sapa, but for the Shifting Sands River country and the Shining Mountains, too.

Riders immediately went to Crazy Horse, Touch-the-Sky, He Dog, Big Road, and their hostile warriors.

The agency Indians were split. Some people said, "The land is lost anyway—let's get what we can for it." The young warriors said they would fight first.

For four days there was no talking. The people were split by the new request like a tree cleaved by lightning.

On the fifth day the Lakota came to the council place, but they were still divided.

At noon 200 warriors charged the council tent, painted, feathered, and carrying their rifles. They circled the tent at a gallop, singing their war songs.

At a signal hundreds more galloped down from the hills. At another signal, hundreds more. The men willing to bargain for Paha Sapa and Shifting Sands River country and the Shining Mountains were surrounded by perhaps a thousand angry warriors.

The agency chiefs knew that these warriors came from both the friendly and the hostile camps. The rumor was that they would kill the first chief to speak up for selling the land. The chiefs talked among themselves, uncertain.

Finally, the warriors opened a way and Little Big Man charged through. Dressed and painted for war, holding his rifle high, his chest bleeding from scarifying, he galloped right into the council tent.

He roared out what he had to say: "I have come to kill the white people who want to steal our land!"

Finally the whites saw it. They were surrounded, outnumbered, outgunned. The treaty talkers were nervous, their women were nervous, the writers and photographers from the newspapers were nervous—even the soldiers were afraid. Even the traders' sons, some of them half Lakota, wished they were somewhere else.

Everyone thought the first person to speak would be shot and the massacre would start.

Everyone looked at everyone else, waiting, hoping, wondering.

It was Young Man-Whose-Enemies who stood up. He fixed Little Big Man with his eyes and stared him down for a long time. Everyone waited for the shot that would end his life and start the slaughter. It didn't come.

At last Young Man-Whose-Enemies said quietly but clearly, "Go to your lodges, my foolish young friends. Come back when your heads have cooled."

Little Big Man stared back. Maybe he would strike at Young Man-Whose-Enemies. Maybe—no one knew.

Maybe the shot would come from outside. Maybe no one would even know who fired it.

Young Man-Whose-Enemies stood, waiting.

Little Big Man stood, thinking.

Finally, he thought of what Crazy Horse would say. Lakota must never raise a hand against Lakota. That way is death.

And he thought: Crazy Horse respected Young Man-Whose-Enemies-Are-Afraid-of-His-Horses.

Little Big Man turned his pony and walked off.

The ring of warriors outside backed away.

The agency chiefs picked up their pipes and blankets and left.

The treaty talkers got up and started breathing again. The soldiers sighed in relief.

Red Cloud announced a price. So did Spotted Tail. So did others. But most of the Lakota went back to their villages. No one signed anything.

The Oglala decided they would make a big winter camp on the Buffalo Tongue River. Crazy Horse, Black Twin, Big Road, and the others thought there would be elk in the bottoms along the river all winter and the bark of the sweet sunpole tree to feed the horses. Last winter they had killed horses to eat. This winter they needed to keep every pony possible alive. Maybe for food. Maybe for fighting soldiers.

SETTING DOWN BURDENS

They didn't find out Plum was missing until they stopped for the night.

When they got to the Buffalo Tongue River camping place, Black Shawl discovered that the old woman had rolled up some blankets to make it look as if she were under the robe on the travois. Then she had walked off. Black Shawl had seen the old woman walk away but thought she was just going to relieve herself. Now they knew better.

Crazy Horse started on the back trail fast, leading an extra pony. He had a panicky feeling. Hawk was restless on her perch.

The very old people did this sometimes. Grandmother Plum knew that food would be short this winter. She had little flesh anymore and didn't look forward to shivering in her robes. She didn't expect to live much longer anyway. The last two nights had been bitingly cold. Today was clear again, and would be bitter. Everyone had heard that freezing was a pleasantly dreamy way to die.

But she had no idea how important she was to him. He had lost his daughter. He had lost Little Hawk. He had lost Hump. For a while he had lost Hawk. He had lost his mother. He couldn't stand to lose Grandmother Plum.

And . . . And . . . He wanted to hear her speak aloud. He was sure she could, and now he was in a rage to hear her talk. He would ask her directly, "Please, speak."

He pushed his pony hard along the lodge trail. The last place Black Shawl remembered seeing Plum was almost back at the start of the day's travel. He would get there after dark.

In his imagination Grandmother Plum did speak to him for the first time in twenty-five winters. What would she say?

"Grandson," he imagined.

"I love you," he imagined.

The people often had not loved him. Our Strange Man, they called him. Even his father had not always loved him.

In his imagination the one person who had never failed him with her love was Grandmother Plum. She had listened to him. They had understood each other without words, which was a deeper way to understand.

Now he wanted to hear her words. He would ask. What would she say?

Crazy Horse spent a while looking for her tracks. No luck. She must have been careful to walk away from the trail on rock. So, as one more chance, he decided to walk where he would have gone, had he wanted to leave no tracks. He led his pony and put one foot in front of the other carefully. It was dark, and the rocks had fissures.

Then he found himself looking at a dark blob. It was a bush. No, it had the shape of a person. It was a bush. No . . .

"Unci Plum?" he tried tentatively.

Her first words after twenty-five winters were English: "Goddamn it."

Crazy Horse jumped off his pony and ran to her. She was crouched on an outcropping, huddled in one thin blanket against the whipping wind. He put his arms around her shoulders. "Unci Plum," he said gratefully.

"I don't suppose you'll leave me alone," she said. "I want to die." She looked into his face challengingly.

"Unci Plum," he murmured.

"Oh, all right, build us a fire." She sounded half-friendly and half-crabby. "It's goddamn cold out here."

He half picked her up and got her in the lee of the rock. He cracked flint against his steel, got sparks on his little bit of tinder, and blew on them. Even here the wind snuffed them out. He repeated the process. This time the wind scattered them everywhere, and they went out again. "This is goddamn good," said Grandmother Plum. "We'll both freeze to death."

After the third failure he had to gather more tinder. His hands were shaking. He got a little blaze started.

"Son of a bitch," Plum said in English, squatting close.

Crazy Horse gathered sagebrush to feed the fire and said nothing. He was surprised his grandmother was so quick with words after all these years and so casual with what the white people said were disrespectful words. Had she been voluble when he was young? He didn't remember. He supposed she had picked up all these white-man words when the people hung around Fort Laramie. Normal then, probably, but they seemed like sand in his food now.

He broke sticks off a dead twisty tree and built up the fire. Finally he broke off most of the trunk of the cedar itself, and they had a fine blaze.

He squatted beside her and offered her a little pemmican. She grabbed it hungrily.

"This is a miserable business, killing yourself," she said. "I don't know why I tried it." She looked sideways at him. "I guess I'm grateful to you," she said. "When I'm not pissed off at you for not letting an old woman die when she wants to."

He felt a chill. Rattling Blanket Woman was hovering near the fire like a specter, maybe beckoning them both into the darkness and to death.

"Unci, after twenty-five winters why are you suddenly talking? And . . . disrespectful words?"

She bit off another piece of the pemmican and made big chewing motions while she stared into space. He saw her face deepen and soften.

"You don't know about me," she said. "Your father and the others never talked about it."

Slowly, hesitantly, she began a story. When Curly was a small boy, she said, she lived near Fort Laramie with the loafers for two years. Curly's band was around there most of the time then, not like now. That was before the troubles. Well, her husband was dead, and she stayed around the fort. To tell the truth, she was drunk most of the time. To tell the rest of the truth, she belonged to any man who wanted her, if he had the price of a cup of whiskey. Since she managed to stay drunk the whole time, she must have had a lot of cups.

"That was when I picked up the white-man words," she said. "Many of us loafers did. The soldiers thought it was funny." She ruminated for a moment. "I walked under the blanket with a lot of soldiers, drunk, drunk, drunk." She looked sideways at her grandson. "Maybe I was forty winters old, but I was still beautiful. Or that's what people said."

She gave him a look that meant, "You were too young to notice."

This must be one of the reasons Worm was so set against whiskey, he thought.

Grandmother Plum rambled on: Rattling Blanket Woman had asked her to come live with her and Worm, who was known as Tasunke Witko then. It would be inconvenient—a husband and his mother-in-law could never speak to each other—but it was necessary. "I had no husband, my parents were gone beyond the pines, Rattling Blanket Woman was my only living child, and I had to live with someone and get away from the fort, get away from whiskey long enough to get my spirit back. Besides, Worm was away all the time that summer, gone against the Psatoka."

He knew that summer was when his father stayed away for months taking revenge against the Psatoka. The time when . . .

"You always blamed your father for what your mother

did," she said. He felt the death of his mother in his chest, like a sack around his heart, a sack full of tears. In his mind she was always hanging by her neck from his lodge pole, a memory he could never look at directly, but one always in the margin of his vision. "But it was not his fault," she said.

She looked at him oddly, her eyes flashing in the light of the fire. "I wonder whether you're ready even now to hear it." She nodded as though to herself and plunged on. "You decided she was distraught because Worm was always gone. But you made that up. She didn't dread his absence. She dreaded his return. Because she had lifted the lodge skirt to a young Sicangu."

Plum barely hesitated and marched forth again. "She didn't want to marry this man. He had seduced her and then told all his friends about how he sneaked into the lodge and what he did inside. And how he would do it night after night—she lacked the will to stop him. She was humiliated."

Crazy Horse was dizzy. Unsteady. He put out both hands to support himself where he sat.

"Humiliated," Plum repeated. "That's why she hanged herself. She couldn't face Worm."

He bit his lower lip hard, and she read his thoughts. "Yes," she said, "you have a lot to apologize to your father for."

She stared off into space for a little. "Me too. I encouraged her. I had had many men. I thought your father was mistreating her by being gone all the time. I teased her about not having the heart to take what she wanted. Another man if she wanted." The old woman snorted. "I didn't care about myself anymore. Drunken fool. I was still sneaking the whiskey when I could.

"Your mother cared about herself. So she couldn't stand what she'd done." Her voice dropped to a whisper. "My fault.

"Yes, that stuff about your father being gone all the time was something you made up." She spoke matter-of-factly. "You missed her. You were not far past your time of sucking at her breast. You didn't think it up about him being gone until later."

Crazy Horse just sat there. He felt the truth of his life dropping onto his head like rocks.

"Why did you stop talking, Unci?"

Grandmother Plum shrugged. Then she went on in a matter-of-fact way. "Didn't want to do anything at first. Not eat, not sleep, not stay awake, nothing. Guilt." She sat looking into the shadows of the past. "When we found her, I just sat down, fell down, almost. Didn't move. You ran outside crying and brought help. I just sat there. I felt so terrible I . . . I didn't want to move, to breathe, to exist. Didn't want to die, just wanted to . . . evaporate."

She fell silent for a while. "Couldn't stop breathing. Holding my breath would have been doing something. Intended never to move again. Wished I could just turn to rock. Know what it was made me move finally? Got up to pee. Wanted to stay there and never move, tried, but it was too uncomfortable. Next morning I drank water, never drank whiskey since. After a while I ate a little. Couldn't help it. Hated it, but couldn't help it."

"But why didn't you talk?"

She didn't answer for a long time. "For many winters I lived like a person walking around underwater. Muddy water. Moved slowly, didn't see anything clearly, didn't hear much, didn't feel anything." She paused. "Finally my spirit started to come back a little and things weren't so murky. But I didn't want to talk, didn't want to feel, didn't want to tell your father what I'd done. I still wanted to turn into a rock, so that I wouldn't feel the rain or the wind, even the winter snow could sit deep on me and I wouldn't feel it.

"It was you that started me back."

She turned her head toward him with a bird-like jerk, and he saw something alive in her eyes. "Twenty winters ago."

He waited.

"Give me your blankets," she said. "I'm cold." She flashed him a crooked grin. "Which is what I intended to be."

He lifted the two blankets off his shoulders and draped them over hers. She pulled them tight.

"You remember when Bear-Scattering was dying? On the Running Water? You came and took me outside and sat me on a log and talked. That . . . reached me. You took me by the arm, sat with me, talked to me. Nobody had done any of that for ten winters."

She seemed to shiver for a long moment.

"I remember perfectly what you talked about. Hawk. Hawk living in your heart. You wanted to know if everybody had a Hawk in the heart." She smiled broadly at him. "No, not everyone does. Not everyone finds his animal guide as a youth, as you did. Some never find it. Most animal guides aren't a constant presence, like Hawk."

She thought awhile. "I knew then that you were very special. You are like her. You have a big gift. I knew then, and I should have warned you: Great trials come to those with great gifts.

"You also wanted to know whether you should seek a vision. I didn't answer you. Force of long habit, partly. But had I felt like answering, I wouldn't have. You knew the answers in your heart. You needed to learn to look into your heart and see them and trust them and act on them.

"Right away you went out crying for a vision. I was proud. When you came back, I saw in your face that you had seen beyond, and seen much. I was thrilled for you, and afraid for you. I couldn't say any of that. Feeling anything was nearly too much."

She stopped. After a little while Crazy Horse went into the darkness to find some more wood for the fire. When the tongues of the blaze rose high, she began again.

"It is for you I have wanted to stay alive these past twenty winters. You walk in a sacred way. In you my daughter walks in a sacred way. In you I walk in a sacred way.

"These are terrible times. Maybe the end of times, I think. In any time it is possible to walk in a sacred way. In some times, like this one, it is the only way to live like a human being. You are doing that."

When she didn't speak for a long time, Crazy Horse asked his question. "Unci, things are hard. What shall I do? What shall we do?"

She answered promptly and softly. "I don't see into the future. Listen to Hawk. Walk as she tells you. Look with the single eye that is the heart.

"Listen for the Inyan, too. Maybe they will begin to speak. Mainly listen to Hawk. Act accordingly. That's all human beings are asked to do."

After a long moment she looked him in the eye. "I don't want to live much longer," she said. "Don't say you need me—you don't. My hands hurt, my knees hurt, my back hurts, the pain is terrible sometimes in the morning. I want to go on. A person knows when it's time to go on."

"Unci," he put in quickly, anxiously, "will you come back to camp with me in the morning?"

She hesitated. "Yes," she said. "Thanks for coming to get me. There's something I must do."

The next day they got to camp about midday, cold, tired, and hungry. That evening Grandmother Plum went to Worm's lodge and stayed a long time. Crazy Horse went to his sister, Kettle. Since she was older than he, she'd recall the months and years after their mother died better than he did. He asked her what she remembered of how his father had taken care of the two children in that difficult time. She told him.

The next morning Crazy Horse started the painting.

First he went to his uncles Little Hawk and Ashes, who were in camp. He got from them detailed accounts of his father's attacks on the Psatoka to avenge the death of their brother, understanding carefully what coups were struck, what enemies killed, scalped, injured, what ponies stolen.

He admitted to them that he was ashamed of himself. Full of resentment of his father's absence, he had never paid attention with sufficient care to his father's formal singing and dancing of these events. His uncles told him of the coups simply, soberly, without reproach.

Then he took a fine, luxurious robe Black Shawl had tanned. He got out his paints, red, white, and ocher from clays of those colors mixed with the fat scraped off a buffalo hide, black from ashes, blues and greens from lichens, bitterbrush, and blueberries.

Slowly, scrupulously, he painted his father's deeds during those months of holy war against the Psatoka. His father mounted, riding fast and shooting arrows. His father throwing a spear, swinging a club. Psatoka wounded and bleeding from the head, the neck, the chest.

It took him six days to finish the painting. Since he was not a skilled painter, the pictures had a certain crudeness, rawness. He hoped his heart showed even through that.

Black Shawl did not understand what he was doing and gave him curious looks. Grandmother Plum knew, voiced her approval, and provided a few details. She understood that the son was honoring the father's war deeds at the time the mother died. Honoring, and saying he'd been wrong.

Black Shawl could hardly get over the fact that Grandmother Plum talked. When Plum spoke to Crazy Horse, Black Shawl hung on every word, tickled. She reported mundane comments to neighbors. Everyone in camp exclaimed about it, hands over their mouths. Plum acted like it was the most normal thing in the world. She chattered merrily at everyone, sometimes with a mordant tongue. Sometimes she made them wish she'd shut up again.

Crazy Horse chose Little Hawk to take the robe to Worm as a gift. Little Hawk returned to say that Worm accepted. They all understood that Worm knew the meaning of the gift. Not only did he see the events depicted, he knew from the beginning what was in his son's heart. He sent word by Little Hawk that he invited Crazy Horse for a meal and a talk the evening after next.

They ate first. Crazy Horse's mothers disappeared into the shadows at the back of the lodge. Worm got out tobacco and *canupa* and they shared the comforting ritual and the companionship of a smoke.

Then Crazy Horse began. "I apologize to you, Ate. I've kept hard feeling toward you in my heart." He simply breathed in and out a couple of times. "When the one we both loved left us, I felt . . ." He had hoped he wouldn't be this poor in words. "You know how I felt, how you felt. My mistake was that I blamed you. That was wrong. I know it. I wanted someone who wasn't there, so I blamed the person who was there. I was wrong. You were doing everything you could for me, I know that now." He looked up into his father's eyes and back down. He was not so much ashamed as sad, infinitely sad.

"After a while I made something up in my mind." This was the worst. "I made it up that she . . . died . . . because you abandoned us, you were gone all the time. I told myself I hated you for that."

Now he looked his father full in the face. "I have behaved very badly. I've acted like you were . . . cruel when you were acting like a true father. I'm sorry for what I've done to you."

He let it sit. He felt a little anxiety, a little yearning.

Worm just looked back at him. Benevolently. After a long while, he said, "A father understands such things. It was natural for you to feel hurt, to act hurt. I'm glad you've set down your own burden. There was no burden on me."

Nine days later the winter's second big snowstorm came. Worm and Crazy Horse were out hunting that day. By turning around promptly, they got their ponies back to the village before the drifts got bad, and not long before dark. At his lodge Crazy Horse asked Black Shawl, "Where's Unci Plum?"

"At your mother's lodge."

He stood there. He was always uneasy about Plum now. Against reason, he said, "I'll get her."

He walked through the softly falling snow. He could see clear sky to the west, over the Shining Mountains. The storm would clear soon.

His scratch brought "Come in." When he lifted the door flap, he saw only his father and mothers.

"How long since Unci Plum left?" he asked.

"A long time," said Red Grass. "Midafternoon."

"Isn't she with Black Shawl?" asked Corn.

She had a head start of a couple of hours.

"Let's go," he said to Worm.

They circled the outside of the village in opposite directions. When they met at the far side, Crazy Horse didn't need to ask. Worm's face showed that he had seen no prints leading away from the village in the fresh snow. They circled again and met back where they started. Almost all sign—children playing, women setting traps, men going out to tear off sunpole tree bark, the prints of the sentries coming to and from the pony herd—almost all sign was drifted in. They found nothing that looked like Plum's moccasin.

Black Shawl, Red Grass, and Corn stood in front of Worm's lodge with worried expressions. "She's not at any other lodge," said Black Shawl.

"No one has seen her," added Red Grass.

Now it was full dark, and the sky was clearing. Tonight would be very cold. Father and son looked at each other and started off. They walked out where it was possible to walk, along the rimrock above the river, and on the slopes where the snow wasn't deep. Then they walked where it might be trouble, through the drifts on the hillsides, in the gullies deep with snow. Wordlessly, they had the same thoughts. She must have left a track somewhere. Maybe she had thrown herself into a drift.

They walked from darkness until night-middle-made, in circles ever wider around the camp. They called her name frantically. They walked faster and faster, for the cold was bitter. They found nothing.

They walked until almost dawn. When they turned back toward their lodge fires, they knew they would not see Grandmother Plum alive again.

ULTIMATUM

In the middle of the Moon of Frost in the Lodge, young men came in from Red Cloud Agency. They had had a hard time coming in the middle of winter. The White Earth River lay far to the south and east. Though not much snow fell, the weather was bitter, cold and windy. Their skin got frostbitten, and they needed nearly a full moon to get here. Now they had things to say in the council lodge.

Their relatives took them to warm lodges, fed them stew, and got them warmed up and rested. Then the messengers and headmen and people gathered in the council lodge. The message from the white agent turned out to be simple enough: All Lakota who did not come in to the agencies by the end of this moon would be considered hostile. The army would come out and drive them in.

Big Road, Black Twin, and Crazy Horse looked at each other. Though the Strange Man was still smoking his short *canupa,* about a hundred lodges of these people regarded him as their leader. The chiefs looked at each other. . . .

Crazy Horse supposed the others were having the same mad thoughts he was. He was amused at the presumption of the whites and outraged, too. Amused further at their stupidity: a journey that had taken young men a full moon was now supposed to be done by a village with children and old people in half a moon. Or maybe it wasn't stupidity—maybe the whites wanted to make an impossible demand to get an excuse to fight.

Sad. The young, the old, and the weak would suffer when war came. Sad, for this turn was likely a sign of the end of their free life.

He was also glad, because this meant an end to the talking and maneuvering, bribing and blackmailing. The issues would be settled now by honorable clash of arms.

The chiefs all drew in smoke and sent it, the breath of the earth, up to Father Sky. They had talked plenty about this possibility in private. They knew what was coming. So did the people. Not many words were needed, and none from Crazy Horse.

Elation was swelling his chest. He wanted to fight. He recognized that fighting might not be best for all the people. So he promised himself that he would seek a vision and ask Spirit what to do. He promised himself further that he would pray constantly with his Inyan, in hope that they would speak.

He could hear, in his mind's ear, Hawk yawping her war cry. It would be a fight.

Big Road was the one who finally spoke up. "Tell the agent the snow is deep, there is no grass, and the ponies are already weak."

After a pause, Black Twin added quietly, "Tell him also that we are not willing to be told where we must live in our own country."

Crazy Horse looked at his fellow headmen and smiled with his eyes alone. No, no words were needed from him.

A CALL TO ARMS

People disagreed, though, about whether they should go in. When the grass greened, some said, the soldiers would be chasing everyone—it would be hard. Others said the soldiers wouldn't wait for the grass: "Remember eight winters ago," they said, "Long Hair attacked the Sahiyela on the Washita River in the middle of the snow time. And killed many women and children." Still others said that they could keep the soldiers out of the country, or at least stay clear of them, as long as their ammunition held out and there were enough buffalo.

Throughout the rest of the Moon of Frost in the Lodge and all through the Moon of Popping Trees, they met in the council lodge and talked about it. Word came by runner from Red Cloud: "Come in, we're waiting for you." But was that what the old war leader truly wanted? Or did the whites make him say it? Or was there a hidden message?

Crazy Horse said privately that each man must decide for himself. He told those who wanted to go in that he understood. A man can't fight when he can't feed his women and children. Each family must do what's good for them.

Publicly, Little Big Man spoke for him. For himself and his family Crazy Horse chose the old way, the ways of the grandfathers, the ways shown them by White Buffalo Cow Woman and Grandfather. To Crazy Horse all ways but these were death. Regardless of the ammunition, regardless of the buffalo, he would stay in this north country.

So the people were divided against each other. During a warm wind in the Moon of Popping Trees, Crazy Horse's cousin Black Elk started for Red Cloud Agency with a few lodges. Early in the Snow-Blind Moon, the last moon of winter, even He Dog left. He took eight lodges toward the Sahiyela camp led by Two Moons on Little Shifting Sands River. From there, when the ponies were stronger, he would go to the agency.

A-i-i-i, a shirtman and one of his oldest friends.

Sometimes it seemed to Crazy Horse that he had to lose everyone who mattered to him: his mother, his daughter, his brother, Little Hawk, his *hunka* Hump, Grandmother Plum. Now his cousin Black Elk and two old friends, Young Man-Whose-Enemies and He Dog, both leaders, both wearers of the shirt, were agency Indians.

Crazy Horse took the only course he could see clearly.

He paid attention to his spirit animal, Hawk. He purified himself in the sweat lodge. He cried for a vision. He listened for word from the Inyan.

The Inyan seemed silent, except for the sound of the beat of the earth. But maybe they weren't silent. Maybe the beat was speaking and he wasn't listening.

The thaw was on. Snow dripped down the trees and bushes. The ground was patchy, white here and marshy there. They were sitting on a log by the river. Horn Chips had suggested it because, he said, he liked to hear the thick river ice make its big cracking noises. To Crazy Horse the cracking sounded too much like soldiers' rifles in camp. The Strange Man had asked his teacher for a talk about the Inyan.

"Sometimes I do think I hear something," said Crazy Horse. "Sort of."

"Tell me about it."

Crazy Horse made a little flinch with his shoulders. He had never been really comfortable with his Inyan, not the shell stone he wore behind his ear, not the moss stone under his arm. To him the Inyan were a little bizarre.

Maybe that was because Chips was a little bizarre. Crazy Horse had long since accepted that the two of them would never have an easy relationship. There would always be an undercurrent of tension, a feeling that Chips was impatient with Crazy Horse's spiritual slowness. He thought Chips liked him but didn't entirely approve of him.

"Tell me," Horn Chips repeated. Their *canupa* sat on their laps.

"I expected words," said Crazy Horse. "Or pictures. Lots of times when I pray and listen I hear nothing at all, see nothing. Feels like trying to walk through a boulder. Sometimes I . . . Maybe I get a sense. Not words, not pictures, not anything . . . A sense."

"Describe it to me."

"It's like hearing a drum but not quite hearing it."

"Does it make you nervous?"

"No, it makes me . . . peaceful."

Horn Chips thought for a while. "Inyan are different for different people. Sometimes they say something exact. I can ask my Inyan where someone is, and maybe I will see. Sometimes Inyan just . . . People listen and without being able to say how, they know what's right to do. Sometimes they're more subtle, much more, they . . . It's like a song with no words, just the music."

He left it for a little. Crazy Horse began to wonder if his teacher was finished. The river ice made a loud snap.

"Just listen," Chips said. "Just listen." He paused again, as though considering whether to speak. "You have a hard path. You are called to be a holy warrior and one who sees deeply. Normally they don't go together. I've told you before that to hear truly, you may have to stop fighting. And stop seeking glory in the eyes of the people."

Chips gave him a knowing smile. Crazy Horse knew what he meant. It made him mad. Give up leadership, give the people up.

"Inyan are the oldest of all living things," Chips said. "Inyan can tell us everything about life. Listen. Just listen. No one can tell what you will hear. Something small or something big, that will be your beginning point."

Crazy Horse supposed so. But was a teacher supposed to be like a sand sticker on a moccasin?

They heard someone coming from the direction of the village. A young man approached and stood respectfully silent four or five steps away. The Strange Man turned to him and raised an eyebrow.

"A messenger has come from Fort Fetterman," he said. "He tells us the entire village of Crazy Horse has been destroyed by the soldiers."

Crazy Horse looked sharply at Horn Chips, half-tickled and half-scared. The village of Crazy Horse?

The stone *wicasa wakan* nodded and smiled.

Crazy Horse got up and walked toward the council lodge.

* * *

Before they could get the council well started, one of the young men came in with a signal from the wolves. People were coming up the creek, weary, with almost no horses or belongings.

They sent food and robes out for everyone and pony drags to bring in the wounded. Crazy Horse and the other principal men rode out ahead.

It was He Dog and the Sahiyela he had joined, led by the headman Two Moons and the seer Ice.

After everyone was warmed and fed, they heard the story. Like He Dog, Two Moons had wanted to go in to the agency. The Sahiyela were not like the Oglala, hostile to the whites. But they decided to wait until the grass was better. The scouts saw soldiers, some out of Fort Fetterman led by Three Stars, the one the whites called Crook. After Three Stars marched on by, the chiefs moved the village into a small, obscure canyon the soldiers couldn't find. They were sure they were safe, though—the Sahiyela were known to be peaceful.

Three Stars' soldiers were almost into the village at dawn before the scouts spotted them. Grabber was with the soldiers. He knew the canyon and had led them there.

"Hai!" people exclaimed.

Grabber was the son of a Mormon missionary and a woman of the islands of the western sea. Years ago, the Hunkpapa had found him and taken him in and made him one of them. Now he led the soldiers against his own. The runners said Grabber thought the village was Crazy Horse's because he recognized the horses of He Dog.

Several men in the council gave each other looks that meant, "Let's kill this traitor."

In the dawn attack the women and children ran. The warriors, naked and afoot, tried to hold the soldiers back. Though the whites stampeded the pony herd, the boys found some old horses that hadn't run far and got the people going. From afar they saw the black, oily smoke of lodges burning, and knew that everything not on their backs or in their arms was destroyed.

Through the snow they made their way here.

Crazy Horse was glad to see that one matter was settled. He Dog had no agency in his heart, not now.

Still, Three Stars was loose in the country. The Lakota had not met the ridiculous deadline, so soldiers could now hunt them like animals. No village was safe.

Everyone decided to move the camp to Chalk Buttes, where Sitting Bull's people were. There would be safety in numbers.

At Chalk Buttes the headmen counciled. Sitting Bull would not go in to any agency, not ever, he said. His position was unchanged: The people must have nothing to do with the whites in any way. Not talk, not make treaties, nothing. Not even go in to the forts to trade.

As for the coming fight, he welcomed it. The people had a little ammunition from the Gros Ventres. They could trade for more from the Slota. It would be expensive, but worth it. He wanted to turn the tables on the agency Indians. "Let's send our runners back to the agencies," he suggested. "Come fight. Bring shells. It's going to be a grand summer against the whites." He looked at the man next to him, powerful in medicine and in war, and added, "Tell them His Crazy Horse will be leading the war."

The Strange Man kept his silence, as always in council, but he was satisfied. Hawk was exhilarated.

Once more Crazy Horse prepared in the sweat lodge. He went onto the mountain to seek a vision. For four days and nights he cried to the grandfathers and all the powers for assistance. He saw. He dreamed. He dreamed pictures of war and of dying. He saw only an eternal fighting, a martial dance. He did not see Lakota women cutting their hair off or scarifying their arms and legs in grief. Nor did he see them dancing in celebration, with brown and yellow and red scalps dangling from the pole.

After sweating again, he prayed for a long time with the Inyan. He heard nothing from them. The dreams of war rampaged through his mind, a war that seemed never to end, blood that pulsed out forever, like a fresh and abundant spring flowing from a wound in the earth.

Throughout that spring of the Winter Red Cloud's Horses Were Taken Away, which the whites called 1876, Crazy Horse left Black Shawl, the wife he had come to love, to go back to the mountain over and over. His dream was always the same.

He was satisfied. It would have been good to see many soldiers upside down, therefore dead. It would have been good to see Lakota men dancing their coups, Lakota women sending up the piercing tremolo. But for a warrior like him, he knew, it was the rise to martial spirit that counted, not the victory.

Throughout that spring, agency Lakota swelled the wild camps. Black Elk's people came back from Red Cloud, disgusted because the peace chiefs intended to sell Paha Sapa. Many young men were also angry and would come to fight the soldiers, said Black Elk, even Red Cloud's son Jack.

The young men did begin to come in, eager to go to war behind Crazy Horse. Northern bands joined the camps: Those Who Plant by the River, Those Without Bows, Sihasapa, Two Kettles, some Santee and Yanktonai, and many Sahiyela.

The soldiers would come too, said all the agency men. At the agencies the whites were even trying to recruit agency Lakota to scout and fight against their own. Three Stars would come out, they'd heard, and other soldiers from the forts on the Big Muddy River. These soldiers were not coming with excuses, not to build a road to the goldfields, to survey for a railroad, to look for gold in Paha Sapa. They were simply coming to kill Indians.

A-i-i-i, it would be a summer for a young man to show what he was made of.

It was also a good summer to stick together, the headmen agreed. They would not go out looking for the soldiers but would stick together in one big camp and wait until the whites were near. They would employ all the strength of their numbers. The numbers were grand—by early in the Moon When the Chokecherries Are Ripe, 450 lodges, 3,200 people, about 800 fighting men.

The young men were not so sure they just wanted to wait. Maybe they would go find the soldiers.

On Rosebud Creek the camp grew so big it had to be moved every few days, for the sake of firewood and grass. For once the scouts found plenty of buffalo, and the hunters filled the camp with meat. Many young men and women got married. The old ways felt strong. And in this strength Sitting Bull was able to see beyond.

He dreamed of a huge billowing of dust leading soldiers from the east against a cloud that looked like the village. When the dust whipped against the village, a great storm raged. When it cleared, the dust fell to the earth, and the village stood strong.

When Sitting Bull told the other headmen his dream, they rejoiced. They also posted extra lookouts to watch for soldiers coming from the east.

A few days later Sitting Bull pledged to give a sun dance, not the annual dance of all the Lakota, but a special dance of his own band only, where he would make a particular sacrifice.

In the first quarter of the Moon When the Chokecherries Are Ripe, the Hunkpapa gave the dance with the other bands watching. Sitting Bull sacrificed fifty small pieces of flesh from each arm, cut away with an awl. Bleeding profusely, he then danced most of the day gazing into the sun. Suddenly he stopped and stared at the sun for a long time. And when he returned from his journey, he told the people what he had seen.

Soldiers came thick as grasshoppers to an Indian village. All of them were upside down with their hats falling off, and their horses were upside down. Some of the Indians were also upside down. "The soldiers do not have ears," Sitting Bull said, "but you are not supposed to take their spoils, or cut their bodies."

The people were thrilled. Lots of soldiers would attack their village. Though some Indians would die, all the soldiers would be killed. But the people must leave their bodies untouched.

The lodge circles simmered with anticipation of a great victory. Soldiers falling into camp, they called their leader's vision.

During this time Crazy Horse also sought to see beyond. Again he saw only blood, killing without end.

The scouts said Three Stars and his soldiers were marching toward Rosebud Creek.

Only yesterday the big camp had left the Rosebud, headed over the divide to the west toward the Greasy Grass River. Now Three Stars was close behind them.

The council was divided. The older men said to leave the soldiers alone until they attacked the village. This was what Sitting Bull had seen in his vision. There was no reason to look for trouble with the whites. But the younger men said the people should not risk the lives of the women and children and the elderly by letting the soldiers hit the camp. They wanted to drive the soldiers away now.

"But you'll leave the village unprotected," some protested. "What if the soldiers seen by Sitting Bull come from the east?"

So they divided the warriors, the young men led by Crazy Horse and Sitting Bull to attack Three Stars, the older men to stay behind and guard the village.

That night Crazy Horse talked to the young warriors and the *akicita* leaders. He told them this was a new kind of war. It was not honorable fighting, where a man demonstrated his physical and spiritual power, but simply killing. The white soldiers didn't have women to protect or children or homes, they were merely killers. If the Lakota wanted to live peaceably on their own land, they must not think of the heroic touch with a hand, but the bullet to the brain. They must all act together, they must charge not as individuals but in bunches, they must fling themselves at the soldiers like hail. And they must kill every soldier they could.

Even Crazy Horse thought it was ugly advice. But it was necessary. The world had changed, and he would walk the new way, despising it.

Gen. George Crook did not believe the world had changed. He believed, without thinking about it, that he was the instrument of the inevitable. So he was comfortable with himself while waiting for his aide-de-camp to set up the table in front of the tent and deal the cards. He was a white man, a soldier, a man of honor.

The general liked soldiering, he liked being in the field, he liked fighting, and he liked whist. He even liked his aide-de-camp, Lieutenant Bourke. The man talked too much. He could charm the birds out of the trees with his stories, or revive a company of exhausted soldiers with his Irish wit. These barrages of talk were to the good, because the general spent words like a miser spends coins.

This morning by 8:00 A.M. the general's cavalry and mounted infantry had ridden for five hours. Here at the forks of Rosebud Creek they were giving the horses a little rest. When the general rested, he played whist with Bourke, even in Powder River country. Especially in places this wild.

"What did you write in that damned diary of yours last night?" Crook asked, taking a trick. Bourke's incessant writing at the end of the day, when other men couldn't even sit up, was a standing joke among the officers.

Bourke answered in the tone of a quotation, " 'We are now right in among the hostiles, and may strike or be struck at any hour.' "

The general nodded. He lifted a commenting eyebrow. "Whether we find them or they find us," he said unnecessarily, "for the record, we found them." Six newspaper-men accompanied the expedition.

"Naturally, General," answered Bourke. The two men understood the politics of army life intimately and played the game with ironic good humor.

The aide-de-camp led a club and took the trick. The general realized he'd been snookered. His aide was going to run the club suit and win the game.

Crook stalled. He thought he heard something. A few minutes ago some sporadic firing had come from the direction of the Crow and Snake scouts he had sent on to the north, looking for the big village of Sioux that was supposed to be here. He had assumed the Indians had found a few buffalo and were making meat. Now what he heard was . . . yes, pounding hooves. Fire and answering fire.

Crook gave the lieutenant a small smile and laid down his cards. A lieutenant shouldn't outsmart a general anyway.

"Sioux, Sir," said Bourke, "behind the scouts."

The man had a good pair of eyes.

Calmly, Crook gave his orders. Captain Mills and four companies of cavalry to secure the hills along the river. Colonel Royall and his cavalry to the west beyond some rocky ledges. Himself and the mounted infantry to that hill at the end of the ridge.

He didn't add, "If we can mount and deploy before they overrun us."

He could see the scouts on the hill now. They were coming back fast. If they didn't slow the Sioux down, five companies of infantry and fifteen troops of cavalry of the U.S. Army would be caught with their pants down. The general liked scatological humor, and the prospect of this sort of report amused him. He was the sort of man who, faced with imminent death, would be slightly amused and hugely curious.

Now he was fascinated to see his Indian scouts turn, fire on the charging Sioux, and start to establish a position.

That slowed the enemy down, for sure. The scouts were fighting hard, and Crook saw that his troops would have time to mount and get ready to fight before getting their tails shot off. This pleased him.

It was time to start for the hill.

Little Big Man was watching Jack Red Cloud's full-length eagle-feather warbonnet flutter in the breeze behind him as the young man rode ahead. The warrior was in a sour mood about that—absurd for a young man who had done nothing to wear such a headdress. But the young men understood nothing and acted like fools. Little Big Man made a motion like spitting, but his mouth was too dry. At least Red Cloud's son wasn't hanging back behind everyone else. At least his foolishness took him to the front.

"Goddamn it," Little Big Man muttered in English. Jack's pony had just gone down. Little Big Man kicked his horse hard toward the young man.

Jack jumped clear and ran for his own line. He didn't stop to take off the bridle, to show that he wasn't afraid. He didn't stop for anything but ran like a coward, the warbonnet drawing attention to his flight. Ridiculous.

The Psatoka scouts bore down on young Red Cloud hard, and Little Big Man could see he wasn't going to get there first. Maybe they would think it was an honor to kill the son of a great Oglala war leader and scalp him. Maybe they would think it was funny to steal the unearned warbonnet. Maybe they would send it back to Red Cloud with a caustic message. Little Big Man wished he'd spoken his mind to Jack. It was bad to die like a fool.

The Psatoka rode alongside Jack and . . . It took Little Big Man a moment to see for sure that they'd unstrung their bows and were whipping the boy with the strings. Insulting. Better to be killed. If the boy had sense enough to know it.

Little Big Man quirted his pony. He heard and felt and then saw Crazy Horse come up next to him.

One of the Psatoka jerked the headdress off Jack. The others yelled that Jack had no right and . . .

When Little Big Man and Crazy Horse got within arrow range, the Psatoka whipped their horses away. The two warriors led the youngster back to his own side, embarrassed to look him in the face.

Crazy Horse didn't like the way the fight was going. It washed back and forth across the valley, bluff to bluff, hill to hill. Each side would drive the other back into cover and then have to retreat. No one was going to take the field or rout the other side or kill many enemies. They were going to swirl around for a quarter- or half-day and quit because the horses were tired.

He did like the way his warriors conducted themselves. Except for a few young men like Red Cloud's son, they worked together nicely. When he whistled for an attack with his eagle-bone whistle, they charged hard and made the soldiers run like prairie dogs when the coyote comes. They took their time shooting and made their shells count. They thought tactically. They operated as a unit. This new style worked. But no lesson was going to be taught today.

So, yes, he would lead a charge.

Crazy Horse talked a little to his leaders. Then he kicked his horse out in front of everyone and galloped across the line and back. He called out war cries interspersed with, "Remember the helpless ones in the village!" He blew the bone whistle shrilly. "It is a good day to die!" he yelled, and finally he charged toward the cavalry line.

The warriors came with him, crying *"Hokahe!"* Little Big Man, Bad Heart Bull, Good Weasel, and a hundred others. As Crazy Horse had suggested, they shot not at the fighting soldiers on the rise, but at the big American horses and the soldiers who held them, four mounts to a holder. They whipped their ponies hard. They would see if the whites' hearts were big.

Crazy Horse's heart was huge. He felt the familiar tingle of excitement. He let it raise his bow and shoot the arrow toward the mounts and the men holding them.

"Hokahe!" they shrieked, and bore down on the cavalry line.

It was going to work. The horses were rearing and bolting. The soldiers, afraid of being left afoot facing a charge, jumped for their mounts and fled down the valley.

Quickly the Lakota were on them, swinging war clubs, jabbing with lances, hitting with the stocks of their empty rifles. Warrior and foe rode hard toward the strong line where Three Stars stood with the walking soldiers. Some Lakota stopped to pick up dropped carbines, and they found the soldiers had had trouble with them—the empty shells wouldn't eject. Other Lakota drove the soldiers toward their own line, laughing and yelling and hitting.

When they came within range of the infantry rifles, which were accurate at longer distances than the carbines, the Lakota whipped the soldiers forward with mocking calls and fell back.

The charge had worked, but it was a big risk for a small gain. The fight was getting difficult—the Lakota and Sahiyela had almost no shells—they'd used even the ones they got with the carbines they picked up.

Crazy Horse decided to try one more trick, a decoy. He did it the old way, retreating with intermittent charges, as though to make the soldiers slow down the pursuit. So they came harder. If he could get them into the narrow beyond the bend of the creek, strung out, between lines of his warriors, in a place where arrows would be effective . . .

But the Psatoka and Susuni refused to go into the little canyon, and the decoy failed.

The Lakota and Sahiyela backed off. The warriors were tired, the ponies exhausted. Even if they had killed many soldiers, they had lost some good men. It had been a tough fight, and it was time to go home.

Not until the next day did they know they'd won something big. Three Stars had turned around and headed for his base camp or maybe for the fort.

In council everyone spoke happily. The soldiers had turned around, the village was safe. A big victory, they said.

But you could not dance a victory in a camp where dead warriors were laid out in their lodges. So they moved the camp down to the Greasy Grass, the river the whites called the Little Bighorn.

When General Crook got back to his supply base two days later, he told his aide-de-camp to sit for dictation of messages to Lieutenant General Sherman. Impatient of niceties of every kind, Crook put things bluntly and left it up to the Irish wit Bourke to find fine words.

"Tell him the Indians have got more starch than we thought," he said. "Lots more." Bourke nodded his head in irrelevant approval. It was good manners to praise an enemy and good politics to give his ability a high estimate. "Tell him I've ordered five more companies of infantry." Crook shot Bourke a jaundiced look. "Tell him I won't venture into the field until they arrive."

"But, General," Bourke protested, trying to sound soft and gentle, "that means you can't join Custer and Terry."

This was a small effrontery. All the top officers here were fully aware of the plan to close in on the Sioux from three sides.

"Tell him," said Crook with caustic emphasis, "that I won't move until I have the infantry."

Bourke wrote it down.

The general proved good as his word.

CRAZY HORSE AND CUSTER

It was *yaspapi,* the time of bitten-off moon, in the Moon When the Chokecherries Ripen, which the Sahiyela called the Moon When the Ponies Get Fat.

It was a good time for the Lakota and Sahiyela. They

had driven Three Stars off. Scouts spotted herds of antelope to the north of their camp. Friends and relatives were coming in from the agencies thick as ducks flying north in the spring. In the six days since the fight with Three Stars, the size of the village had more than doubled. Now about eighteen hundred fighting men were in camp. If they were strong against Three Stars, they would be overwhelming against any soldiers that would dare to come, even like storm clouds from the east. They were confident. Now everyone was seeing soldiers falling into camp.

When they thought about it, they judged that the whites deserved what was coming. Had they not tried to steal Paha Sapa? Did they not kill women and children wantonly? Did they not act without honor?

The big camp used up grass and firewood fast, so the village moved downstream one sleep, toward the antelope herds. There they put up seven big circles of lodges: at the upstream end along the river, Sitting Bull's Hunkpapa. At the downstream end, Sahiyela. Behind the Hunkpapa, Blackfeet. Along the river from upstream to down, Mniconjou, Itazipicola, Sicangu. In back of these, the Oglala of Crazy Horse. For the Lakota it was a stirring sight, one they hadn't been treated to in a long time. Seven thousand of the people together, strong, unified, of one mind and heart. They smiled to think what the sight would do to the soldiers.

Many of them thought the soldiers would steer clear. Even white people were not that dumb.

That's why the Lakota were spending a lazy afternoon when the wolves came dashing back. Soon the camp criers were bawling out the warning: "The soldiers are coming! From the east!"

It was also a good time for Lt. Col. George A. Custer, commonly called by his brevet rank, General Custer. He was a man enraptured by his own vision, entranced by the blazing sight of himself in the heaven of military and political prominence in the summer of 1876, the nation's centennial. He saw that good luck attended him at every turn, but it seemed far more than good luck, more a destiny of shining eminence. It lay seductively within the reach, Custer saw, of any white man with the vision and boldness to stick out a gauntleted hand and seize it, and the élan to wear it dashingly.

Yes, he had been in trouble. Had been court-martialed and set down. Had gotten into trouble even this spring. But his difficulties came from passion, from burning desire. If this waywardness sometimes brought disapproval from his superiors, it was not a quality the army truly condemned. They tut-tutted but secretly admired it. Politicians admired it. The American public loved it.

In fact, General Custer thought it might be about to vault him over the heads of those stuffy superiors and into highest office. The Democratic party would be holding its quadrennial convention next week, its main purpose to nominate new candidates for President and Vice President of the United States. Certain influential men had dropped a word to the wise: A young, chivalrous, dashing general of the army would make a good nominee for Vice President, certainly. In fact, many generals had become President in the last half-century.

What could be more perfect! thought the lieutenant colonel in his heart of hearts. *A really extraordinary man rewarded in the right way!*

What was needed, hinted these influential men, was a smashing victory against the Sioux. The American people were impatient with a government that could not keep savages in line. They would not tolerate letting the Sioux chase buffalo through the Black Hills, where millions of dollars' worth of gold waited to be mined. Ridiculous. They would respond to a man who put a resounding end to such nonsense.

So Custer listened to General Terry's plan. Custer was to lead the Seventh Cavalry up the Rosebud and follow the lodge trail to wherever the big Sioux village was, probably on the Little Bighorn. Meanwhile Terry and Gibbon would get their soldiers, slowed by the infantry, into place. It wouldn't do to hit the village and let the Indians run, as they always did. Custer was to strike from the east. If the Sioux fled downstream, Terry and Gibbon would be waiting. If upstream, they would be running into the arms of Crook.

Custer was willing. He was eager. He was an experienced Indian fighter—the victor of the Washita—and knew what to expect.

Custer believed he knew Indians. He even admired them, as a hunter admires the buffalo, the mountain lion, the grizzly bear. He didn't think of them as men and women with children, people who got hungry and cold and loved the feeling of being alive. He thought of them as a slightly magnificent but utterly doomed species, more animal than human.

Had someone told him that men of spiritual power were in the village he meant to destroy—Crazy Horse, Horn Chips, Sitting Bull, who saw soldiers falling into camp, the young Black Elk, beneficiary of a great vision—Custer would have smiled in amusement or rolled his eyes. He thought his job was finishing off a benighted people, a job Nature herself was doing, but too slowly.

Yes, the only danger was indecision. The only issue was sufficient will. The only strategic concern was to force the Indians for once to choose fight, not flight.

So when Terry spoke of caution, of coordination with the other forces, of prudence, Custer wasn't listening. These were the worries of the official army. The truth was that neither the army nor the public loved such old-maidish stuff. They rewarded the men who were not afraid, men who saw opportunity and seized it, men with the courage to ignore such mutterings and win the day.

He knew that he was such a man.

The Seventh Cavalry found the lodge trail on the Rosebud and marched along it toward the Little Bighorn. All was going according to plan. Custer would rest his regiment on June 25 and attack the next day. On the morning of June 25 Custer's scouts spotted the village to the northwest. They pointed out the campfire smoke to the general, and the pony herd on the hillsides beyond. A big village, they warned him. They also told Custer they thought the regiment had been spotted or would be spotted any moment.

So the Indians might escape after all. Custer reacted with élan. Instead of reconnoitering, he decided to gather information about the lay of the land and the nature of the enemy on the attack. He sent a battalion under Captain Benteen south to make sure no lodges sat down there. He sent another battalion under Major Reno down a creek with orders to attack the upstream end of the village. He kept a third battalion under his own command to ride north and hit the village right in what appeared to be its center.

His only worry was that the bastards might get away.

The plan: Reno would hit the upstream end of the village. The warriors would rush to that point. Then Custer would hit the downstream end, scatter them, and mop up.

For the valiant, life was delicious.

On the afternoon of June 25, 1876, guidons flying, his command cantered down Medicine Tail Coulee.

Major Reno followed his orders, at least for a while. His battalion crossed the Little Bighorn and attacked the lodges at the south end of the big village.

The warriors were scurrying—getting their horses, most of which had been turned out on the hillside. Getting their weapons. Painting themselves. Making medicine. Readying their spirits. So the soldiers came hard. When they got within rifle shot of the village, the warriors laid down such a fire that the soldiers got off and fought on foot.

Still, gunfire damaged the village. These were Hunkpapa lodges, people led by Sitting Bull and Gall. As it happened, Reno's soldiers killed some women and children in that initial fire. Among them were Gall's two wives and three children. Up Gall's gullet surged a murderous rage.

Crazy Horse came riding with a strong bunch of Oglala warriors from their village downstream. He was dressed and painted as the man anointed Rider should be—his light hair hanging below his waist, shirtless, hailstones painted on his body, a streak of lightning on his face. Most important, the red-tailed hawk was on his head and Hawk flew above him. He could feel her like a throb in his blood, and without sound could hear her barbaric war cry, KEE-ur, KEE-ur.

She was huge in his heart.

He saw the warriors getting ready to charge and wondered if they had enough bullets to win. Then he thought of the fight on the Rosebud a quarter-moon ago, when the soldiers' rifles got so hot they wouldn't eject the spent shells.

So he kicked his horse into the no-man's-land between white and Lakota warriors. He rode in curves, circles, slants, every which way, drawing the soldier fire. As he rode, he felt himself in a swirl of time and place between one world and another, a place of spirit, a place utterly protected against not only the bullets ripping through the air at him but the physical world itself. He was Rider, and invulnerable.

He rode hard back to his own side, where the warriors were shouting his praises. "Hold your fire!" he shouted.

Back into no-man's-land he rode, exhilarated, serene in the confidence that he couldn't be touched. He made a show of riding tricks. He called mockery at the soldiers who couldn't hit him.

He felt like Rider today.

Back to his warriors at a gallop. "Wait!" he shouted. "Soon!"

And once more toward the whites.

The fire was heavier now. He could feel the anger and frustration of the soldiers in it. But it was impotent.

So he circled back toward his warriors, blew the whistle meaning "Charge!" and rushed the whites' left flank head-long. He felt the surge of Lakota fighting men behind him.

The soldiers broke and ran.

The Lakota killed some from behind. Before long, though, the soldiers reached some trees on a little rise by the river.

The fight slowed. It was hard to attack them in their good cover.

Soon the whites broke again and ran for the river. Straight off the high bank they jumped their horses into deep water where there was no crossing.

The Lakota caught them from behind. They clubbed the soldiers off their horses into the swift and flooding stream. They used arrows. They killed mercilessly.

The whites who got across the river climbed a hill where they were hard to reach.

Some of the warriors stayed up on the hill and kept the soldiers pinned down there.

Most of them came back and started picking up aban-doned rifles and shells, grinning at each other, exulting. They jabbered and joked with the queer nervous energy that follows a wrestle with death.

Until a big shout came. "Soldiers!"

A messenger, riding hard from downstream.

"More soldiers!" he yelled. "Down that ridge where the dust is!"

Another fight. No one was alarmed. Yes, that was the middle of the camp, where the women and children had fled from this first attack. So it was simple—they would kill the soldiers.

Energy coiled and gathered in them. Another fight. An-other look at death. Yes, they were ready. This was their day, supremely their day.

These soldiers were coming directly from the east. The warriors looked at each other speculatively. Maybe these were the ones Sitting Bull saw falling upside down into camp.

"*Hokahe!*" some of them yelled. Others looked at each other appraisingly. *Yes, let them come. Yes, let's go get them.*

Gall and Crazy Horse drew the warriors together with their whistles. They asked for a charge. The women and children were down there, and the lodges were half-down. They must strike hard.

The martial spirit was huge in Gall—his wives and children murdered. The warriors saw it and felt it.

"This is a good day to die!"

"This is a good day to die!"

They roared downstream.

Crazy Horse circled through the Oglala village. His pinto was played out. Black Shawl, anticipating, was holding a second mount for him. He saw Sitting Bull briefly. The Big Bellies were staying in the village, ready to fight or flee if the soldiers got too close.

A pretty young woman, unmarried, was singing encouragement:

> "*Brothers-in-law,*
> *now your friends have come.*
> *Take courage.*
> *Would you see me taken captive?*"

Crazy Horse gathered up some warriors and galloped for the river.

Gall and his forces were just getting there. Four Sahiyela flanked each other on the far side of the river, facing the soldiers, four alone against two or three hundred. They laid down a fire that slowed the whites down. *Brave men,* thought Crazy Horse.

Galloping toward the river, he saw that Gall was crossing now. He appeared to outnumber the soldiers easily. As his men charged the white line, the soldiers started falling back. The village was going to be safe.

And now Crazy Horse saw what was going to happen. Gall was pushing up the hill hard. Other warriors from the lower circles were crossing the river behind him. The front of the double column of soldiers was getting hit bluntly and hard, the whites would have to . . .

Custer was determined to get his five companies back together and make a defensive circle, damn it. The ones who descended to the ford were being driven up the coulee and onto the hill to the north. The general and his companies above were fighting their way north to join them. They would kill the horses if they had to, use them for breastworks, and lay down a fire these savages would never forget.

Custer looked merrily across his horse's neck at his brother Tom. "It is a good day to kill!" he said mockingly.

They had to get together first. He yelled, he fired, he used his spurs. The enemy was pouring up the hill. Where had all these Injuns come from? Where had they gotten all this ammunition? Why had they suddenly decided to fight instead of run?

When General Custer saw that fellow, the correspondent of that Bismarck newspaper, he would have some choice words for the high command. The newspapers always liked it when field officers said what asses the generals back in their headquarters were.

The enemy fire was heavy. Some men of these companies weren't going to get to that high ridge where the stand would be made. He grinned sardonically to himself. Not everyone was chosen by fate.

Crazy Horse saw it. The coulee running upward, the hill behind. Beyond that he remembered the long ridge stretching to the northwest. The battle laid itself out in his mind. He watched the white soldiers going for the high ground where they would make their stand. He saw himself and his warriors coming at them from behind. He thought so. He was almost sure.

He got off his fresh pony. He threw gopher dust on it to confound the enemy. He put spears of grass into his long hair to suggest snow that drives creatures before it. He called upon the power of the wind to confuse the enemy. When enough warriors were gathered, he blew the eagle-bone whistle. For once he raised his voice: "Let every Oglala," he cried, "every man of any circle who wants to, follow me!"

They whipped their ponies after the war leader Crazy Horse, and he felt the power of all these men propel him forward.

He rode for the river and turned downstream, away from Gall's fight, toward the hillside that would lead him up to the far end of the ridge. He saw it. As the soldiers came up the hill, firing back down at Gall, he would hit them from the other side. He would turn the place of their stand into a trap. But nothing was certain yet.

He rode hard, rode furiously, rode eternally.

When Crazy Horse came up the last rim below the highest ridge, he saw them, yes, the backs of the first soldiers to the top. Not forted up yet, just arriving. It was perfect.

He looked. He felt the sun on his face. He felt Hawk in his heart, jubilant. This day was radiant as the one in his boyhood vision more than twenty winters ago.

Now was the time. Yes, he would charge straight into the whites, trusting Rider's power. When they saw the strength of his medicine, his men would follow him. The surprised soldiers would scatter like prairie hens. Then there would be nothing left but the killing.

He put his quirt to his pony and screamed. "KEE-ur! KEE-ur!"

PART **FIVE**

GOING HOME

*In the twilight
the spirit of His Crazy Horse
  stands
on the sundance ground.
He raises the sacred canupa
to the sky and intones a prayer:*

*"In a sacred manner I send a voice
  to you.
In a sacred manner I send a voice
  to you.
To half of the sky
I send my voice in a sacred manner.
In a sacred manner I send a voice
  to you."*

*As the light grows,
he continues to pray.
Hundreds of Lakota people
rise up around him,
dancing in celebration.
Over the thumps of feet and drum
we cannot hear his words.*

The victory tasted delicious. The big villages moved off from the site of the battle and held big dances to celebrate. The men chanted, sang, and danced their deeds in the fight against Long Hair by the Greasy Grass. Crazy Horse noticed that they sounded like hero stories of old. Lakota warriors struck so many coups that many of them had not been witnessed.

Men made new songs about the fight. Some were mocking:

> "Long Hair, I had no guns.
> You brought me some.
> I thank you.
> You make me laugh!
>
> "Long Hair, I had no horses.
> You brought me some.
> I thank you.
> You make me laugh!"

One of the songs Crazy Horse liked best pointed at the way the whites were always condemning people different from them:

> "A charger, he is coming.
> I made him come.
> When he came, I wiped him out.
> He didn't like my ways,
> That's why."

What he was happiest about was that the people had joined together and acted as one people, not a lot of quarreling bands and chiefs. Also, the Lakota had fought the new way, not individually but as a unit, not for honors and glory but to kill.

Other war leaders paid him a compliment. When they

saw that Gall would chase the soldiers up the hill, the warriors following Crazy Horse rode away from the fight, around in back of Long Hair, and surprised him from the rear. They added that only Crazy Horse could have led the men in that roundabout attack.

People said the spirit of Sitting Bull's vision had been realized. Others said that because of some mutilations and stripping of bodies, a terrible price would be exacted later.

Many Lakota wondered what the soldiers would do now. "Respect us," some said, "and leave us alone." "Get revenge for Long Hair," others said, "by sending ten soldiers for every one they sent to the Greasy Grass."

Crazy Horse did not participate in these arguments. He said in private that they would simply have to wait and see what the whites would do. There was nothing to be gained by guessing about it. He had another reason not to talk, though, to withdraw and be quiet and listen: Something was more and more insistent in his mind—the beat of the drum.

The soldiers made their choice: They withdrew from the entire country and waited until one full moon had passed and half of another, the Moon When All Things Ripen. Even then they marched all around and found hardly any Indians and had indifferent success when they did.

In the meantime Crazy Horse went to Paha Sapa against the miners. He thought the people mustn't lose the Hills. But regardless of what the army did, more miners crawled over the hills every day, tearing up the earth looking for gold. He took groups of young warriors. They slipped through the canyons silently, used arrows instead of guns, and killed miner after miner.

They stole wagonloads of goods that were welcome in the camps.

When the young men dragged their feet, wanting to enjoy themselves, Crazy Horse went back to the Hills alone and killed more miners. He was quiet and effective. He felt more murderous than he had since the days when he avenged Little Hawk's death.

It was He Dog who figured out what Crazy Horse was doing and upbraided him.

"And what do you do?" He Dog asked a little sharply, talking about the lone trips.

"Kill miners," said Crazy Horse. It required no explanation.

He Dog sucked at his *canupa* and said nothing for a while. Then he spoke softly and intensely. "My friend, you have no right." He looked Crazy Horse in the eye. "You have no right. You belong to everyone now."

He let it sit. They both were thinking how Crazy Horse had belonged to everyone as a shirtman, pledged to think of all the people first, and how he had lost that status and those duties.

"Things are different now," He Dog said. "The Big Bellies are agency chiefs. We have not made any new shirtmen for a long time. The people choose the leaders they want in the way they want." He gazed at Crazy Horse directly. "They've chosen you. You are their hero. They follow you."

Crazy Horse listened to the beat of the drum.

He Dog was quiet for a while. "This is a terrible time," he said. "The hoop of the people is broken, some of us living the old way, some of us begging from the whites. To mend the hoop we need leadership. You cannot throw your life at the feet of some miner who happens to see you first."

Crazy Horse stayed in camp. It was time for the fall hunt anyway, if anyone could find buffalo.

When the meat was in the packs—well, some meat—came the awful news. The Big Bellies had sold Paha Sapa. The Black Hills, whites called them, and the whites "owned" them now.

People listened to the messengers in the council lodge in a hubbub. They spoke out of turn and even interrupted each other. Men called *"Hunhunhe!"* in regret. Some women wailed.

"They can't sell any land," said someone. "The paper says three out of four of us have to sign."

"The whites say it's done," answered the messengers.

"How many signed?"

"Thirty or forty."

"Out of all the people?"

"Thirty or forty."

Worm said, "They see how few of us are left."

"Why did they sign?"

"They were drunk," someone put in.

One messenger held up a hand. "Red Cloud refused to sign," he said. "Spotted Tail refused to sign. Then the agents said no more food would be given to anyone until they signed."

No more food at all. The children would starve to death.

The warriors looked at each other. No one said the obvious. If you took the white man's word, his food, his clothing and blankets, then he would starve you whenever he wanted more.

At this revelation Crazy Horse, silent as usual, got up and left the council.

He walked out into the hills near camp. He sat and looked around and saw nothing. He was in a rage.

He tried to quiet enough inside to listen to Hawk, to sense Hawk's mood.

Maybe she was still. At least he couldn't feel her.

Besides, she was his guide in war.

Who would guide him when he won on the battlefield and lost everything to a piece of paper?

WINTER OF THE SOUL

Crazy Horse watched them walking knee-deep through the soft snow, gliding through the flakes that drifted down, gray, misty shadows barely moving. Many took just enough steps to keep from freezing to death. When they stopped, they looked thin and bare and quaking, like the leafless aspens they walked through.

Easing down, the snow made them lavender silhouettes against the pink dawn light. Yes, they had a kind of austere beauty. Sometimes he thought death was beautiful. Sometimes he felt its call, soft and alluring. Sometimes the call seemed to come from Hawk. Sometimes from the mother whose name he would never speak. Sometimes from the beat of the drum.

It was not time to listen to it, not yet.

He stood in the deep snow among the aspens and watched the Sahiyela village of Morning Star walk toward Crazy Horse's camp on Hanging Woman Creek above the Buffalo Tongue River near the Shining Mountains. The village had been hit by Three Stars' soldiers, and for three-quarters of an entire moon, a moon of death, they had walked through the terrible cold to seek succor from Crazy Horse.

He was afoot because he had given his mount to a young woman with children of about six and two winters. The woman could barely stand up on her frozen, bloodied feet. *Akicita* men would be here soon with plenty of ponies, but Crazy Horse wanted to ease the woman's pain immediately. He would walk back to camp. Sometimes walking made his mind and spirit reflective, and he saw into things.

This time he could barely stand to see. The word was that eleven babies had frozen to death in their mothers' arms. Clearly the soldiers had destroyed most of the village's possessions—horses, lodges, food, clothing, blankets, everything. And left them to walk through the cold, dying.

This moon, which the whites called November, had been the coldest Winter Moon he could remember. The snow that began last night at dusk had warmed Mother Earth a little. Otherwise more children would probably have frozen to death in their mothers' arms just last night.

Now his village's camp was on Hanging Woman Creek. The name was from the Psatoka, who said that an older woman had hanged herself from the lodge poles here when her man took a second and younger wife. Still, the name seemed . . . fateful.

Sometimes he felt mesmerized by the beat of the drum.

He shook his head and forced himself to think not about his birth mother but the soldiers. They had done such things before to the Sahiyela, on Sand Creek, at the Washita, and just last winter at Two Moons' camp, when He Dog was there. Such soldiers were incomprehensible to Crazy Horse. "Understand your enemy" was a first principle of war. He did not want to understand these enemies. But he did want to kill them.

Morning Star told the story in the council lodge, but so feebly it hardly made sense. The Sahiyela thought the soldiers had missed them. A youth captured by several Snakes had given the location of the village away before he realized the Snakes were scouting for the army. The pony soldiers struck at dawn. Morning Star's young son had been killed in the first charge. The soldiers got straight into the village. The warriors had to hold them off from a nearby ridge while the women and children fled. Over thirty Sahiyela were killed. And the soldiers burned the entire village, everything the people owned.

Exactly what had happened didn't matter, though the Sahiyela seemed not to be good at watching for soldiers in winter camp. What did matter was that here were nearly two hundred lodges, about thirteen hundred people, without shelter, without clothing, without blankets, without food.

Sitting next to Crazy Horse, He Dog assured the Sahiyela that their people would be fed and kept warm by their brothers the Lakota.

Crazy Horse held his short *canupa* up and asked the blessings of the powers upon this village. They were going to need blessings, he thought. To get enough food and enough to keep warm for all these people through the winter—now that was only a gray, misty hope.

In the next moon, the time of the shortest days of the year, Lakota men came into camp from Red Cloud Agency with an offer. To persuade these men to ask the free chiefs to bring their people in, Three Stars had made two promises: He would quit chasing the Indians in the winter, and they would get agencies here in their own country, not far off on the Muddy Water River, the Missouri.

"A white-man promise!" exclaimed Little Big Man.

Besides, the messengers had to admit that last moon Three Stars had confiscated all the ponies and guns at Red Cloud Agency, every one of them. It was humiliating. The army had sent the scouts of the Pani, their oldest enemies, to confiscate Lakota property. The Pani had marched right into lodges, thrown things around, taken every gun they could find, and even burned some lodges.

"Why?" asked Little Big Man sharply. "Why take the horses and guns?"

Three Stars said it was because the Oglala had moved away from the agency after they signed the paper selling the Black Hills. But Red Cloud's people thought it was to keep the agency Indians from helping their free cousins.

Then Three Stars showed how angry he was at Red Cloud. The soldier chief set Spotted Tail as headman over the Oglala as well as the Sicangu.

The leaders looked at each other wide-eyed. Go in? And have every horse and every firearm taken by the soldiers? How would they live? What good would an agency in their own country be if they couldn't move the village or hunt? They would be prisoners, dependent on handouts.

No, they said with bitter laughter, they wouldn't go to Red Cloud Agency. There the air would be thick with the old troubles among the Oglala anyway. And the Oglala would be under a Sicangu chief.

But they were very hungry. Every day they ate horses, usually the American horses captured from the soldiers last summer. Though they'd run cattle off from Bear Coat's new fort at the mouth of Buffalo Tongue River, that beef was butchered and gone.

No one mentioned it, but the extra Sahiyela mouths to feed were a heavy burden.

Crazy Horse struggled to keep his mind on helping the people. His spirit was off in the forest, alone, listening to the song of songs, the beat of the drum.

One morning thirteen lodges were gone, headed for Red Cloud Agency. The headmen had talked about this and agreed: All the people in this camp, 600 lodges of Oglala, Mniconjou, and Itazipicola, would stay until everyone decided what to do. They would not fragment themselves, not during this hard winter. No one liked to make such a decision—it went hard against the Lakota sense that each man owned his own life and directed it by his own insight into Power. But sometimes individuals had to govern themselves for the best for all.

So the *akicita* men followed the lodge trail in the snow and brought the deserters back. By instruction they unstrung their bows and whipped the men to shame them. They also took their weapons and broke their lodge poles.

The next day four lodges of people left with the messengers from Red Cloud. The chiefs let them go—the soldiers were holding the families of these people hostage at Fort Robinson until they came in.

So the headmen talked long and seriously among themselves. People were suffering. Something had to be done.

They decided to send messengers to Bear Coat, the whites' General Miles. Four hundred lodges of Hunkpapa had gone in to Miles at the soldier house at the mouth of the Tongue River and were given plenty to eat. Maybe Bear Coat would give them food, let them keep their mounts and weapons and live in their own land.

The headmen went down to the fort, Crazy Horse, He Dog, Big Road, Lame Deer of the Mniconjou, and a score of others. They sat their ponies on a ridge and sent forward Drum-on-His-Back, the Oglala who had learned to read. Seven other messengers rode with Drum-on-His-Back, under a white flag of truce, as General Miles had instructed.

As the headmen watched, their old enemies the Psatoka, who were scouts for General Miles now, opened fire on the peace messengers. Drum-on-His-Back and four other men were down before the rest could get away.

The soldiers rode out fast and stopped the shooting and called and signaled for the Lakota to come in.

Crazy Horse said disgustedly to Little Big Man, "Yes, after five good men are dead."

They rode back up Buffalo Tongue River.

Crazy Horse didn't know how they would survive the winter.

Maybe he had to face it: What was a life for him was not a life for the people.

He didn't know. It seemed possible. The agency was death for him. But . . .

He went to Horn Chips. They smoked. He stated as clearly as he could the case against agency life: People would say anything, do anything, for whiskey, coffee, sugar, or enough food. They became white people: Morning Star said sixty of the scouts who had come against his village were Lakota.

Worse, what had happened at Fort Laramie would take place more swiftly and severely now. Medicine would be forgotten, *akicita* would lose influence, no one would become a shirtman, ceremonies would disappear. Those who became Big Bellies would be those good at currying favor from the whites, not those proven to have the good of the people at heart.

If the Lakota fought, the whites would kill them. But if they no longer cared about the powers, no longer kept the awareness of Spirit at the center of their lives, they had killed themselves. The hoop of the people would be broken forever, and the flowering tree would wither.

Horn Chips listened carefully. Crazy Horse thought the man of stone medicine might have wise words, for he had lived with the agency Lakota as well as the wild ones. But Horn Chips seemed to have no specific advice to give. He only said that they would sweat and prepare Crazy Horse to seek to see beyond.

In the sweat lodge Horn Chips prayed for insight to be granted on the mountain to this leader of the people. One of the sentences of his four prayers Crazy Horse marked down in his mind: "Help us to remember that the hoop contains both the red road and the black road, contains peace and harmony and discord and hardship, and all these are part of the embracing circle of life."

As they walked to the site of the vision-seeking, Chips made one suggestion: "Remember," he said, "sometimes we ask Power to be on our side. This time you must ask how to be on the side of Power."

So Crazy Horse cried for a vision on the mountain, naked and forlorn. He asked the four directions for their help, and Father Sky and Mother Earth, and all the grandfathers. He paid attention to Hawk in his heart for guidance. He touched the stone behind his ear with a finger and squeezed the moss stone he had gotten at the Split Rock against his ribs. He listened to the beat of the drum of the earth, a language older than the stone language. He sat for days, waiting for counsel.

During this time he had no new thoughts about how to deal with Three Stars or Bear Coat or the people's agency relatives. He did not see where herds of buffalo stomped in the snow. He did not see anything in particular.

For himself he felt a kind of peace. He wanted to fight. He would fight. That was his way.

For the people he saw no peace yet. Maybe somehow,

somewhere, a way he did not see opened ahead for them. Though it seemed that the sacred hoop must be broken, he tried to remember that the hoop held not only the good red road of peace but the black road of war. He reminded himself that the people had undergone great changes in their way of life before, like the one marked by the coming of White Buffalo Cow Woman. Maybe this time was the beginning of one of those changes. If he did not see the future, maybe someone else would.

Sometimes Crazy Horse had hope that his young cousin Black Elk, the son of the elder Black Elk, would see the way. The boy had been granted a great vision. Maybe some power lay in that vision for the people.

But he did not see it. Yet. The drum beat forever, but did not explain itself.

In front of the sweat lodge, after Crazy Horse told Chips what he had seen, Chips asked him whether the Inyan spoke to him.

"No," said Crazy Horse. "I sit with them. I pray with them, perhaps not as often as I should. They don't speak to me. They give me something, though. When I put my mind on Inyan, I feel the way I used to feel with my *hunka* when we were youths." He could not say Hump's name. "We would sit on a ledge, a secret place we went, and talk all night. Especially we would talk about the stars, and Hump would tell the star knowledge he got from his uncle. Then sometimes we would fall silent for a long time and just look at the stars. Just look. Somehow then we felt together, with each other and with the stars, and with the earth and all things. I believe we heard the drumbeat, the pulse of the earth, the same pulse. A feeling, not words. But it was strong. It was a bond between us."

Crazy Horse felt his eyes moisten. He had not often allowed himself to remember his *hunka* so vividly.

Horn Chips said, "Then the Inyan are speaking to you. Listen."

A LEADER'S CHOICE

What Crazy Horse heard didn't come from the drumbeat or the Inyan or from Spirit but from the scouts: General Miles was coming up the Buffalo Tongue River with about five hundred walking soldiers.

Chasing Indians in the snow again. This was what the villages could not stand. The ponies weren't strong enough to travel much. The snow slowed everyone down. The weather took a toll. If you didn't keep a good watch, the soldiers would drive off your horses, take your food, and burn your homes.

The women and children packed up and moved back. The warriors, more men than Miles had but with little ammunition, held the soldiers off from a ridge.

The headmen were worried. They started the pony drags toward the Greasy Grass. If the soldiers stayed in the field and did not let them settle down, children and old people would die of exposure, hunger, and weakness.

Late that afternoon it started to snow, hard. Crazy Horse sent the warriors fast after the women. He and He Dog and two Sahiyela stayed behind to guard the rear. Occasionally they shot a soldier. Sometimes they recovered some bullets from the bodies. They kept up enough fire that the soldiers did not know the village was gone.

That night the village traveled through the snow and the darkness, crossing as fast as they could to the west, over the divide toward Rosebud Creek. When the snow was coming so hard it filled a hoofprint quickly, Crazy Horse and the others followed.

The next day Crazy Horse's scouts said General Miles had gone back down Buffalo Tongue River. Probably they were nearly out of food.

* * *

Messengers came with presents from White Hat, the young officer at Fort Robinson. Though they promised that the Crazy Horse people could have an agency in their own country, none of the chiefs would accept the presents.

Messengers came with presents from General Miles. The chiefs refused to touch the presents. Crazy Horse was on the mountain, they said, seeking a vision. They could not say what to do until they talked to him.

Crazy Horse hardly saw Black Shawl or his own lodge the rest of that winter. Over and over he went to the mountain seeking a vision. The elder Black Elk found him there one day. Crazy Horse told him not to worry. "Cousin, I can live well enough in caves. Maybe the powers will show me something. We don't have much time."

He listened to the Inyan and heard nothing. He listened to the drumbeat and heard everything, but saw no path in it.

In the Snow-Blind Moon, Spotted Tail came to appeal to Crazy Horse, with lots of lodges and lots of food.

"My son is on the mountain," Worm told Spotted Tail. The Sicangu leader understood that his nephew was seeking guidance. His wives put the lodge up, and they waited. Since Spotted Tail seldom saw his two sisters and brother-in-law, he was glad of the chance. And he was glad to have the chance to talk quietly with many people of the village and find out how their spirits were.

It was as he suspected: Half the time they were enamored of being the last holdouts, they and Sitting Bull's people. When they felt that way, they were ready to fight to the end. Or ready to go to Grandmother's land, Canada, with Sitting Bull. The other half of the time they were weary of being heroes. Hardly a woman among them had not lost someone, a brother or husband in war, a parent to starvation, a child to freezing. Every one of them had suffered severely, traipsing over the high plains in winter to avoid soldiers when they ought to have been tucked snugly in a warm canyon.

Yes, they gloried in the whipping of Long Hair last summer. No, they didn't want to die. True, this clinging to the hunting life felt grand. But it wouldn't keep a baby warm. When Spotted Tail gave out the presents of food he'd brought from the agency, the women's faces were so avid that he was embarrassed.

He also found out something personal about his nephew. His wife, Black Shawl, had the coughing sickness. When Sitting Bull had proposed that all the wild Lakota go to Grandmother's land, Crazy Horse said the winters were too cold and too long and even the summers too cool. His wife would die of the coughing.

Spotted Tail was moved to pity. He thought his nephew was not often enough moved to pity.

He admired his nephew as a man, as a warrior, and especially as a war leader. The young man had more power than anyone had hoped, even his relatives.

Spotted Tail did not admire Crazy Horse as a leader for all the people. He thought his nephew shortsighted and self-absorbed.

So he went to see Horn Chips. He couldn't suggest that Crazy Horse's spiritual counselor guide his nephew in this direction or that, not at all. But speaking his thoughts to the man might help, and listening might reveal the future.

They shared some food and some smoke. They spoke of relatives. They exchanged news and gossip. Spotted Tail sat his full height and consciously made himself physically imposing. He watched Horn Chips carefully. Did this man think of him only as a white-man chief, a conciliator? Or did he remember that Spotted Tail had knocked thirteen soldiers off their horses at the Blue Water? And had many other coups? Did he realize what Spotted Tail had truly done in taking his people to the agency?

Spotted Tail couldn't be sure. Finally, he asked one of the questions that bore on the truth here. "The young men in this camp seem to believe that no good life is possible at the agencies. Do you think so?"

Since Horn Chips measured his response carefully, Spotted Tail knew he understood the full weight of what he was being asked.

Then Horn Chips delivered a discourse on the nature of life. At first Spotted Tail did not see how his question was being answered. At last he did see. And then he wanted Crazy Horse to hear these words. He knew Crazy Horse needed to hear these words.

At the end Horn Chips waited awhile. Spotted Tail was silent out of great respect. Chips smiled. "You want your nephew to hear these words, I know," said Horn Chips. "I have thought about it a long time. It's hard to guide him. He has his own way to see. But yes, I want to say all this to him. When he gets back, I will invite you and him to eat."

Spotted Tail was delighted.

When his nephew came down from the mountain, all the leaders sat in the council lodge and talked things over. Crazy Horse said how glad he was to see his relatives and thanked Spotted Tail for the many gifts. The Sicangu chief relayed the promise of the soldier chiefs to Crazy Horse: If he came in, he would be given an agency here in his own country.

Crazy Horse said nothing, as Spotted Tail had expected. The other leaders were noncommittal. Spotted Tail could not divine what his nephew would do. He held out hope for when they talked to Horn Chips together.

The dinner Chips gave for Spotted Tail and Crazy Horse was not congenial. All the conversation had to be carried by the agency chief.

Finally Horn Chips surprised his guests by saying he wanted to talk to the two of them about what his own Inyan told him. It was rare, and a privilege, to hear a *wicasa wakan*'s communications from his Inyan. Then Chips surprised Crazy Horse again by seeming to tell the story of the creation of the world.

"From the beginning," he said, "there was Inyan, rock, the first of all things, who was then soft and shapeless as a cloud. Inyan wanted to use His powers, so from part of Himself he made Maka, Mother Earth. In creating Maka, Inyan let too much of his blue blood flow away, and it became the waters. Since power cannot stay in the form of water, it changed itself into the sky god, Taku Skanskan, which means what makes motion move, that which moves and changes. And from Inyan and Maka, Skan created Wi, the sun. These are the four principal powers," said Chips. "They are the shapes creation takes.

"From these comes everything we see." He proceeded to mention the creation of the four subordinate powers: Moon, Passion, Wind, and Thunderstorm. He spoke of the star people, of sands by the waters, of growing things and rain, of monsters that could abide in the waters and go upon the lands, of crawling, winged, and four-legged people, and of the buffalo and the human beings. "My stones are Inyan," he said. "Inyan is all substance. Everything is Inyan," he said, "and Skan, the force that moves it.

"One of the teachings of the Inyan," Horn Chips declared, "is that in each stage of this making of the world in its present form, Skan was, and life was, but changing, always changing shape. In each time since then, including the time of the two-legged creatures," he said, "Skan was, and life was, but changing, always a new way to live. Always, including many ways that are lost from the memory of the people.

"Many generations ago, White Buffalo Cow Woman came and gave the people a new way to live, by the buffalo and the sacred *canupa*. That is one of many ways for two-legged creatures to live. Ways change," said Horn Chips, "but life is, and Skan is.

"Big changes come sometimes," he said. "Skan circles, life circles. Not every seven generations, but seven times seven or a hundred times seven, changes come that are too great to foresee, far too great to understand."

He looked at them somberly. "I believe this one of the teachings of the Inyan: When the old ways are dead," he said, "it means that a new way is upon us. We cannot discern it yet, but it is at hand."

Horn Chips lifted the sacred *canupa* that lay across his lap. He pointed the stem representing Mother Earth to the sky. He touched the bowl representing the buffalo and the entire universe to the spirit place in the top of his head. He held the *canupa* straight before him. Carefully, delicately, he separated the bowl from the stem and held them far apart, one in each hand. Then he looked his two friends directly in the eyes, and they all understood.

Crazy Horse's heart chilled. A way of living, the sacred way of the buffalo, separated from the earth, and made powerless. Fecundity turned to death.

"I think we will not see the new way," Horn Chips said. "I think it will not become visible for seven generations. In that time the hoop of the people will seem to be broken, and the flowering tree will seem to be withered. But after seven generations some will see with the single eye that is the heart, and the new way will appear."

He looked directly at Crazy Horse. "The old way is beautiful. We turn backward to it and in taking leave we offer it our love. Then we turn forward and walk forth blindly, offering our love. Yes, blindly."

Horn Chips was quiet for a long time. "No one man must walk forward," he said gently. He looked straight at Crazy Horse. "But the people must."

After a while the visitors rose to take their leave. Horn Chips and Crazy Horse agreed that they would prepare the sweat lodge tomorrow, and the leader would go onto the mountain to ask one last time for guidance.

But he already knew what he would do. They all knew.

* * *

On the mountain he prayed for the prosperity of the people on the new road. He asked the four directions and the grandfathers and all the powers to make the new way a good, red road. He asked for courage for the people to follow it now, in blindness. For three days he prayed incessantly for this succoring.

On the fourth day he prayed for help for himself. In the constant running these last months, keeping away from the soldiers, worrying about food, coping with messengers from the soldiers and from the agency Indians, in all these responsibilities, he felt himself becoming someone alien. So he was slipping into the grip of a profound melancholy.

He asked for strength to carry the robe of leadership as far as it must be carried. He asked for courage to walk into the darkness that loomed ahead for the people. He asked for the will to complete the tasks of the next few months.

"Then, O Grandfathers," he prayed, "I ask the freedom to wrap the robe of chieftainship around another man's shoulders. Remember, I, His Crazy Horse, sought always only to become a warrior. In my youth vision I saw myself riding into battle. Later I was uneasy even with the responsibilities of the shirt. Now I feel unsuited to lead my people. They came to me, I did not seek them, and I have never felt right as their leader. I beg now to be permitted to return to my own way. I want to listen less to the cries of the hungry and more to the beat of the drum of life. I want to turn my mind from time to timelessness."

He hesitated. He had spoken of this next to no one, not even his spiritual counselor, Horn Chips. It was too difficult to voice.

"I ask this because I have lost my oldest friend, one closer to me than my *hunka* Buffalo Hump, more intimate even than the mother I suckled as a child." Tears were running down his face now. "I have lost Hawk."

Father Sun was going down on the last day, a remote, clouded half-disk among pink and purple clouds. Crazy Horse faced it in the west, naked and shivering.

"I cannot find Hawk in my heart, Grandfathers," he said

softly. "I cannot find Hawk in my heart," he murmured again. "I do not even know the day she left me," he said. "It was when I was deciding to go to the agency." The next words were agony. "Inside my heart are the hardness and deadness of stone."

He lifted his arms to Father Sun. "Return her to me. Without her I cannot live as a man. Without her I cannot die as a man. Return her to me. Let me feel her again alive inside me."

He stood that way a long time, waiting for the sense of an answer. He sat up all night, wrapped in a buffalo robe, listening for a reply that might come from the beat of the drum.

He heard nothing but the pulse itself, endless and mute.

UNTYING THE HORSES' TAILS

Lt. William Philo Clark was struggling not to feel small, which was new to him—he was not short on ego. He watched the pipe make the circle of men in the council lodge and reflected on the names, names he'd heard incessantly since the beginning of the Sioux campaign a year and a half ago—Crazy Horse, Little Big Man, He Dog, Little Hawk, Big Road. And these were merely the men in the front circle.

Trying not to seem rudely curious, he studied the Indians' appearance. He considered himself an astute student of Indians and knew well that all the decorations had meaning, that they were signs of coups or visions, or status in warrior societies or chieftainship. All this was like insignia on a military uniform, known completely to every man in the outfit but to outsiders mere baubles. He could accept that, though the decorations were strange. Some men dangled human hair from their lances. Others fringed buckskin shirts with scalps.

By will he kept his stomach from turning. He would no

more have hung a scalp from his sword than he would have worn a necklace of slain enemies' ears or a sash of enemy intestine. Even the thought of touching a scalp, a cap of human skin, shriveled, with dry, dead hairs hanging from it—it made him smile sardonically. Sometimes it made him feel like cringing.

The pipe made its circle. Yes, these men were intimidating. Lieutenant Clark was young and inexperienced beside them. He had only a few weapons: He was privy to some of the purposes of the army, which they had no idea of. And he was ruthless, willing to do what was necessary.

He had to give them credit, though—they were true warriors. In the space of eight days they had whipped his present commander, General Crook, at the Rosebud, and then the army's best-known Indian fighter at the Little Bighorn. When he himself was with the cavalry under Crook that engaged them at Slim Buttes, his outfit had made no impact on them. In fact, these Indians had stayed out in their country, two steps ahead of General Crook and General Miles, for a year and a half. They had inflicted a terrible defeat on the army at Fort Phil Kearny a decade ago and one on Grattan's men a decade before that. All the army's "victories" had come against these men's women and children.

Yet none of that impressed him particularly. It was his job to understand them—he had studied their sign language, their spoken language, their habits, their customs, had cultivated influence among the friendlies. What made him feel a tad uncertain of himself was what he saw in their faces today. These were worn faces, lined by caring, facing up to hard decisions, making desperate flights in the dark and the snow with women and children. Faces that looked down on sons and daughters while they died. Faces that had known elation and exhilaration and hardship and tragedy and . . .

He pondered it sometimes. They had done all their fighting not for some abstract ideal like conquering territory but for the simple need to protect their families. They had not gone into a foreign land, as he and the men under him had done, to take something from others. They had defended home, hearth, family, and tribe. They had tried to get enough food and something to keep the cold away.

Well, all this was not his concern. He was aide to General Crook, he was ordered here to get these Indians settled onto a reservation with a minimum of trouble, and his job was to acquit himself well in the eyes of his superiors.

He did not know for sure why these hostiles had come here to surrender today. Was it the chasing of Miles and Crook? Was it the reassurances of their relatives sent to persuade them, first Spotted Tail and then Red Cloud? Was it an overwhelming realization that change had come and was irrevocable? The lieutenant didn't know. Surely they had faced terrible realities and made terrible decisions. They came here today with the simplicity and sere tragedy of these realities and these decisions written eloquently on their faces, for those willing to read.

It almost made him feel callow. He looked into these eyes and saw texture, grain, shadow, depth he felt lacking in himself. He thought maybe they understood life and he did not. At least they had experienced it and he had not.

It also made him feel guilty. He remembered what General Crook had said when a reporter asked him what was the hardest thing about fighting Indians. Replied Three Stars, "Knowing you're wrong."

Lieutenant Clark—White Hat, as the Indians called him—reminded himself that he represented the armed forces of the government of the United States and, as his enlisted men said, he could be a right son of a bitch.

So now he would do his job and do it well. He would listen carefully to the Indians, and that included knowing enough of the Lakota language to prompt an interpreter sometimes to a better, fuller translation. It meant understanding the ceremonial gestures, such as the handling of the sacred pipe. And remembering the courtesies. So he would now wait for the slender man behind the center fire to speak the crucial words of this meeting. He had heard often that Crazy Horse never spoke in council. He didn't know whether this was meant literally—it was hard to believe the headman never uttered a single word—or whether Crazy Horse would say a few words on an occasion of great moment, like this one.

As the pipe circled, Clark tried to study Crazy Horse without appearing rude or showing astonishment at his appearance. The great leader of the Oglala was anything but imposing. To begin with, he scarcely looked Indian at all. His skin was light, his hair sandy and down to his hips in braids. His figure was boyish. On his torso he wore nothing, below it only a simple leather breechcloth, undecorated leggings, and plain moccasins.

He was not quite naked of adornment. On his head perched the full skin of a red-tailed hawk. White hail spotted his chest, and blue lightning streaked down one cheek. This paint, though, indicated only dreams, not accomplishments.

Clark had spent a week with the half-breed Billy Garnett studying drawings of Lakota men painted to show their achievements. For Crazy Horse it had been a waste of time.

Strangely, Clark felt a surge of attraction to the man. He wanted not only to know him but to be close to him physically, to touch him, like an object of . . .

He cut off his thoughts. The pipe had returned to Crazy Horse. The headman cleaned the bowl and emptied the ashes into the fire. Then he looked Clark fully in the face for the first time. He had a mesmeric gaze, and the lieutenant felt his chest tighten.

In a soft voice Crazy Horse said, "My people untie the tails of their horses."

And that was all. The translator, as Clark had requested, rendered the chief's statement literally. A warrior tied the tails of his horses up when he went to war. So Crazy Horse was saying that these Lakota would fight no more. Evidently, that was all he intended to say.

"Thank you," said Clark. After he said it, he wondered

if "thank you" would look good—sufficiently triumphal—in the record.

The translator, Billy Garnett, added that Crazy Horse was acceding to everything essential. He would surrender. He would instruct the people to turn over their guns and their horses to the army. They would agree to give up their roaming ways and live on an agency. They did all this in return for a promise of peace, food and other necessities to be given to the people immediately, and eventually an agency in their own country.

Barely more than a boy, Garnett had a simple face and simple speech. In a world of the clandestine, Clark trusted him.

Now the warrior next to Crazy Horse spoke up. Clark had been told this was He Dog, a shirt wearer and a lifelong friend of the Strange Man. Clark caught the idea before Billy rendered it into English. "To show their sincerity, the chiefs will shake hands with you. Instead of the right, which does much mischief, they will shake with the left hand, which is the one closest to the heart."

Lieutenant Clark nodded. Crazy Horse came first, grasped Clark's right hand firmly with his left one, and sat down. One by one He Dog, Big Road, Little Big Man, and Little Hawk did the same.

Clark was actually moved. He looked into the chiefs' faces and believed them. They wanted to stop fighting the soldiers. That's what they would do—it was simple.

He Dog spoke up again. "Crazy Horse wants to give you a headdress." *Damned straight,* thought Clark—this is a surrender. "But he owns no headdress." Yes, that was the Strange Man's medicine, Clark had heard. It prevented him from acquiring splendid clothing, signs of his accomplishments, or even fine horses. "So," He Dog went on, "I will give you mine."

The shirt wearer reached behind his back and brought out a painted rawhide case and opened it. Slowly, gingerly, he drew forth an eagle-feather bonnet, one that draped all the way to the ground. It was a magnificent artifact, thought Clark, lovingly cared for. Very few men would ever strike enough coups to earn the right to wear one of these bonnets.

He Dog handed his headdress to the young officer with a gentle smile.

"Crazy Horse," He Dog continued, "wants to make you some other small gifts." Garnett added that since the Strange Man owned no fine things, these items also belonged to He Dog.

The first was a long medicine pipe, painted and adorned with eagle feathers, a ceremonial pipe. Clark accepted it soberly, the stem that represented Mother Earth, the bowl that represented the universe, and the lovely quilled pipe bag. Billy Garnett spoke the officer's thanks.

The second was a war shirt, beautifully beaded on the shoulders and arms and fringed with scalps. Garnett did not need to tell Clark how much fighting and how much war medicine the scalps represented.

The third was a small beaded bag of the sort that Lakota men often wore around their necks.

In spite of himself, Clark was enthralled. He stood up and took off his uniform coat. Then he thought to look at Garnett for confirmation that this was a good idea. Garnett gave a tiny nod. Clark put on He Dog's war shirt. He looked at the gleaming beads on his shoulders, arms, and breasts. Hesitantly, he touched the scalp hair. He felt a primitive thrill.

Now he hung the beaded bag from his neck. He wondered what he would put inside. Something small but of singular importance to his own life, he thought. His father's ring, perhaps.

He lifted the warbonnet onto his head. He Dog himself rose and helped to arrange the eagle feathers, the ones standing above the head and those trailing all the way down the back and legs. Clark felt self-conscious. He felt proud. He looked into the eyes of the chiefs surrendering to him and felt their generosity, the tribute they were offering, the honor they were giving him. He thought, *Watch out, you idiot, or your eyes will moisten.*

He wondered whether Washington and the high command had any idea what these people were really like. He knew it didn't matter.

Remembering his orders, Clark sat. There was still a considerable distance to go. There was the signing of a paper of unconditional surrender, and other necessities.

Clark instructed Garnett to tell Crazy Horse that he was invited to Washington to see the Great White Father.

Now Little Big Man put words in. "Crazy Horse says that he would be honored to speak with the One You Use for Father. He will make that journey when he knows where our people's agency will be."

So the chiefs were not abject in surrender. Clark liked that.

"He says that the headwaters of Beaver Creek, on the west side of the Black Hills, would be a good place," Little Big Man went on. "It has good grass for the horses, and some game."

So Crazy Horse didn't intend to go to Washington, D.C., to meet with Rutherford B. Hayes until he was given an agency where he wanted it. Clark smiled. Surely the chief didn't know that a photograph of himself with Crazy Horse, the conqueror of Custer, would be political capital for the new President. Certainly he didn't know that Hayes, elected amid sharp dispute, needed all the political credit he could get. Clark smiled to himself. It was funny that Hayes didn't have his people's confidence in the way that this simple tribal chieftain did.

"Or Goose Creek, by the Shining Mountains." The Bighorns, Garnett translated. "That is a good place," said Little Big Man. "If His Crazy Horse cannot have Goose Creek, he will accept Beaver Creek."

Clark felt the steel in the words. Surrendering but not defeated, these chiefs. They wanted an agency in their own country, so that surrender would change their lives less. They wanted it as far from Red Cloud and Spotted Tail as possible, because of old rivalries.

What's more, they were hinting that giving up their horses and guns would only be temporary. They wanted their agency in a country good for hunting. They were even hinting that they knew the Great White Father wouldn't feed them, as promised.

It was all subtle, indirect, and done without a hint of offense. Clark knew it wasn't unreasonable. Everyone knew that the agents and freighters stole rations until the Indians got only the crumbs and the worms.

Handling them would require all his skills. But he had no authority to make any such promises. He had to suppress an ironic smile. He could make a recommendation—he would do that. Colonel Mackenzie, the commanding officer at Fort Robinson, might support that recommendation to his superior, General Crook, or might oppose or suppress it. General Crook might make a recommendation to Gen. Philip Sheridan, Military Commander of the Missouri. Sheridan in turn would have something to say to his superiors, who ultimately would confer with the President of the United States.

Each of these men would have a stake in the decision. Like Clark himself, each would see himself as gaining or losing influence, showing strength or weakness, rising or slipping in the eyes of the public. The new President especially would view it that way, a man who had nearly become the first Republican Presidential candidate since the start of the War between the States to lose an election to the Democrats.

How enviable for these Indian leaders before him, to have the consent of your people and to speak for them directly, saying exactly what you mean.

Well, Crook would have the welfare of these Lakota people at heart, at least in part. He would want to keep whatever promises he made to them. But as the question went higher and higher, the men in power would care less and less. Some of them, in fact, would be in the grip of the fever to avenge Custer.

Therefore, knowingly, Lieutenant Clark said that he would pass the request of the headmen for an agency on Beaver Creek or Goose Creek on to Three Stars, with his personal support.

They all understood that the question of Crazy Horse's going to Washington, D.C., was left hanging.

Clark said that a week's rations were in the wagons outside, plus blankets, pants, shirts, and cloth. He would dispense them now. Perhaps it was not enough, he admitted. The agent would be getting more freight soon.

The leaders suppressed smiles. They had heard that story before—more rations soon.

SURRENDER

In Pehingnunipi Wi, the Moon of Shedding Ponies, which the whites called May, horsemen waited on the white, cedar-dotted bluffs above the White River. They watched, silent and motionless as the cedars, looking impervious to weather and time. They were Lakota, agency Indians, followers of Red Cloud or Spotted Tail.

Below, spread along the river valley, waited thousands of Lakota people, mostly of Red Cloud's agency. The sense was in the air, the knowing. Like the feeling of springtime renewal in the earth, people could sense it in the wind, in the sunlight, in the way their feet felt on the earth, in a dozen ways they did not name. Something big was happening today.

Fort Robinson sat in the wide valley below the cliffs and the agency a little way on down the river, to the east. Everyone was looking up the river, up the lodge trail that came this way from Powder River country.

The sentinel horsemen sat on the cliffs, and below thousands of Lakota watched for their signal. Others watched, too—white soldiers, some Sahiyela, Mahpiyato, and members of other tribes. They were all watching for the great event to begin. Tasunke Witko, Crazy Horse, the man they thought of as the one true leader of the last free Lakota, was coming in to the agency today.

It had begun a month ago, when he had started moving his village this way from Powder River. Yes, it had been anticipated—over a hundred lodges had already come in from his camp in the past quarter-moon, those with stronger ponies, those without too many of the weak and helpless. Yes, it had been partly accomplished three days ago, when Crazy Horse met Clark and shook his hand in surrender. The left hand, people said, because it was the one closest to the heart. And they looked into each other's eyes with the sense of something momentous taking place, and hope and despair and love all at once, and sometimes envy and rivalry and even hatred. Many Lakota had shed tears quietly last night, off to themselves. Some would shed them openly today, when they saw their Strange Man walking quietly behind the soldiers.

Today would be the occasion. Today the heart of the Crazy Horse people would come in, with all the shirtmen and war leaders, roughly a thousand people. When they got here, they would first give up their ponies, that was the agreement. Then they would hand over their firearms.

Though the wild ones had promised, people wanted to see them actually hand over their horses and guns to the soldiers. Some people thought that at the last moment they would refuse and a big fight would start, and plenty of killing. But most people said that if the Strange Man agreed and gave his hand on it, he would do it.

When the free Lakota had surrendered those two strengths, their only way to travel and so their only way to hunt and their power to fight, it would all be over, truly over.

Now two horsemen at the west rode their horses in a

circle, the traditional sign meaning, "Many people are coming."

Clark and Red Cloud rode first, with some of the principal agency Oglala alongside their leader, the one-time Pretty Fellow, now called Woman Dress. Alongside them his brother Standing Bear, White Twin, and his brother No Water.

Red Cloud's eyes glinted with a kind of pride. The people regarded their chief with two minds. One said, *This is not a man of honor—he is the murderer of Bull Bear, he schemes for himself instead of the people, he would do anything for attention and status—see, even now he pretends to be bringing in the Strange Man, though that is not truly his accomplishment.* The other said, *This chief and Spotted Tail are the only ones who understood long ago that we must make accommodation with the whites. They saw the only road that could be walked. Through every kind of difficulty, and with sorrowful hearts, they have kept us on the road. They deserve our gratitude.*

"Where is Spotted Tail?" some people said. They thought His Crazy Horse's uncle, his mother's brother, should be the one bringing him to the agency. Many of them said it was Spotted Tail's words that had changed the heart of the Strange Man, and Red Cloud went out only later. But the soldiers had made a deal, the people whispered. Red Cloud was to appear to bring the free Lakota in. In return he would be restored to chieftainship. That was good, thought most of the Oglala. They needed one of their own as leader, not Spotted Tail. So the Sicangu stayed home today.

Behind Clark and Red Cloud rode Clark's detachment of bluecoats, and behind them the Indian police. The people looked at each other with knowing eyes. To be a tribal policeman, that was an honor, well, a sort of honor. The *akicita* men had always been important to the people, enforcing the discipline needed to act as a group, whether moving the village or conducting a big buffalo hunt. *Akicita* men made people follow the rules, but that was for everyone's protection. It was the same now, in a way. Except that these Indian police were responsible to Clark, and so to the whites. Now they enforced the white men's rules. "It is the only way," most people said reluctantly. Other people said bitterly, "It is the white man's way."

The only way.

A way of death.

The *only* way.

Behind the Indian policemen there seemed at first to be nothing but a cloud of dust. Then, after a long space, the front rank of the last free Lakota.

When the first watchers saw them, voices raised in song.

At the front of the traveling village rode a rank of its leaders, not only Crazy Horse but one of the ones he called *ate,* Little Hawk, along with Little Big Man, He Dog, and Big Road. They were impressive-looking men, strong, physically vital, proud, conscious of position. As befitted a ceremonial occasion, they were outfitted in the regalia of rank. They wore the emblems that showed their status, the shirts of the shirtman, the staffs of honor and leadership in warrior societies, the signs of coups, the scalps of their enemies, and full-length bonnets of eagle feathers. With paint, feather, and fur they spoke their personal achievements and their rank in the tribe.

Except for Crazy Horse. He did not wear the sign of a single achievement. Among his resplendent lieutenants, he looked small, thin, barren, poor, almost nude. To the many agency Lakota who had never seen him, he looked less like a great leader than a boy among men.

A teenage girl who had stood on her tiptoes and craned her neck to see him cried, *"Hinu, hinu!"* in astonishment, then looked with shame at her mother.

More than one young man wondered if he could not outshine this man, and wondered where he'd gotten his reputation.

"Our Strange Man," people murmured throughout the

crowd, and many saw some of its meaning for the first time.

Perhaps it was worse because most of the people were dressed poorly today, as they were every day. The women were wearing calico dresses or even dresses made from stitched-up flour sacks. Men wore breechcloths not of blanket or buckskin but scraps of cheap cloth crazy-quilted together.

The whites, especially the women of the fort, thought these clothes were an improvement. "At least they're wearing *cloth*," one army wife said. "They're out of animal skins," agreed another with a droll smile.

But the people did not feel that way about it. Who would prefer cloth to buckskin? Cloth would tear on the first bramble. Hide would last for decades. Who would prefer the white man's calico to quillwork done patiently over many long evenings—which one showed more love? Who would rather have the calico pattern than decoration in quills and beads and paints and furs? Who would rather have the impersonal figures of a manufacturer on his clothing than the tale of his own life and his own medicine?

They wanted to see the leader of the wild Lakota looking splendid. Instead they saw what they feared was their future, not simplicity but poverty.

Yet the people knew. Everyone knew who this man was, what he had done.

They responded with every kind of feeling—adulation, excitement, a sense of glory, pride, admiration, curiosity, envy, rivalry, and fear.

A few of the people, understanding the event, had decorated themselves as best they could in paint, feather, and fur. Their minds and spirits were not debased, and they wished to salute a great occasion. Many of them, hungry, had still traded food for a little paint or some bright cloth.

These were the ones who sang. They did not sing together, some great chant of lamentation or acceptance or a new vision of peace and harmony. Each sang his own song, reflecting the meaning of this occasion in his own life.

Red Roach, for instance, stood close to the lodge trail at the far west. He was one of the first to see the free Lakota coming and the first to sing. In front of his scalp lock he was wearing the roach that gave him his name. It signified that he had attacked an enemy while the enemy was protected in some way.

He was also painted with the long story of his life of many winters. His face, arms, and trunk were yellow, showing that he was a member of the Kit Fox Society. His legs and feet were painted red, indicating that he had danced a sun dance. The red on his hands declared that he was in compliance with Lakota ceremonies, and so entitled to touch sacred objects. Horizontal lines of red on his yellow arms and chest showed the exact number of battles he had been in, six. Dabs and dots of red said that he had been cut by knife, arrow, and spear twelve times.

He wore many other small signs of his accomplishments, all of them clear to an initiate but a mystery to the whites, who neither understood nor cared.

His membership in the Kit Fox Society was also bespoken by the fox skin that dangled from his right hand. This society had been formed to aid the poor and helpless. One of a member's models was the activity and cunning of the kit fox. The eagle feathers on the skin showed that he was a leader in the society and the red feathers that he was a leader in war.

Red Roach's face also told a story. It was hardened and burned by sun and wind and deeply crevassed. His clear eyes spoke a long transit on the earth, much living, much gladness, and much sorrow. On this day, as the last of the leaders of the old way surrendered, his eyes were springs, and their tears flowed down his ancient cheeks. From his mouth flowed a song, and its words spoke the time-honored pledge of the Kit Foxes:

"I am a Fox.
I am supposed to die.

> *If there is anything difficult,*
> *if there is anything dangerous,*
> *that is mine to do."*

Over and over he lifted this song to the sky. Though he no longer possessed much strength, he promised what he had to the people, today and forever.

Another warrior, much younger, was a wolf, and wore the four striped feathers of his office. He had painted his upper face red to say that he was in compliance with Lakota custom. He had painted his trunk and arms yellow to show that he was ready to go to war. He sang for Crazy Horse an honoring song:

> *"Tasunke Witko,*
> *He whose heart for greatness is known."*

It was simple in words, heartfelt, tender, and gently eloquent in its melody. He sang it in a beautiful, high voice, repeatedly, from the first moment he could see Crazy Horse until the Strange Man was out of sight.

Several men recognized the end of an era here, and so sang their death songs. Blue Hawk sang an honoring song of the Strong Heart Society, a beautiful melody in a minor key with the feelings of a slow, sad march:

> *"His Crazy Horse,*
> *Take courage.*
> *A short time you live."*

Crazy Horse and his main leaders so passed down the lodge trail toward the fort and the field beyond where they would give up their possessions, and surrender to a future they could not see. Behind them rode nearly a thousand Oglala, first the older warriors, then the pony drags, alongside these the women and children and the aged, and behind them the herds, nearly two thousand horses.

Like the ponies, the people were skinny and run-down, showing the effects of a hard winter. They needed more of the food promised them by Clark, needed it immediately. They also needed the blankets, awls, hatchets, tobacco, and cloth. They were poor.

But this noon they were proud, too. They walked into the Red Cloud Agency through a corridor of song, of feelings given voice, of hearts lifted to the sky. In the many voices they heard honor, praise, lament, and acceptance. In every voice they heard the sense of the sacred, throbbing.

A group of officers, most of them young, stood outside Fort Robinson to watch the rebel leader give up. This was a great moment for the army. For a year and a half the soldiers had chased these people desperately and had gotten whipped too damn often. Then there was the one whipping so disgraceful you seldom mentioned Custer's name.

They mostly just watched, these officers, with feelings even they hardly knew—rage, admiration, regret, celebration, doubt, savage satisfaction. They could not, dared not, speak their real emotions.

Sometimes one would make a sarcastic comment. There were several remarks about the goddamn devil music. Yet they were all mesmerized, entranced by the spectacle and the sound. They were beholding the ending of an age.

After the soldiers and police came the wild Indians. The officers coughed and sputtered and looked strangely at each other when they saw the leaders and the slight, insignificant-looking man at the head of all. They knew that somehow this man had raised in his people a spirit no one thought they had, not even themselves. Most of the officers just gawked, stupefied. The brightest marked Crazy Horse down as someone to study, someone to learn the true nature of leadership from.

The songs reached a new intensity as Crazy Horse passed in front of the fort. Every soldier's eye was on him, every man held by his simplicity, the eloquence of his posture and his carriage. Just as the Strange Man drew even with them, one officer said out of the side of his mouth to another, "This is not a surrender. It's a goddamn triumphal procession."

Crazy Horse did not feel triumphant. He saw that people were curious about him and his fellow holdout leaders. He saw that some admired him. He knew others envied him. He noticed that the people used this occasion to celebrate the way the Lakota had lived for hundreds of winters. To celebrate it, and to say a tender and regretful good-bye to it. He shared those feelings. He knew that he personally and the brave men who rode beside him were merely the vessels of the feelings.

To be such a vessel seemed to him an honor, and it touched him.

Yet in his heart was muted, melancholy music. As he accepted this honor offered, he would have to accept the envy, jealousy, and rivalry that would come his way tomorrow and every day from now on. That was the nature of being a chief. He was weary of it, deeply weary. It was past time to lay leadership down.

Many arrangements needed to be made. He might have to go to Washington to see The One They Use for Father. He needed to obtain an agency back in Powder River country for his people, so they could be away from the Red Cloud people and the Spotted Tail people and all the maneuvering and manipulating that came from being too close. Besides, they wanted to live in their own homeland. He needed to get back enough ponies to hunt, and some ammunition. Perhaps he had the power with the people and the soldiers to get these things done, and that would be the last.

Below those commitments, those awarenesses, pooled desolation in his heart. As he looked around at the agency Indian, dependent, destitute, spiritless, it was clearer than ever that an agency offered no life to him and no prospect for the return of Hawk. The people might be able to live here, he didn't know. Hawk would never come to him here, and he would die. And until his death, live gutted of spirit.

He walked his pony and felt in its hooves the pulse of the drum, tapping the earth. Maybe that beat would help him against his melancholy. Soon he must go to the hills alone and listen for Hawk. He felt the meaning of the song Hawk would sing without words. He deliberately did not think of the high hills and the secret, lonely places, not yet. For now he had to sink into this cold bleakness, a body at the bottom of a lake. He hoped that, later, Hawk would lift him from the waters of desolation.

SPIRIT CATCHERS

Lt. William Philo Clark of the Second Cavalry declined another cup of coffee with his hand. Crazy Horse poured himself one. The chief was very fond of coffee, the lieutenant had noticed, and with lots of sugar in it. Sometimes it was the small things that converted a barbarian to civilization, the lieutenant thought—something sweet to eat or the small luxuries women liked, like needles, soft cloth, or bright ribbon.

Tonight Clark had made Crazy Horse a gift of an army coffeepot, three pint tin cups, two filled with roasted coffee beans and one with sugar, and a tin coffeepot. He was at once pleased and ashamed of his gift. Pleased because it was politic, and they really did appreciate it. Ashamed because the coffee offered no nourishment, and the Crazy Horse people were half-starved.

He wasn't responsible for their lack of food. Not him and not the army either. It was the damned agent and freighters and the whole Bureau of Indian Affairs. They were slow, they were inefficient, and their contractors stole every time provisions changed hands. Or the goods got lost. Or the wrong things came. Recently Clark had supervised a distribution of rations of wool cloth in the middle of summer, pots for the meat the people didn't have, rancid bacon, flour they wouldn't eat, and two cows. This for a thousand people. And then he had to refuse the men permission to leave the agency to hunt.

It was a disgrace. As Crook had told him, the army might shoot the Indians, which was honorable, but it wouldn't starve them to death, as the Bureau of Indian Affairs did, children and old folks first.

Still, Clark thought Crazy Horse knew the difference between his government's ineptitude and his personal generosity. He'd nipped these items from the quartermaster's store, and he couldn't do much of that. Now he and Crazy Horse had told stories all evening, war stories, hunting stories, the kinds of tales men of action tell on the way to becoming friends. Crazy Horse had told how his people's leaders had bargained away what the soldiers had won on the battlefield. Which was how every every soldier felt.

"Did I tell you about the first time my mother got coffee?" asked the chief in signs.

Clark gave his smile, tight on his face. "No."

"It was before I was born—it's one of my father's favorite stories. The people went in to Fort Laramie when it was first built. We traded for many things, including Spanish beans and American beans." Clark knew this meant pinto beans and coffee beans. "That's how we discovered that the Spaniards are much smarter than the Americans. The Spanish beans cooked right up, and they tasted good. The American beans never did get soft enough to eat, no matter how much you cooked them."

Clark laughed, really laughed.

Crazy Horse poured from the coffeepot, but it was empty. "It's time to go," said Clark. Crazy Horse didn't demur. The lieutenant wondered whether he'd almost overstayed his welcome tonight. He rose, and said *"Ake wancinyankin ktelo,"* until I see you again. His command of

Lakota was improving. He stood and offered his hand. After a hesitation, Crazy Horse shook it. Clark lifted the door flap and stepped out.

Yes, it had gone well. He was gaining this chief's confidence, as he had gotten the confidence of Red Cloud. He looked up into the summer night with a feeling of satisfaction.

A hand grabbed him. Clark recognized Grouard's sleeve before he struck. Then he gave the scout a look that would blanch blue out of the sky. Grouard dropped his arms and stepped back and began to stutter. Clark brushed by him, paying the beggar no mind.

This Grouard was a contemptible nothing, the son of a Mormon missionary and some native woman, one of the innumerable whores of the innumerable islands of Polynesia. The Lakota called him Grabber—Sitting Bull himself had adopted the fellow as a gadabout teenager. But now the Indians despised him. He had led Colonel Reynolds to the hidden camp of Sahiyela and He Dog's Oglala a year ago March, before the big fights on the Rosebud and the Little Bighorn. At a skirmish at Slim Buttes Grouard had been so afraid they'd get even for his betrayal that he hid at the rear. Now he was sure that a knife would come out of the blanket of a hostile at night and his miserable life would ooze into the dirt.

"Lieutenant," rasped Grabber, "you must not come to this lodge alone."

Clark turned and faced the man. Clark disliked him, if only for his uncouth features and his yellow, sick-looking skin. Had the bastard lurked in the darkness to tell him this? His job was to get familiar with these Indians and report to Crook exactly what was on their minds. He certainly wasn't going to reject the friendship of one of his main targets. But did this lowlife know something?

Clark motioned the man to keep up with him and walked toward his picketed horse.

"He is dangerous, this Crazy Horse," Grabber went on.

"He broods. He plots. You must not go to his lodge without me to protect you."

Clark almost laughed. Grouard was not protection, he was a magnet for trouble.

He looked at Grouard hard. "How do you know he's plotting?"

Grouard shrugged. "He looks no one in the eye. His mind is always off somewhere."

Clark stared the man down. Well, it wouldn't hurt to be careful. Everyone on this agency distrusted everyone else. The biggest danger to white man or red was a knife in the back. He lifted his foot into the stirrup.

"Is it true that the government is considering making Crazy Horse the head of all the Lakota?"

Clark snapped his head back at Grouard now. He thought he saw a gleam in Grabber's eye. Maybe the scout was cunning enough to see the games being played here. Well and good. "Good night, Grouard."

"Good night, Lieutenant. Remember, you cannot be too careful."

Clark touched his heels to his horse. Crazy Horse the head of all the Lakota? Where did that rumor come from? Not the army, not likely. It wouldn't do to put Crazy Horse above Spotted Tail. And Clark himself had promised Red Cloud reinstatement if the old leader brought in Crazy Horse. This Red Cloud had done, or at least made it appear so. If Red Cloud wasn't put back as chief, it would be Young Man-Whose-Enemies. Not Crazy Horse, either way.

So where did the rumor come from?

Clark shifted his weight in the saddle and smiled. From some of the Indians themselves. The longtime agency chiefs clearly resented the attention given their younger rival. Especially that old bastard Red Cloud. And for good reason—Clark found Crazy Horse a better man than any of them, modest, straightforward, courageous, sincerely concerned first for the welfare of his people. Yes, this rumor would make many Indians angry.

Clark savored the thought. His policy was divide and conquer. Divide the chiefs and conquer. Divide all the Lakota and conquer. So he certainly wouldn't deny this fine bit of claptrap. He thought of what he was supposed to say: "The government will do whatever is best for everyone." He repeated the words in his mind to the clop of his mount's hooves. *The government will do whatever is best for everyone*. He smiled at whoever would believe that.

Crazy Horse saw Black Buffalo Woman sitting under a tree working with her awl. Two children were playing nearby, a boy of about eight and a girl about six, separately, their backs to each other.

He was coming back from a smoke on Crow Butte. He had gone out there to think about what was happening. So far no agency in his own country, and even talk that all the Lakota would be moved to the Missouri River—the Muddy Water, where not even a dog would drink. He thought about his promise to untie his horses' tails. He had meant it, forever, and still meant it. But what if the whites didn't keep their promise?

Altogether the smoke brought him no peace. He could see no answers. He still didn't feel Hawk inside.

When he saw the woman, he stopped his pinto. Memories flooded on him, and feelings. The day he sat above the village mourning his uncle Spotted Tail. Black Buffalo Woman came to him, and they soared into the sky of their passion and at the same time dived into the cold sea of Spotted Tail's death. The ring he carved from elk antler for her, and the day she accepted it. The heady anticipation of having her as his woman, in his lodge every night. The agony of hearing that she was walking under the blanket with No Water. The wild elation of thinking she might still be his. The solemn triumph of their elopement. The unspeakable pain and shame that followed.

His failure to remember his medicine, and his punishment.

He put a finger to his scar.

Now she lifted her blanket over her head, indicating that she didn't want to be talked to or even noticed. He hesitated, and decided he would honor her choice. He'd heard she lived in a small lodge behind No Water's, alone with her children. He wondered if it was true. Life seemed to him loneliness. But he was not as lonely as she. He had Black Shawl.

Suddenly, he saw the boy glaring at him. So. No Water's son had heard stories. Crazy Horse wondered who told them. It didn't matter. He smiled slightly at the boy.

The girl. She was an appealing little creature, playing near her mother with rawhide dolls. They said she was born nine moons after the elopement. He guessed she was a little light-skinned, as they said. She didn't feel like a daughter. His daughter was They-Are-Afraid-of-Her, and her bones rested on a scaffold in a country that was no longer his.

He could feel tension radiating from the blanket over the woman's head. He flicked the reins and his pony walked on. Yes, life was loneliness.

Red Cloud sent for his relatives. He got out his pipe and sat behind the center fire. He was angry, but he wouldn't let it show. Today he'd seen Clark, who'd promised to put him back as head chief at this agency. The officer avoided saying anything about his promise, but he had plenty to say about Crazy Horse, all of it praise. "He's so modest," said Clark. "He's so unpretentious. He's a good listener. He's fun to trade stories with."

Then suddenly Clark announced that he was dismissing most of his scouts, who were like the *akicita* men, a kind of police. He would hire 250 new ones, many from the Crazy Horse people. Wasn't that good? The Crazy Horse people were behaving well, and deserved it—didn't Red Cloud think so? Certainly Crazy Horse people would make excellent scouts.

Yes, Red Cloud was angry.

Woman Dress came in with his brothers Standing Bear

and Little Wolf. They waited awhile for No Water, talking idly. Red Cloud was pretty sure that these Bad Face relatives had enough anger for them all.

After they'd smoked, Red Cloud told them about the hiring of Crazy Horse and his followers as scouts. He didn't have to add that meant they would be given guns, and horses. "Clark is putting trouble in their hands," Red Cloud said.

"This is what we get for behaving ourselves," said No Water.

"Loyalty," said Little Wolf bitterly.

"I even heard that the whites are thinking of making Crazy Horse head chief of the agency," said Woman Dress.

"Head chief of all the Lakota," added Standing Bear.

"They ought to give a bounty for his scalp," muttered No Water.

Red Cloud said nothing, just watched No Water. He thought this Bad Face was not the only Lakota who would kill Crazy Horse if given a chance. The problem was the fools who made a romantic hero of him in their minds and would take revenge for his death. *Heroes,* thought Red Cloud, *are for teenage boys and fools.*

He responded to Woman Dress. "Clark has told me that he will make me chief of this agency again," he said evenly, with more assurance than he felt. The rumor going around in fact made him furious. He had asked Clark about it and gotten only evasion. Even if the rumor was false, as he was pretty sure it was, the fact that Clark didn't deny it quickly and firmly infuriated him.

"I think you'd better speak to your white friends," Red Cloud said to Woman Dress. Since Woman Dress was a scout, he knew the soldiers well. He nodded to Red Cloud, who added, "Let them know they're flirting with a dangerous man."

"He won't be dangerous if I can catch him," said No Water.

Red Cloud regarded him. It was good to have an angry

man as a weapon, provided you could control him. Two angry men. Woman Dress had not forgotten that broken nose of many winters ago.

Crazy Horse chief of all the Lakota. Red Cloud didn't think so, but you never knew about white people. What would Spotted Tail say when he heard this tale? Would he feel like an uncle to his nephew? Or would he take steps to protect his position? Red Cloud had known the Sicangu leader well more than twenty winters. He thought the man would protect himself. And protect his people against this rash, moody, romantic fool.

Then they talked about other things, as though the thought of Crazy Horse didn't fever their every waking moment.

Spotted Tail and Crazy Horse, uncle and nephew, teacher of hunting and warfare and his pupil, sat beside the coffeepot and drank hot, sweet black liquid from the new tin cups. Spotted Tail recognized them as white-man gifts and was glad that his nephew was amenable to accepting small presents from the white people. It was part of getting along.

"They say you are morose, *tunska,* bad-hearted, and maybe dangerous," Spotted Tail said with a smile. Crazy Horse didn't smile back. Spotted Tail had heard he smiled seldom these days.

They both knew what everyone was saying about Crazy Horse. Whenever you disagreed with the whites about anything, they called you bad-hearted. It was worse now—the agency Indians were saying the same thing. As for morose, Spotted Tail thought his nephew had always been inclined to melancholy. Maybe because his birth mother had died when he was a child. Maybe because he always had his mind on things no one else saw or heard. Maybe just because that was the spirit he was born with, melancholy.

Spotted Tail felt sorry for Crazy Horse. Not only because all the maneuverings and schemings would be alien to him, unpleasant, and difficult, but because the young man didn't respond to the everyday oddity of life by feeling tickled. It was so quirky and . . . intriguing. Crazy Horse didn't see that.

It was difficult, this agency life. No one had quite enough to eat. Rations were always late and never enough. You weren't permitted to leave the agency, so you could only hunt where everyone else had hunted and the game was gone. Sure, a lone man could slip away for a couple of days and maybe take an elk, and that helped one family, but did little for the people.

This wasn't the worst. In the winter, travel would be harder, game scarcer. The whites would say that wagons couldn't get through to the agency with the food. (Somehow troops got through always, supply wagons seldom.) Men would have even less to do. They would watch their children and their old people get hungry and then sick. Many would die. Men would feel so useless that they would stay drunk or pick fights with others or maybe kill someone. The winters were bad. His nephew did not know the half of agency life yet.

The trick was to survive this somehow, and Spotted Tail wanted to help his nephew if he could. All he could, short of endangering his own people. That he was pledged not to do.

"They say you're angry that Crook has not kept his promise, and that you're ready to go back to war," said Spotted Tail. That brought some life to his nephew's eyes, he noticed, a flash of denial.

Crazy Horse reached for the coffeepot and refilled both cups. Spotted Tail wondered whether his nephew was getting a craving for this coffee. It happened, he had heard. Some white people would trade for coffee and short themselves on food.

Crook was why they were here. After almost a full moon the general had finally journeyed to Fort Robinson to talk about his promises with the hostile Lakota who had come in. This afternoon the council would get started right here on this prairie. Spotted Tail had come early because it was a long ride from his agency, a full day, and because he wanted to sit down with Crazy Horse. He wanted to know which rumors were true and which weren't.

At last Crazy Horse said simply, "My people have tied up their horses' tails."

Spotted Tail believed him. Crazy Horse was not the sort of man to vacillate or deceive. As a leader he would keep his word.

"All the people?" Spotted Tail asked.

"Each Lakota is free to do as he chooses," said Crazy Horse, emphasizing the words a little. He was saying, "Some things change. Basic things do not. A man must live his life as his powers show it to him." "I will not lead the people into war again."

"But maybe you'll live alone?" pressed Spotted Tail.

Crazy Horse hesitated, and Spotted Tail could see he'd thought about this. "I've guided the people onto the road everyone says is red. I may still ride my own way," Crazy Horse said simply. Spotted Tail thought this was what was on his nephew's mind. He felt sympathetic, as long as Crazy Horse didn't take the people with him. The idea was naive and romantic, but so was his nephew.

Spotted Tail stalled by pouring coffee for his nephew and himself. "You have a fine new pony and a fine new rifle, Nephew," said Spotted Tail. The pony was staked a few yards away.

Crazy Horse smiled. "We are bluecoats," he said. "They have taught us to ride in straight, white-man lines and then do tricks. We will give you a riding show before the council."

Spotted Tail knew. Crazy Horse and about twenty-five of his warriors had been chosen as scouts under the command of Clark. Little Big Man was one of these new scouts, as were several of Crazy Horse's other most ferocious warriors. Well, they'd been good fighting men, and now they would be good policemen. Times changed.

This was the soldiers pacifying the hostiles as best they

could, giving them uniforms and guns and positions of honor. It would also annoy Red Cloud and his relatives no end. They wanted the hostiles punished for holding out and themselves rewarded for being good Indians. Spotted Tail smiled to himself. Anything that annoyed Red Cloud couldn't be too bad.

Red Cloud or not, it was a good idea. Clark had been drilling them in cavalry maneuvers. The funny part was, none of the white cavalry could ride like Lakota.

"Is it true that Clark has announced an issue day tomorrow?" the older man asked.

Crazy Horse looked up at his uncle regretfully. This was a sore subject. "Yes," he said. *Issue day* was a new term for the Lakota, meaning the day the whites handed out rations.

"Are you going to have a buffalo hunt?" asked Spotted Tail, smiling.

"Buffalo hunt?" Crazy Horse was puzzled.

"Yes. The young men ride down the spotted cows." Meat was usually given to the people on the hoof, and they shot the beeves in the corrals where they were unloaded.

"My young men turn it into sport," Spotted Tail explained. "We let the cows out of the pens, run them hard across the prairie, ride up alongside like they were real *pte,* and bring them down with an arrow to the brisket."

The two men looked at each other, half-tickled and half-saddened.

"The young men learn from it," Spotted Tail went on. "But spotted cows come down more easily than *pte.*"

A loud voice interrupted them.

Crazy Horse saw two men, one with a shadow-catching box, walking across the grass. They were shading their eyes against the midday sun, and one was hollering rudely in a language no one here understood. You had to learn patience with white men.

Spotted Tail called softly to his daughter in the lodge

and asked her to get Bordeaux from the next lodge to translate. James Bordeaux was one of the traders' sons. Then Spotted Tail motioned the shadow catcher to come closer. The one fellow came dragging his big box.

"Chief, chief!" cried the one without a shadow box. Bordeaux was coming up. "Sir, can we get a picture? Sirs?" This one was running ahead, the other one struggling. The shadow-catcher box was heavy. "The Great White Father would like to see your picture, Mr. Crazy Horse. Are you Mr. Crazy Horse? You too, Mr. Spotted Tail."

Crazy Horse looked at the man without understanding a word. He also didn't understand the look on the man's face, a kind of avidity, a little like a hunter's excitement, combined with self-consciousness and self-importance.

Bordeaux said in the Lakota language, "He says The One the Whites Use for Father asks for your face on one of the shadow plates, which is a lie. This fellow wouldn't know The One They Use for Father from one of their pay women. But someone told him your name, and they'll give him pay money for your shadow. He loves the pay money, and even more he loves the thought of himself as The One Who Captured Crazy Horse's Shadow. He will not count the coup honestly but will make it sound like he rode bullet-proof through the fire of a hundred warriors to catch the shadow. That will make him so happy he'll go get a disease from one of the pay women and for half a moon will walk funny."

Spotted Tail was laughing out loud. Crazy Horse smiled. Bordeaux was fun.

"General Crazy Horse? Chief Crazy Horse? May we take your picture?"

Said Bordeaux, "He's using fancy titles. He wants to make you feel so flattered and so important that you'll give him what he wants. Children they are, the whites. He doesn't care a bit if you're willing to have your shadow captured, but he has to get you to stand still while he does it. And he's heard that you cut off the noses and penises of white men you don't like and feed them to devils after night-middle-made. So he's trying to be courteous. Which is against his nature."

The other one had the shadow box close now and was setting it up.

Spotted Tail contained his laughter.

"No," said Crazy Horse quietly to Bordeaux. He was uncertain of his connection with Hawk as it was. He didn't intend to let any white men look at his *nagi,* spirit. He felt glad he was talking to Lakota, not the whites, and a simple "no" would be enough, without questions.

"They've got no manners," said Bordeaux.

"Go into my lodge," said Spotted Tail. "They won't bother you there."

Crazy Horse walked quickly without appearing to hurry.

"Mr. Crazy Horse! Sir! General!"

He slipped inside.

Spotted Tail spoke in Lakota, and Bordeaux made the words in English. "Would you like a picture of me with my family? My wife and my daughter?"

"Of course, Mr. Spotted Tail, but . . . General Crazy Horse?"

Bordeaux nodded at Spotted Tail. The chief raised his big frame off the ground and put his head under the door flap of the lodge.

"Come outside," he said to the two women. "We'll have our picture taken. Since they think we're children, they'll probably give us a few beads, or maybe some of that good lemon candy. Bring blankets," he added. "They like to see us in blankets, even on the hottest day of the Moon When the Chokecherries Ripen."

The women stirred themselves without a word. In the lodge Crazy Horse sat down and took out his short pipe for a little smoke.

"Nephew," said Spotted Tail to him, "I am your relative. I will help you any way I can. Unless it harms the people. Any way I can. Come to me."

Crazy Horse nodded his gratitude. But Spotted Tail thought his eyes looked far, far away.

Young Man-Whose-Enemies welcomed General Crook formally to the agency and the council and then said he was ashamed. Crook had promised him and his fellow peace chiefs, he said, agencies in their own country. On his word they had urged Crazy Horse to bring in the last hostiles. Now the army was talking about sending everyone to Indian Territory, a bad country far to the south, or to the Missouri, which they knew and disliked. "We are shamed before our kinsmen," he concluded. "We remind you of your promise."

Strong talk. Crook acknowledged it with a nod and turned to Crazy Horse.

His uncle Little Hawk stood and spoke in a splendid voice. He was proud to be called a hostile, he said. That meant one who lived in the old way, given to his people many generations ago, in his own country. The soldiers came there without any right and shot at the people, he declared. What could they do? The whites kept pushing in everywhere.

"In the Moon of Sore Eyes," he said, "our relatives came and said to stop fighting. If we would come in, they said, you would give us an agency in our country." He looked around dramatically. "Here we are. Now what do you say? You want us to go far away!"

He stared at Crook. The general told the interpreter, Billy Garnett, to hurry him up.

"Yes," said Little Hawk. "I have only one more thing to say. Are you Three Stars? The one our relatives told us speaks with a straight tongue?"

Murmurs ran through the Indians. Would Crook permit this kind of strong talk?

Crook stood up to speak. He looked them in the eyes, letting them know he meant exactly what he said. He didn't like not being able to do everything he said he'd do, but by God, he had nothing to be ashamed of. He started by saying that he personally had never wanted to fight the Lakota. He just followed the orders of the Great White Father and had no choice in that. Besides, the Indians shot at him when he came.

Half-voiced protests spewed out, but the Lakota themselves shushed them. Let the soldier speak.

"There is a new Great White Father," he said, "not the one some of you met in Washington City." Rutherford B. Hayes, a politician. Good Lord, could anyone understand a politician? A Janus? On Crook's way here the clack of the rails had drilled a line of doggerel into his head about Hayes. If he'd been a versifier, he'd have written a caustic lyric about his commander in chief. As it was, he had only the last line, which repeated mockingly—"Rutherford, Rutherford, Rutherford B."

Now his job was to make some plausible excuse for this Great White Father, and what he said would go into the record. "He is very busy. In the autumn we will go there together, and I will ask him to help you." And maybe for once good sense would prevail and the government would leave these people where they'd always been and wanted to be. But maybe not. He didn't let his thoughts show.

Rutherford, Rutherford, Rutherford B.

"In the meantime, in the late summer you may go on a buffalo hunt to the north country. Come back with no trouble, and I will go to see the Great White Father with you."

He wondered if Crazy Horse would come back. Wouldn't that be a coup for Rutherford, Rutherford, Rutherford B.? Wouldn't the newspapers love it?

There was nothing more to say now. He looked the principal chiefs directly in the eyes, man to man, Crazy Horse, Spotted Tail, Red Cloud, and some others. They wouldn't meet his gaze. He sat down.

* * *

As they got up to go to the feast, Crazy Horse said to Little Hawk, "The promise is changed." No guarantee of an agency in their country now, just a request for such an agency to The One They Use for Father.

Little Hawk said, "Yes, the whites get hard and get soft, get hard and get soft, like mud." He laughed and pushed on with his mockery. "Regardless, they're all dirt."

Crazy Horse talked with Worm and Touch-the-Sky after the feast. They had moved their camps up to Spotted Tail's agency, Touch-the-Sky with most of his Mniconjou lodges. "We aren't known to all the newspapermen," said Touch-the-Sky, "so we can go where we want."

Crazy Horse noted the irony. The officers and the men who wrote things down for the newspapers and the men with the shadow-catching boxes made a fuss over Lakota who were "famous." Since the whites had made a big man of him, he would be watched carefully, his every movement reported, and he could not slip away to hunt. The whites could take away your freedom without putting you in the little room with chains and barred windows.

He asked his father and his mothers' brother about that agency and got the impression that things were better there. Spotted Tail got along well with the agent and the commanding officer at the fort. Things were settled. Lakota weren't scheming against each other all the time.

That night Crazy Horse told Little Hawk, He Dog, and Big Road he thought his band perhaps should move upriver to live with Spotted Tail's people until the Oglala got their own agency.

He Dog nodded. "It would be good to be with your relatives there," he said. His implication was that He Dog and Big Road, being related to Red Cloud's people, might want to do otherwise.

Crazy Horse nodded, understanding. "We would have to get permission," he went on. "Maybe White Hat would help us. Will you go to White Hat and ask him?" said Crazy Horse to his uncle.

Little Hawk said yes. He Dog watched this older man look into the eyes of his nephew, one of the nephews he called son, for a while. They all knew what was happening. More and more Crazy Horse was trying to back away from leadership, to turn it over to his father's brother. Sometimes this made He Dog impatient with his old friend. A man was supposed to understand that as he grew older, he accepted more responsibility and lived less for himself alone.

"Will you go with me to talk to Clark?" asked Little Hawk.

He Dog and Big Road said yes.

On the other hand, thought He Dog, maybe it would be good for Crazy Horse to set down leadership. Many of the people admired him excessively, and many of the leaders were jealous of him. If Crazy Horse were not a chief, life would be simplified.

Leadership didn't suit him. Never had. His eyes and ears were always on something else, something no one else saw. He Dog was Lakota and knew deeply that every man's red road was different. As he took his leave, he was thinking affectionately, *My friend, you are truly Our Strange Man.*

SUN DANCE

Crazy Horse found it sad. Lakota people came from all the other camps to pitch their lodges in his circle. Even with the tipis crowded together, walking around the circle would take nearly a quarter-day. He knew why. He raised his eyes to the sacred sun pole in the center, defining the dancing place, and the pole shelter built around it. These agency Lakota had not done a sun dance in the truly old way for many winters. They wanted to dance with the hostiles, the Lakota who still knew the old ways.

Though Crazy Horse did not participate in dances himself, he believed in them. They led most Lakota along the red road. Days of listening to the pulse of the drum, whether you let your body move to it or not—that was a true way to set your feet on the red road. The lack of a true sun dance at Red Cloud Agency, well, that was a powerful sign of why agency life would be a black road. It was part of why his soul felt desolate.

He saw White Hat walking toward his lodge. Crazy Horse would share his short pipe with the man. The whites were here, too, big numbers of them, soldiers and their wives, traders and their families, half-blood traders who had been among the people for a long time—everyone wanted to see the sun dance done in the old way, White Hat included.

"Hau, kola!" said White Hat. The officer was without a translator. He didn't understand Lakota too badly, and would talk with halting words and signs.

Crazy Horse motioned for him to sit and lit the pipe. He wondered what the man would say. Clark had heard that Crazy Horse was thinking of moving his people to Spotted Tail Agency, and he wouldn't like that.

After the pipe went back and forth, White Hat opened with, "The people are glad to have this dance."

"Hecitu welo," said Crazy Horse in agreement.

"I will be glad to see it," said White Hat.

Crazy Horse nodded. *I will be glad to see it.* They were funny, these whites. They called the old ways barbarous, or some word that meant more like the ways of four-legged than two-legged people, yet they wanted to see the dances.

Crazy Horse played it out in his mind.

White man: May we write everything down?

Crazy Horse: Yes.

White man: May we make shadow pictures and show the dance in the newspapers?

Crazy Horse: No.

White man: Why not?

Crazy Horse: Just no. It isn't right.

White man: Well, your ways are wrong, and you need to learn about the One Big Spirit, the one the blackrobes tell about, and you should change to our ways.

Crazy Horse: Yes, we need to become like you, and you need to become like the bird that smiles at shit, and magpies need to become blackrobes.

He smiled to himself. He had never imagined a people so avid to make everyone like them.

For himself, he wouldn't mind having ways like the four-legged and crawling and winged people. Blood pumped to the pulse of the earth in them as it did in him. They too were born and made young and hunted for food and got cold and hungry and died. *Mitakuye oyasin.*

In fact, some of their ways were better than the human beings'. They didn't have wars and kill their own kind. Nor did they scheme to control each other. Strange that the worst two-legged creatures he had known, the whites, had the most weapons and were the most desperate to make others like them. As much as they liked killing, whiskey, and taking other people's women, they liked controlling most of all.

Crazy Horse decided to give White Hat an opening to talk about the move to Spotted Tail Agency. "Maybe I will go live with my uncle."

White Hat shrugged and smiled. That was one of the things white men did when they didn't like something: pretend. *Who already told you?* Crazy Horse wondered. The man had ears everywhere. One day Crazy Horse and Little Hawk had discussed it with the heads of a few families, and the next day White Hat was talking to his friends among the Indian police about how to stop this move.

"It is good to live among relatives," Crazy Horse tried again.

"You have relatives everywhere here," said White Hat.

"Yes, but Spotted Tail is my uncle, and my father and his wives pitch their lodge there." He waited, but White Hat stared out into space.

Well, Crazy Horse would be amused to see how this white man would try to outsmart him and get him to do what the white man wanted.

After a while they broke up the talk. Crazy Horse shook his head. The silliest thing *wasicu* did was maneuver and maneuver and maneuver.

Clark ran like hell toward the sun dance. He didn't pay any attention to the damned heat or the prairie-dog holes or the prickly pear or his hat, which flew off, or his dignity or any damn thing. He ran like a rabbit in a lightning storm.

Because that was live gunfire—a soldier's ears knew—and a lot of it.

Whites were running away from the sundance circle. Indians were running away, men, women, children, old folks, even dogs. Dust was up, and someone was getting shot.

Lieutenant Clark ran toward the sound of firing. Oh, Christ.

He tripped over something, sprawled straight forward, hit on one shoulder, slid in the dust, jumped up, and ran like hell.

Oh, Christ. Crook would have his ass.

Suddenly, everything went quiet.

He slowed to a trot. He could hear a voice, barely. It repeated the same words, something about friends.

Hell, yes, Crazy Horse's voice.

He pushed roughly to the front of the circle.

Crazy Horse stood alone in the center of the dance ground, near the sun pole with its prayer flags. Near the outer edge, where the prayer sticks stood like fingers, men were picking themselves up and hauling themselves off. Ponies were struggling to their feet, and their riders were leading them away.

Clark got next to Billy Garnett and asked in a whisper. He wanted to be sure of what Crazy Horse was saying.

The Strange Man repeated it. " 'Friends!' " Garnett murmured. " 'You are shooting at your own people!' " In a tone of finality.

Not a single body lay on the ground. Crazy Horse had come in time.

Clark looked at the Indian. Light-haired, slightly built, poorly dressed, unprepossessing. But he commanded the space in the middle of this dance ground, a master. He commanded the crowd, a master. Christ, he must know a hundred Indians at this place would shoot him in an instant. Evidently, they had just been shooting at each other. But the man rose up and dared them, and from the force of his spirit and the fear of retribution, they dared not. Remarkable, and just like him.

As commander of the scouts Clark was supposed to be the leader of most of these men. He felt envious of their real commander, Crazy Horse.

Clark stepped into the arbor, under the shade. He would write to Crook again tonight. This man could *compel* the Indians. He alone. The government must have him on its side or be rid of him. They must win his heart. Or take him to Washington City and overawe him. Or put him away very permanently. The Dry Tortugas had been mentioned, some godawful reef off the coast of Florida, a federal prison on a barren rock surrounded by ocean and sharks. Yes, that would do. Miles of shark-infested sea. A one-way ticket in irons.

Jesus, but he was a man.

Crazy Horse started walking away. Suddenly he seemed to sag, and to become ordinary.

Clark and Garnett intercepted the Strange Man. "What happened?"

Crazy Horse shrugged lightly and gave a half-smile. "The Greasy Grass fight," he said. Garnett's voice softly changed Lakota into English. "Our Oglala played themselves, riding up the hill." The slight man gestured to the dance circle. "The agency Indians and the traders' sons played Long Hair and his Yellow Legs. They got overexcited."

"That's one way of putting it," added Garnett. "The Oglala started hitting the friendlies too hard with their bows. A couple of friendlies pulled their pistols and fired. The Oglala ran off, but they were back in a hair's breadth with guns." Clark and Garnett looked at each other. No matter how many times you disarmed Indians, they always came up with guns.

"I heard the firing," said Clark.

Garnett told Crazy Horse what he had told Clark.

"I spoke to them," said Crazy Horse. "It is not important."

"Maybe not," said Clark. He nodded to himself. "Let's have a smoke." He thought, *The man who can stop fighting with his presence and his voice is damn well important.*

It wasn't just a little smoke. Before long He Dog and Little Hawk were sharing the pipe, and pretty soon Young Man-Whose-Enemies and Little Wound, too. Crazy Horse passed his short pipe around several times. White Hat offered tobacco, and Crazy Horse accepted it, wondering why all these influential men were sitting in front of his lodge, smoking the short pipe that an insignificant man must carry. All the while the sundance drums beat in the background, and the singers' voices lifted up to Wakan Tanka.

It was Young Man-Whose-Enemies who broached the subject. "Do you like Nellie, the daughter of Joe Laravie the trader, the girl who helped the doctor?"

Crazy Horse remembered. The trader's daughter who translated when the white doctor examined Black Shawl for the coughing sickness, thumping the back and listening at the chest, the girl who explained what the doctor was doing. "Yes," he said. A very appealing young woman, gay, always laughing, never serious, and with a truly, truly beautiful face.

"We your friends want to honor you," said Young Man-Whose-Enemies. "Clark asked how the army could honor you. Little Wound and I, your friends among the agency Oglala, suggested the Laravie woman. If you like her. Little Hawk and He Dog agree. If you like her."

Crazy Horse let his eyes smile a little. Not much that was funny happened these days. The white people opposed a man's having more than one wife. But they would pay horses to Joe Laravie to buy a chief a second wife, if they thought it might influence him. This was how the whites tried to outsmart him.

He emptied the pipe, filled it with the good tobacco White Hat had brought, lit it with a coal, drew deep, and his mind offered the smoke to Father Sky.

Ordinarily, he could not refuse. To refuse honor was to insult your friends. To refuse a gift from the whites and from rival chiefs would be to refuse their friendship. Dangerous, very dangerous.

He wondered, though, if he might refuse as a way of laying down chieftainship. Say that he knew they wanted to honor the leader of the free Oglala, but he was no longer that man. Could he convince them that his friendship was no longer pertinent? That he was no longer an important man? Perhaps. He doubted it.

He looked his uncle Little Hawk and his friend He Dog in the face. Since they were involved, there was no treachery here. Those who cared for him thought Nellie Laravie would be good for him. Little Hawk would have consulted Crazy Horse's father, who evidently thought it good.

This last notion pained Crazy Horse. Yes, Little Hawk would have consulted with Worm. Which meant leaving the agency without permission to go to Spotted Tail Agency—you couldn't even visit your own brother without permission. Which meant riding at night, concealing your horse, keeping Worm's lodge flap shut tight while you were there, and avoiding friends or even anyone who would recognize you. What a world the whites made.

He forced his mind to the girl. Yes, very appealing.

Black Shawl would be glad of a sister in the lodge, he thought. Though the doctor said she would get better with rest, she was often sick and weak. If he escaped this place, a second woman would be a great help to Black Shawl back in the hunting country, when Crazy Horse would often be gone.

But what would the whites want in return for this bribe?

He shook his head. He didn't want to live like this. But refuse an honor from his fellow chiefs?

He answered softly, and in a measured way. "I thank you for the high honor you offer me," he said, "and I accept."

"THIS AGENCY LIFE IS FOR POLITICIANS"

The word from Crook came in a telegram: The Lakota of Red Cloud Agency, friendlies and hostiles alike, could go on a buffalo hunt back to their own country. After the hunt, in the Moon When Leaves Turn Brown, they could go to see the Great White Father to tell him why they didn't want agencies on the Missouri.

Clark read the paper to the assembled headmen with big smiles, and Grouard translated ingratiatingly, as though something grand had been accomplished in getting these permissions. All the principal men were there, not only Crazy Horse, Young Man-Whose-Enemies, and Red Cloud, but three score of the smaller leaders—He Dog, Black Elk, Good Weasel, Little Big Man, Jumping Shield, and Little Hawk of the Crazy Horse people, Red Dog, Big Road, Black Twin, Woman Dress, and No Water of the Red Cloud people, Little Wound and American Horse of the True Oglala, Sword of the Oyukhpe, Yellow Bear, and many others. The old ways of describing the bands— Hunkpatila, Bad Faces, Bears—didn't apply well anymore, for the agency had changed everything, and the groups were intermingled.

Before dark Clark heard from his various informants that the response to Crook's proposal was less than enthusiastic. Some hostiles said again that a hunt and a trip to Washington City were not what they'd come in for—they'd been promised an agency in their own country. And some still said that waiting for the white man's permissions, to hunt or to do anything, was intolerable. Besides, they muttered, the rations at the agency had been short this summer. The white man was using the threat of starvation, some said.

Clark had anticipated these objections. He called the chiefs back together. When everyone was seated, Clark announced enthusiastically that he had asked Dr. Irwin, the new agent, to issue cattle and coffee and sugar for a feast. Through the mouth of Grabber, Grouard, he added, "You Indians can decide who will have the honor of hosting the feast."

Young Man-Whose-Enemies was first on his feet. "Our relatives from the north have been among us for more than two moons," he said, "and have not been given the food to hold a big feast. So I say His Crazy Horse and Little Big Man should get this honor."

Crazy Horse listened to the murmurs. *Always the maneuvers,* he thought. *I am to be grateful to the white men for giving me the food to feast my people. Half of them will rejoice at a feast in my village. The other half, the Red Cloud people, will resent it. Why should I be rewarded for holding out? they will say. Instead they should be rewarded for their many winters of loyalty to the white man.*

In fact, Red Cloud and Red Dog, his shadow, were walking out of this meeting right now. Crazy Horse averted his eyes from them, not wanting to invite a confrontation.

Despair touched him in the chest again.

No one else had much to say. The suggestion of Young Man-Whose-Enemies was accepted. The feast would be in the camp of the recent hostiles. Crazy Horse and Young Man-Whose-Enemies traded glances subtly. Yes, here was another cause for resentment.

Though darkness was falling, Crazy Horse indicated that he wanted to stay outside. His new wife, Nellie, brought light blankets for both him and Little Hawk. For the hottest moon of the year, Middle Moon, it was a cool evening. Little Hawk liked the cool evenings and nights of this northern country. He didn't want to go to the south where the government wanted him, Indian Territory, they called it. There the summer nights were hot and the water was bad.

Nellie went back into the lodge for the coffeepot. Little Hawk wondered whether Crazy Horse didn't want her to overhear their conversation, whether he was afraid she might say something unknowingly to her relatives that would cause trouble. It was true that trouble was everywhere, and even a well-meaning wife could make it worse.

Little Hawk had watched Nellie and Crazy Horse, and Black Shawl too, during dinner. Nellie was clearly enamored of Crazy Horse. Why not? He was a man of real power, physical, spiritual, even political. Little Hawk's nephew's eyes seemed livelier than they had since that day on the Greasy Grass. Maybe it was the new wife. And the improving health of Black Shawl. Now Nellie poured the coffee. Little Hawk felt that he had done right to encourage this marriage.

He had some things to say to his nephew. When he had taken a sip, he said, "How subtle the whites are, especially Clark."

Crazy Horse smiled and nodded. "He thinks to bribe me with a woman. Result—I am happier, and he gets nothing."

"I was thinking of the feast."

"Yes," murmured Crazy Horse.

"He yokes you and Little Big Man together in honor. The wildest one, the one they're afraid of, and the wild one who has become the biggest peace man." Since Little Big Man had become a scout, a policeman of his own people, he had taken his duties very seriously. Crazy Horse was an officer in the scouts because of his position. Little Big Man, on the other hand, was earning high office by hard work and close attention to what the soldiers wanted.

Crazy Horse nodded. He had realized. He didn't miss much, even if he did hate politics.

Little Hawk said with a sly smile, "Watch out, Nephew, the white men have ways of doing you favors that can get you killed."

Crazy Horse smiled.

"What do you think about going to see The One They Use for Father?"

Crazy Horse looked at his father's brother questioningly.

"It is said you might go and not come back." Each man looked at that in his mind for a moment. "The whites might kill you, or they might send you to jail in a hot place far to the south."

"They will never put me in one of their jails," said Crazy Horse sharply.

Little Hawk was glad. Some compromises were not possible for a true Lakota. He wondered if his nephew was thinking that Spotted Tail had gone to jail and come back half a man.

"They want you to go. They flatter you with honors so you will do what they want."

Crazy Horse didn't respond for a while. "You would speak better than I for the people to The One They Use for Father."

Unspoken: And they wouldn't kill you or jail you.

Also unspoken: Here at the agency you will make a better leader than I.

Little Hawk waited. He could see more on his brother's son's mind.

Crazy Horse picked up his short *canupa*, filled it, lit it, and offered the smoke to the four directions, Father Sky, and Mother Earth.

"Ate," he said, "I cannot bear this agency life." He grinned suddenly. "It is for politicians." His eyes got far away. "I think a man could still live with a very few lodges in the Shining Mountains. Don't you? If he slipped away quietly? As long as he killed white people only once in a great while?" The grin again. "Or left the moccasin prints of the Psatoka near the bodies?"

Little Hawk watched his nephew's face. It was smiling, but Little Hawk thought despair was not far away. In his mind, thought Little Hawk, Crazy Horse was crying to see a way.

So. Little Hawk wondered. If Crazy Horse went to the Shining Mountains, would he be able to avoid the appearance of an outbreak? If the hard choice actually came, how many of his friends would go with him? Was there still a life for a man like this?

Little Hawk felt a twist of emotion, pungent as the smell of sweetgrass, a breath of love and loss.

"Yes," he said, "and you would not be able to get this coffee, which some of us like too much," said Little Hawk. They smiled at each other, raised their cups, and drank.

The next morning the new agent, Dr. Irwin, spread the word that the feast would be postponed. He offered no explanation. Everyone assumed Red Cloud's people had objected too strenuously to its being hosted by Crazy Horse.

A few mornings later Crazy Horse's warriors went to the trading houses to get rifles and ammunition for the hunt and were refused. No hunt, the traders said. They showed their orders from the agent. No guns or ammunition to be traded to the people of Red Cloud Agency.

So Crazy Horse sent friends to find out the explanation of this broken promise, friends with good contacts among the whites. Among them he sent Little Big Man.

His old friend talked to Billy Garnett and Grouard—

Grabber—and others and pieced together the story he brought to Crazy Horse. Because ears seemed to be everywhere these days, and lying tongues, they talked inside the lodge.

Much of this information came from Billy Garnett, said Little Big Man. Though he was young, they had known Billy a long time and he had lived with them, and you could see he worked hard to tell everyone the truth.

"The night Young Man-Whose-Enemies-Are-Afraid-of-His-Horses asked that you and I give the feast," said Little Big Man, "two of Red Cloud's people went to the agent, Irwin, secretly, their faces covered with blankets. Some say No Water was one of them. Others say Grabber was there, and Red Cloud's confidant Red Dog, and Standing Bear."

Crazy Horse sniffed. Standing Bear, the brother of Woman Dress. After all these years the sly hand of Woman Dress worked against him. The most foolish thing Crazy Horse had ever done was break Pretty Fellow's nose by accident.

"No one knew for sure who went," Little Big Man went on, "but they came from Red Cloud's side. They told the agent, who was brand-new to the reservation, that he didn't understand who Crazy Horse was. A troublemaker. Even the chiefs had thought so for a long time—they took the shirt away from you seven winters ago. The chiefs still don't trust you, these men said. You were hostile to the white people. No one ever knows what you're thinking. You're a bad influence among the young warriors. It wouldn't do to let such a man give a feast."

Crazy Horse just waited.

"Irwin told them he was surprised. 'The officers like and respect Crazy Horse,' he said. 'Even Crook does.'

"The Indians gave a stern warning. If the agent lets the Crazy Horse people trade for rifles, they will go back to their country and go on the warpath. They won't kill buffalo—they will kill white people."

The two old friends looked at each other. Something was slipping away here.

"The next morning telegrams flew from the agent to Crook and back. Also to Spotted Tail Agency and back. Crook decided the hunt was too risky. Some said that even Crazy Horse's uncle Spotted Tail doubted the wisdom of the hunt—he too said that if his nephew left the agency, he might never come back."

"E-i-i-i," Crazy Horse said regretfully to Little Big Man. He was hurt. Spotted Tail knew that a Lakota chief keeps his promises.

The two men sat and stared into the fire. Their friendship had been forged in the hardships and dangers and loyalties of the war trail. Yes, Little Big Man had held Crazy Horse's arm from behind against danger, but even that was a closeness. Crazy Horse rubbed the scar below his nose with a forefinger.

Little Big Man had come to Crazy Horse as a passionate young man, eager to show his power in war. Then he had become a respected war leader, now an officer of the Indian police. Always he'd been a determined defender of the people—no one had been more obstinate about keeping the Black Hills. No one had been more zealous to stay in the hunting country and fight the whites. He was a good man. Yet now even he was changed.

Crazy Horse took a little sweetgrass and put it on the fire. The smell always brought him a kind of tranquillity. He had liked to use it when he wanted to sit quietly and be with Hawk. He missed Hawk. Right now he burned the sweetness to invite the spirits to attend this talk. He watched the pungent smoke waft up toward the smoke hole.

"My friend," he said, "look what we've just done. I asked you to creep around and ask questions of this person and that one and put the answers together so we know what's going on. Now, in the same darkness, we think of doing something back and hope we get what we want, maybe, sometimes, depending on who outschemes who." He paused. "And who are we scheming against?" Crazy

Horse shook his head. "Other Lakota. Even other Oglala. "I can't live like this."

They let the words sit. Little Big Man didn't deny them.

"I think Little Hawk will be a better agency leader than I am. He is a good speaker, and lets the whites know how a real Lakota feels." Crazy Horse smiled a little. "As for me, I think I want to live quietly, and maybe somewhere else." He waited. "Out in the hills somewhere." He listened for the beat of the earth, but for the moment he heard nothing. He rubbed the scar on his upper lip. "Would you like to smoke?" he asked. Then he lit the short *canupa* once more. Both of them were thinking how short it was.

PARTING OF FRIENDS

Crazy Horse made time often now to listen to the Inyan. He went down to a quiet place he knew by White Clay Creek, where no one could see him or was likely to come on him by chance, and prayed to Inyan, Stone, the first power, which came before anything else. He never heard words from Inyan, but he knew now he was hearing something. Not words, as he had expected, but the beat of the drum, which was the beat of his pulse, which was the beat of life upon the earth. Yes, he had heard it all these years and never known it as the song of Inyan, the song of the oldest creatures on the earth.

Sometimes he got a whisper of what more there was to hear, an understanding. It didn't come as words, but as something wispy, like the sound of wind when it isn't quite loud enough to hear. An awareness, a sense.

He didn't know what this whisper meant. It was tempting, seductive. It was also tranquil, sweet, at rest with the world. Nothing else in his life seemed sweet or tranquil now. He would sit for days and days beside Inyan, his mind within them, savoring this feeling.

He thought that if he felt Hawk again, it would be here. If he felt Hawk again. He was still desolate.

But the soldiers did not like for Crazy Horse to be off by himself somewhere, no one knew where. The rival chiefs liked it even less. "He comes back with a faraway look in his eyes," they said. "He doesn't seem so ready to sit around the fire and tell stories anymore. He's morose, and we can't tell what's on his mind."

So they sent word for the village of the recent hostiles to move in close to Red Cloud's village for a big council.

When the headmen discussed it, Crazy Horse said he didn't want to go. He was starting to talk often in council, and he thought that was another sign that he was leading a life that wasn't for him. "I see no point in going," he said. "They have broken their promise about the hunt. I am not willing to talk to them about anything. Let them send word that we can have our agency back in our country. Then we'll talk about trading so we can leave."

Crazy Horse went on, "Every man can do as he wishes. Whoever wants to move next to Red Cloud for this council can say so by moving his lodges across the creek."

For once He Dog opposed him. "This is not the time to make a stand," he said. "I will move across the creek. Everyone who doesn't want his wives and children shot by soldiers, come with me."

No one knew why He Dog was so sure of a crisis coming. He would say nothing but, "Trouble is close."

Soon two soldier chiefs came to visit Crazy Horse, one of them Col. Luther Bradley, the new commanding officer at Fort Robinson. To show hospitality Crazy Horse offered them coffee, but he drank none himself. Though he was fond of the sweet taste, he had decided it was another *wasicu* weakness and had made up his mind never to touch it again.

The soldier chiefs gave him a new knife in a leather scabbard and asked if he was willing to go to Washington City.

If they wanted him to go before giving him an agency in his own country, Crazy Horse replied, he would have to think about that. Maybe his uncle Little Hawk should go.

Crazy Horse hinted again that Little Hawk was a better man than he to lead the village now and the soldiers should look to him. But he could see they only thought he was being uncooperative.

He said he had no more coffee, and they understood that he was breaking off the talk and left. He appreciated that. He wanted to go down by White Clay Creek and pray over Inyan and listen to the beat of the earth, hoping to see toward a future.

Leaving, the soldier chiefs marked him down as sullen and evasive.

He Dog thought he was changed, too. His friend had always been quiet and sometimes remote. Now he seemed even more withdrawn. "You seem different," he said to Crazy Horse. "I wonder—if I move across the creek, will we still be friends?"

Crazy Horse laughed easily. He Dog was glad to hear his laugh again. "Only white men draw a line and say, 'If you camp here, we are friends. If you camp there, we are enemies.' There's plenty of room, my friend. Camp where you want."

But the big council never happened. Clark gave He Dog the food to host a feast so the soldier chief could talk to Crazy Horse. But the Strange Man didn't come—he sent a message that he saw no point in talking to the soldiers anymore.

He Dog considered before he spoke to the soldier chiefs. "His Crazy Horse has strong medicine," he said. "I think it is warning him. Warning him of what? I don't know."

"Is he going to break out?" Colonel Bradley asked in a demanding way.

"No," said He Dog. "He has said over and over that he came here for peace. He will stick to his word."

Bradley and Clark seemed to accept that.

Crazy Horse spent more and more time with Inyan, listening, sometimes praying, often simply sitting with them. For entire days he waited over Inyan in the warrior way that Hump had taught him, paying attention only to his own breath, becoming in that way stiller than anything living could normally be, still as the living Inyan itself. Stronger and stronger came the sound that was not a sound, the pulse of the earth.

He waited as a warrior waits, fully aware, fully ready, surrendering expectation, giving his being to awareness, to welcoming anything in the forest or on the plains or on Maka, Earth, that might come to his consciousness. Now, more than in his youth, that might include visitors from the realm of spirits, or dreams, or ideas, or visions.

He had gone to Horn Chips to talk about his time with Inyan. Though he didn't hear words from them, he said, he was hearing something, not with his ears, not even with his mind, with . . . He heard the pulse of the earth and of all living creatures. "In this pulse is a sense of vastness," he said, "or something like vastness. Like the feelings you get when you sit all night in the warrior's way, breathing as a warrior, and the prairies begin to get light, and that light *is* the prairie, and is you, and you are it, touching everything in the prairie, Inyan and Maka and all the creatures that grow, and the air, and the light is the air, and you are the air, and you are within everything, and everything is within you. And then Father Sun rises. . . ."

After a moment he went on. "When I have that feeling, I can't be angry or rash or foolish. It makes me want to spend day after day with Inyan."

Horn Chips said, "Inyan is speaking."

Crazy Horse said, "I don't know what the stones are saying."

Horn Chips' only other comment was, "Keep listening. Expect nothing. Listen."

As Crazy Horse left, Chips remarked to his wife that he saw that his friend's spirit was better, and he was glad.

Though Crazy Horse concentrated on waiting without expectation, one of his thoughts was that Hawk might return to him if he spent his time this way, his heart open, his being receptive. Sometimes he had a sense that Hawk was near, just out of reach, close but not yet back in his heart. He knew better than to lurch toward this presence he felt hovering. Hawk would come when she was ready.

His sense of the nearness of Hawk was not vague or ephemeral. It was definite, as Hawk's perch in his heart had been unmistakable, and it clearly did not yet include Hawk. She was not within.

His heart began to recover now. He recognized again the feelings of his youth and young manhood, tentative yet returning—aspiration and hope, a sense of possibility, the prospect of welcome challenges.

Sometimes he thought the coming challenge was living wild again. Other times he thought it was his own death. Either way, desolation seemed to be loosening its grip on him.

As he sat breathing, he thought often of the *cante ista*. He knew that when he was listening to Inyan and the beat of the earth, he saw with the single eye that is the heart. He had no words for what he saw and heard. It was just a sense of the rightness of things. It was healing.

He would be willing to die if he could have Hawk back, and be healed.

Crazy Horse called his friends to him in twos and threes, men he had ridden the war trail and the hunting trail with, men who could keep a secret and who were of like minds, as unsuited for agency life as he was. Red Feather, the younger brother of Black Shawl. Black Elk. Ashes and Bull Head, his father's brothers, his *ate*. His father and Touch-the-Sky, his uncle on his birth mother's side, slipped down from Spotted Tail Agency one night, and he talked all the next day with them. Club Man, his sister's husband. Little Killer, Little Shield, and Short Bull. Good Weasel, his lieutenant through the last years of war. He wanted six or eight companions, with their families.

He made them all the same proposition. He was weary of chieftainship, he said, and was setting it down as fast as the *wasicu* would let him. Little Hawk would be much better than Crazy Horse at facing the new challenges of agency life. For himself, he said, agency life was no life. His spirit was dead here, his medicine sapped. "Maybe agency life isn't for you either," said Crazy Horse to each one.

"I have given my word," he declared, "and I will not lead the people off the agency and back to the free life. I have given my word. But a few of us can slip away, and live as we like. Maybe you would like to do that on your own. Or maybe you have relatives with Sitting Bull in the Land Their Grandmother Claims. Or maybe you would like to do it with me.

"Whoever wants to go with me should slip away quietly, one lodge at a time, without making any fuss. We will all meet on Goose Creek near the Shining Mountains in the first half of the Moon When the Leaves Fall," which was more than a moon away. "Maybe we will be able to live in the Shining Mountains. Maybe farther north. Maybe in Grandmother's Land. Now that Black Shawl is better, I may be able to live there."

He used the old Lakota words for things and places. He had noticed that younger Lakota were changing some of these words—Maka Sika they called "the badlands" or "terre mauvais," and White Earth River they referred to as "the river where the agency is." He had let some of his own language change. Now he consciously used the oldest names he could remember.

"Don't answer me in words," he said. "Come back and ask questions if you like. Then come to Goose Creek, or don't, whatever is best for your family."

Red Feather and Good Weasel, young men of high spirits, were elated at the proposal and said immediately that they wanted to go. Most of the men said how attractive it sounded and promised an answer in a few days. Some looked worried.

Worm said simply and briefly that he would come with his son.

Touch-the-Sky said he would consider the suggestion, but his village weighed heavy on his mind. The people owned him, and maybe he was not free to seek a life good for himself alone.

Little Big Man pondered his answer a long time before he spoke. "I will always be your friend," Little Big Man said, "but I will not walk beside you on this journey." Then he laughed a little. "Maybe that's good. I won't be able to hold your arms if anyone shoots at you." They had teased each other occasionally about that. Tonight Crazy Horse didn't feel like any teasing. He was thinking that if he died here at this agency, it would be because his own people were holding him back in some way.

"I can't go," Little Big Man repeated. "I've set my feet on a new road, the agency road, and I will ride it as hard as I ever rode into battle." He looked Crazy Horse in the eye. "I'm an *akicita* man. That is my promise to the whites and my duty to the people.

"Many times it looks like a black road to me," he said. "Many times. I see much that you see. But I have promised myself, my family, Clark, the people of the village that I will walk this road." He paused. "And I will do whatever it asks of me."

He let this sit a long while. "I'm glad you're going. I think it's right for you. I think this place will kill your medicine." He hesitated. "I'm also glad for myself. I'm afraid Clark might ask me to arrest you." He shifted his weight on his bottom. "They never say so, but I think that's on their minds sometimes." He smiled wryly. "You would be less trouble a hundred sleeps away in a jail, they say to themselves." Hesitation. "I couldn't stand arresting you. But if I was ordered, I would do it."

The two friends looked at each other in the eerie flicker of the fire. E-i-i-i, thought Crazy Horse, *the world has turned itself inside out. . . .*

"So go, my friend. Go soon," said Little Big Man, getting to his feet. "Part of my heart will go with you."

Crazy Horse thanked him. As always, he did not say good-bye, but, *"Ake wancinyankin ktelo,"* meaning, "Until I see you again."

A MISTAKE OVER WORDS

Late in the Moon When All Things Ripen, which the whites called August, Clark summoned the leaders of the Crazy Horse people and of the agency people. Since Touch-the-Sky had been called down from Spotted Tail Agency for the occasion, Crazy Horse knew it was important. As the headmen walked into the building next to his nephew, Crazy Horse said quietly that he wondered what was going on. "Do you think this is the big bribe?"

Touch-the-Sky didn't answer. The rumor all this moon had been that the *wasicu* would offer Crazy Horse chieftainship of all the Lakota in return for leading the people to the new agencies on the Muddy Water. The two leaders had shaken their heads ruefully about it. "They don't understand you at all," Touch-the-Sky said.

But the news Clark gave them in the council room was something else entirely: Led by Chief Joseph, the Nez Percé had broken off the reservation. No one knew where they were going or what they would do. They were in the Yellowstone River country. This was one of the reasons the Lakota couldn't be allowed to go there to hunt, added Clark, but this was a lie: The hunt had been refused half a moon ago.

"Well," the lieutenant went on, "we would like your help, the army would like your help. General Crook and General Miles are going to the Yellowstone country to fight the Nez Percé, and Crook wants your scouts to go with him."

Clark looked at them eagerly while Grabber translated. Bordeaux was there too, up from Spotted Tail with Touch-the-Sky, but he let Grabber do the translating.

Everyone was too surprised to say a word. Finally Little Hawk said, "Fight?"

"Yes," said Clark. "Your scouts fight the Nez Percé."

The Indians talked quietly among themselves, the Crazy Horse people and Mniconjou Touch-the-Sky on one side of the room and the Red Cloud people, including No Water, on the other.

Fight? This was unexpected. There were various opinions. Some said the young men would be glad for the opportunity and it would be good for them. Others said they had quit fighting forever. Others said it was a only trick by the whites to make it look like they were going to war.

Finally Little Hawk answered for the Crazy Horse people. "You whites always ask one thing and then another. You wanted us to come in, we did. You wanted us to give up our horses and our guns, we did. You wanted us to go on a buffalo hunt, we said yes. You asked us to go to see The One You Use for Father, we said all right. Now you say go to war."

Little Hawk paused in his oratory for effect, and some of the headmen made the sound of approval. "Our people have untied their horses' tails," he went on. "We want the peace we were promised. We are tired of war. We want to go to the Yellowstone to hunt buffalo."

Without even waiting to hear from the Red Cloud side, Clark burst out, "That's impossible. We can't have you in that country. There's trouble up there. Everyone will think all the Indians are off the reservation. Who knows what would happen?"

He talked loudly and blusteringly. The Lakota looked

surreptitiously at each other. Some of them felt ashamed to be shouted at this way. Others felt embarrassment for Clark, that he allowed himself to act like this. The most experienced around the agency just said to themselves, *The white men are acting like white men again.*

While Grouard, Grabber, translated Clark's words, they were only half-listening. You don't listen to the words of a man who has lost control of himself.

When Grabber finished, they all sat and thought, wondering how to answer this odd white man. To Touch-the-Sky's surprise, it was Crazy Horse who finally spoke up, softly and deliberately. "We want peace," he said. Crazy Horse did not sound reticent or self-effacing now, but like a man sure of his powers. Touch-the-Sky thought it was a shame that he would lay down chieftainship just when he had grown into it fully. "We want peace," he repeated. "We are tired of war."

While Grabber made these words into English for Clark, Crazy Horse held the floor with his commanding gaze. "The *wasicu* have lied to us and tricked us from the beginning, when you tried to put Bear-Scattering over us all, and thus killed him. You are still trying to trick us."

The Indians in the room were perfectly still while Grabber translated. They were dazed by Crazy Horse's taking command like this.

"Nevertheless," Crazy Horse went on, "we want to do what is asked of us. If The One You Use for Father wants us to fight the Nez Percé, we will go to the north country and fight until not a Nez Percé is left."

As soon as Grabber had translated the words, Clark started shouting at Crazy Horse. He was on his feet, red-faced, bellowing like a crazed bull in his incomprehensible language. Neither Touch-the-Sky nor any of the other Indians knew what to make of this outburst. *Impolite* didn't begin to describe it.

"But Crazy Horse said he will do what you want!" said someone near Touch-the-Sky.

Suddenly one of the Red Cloud headmen, Three Bears,

was on his feet, too, pointing at the sandy-haired one. "If you want to kill someone," he yelled, "kill me!"

Suddenly the two interpreters were arguing, Grabber and Bordeaux. "You liar!" Bordeaux said over and over in Lakota.

Grabber hollered back at Bordeaux—some of the Lakota recognized the bad white-man word *bastard*—the traders' sons were acting as bad as white men.

Grabber jumped up. For a moment Touch-the-Sky thought he was going to strangle Bordeaux. Suddenly the half-breed stopped himself. He glared at Bordeaux. Then he turned slowly and gave Crazy Horse the queerest look. Touch-the-Sky thought the face glimmered with triumph. In an instant the look was gone, and Grabber stomped out of the room.

The door slammed the room into silence. Bordeaux stuck his head down angrily. The Lakota fell silent—no one wanted to argue in front of a white man. They all waited in tense wordlessness. Touch-the-Sky thought everyone looked agitated but Crazy Horse. His nephew seemed recovered from his melancholy of the last several moons, in fact serene in the eye of the storm.

Fear shot through Touch-the-Sky like lightning, fear for Crazy Horse.

He looked at the door Grabber had slammed behind him. *What now?* he wondered. *What has this trader's son done?* But the door was blank and mute.

Lieutenant Clark asked Bordeaux to interpret, but the trader's son refused. Clark didn't know the man well anyway. He was from Spotted Tail Agency. So he told a soldier to go get Billy Garnett to finish the council.

He was irate. This wasn't just a government problem—it was a personal betrayal. Crazy Horse had promised Clark personally that he had quit war forever, and now he declared that he would fight until not a single white man was left alive.

Insolence and effrontery!

He thought they were friends!

It proved all the nasty rumors flying around the agency were true. Crazy Horse hated white people. Though he pretended friendship sometimes, he was a reactionary who would fight until he was dead, and all his people were dead.

Clark waited for Garnett. He had to finish this council somehow, get out of here without a knife in his back, and telegraph Crook quick.

Touch-the-Sky noted the first words Garnett translated from Clark: "Would Crazy Horse change his mind and go fight the Nez Percé?"

That was what the sandy-haired one had already promised to do, and Crazy Horse said so calmly.

Touch-the-Sky studied Clark. He was agitated, anyone could see that.

"You will take the scouts and fight the Nez Percé?" repeated Garnett.

"Yes," said Crazy Horse, "and take some lodges and women too and make a little hunt."

At least a little of this council began to make sense to Touch-the-Sky. His nephew was angling to get the hunt back. That's why he wanted the women, to do the butchering. For sure he was worried about the people having enough to eat this winter. And maybe he was wanting to get up to the north country himself, so he and some companions could disappear. Another reason to take the families.

Clark got angry again at this. "You can't fight with women along!"

Crazy Horse was not rude enough to shrug visibly. "We've done some good fighting with them there," he said softly. No one smiled. Everyone supposed Clark got the reference to the Custer fight.

"No!" shouted Clark. He made a lot more words, but Touch-the-Sky only knew he was yelling again.

Crazy Horse didn't even wait for Garnett to tell what the white officer said. He got up and told his headmen he wanted to go home. "We've talked too much here," he said.

Outside in the night air Touch-the-Sky waited for Bordeaux. "Tell me what happened," he said.

The interpreter acted like he was going to walk on without answering.

"Why didn't Clark understand that His Crazy Horse agreed to fight the Nez Percé?" Touch-the-Sky asked.

Bordeaux wheeled on him. "That *bastard* Grabber," he said, spitting out the one ugly white-man word, "he changed what the Strange Man said. When he told the words to Clark, he made them, 'We will fight until every *white man* is dead.' "

Bordeaux spun and stomped off.

Touch-the-Sky was standing there seeing the future. This mistake—this dirty trick—was going to cause a lot of trouble. Maybe more than he could straighten out. He could kill Grabber—he might kill him—but that might not save Crazy Horse now.

HAWK

Crazy Horse was also seeing the future. Or was it the past? Or a time neither future nor past nor present but somehow always? He didn't know, but he knew he needed the seeing.

That night he dreamed part of the vision he had had as a youth, near the Running Water:

Now Rider was stripped to nothing but a breechcloth, and rode harder, faster, in a martial vigor. But hands flailed at him, clutched at him from behind, slowed him down. He tossed his arms backward like a man slinging off an encumbering shirt. The hands kept pulling at him, holding him back, the hands of his own people.

He felt threat in them. He shook them off and shook them off and rode on and rode on, but the hands did not relent. Rider shook and shook and shook at them. He feared the hands behind more than the bullets before.

He saw it over and over, over and over, and sometimes it was oddly varied: Sometimes he saw the picture of Rider galloping into the bullets and being clutched at from behind, as he had in his vision, a brilliantly colored moving painting, more vivid than anything ordinary eyes could ever see. Sometimes he *heard* words chanting the story of Rider going into fire, and saw discontinuous pictures, as through shifting fog, or gun smoke blown by the wind. Sometimes he saw shifting pictures and heard not words but drumbeats that in their throb told the story once more.

But the story was always the same. All night, in one form or another, he dreamed of Rider invulnerable to his enemies, vulnerable to his people.

When he woke up, Hawk was in his heart. She perched there. He could feel her heft and her body warmth and an occasional clasping of her claws and brushing of her feathers.

She was with him.

He sat up in his robes, quiet, simply attending to her. He touched Black Shawl, still asleep next to him, on the shoulder. He watched the dawn light slowly brighten the dark tipi with a rose light.

"Tunkasila, pila maya," he said. Grandfather, thank you. He felt whole again.

All that afternoon people came to him with unhappy tales. The telegraph wires were singing. No one knew much of what was being said, but the Red Cloud agent and the commanding officer at Fort Robinson had been sending and getting words from Spotted Tail Agency and from Crook.

They'd heard what Clark said. He'd told Irwin, the

new agent who still didn't know the people, that Crazy Horse was going to take his people and make a run for the north country. When the agent asked Red Cloud and the other agency chiefs, they all said the Strange Man was wild and they couldn't control him.

Crazy Horse smiled at this. He was wild—he was returned to his original warrior self—and he couldn't be controlled. That much was absolutely true. And he was no threat to anyone.

Little Hawk asked him why the agency chiefs weren't reassuring the agent. They had heard Crazy Horse promise to do what Clark wanted, go fight the Nez Percé.

Crazy Horse shrugged.

Yes, yes, there was white fire coming at him, and the hands of his own people were grabbing at him from behind, and he might be hurt. He felt the rightness of it. He wanted to survive, but maybe he wouldn't. He would ride and feel the rightness under him like a fine, spirited pony.

He Dog came and explained part of it. It was Grabber. Little Hawk muttered, "Grabber again. They should have killed him. Grabber changed the sandy-haired one's words at the council, He Dog said. Bastard, saying Crazy Horse would kill every white man, not every Nez Percé."

Little Hawk was incensed.

Crazy Horse said he was not so surprised. That was what happened when you spent your days begging for life instead of living.

That night a rider came to Crazy Horse from Touch-the-Sky. The Mniconjou had talked to Agent Lee at Spotted Tail Agency, the messenger said, and the agent understood Grabber's deception.

"It will be all right," Crazy Horse told his uncle through the messenger. Though the family had barely enough to eat, he gave the man a little jerky—it was a hard ride from Spotted Tail Agency to here and and back. Maybe Nellie would go to her father's trading post and beg some more food tomorrow.

His Crazy Horse was quietly noticing Hawk in his chest.

Hawk didn't feel martial yet. But Crazy Horse sensed he would be a warrior again before long, and only a warrior.

The next day the Crazy Horse people loafed around the fort hoping for word.

Crazy Horse was far from the fort, on the creek. The Inyan creatures were set before him. He was breathing in the warrior way, attentive, accepting, aware. He said to Inyan the word Horn Chips had taught him, *"wanisugna,"* living seed within the stone. He heard the earth pulse. From time to time he murmured the prayer, *"Mitakuye oyasin."*

His people wanted to find him to tell him that signs of trouble were everywhere. Crook had come fast on the railroad. Agent Lee was here from Spotted Tail Agency. Pony soldiers were on the way from Fort Laramie, and all the white men were holding talks.

Clark refused to believe that Grabber had fooled everyone or even made a mistake—he insisted that the Crazy Horse people were about to bolt.

Lt. Jesse Lee, agent from Spotted Tail Agency, claimed it was all a mistake, though, and an injustice to Crazy Horse and his people.

The agency headmen would only say that Crazy Horse was young and wild and uncontrollable.

Crook had come and would set things right. He had called a council for this afternoon to hear what Crazy Horse had to say. He did not necessarily believe Grabber—his mind was open.

At first they couldn't find Crazy Horse to tell him all this news. Red Feather, Black Shawl's brother, had an idea where the Strange Man was. He found him at his private place on White Clay Creek and stood respectfully a long way off until the sandy-haired one put away his Inyan and signaled the young man to come close.

After Red Feather told his stories, the two came back to camp. "I will go to the council and tell Three Stars the truth," Crazy Horse said to Red Feather. "But my young friend, it will make no difference, not for me." They walked along quietly for a moment. Crazy Horse murmured, "Begging a *wasicu* for a place to live, or food, or the right to go hunting or visit my father," and shook his head incredulously.

Inside he turned his mind to Hawk, felt her warm presence, and smiled to himself.

GEN. GEORGE CROOK

Crook was on the way to White Clay Creek with Lieutenant Clark in an army coach called an ambulance. Crook would have preferred to ride horseback, he would have preferred to dispense with ceremony, but this was the way of the world.

Gen. George Crook was an impatient man today. He prided himself on his understanding of Indians and on his reputation for fairness. He knew as well as the next man the truth of Abraham Lincoln's declaration that an Indian reservation was a place Indians lived surrounded by thieves. "And liars," Crook would have added.

Now he suspected that the Lakota at this agency were being treated treacherously. He suspected that the interpreter had translated the words of Crazy Horse falsely. And he suspected that the young lieutenant beside him, his own aide, whom he knew with some affection as Philo, was playing the fool. Philo had gotten infatuated with Crazy Horse and with the idea of having a famous wild Indian as a friend. The first time Crazy Horse acted like an Indian, Philo felt personally betrayed and turned into his enemy.

So Crook suspected. He intended to meet everyone in council right now and straighten everything out. Crook was not a man to put up with lying or equivocating or virginal hesitating or fandangling around. He wanted the truth and he wanted it now. Then he would want action, immediately.

An Indian in a scout's uniform rode up to the interpreters in front of the ambulance and motioned for them to stop. He spoke to Big Bat Pourier and Billy Garnett—Crook didn't want to give that damned Grouard another chance to lie at this council. He trusted Garnett and Big Bat.

Whatever the Indian was telling them, Big Bat didn't like it. He sneaked a sidewise look or two at Crook. The Indian was a fellow with soulful spaniel eyes, and the spit and polish of a man who'd had his head turned by a uniform. Not the sort of man Crook was inclined to think a straight shooter. Finally Crook said, "Spit it out, man. What's he saying?"

Garnett explained, "This man is Woman Dress. He says one of his brothers, Little Wolf, was outside His Crazy Horse's lodge last night when he and his warriors had a big talk. He heard what they said, he told his brother Standing Bear, and Standing Bear told Woman Dress. The Crazy Horse Indians plan to kill you today."

Crook snorted. "Exactly how does he say they're going to do this?"

Garnett seemed boyishly embarrassed by this conversation, but he proceeded with the facts. "Sixty of His Crazy Horse's men will be there. When His Crazy Horse shakes your hand with one hand, he will kill you with the other. Then his warriors will kill all the rest of the whites. Woman Dress says you better not go there."

"I knew it," hissed Clark.

Crook shot the fellow a look to shut him up. He didn't intend to be deterred. But he pondered. Finally, he said to Garnett, "What is this man's name again?"

"Woman Dress."

"Who is he?"

"The son of Chief Bad Face, the grandson of Chief Smoke."

Perhaps a reliable man then.

"Does he have a reputation for telling the truth?"

Billy Garnett had lived in Crazy Horse's camp and knew the Strange Man and Woman Dress hadn't liked each other since one was called Curly and the other Pretty Fellow, but he didn't know why. Surely Crook knew Woman Dress was an agency Indian. Garnett thought he himself was maybe prejudiced in the sandy-haired man's favor. So he said, "What do you think, Big Bat?"

"Woman Dress, he's straight," said Big Bat.

Billy started to add that Big Bat was Woman Dress's cousin but thought better of it.

"Private, let's go," said Crook.

"Sir!" protested Clark. "You can't go there now."

"I never set out for anywhere and got scared off," said Crook.

"Sir!" exclaimed the lieutenant. "You don't know what's been going on here. Crazy Horse has been moody, sour. . . . Even the other Indians don't like him. And don't trust him."

"Lieutenant," said Crook, "thousands of men have tried to kill me. If I retreated because of that, I'd need a horse with eyes in its ass."

"Sir! Truly!" Clark really did seem alarmed. "We've lost one good man to Crazy Horse. We can't be made fools of again."

This made some impression on Crook. The army had looked like a three-legged catamount often enough in this Sioux War. Clark started in again, but Crook wasn't listening. It was all right to be mule-headed, he told himself, but not addle-headed. "Enough!" he said to Clark.

He waved Garnett and Big Bat over. "Go to the council place and say I've been called to the railroad," he said. "Then, without letting Crazy Horse know, bring the reliable chiefs and scouts to the fort."

The interpreters nodded. Clark named off some "reliable" chiefs and scouts for them, all agency Indians, mostly Red Cloud people.

"I'm going to get to the bottom of this," growled Crook.

Crook watched the agency chiefs file into the room and sit, against the walls as they preferred. Agency chiefs. He had to have men whose friendship he was sure of. Garnett had come back from the site on White Clay Creek with word that Crazy Horse hadn't shown up for the council anyway. No telling what was on his mind. So only longtime friendlies here—Red Cloud, Red Dog, Little Wound, American Horse, Three Bears, No Flesh, Yellow Bear, High Wolf, Slow Bull, Black Bear, Blue Horse, No Water, and Young Man-Whose-Enemies.

No, it wasn't ideal. He thought some of these chiefs were jealous of Crazy Horse, and certainly Red Cloud could be a devious old bastard. But Crook thought he could see through jealousy. And surely in the end the chiefs would not sacrifice one of their own unjustly.

He motioned to Philo, who brought Woman Dress into the room. At Crook's instruction the Indian began to tell once more the story of what his brother Little Wolf had heard outside Crazy Horse's lodge last night and told to his brother Standing Bear, who had told him, their brother, the scout Woman Dress.

No Water watched with his face carefully neutral. He wasn't going to let his own people see his emotions, much less the white men. But this time it was hard. *Goddamn,* as he had learned to say from the white men, this was delicious.

He felt a hot rock in his chest. The rock was not burning so much from seven winters ago, when Crazy Horse had humiliated him, stealing Black Buffalo Woman away forever, even if she had come back in appearance. No, that was not when he had first felt the hot rock in his chest. That was a day twenty winters past, when the whites were supposed to hang Spotted Tail and No Water had watched from the bushes while Crazy Horse topped Black Buffalo Woman over and over. That day he saw all their ecstasy and felt it all in reverse, as agony. That day the rock first clogged his chest and his breath and his being. Today he would spit it out.

He paid no attention to Woman Dress's story. He had helped Woman Dress and Standing Bear invent it. Woman Dress also hated the Strange Man. This tale was just a way of taking an opportunity.

He looked at around at his fellow headmen as Crook questioned Woman Dress about the story. No Water wondered how many of the other headmen knew this story was made up. He and the two brothers had told no one, not even Little Wolf, who was actually off in the Maka Sica hunting. *Goddamn,* some of them must suspect. But he thought they would go along. He hoped Young Man-Whose-Enemies didn't suspect. That was the only big risk.

Young Man-Whose-Enemies sat quiet while Red Dog answered Three Star's questions—Red Dog, Red Cloud's mouth and tongue these days. Red Dog was telling the truth, with some extra sourness: Crazy Horse wasn't really converted to the new life, he just pretended. He was an unsettling force among the young men, who kept hoping he would lead an uprising, whip the army, and take all the people back to the Yellowstone and Powder River country. He attracted everyone on the agency who was dissatisfied, and there were plenty, and gave them a leader to rally around. In general, he was trouble. And since he was closed-mouthed and morose, you never knew what was on his mind.

Despite the acrid tone, it was a fair summary. Almost every headman in the room agreed. Young Man-Whose-Enemies himself did, with a split in his heart. But Young Man-Whose-Enemies had made up his mind to walk the new road, and he would do it.

Young Man-Whose-Enemies did wonder about Woman

Dress' story. These Bad Face brothers and their friends had envied Crazy Horse for maybe twenty winters. If the whites wanted to run things, they needed to know more about the people.

Still, if the Bad Faces were exaggerating, it probably didn't matter. Crazy Horse was a problem. Something was going to have to be done. Probably the whites would have him arrested. Maybe Young Man-Whose-Enemies could have his old friend put in an easy kind of jailing, like the one Spotted Tail had all those winters ago. Maybe the jailing would soften Crazy Horse's heart, as it had Spotted Tail's.

Young Man-Whose-Enemies felt a vast oppression of misery.

After Red Dog finished, another man or two spoke to Crook in the same vein. The white man heard no dissension.

Crook asked, "So say you all?"

No Indian spoke up. Crook looked straight at Young Man-Whose-Enemies. The headman glanced at Clark, who was staring at him challengingly. The chief looked back at Crook and nodded slightly.

George Crook was not a man who had difficulty making decisions. "Lieutenant Clark, I instruct you to arrest His Crazy Horse at a time and place and in such manner as you deem suitable. You will detain him in the Fort Robinson guardhouse pending further instruction." He got to his feet. "Now I must go to the railroad."

Garnett translated the words for the chiefs. Crook tried to translate the expressions on their faces. Relief, for sure. Malicious satisfaction here and there, he thought—these men weren't any better than anyone else. And genuine regret, he thought, on the face of Young Man-Whose-Enemies.

Yes, it was a damn shame. Crook thought Crazy Horse was a fine man. Crook was honored to have been his rival and under other circumstances would have felt privileged to be his friend. In the last analysis, though, a man who stood in the way of the great river of civilization got washed away. Even the finest man.

He started shaking hands, wishing he didn't have to. The thought crossed his mind that these were the palms of Judases. As he squeezed hand after hand, he wondered if they had heard what the federal prison of the Dry Tortugas was like.

Crazy Horse looked at Red Feather, waiting.

"Crook has given orders for your arrest," the young man finally stammered.

Red Feather had rushed to the lodge of his sister Black Shawl and his brother-in-law the sandy-haired man. He'd gotten the news from Billy Garnett.

He told everything. The meeting with Crook and Clark and the agency chiefs. The story told by Woman Dress.

Kill Three Stars? Crazy Horse and Black Shawl looked at each other in amazement. Crazy Horse kill Three Stars? After he gave his word to untie his horses' tails?

A story passed from three pairs of lips, brother to brother to brother? From Crazy Horse's old enemy? And Three Stars believed it?

"Arrested," Red Feather repeated.

Arrested. That was the word the *wasicu* used when they took away your freedom. Sometimes the prisoners came back changed, like Spotted Tail. Usually they didn't come back at all. Either they were killed trying to escape or they hanged themselves.

The Lakota had talked about it and decided the whites understood perfectly how calamitous being locked up was for a Lakota. Living without being able to face Father Sun in the morning, or see the star people, or the *wakinyan*. Without being able to purify yourself with burning cedar, or invite the spirits with burning sweetgrass, or go to the sweat lodge. Worse than death—life without medicine, life without Spirit.

Crazy Horse felt a painful twist in his chest. He had just

gotten Hawk back. Hawk could not live in a jail. If he went to jail, he would lose Hawk forever.

He gave Red Feather a sharp look. "I will never let them arrest me. Tell everyone," he said low and with an edge in his voice, "I will never let them arrest me."

Red Feather looked distressed. "There's worse," he said.

The Strange Man said simply, "Tell me all of it."

"Crook went to the railroad. Then Clark and the agency Indians made plans to come against our village, to surround us all so we couldn't run away, and kill you. Clark said he would give $200 for your scalp." He paused. "No Water said that would be a brave act, to bring back your scalp."

Crazy Horse rubbed the scar on his lip with a forefinger. So he would be hurt by his own, like the last time.

"But that plan is off for tonight," Red Feather added. "Colonel Bradley forbade it. They will come tomorrow. For all of us, Billy Garnett said."

"Who intends to come against us?" asked Crazy Horse.

"Red Cloud, Little Wound, American Horse, Yellow Road, No Flesh, Big Road, No Water, and Woman Dress," said Red Feather. "And Little Big Man." He added this last name with shame.

Crazy Horse looked at his young brother-in-law, waiting.

"Young-Man-Whose-Enemies-Are-Afraid-of-His-Horses," the young man finally added.

Crazy Horse nodded his head. His friend from childhood. His companions in last winter's fights. His old comrade in war. *Well,* he said to himself, *maybe they are coming to prevent trouble, or an accident.*

He noticed Hawk. Though the news was awful, unbearable, Hawk was gathering her spirits. Hawk was perhaps even eager. He smiled. He had lost nearly everyone, but not his spirit guide. She was ready to go to war with him.

He thought for a while. He signaled Black Shawl to sit beside him. Nellie was off visiting her father. "We will leave in the morning," he said. "We will go to Touch-the-Sky at Spotted Tail Agency, just the two of us."

To Red Feather he added, "Tell everyone I go alone, not inviting the people of the village to come. Tell everyone." He felt satisfaction. He was done with being a headman. Now he was simply a warrior again.

THE CHASE

From out in front No Water saw two rider shapes just as they disappeared behind a distant ridge. Crazy Horse and Black Shawl, surely. No Water signaled the twenty-five warriors behind him, and they sprinted after the pair.

It was a grand day. This morning agency Indians had marched out hundreds strong toward Crazy Horse's camp from Fort Robinson, with almost every important leader except He Dog, the force of all the Oglala turned against the Strange Man. Never had No Water felt such vindication.

And though a few of Crazy Horse's warriors slowed them up with a smoke and a talk, the march was unopposed. The camp was breaking up as people ran to their relatives in other villages. Then the marchers found out Crazy Horse was already running for his two uncles at Spotted Tail Agency.

Running like an old, tired bull, No Water thought, chased by many hunters on fast horses.

Clark had given No Water permission to take twenty-five scouts after Crazy Horse and bring him back, or bring his $200 scalp back.

And now they had almost caught up.

No Water hand-whipped his pony hard. He would ride up alongside the old bull and bring him down.

Uphill, downhill, across the flats, up again, No Water didn't seem to be gaining much. His scouts were strung out behind him now. He smiled grimly. No Water was far bigger than most of them, more for a pony to carry. But if they weren't willing to push their ponies as hard as he did, he would get the $200.

He trotted his pony uphill at a slant. The beast wouldn't go straight up. It was wheezing. No Water wasn't close enough for a shot yet, even a shot with almost no chance. He wondered why he wasn't gaining faster.

He had heard that Crazy Horse had gopher medicine, something he used to confuse his enemies. But No Water wasn't confused at all. He had never felt clearer, or happier, in his life. So that medicine wasn't working.

He had also heard a story about Crazy Horse's name. One story was that the name meant "Horse Spirited in Battle," another that it meant "Horse Magically Obedient." But No Water had heard a third story, that the name meant "Spiritless Horse." Crazy Horse's ancestor had gotten that name by learning to ride a traveling horse so skillfully that he got every hint of energy from it, leaving it alive but sucked dry of spirit.

No Water was more interested in Crazy Horse's blood than his horse or its spirit. But maybe the Strange Man did have the ability to get everything out of a pony.

At every ridge top No Water searched the country ahead for the sandy-haired man and his wife, and saw them only occasionally, too far ahead. He had noticed that Crazy Horse did not run the horses uphill but walked them, and ran them downhill hard. Maybe that was part of the secret.

But secrets would do the Strange Man no good today.

No Water could not bring himself to shoot his horse. He was so angry at it that he wanted it to suffer. Clearly it was never going to get on its feet again.

He looked down the White Earth River. Somewhere ahead Crazy Horse and Black Shawl were riding toward Spotted Tail and now would get away.

Probably someone else would get the Strange Man's scalp. It made No Water want to vomit.

Two of his scouts topped the hill behind and came to the man standing beside the dying horse.

No Water yelled at them until the younger dismounted and gave the leader his pony.

As No Water disappeared over the next hill, he heard the gunshot that ended the life of his worn-out mount. He grinned.

No Water saw the man and woman ride fast into the camp of Touch-the-Sky, Crazy Horse's uncle. There was not much to be done now. He sat his borrowed horse until some of his scouts came up. When they saw mounted warriors sprinting out of Touch-the-Sky's camp toward them, they hightailed it for Spotted Tail Agency.

The messenger said Burke, the commanding officer at the military post at Spotted Tail, wanted Crazy Horse right away.

Amazing. Since he had come in to an agency, four moons ago, Crazy Horse had been dealing with *wasicu* who sent for him, instructed him to go somewhere for a talk, or told him where his village could or could not camp. Now Burke simply sent for him. Right away. Such was the road he gave up the hunting life for.

When everyone understood he was a warrior and not a headman anymore, he would not be ordered around. Or at least when he was living far from *wasicu*. Choice, your own direction, was a funny thing.

For now he would cooperate. He left his wife in his *ate*'s lodge and rode in to see the commanding officer, Burke, and the agent, Lee, who was another soldier and under Burke's command. He rode under the protection of a Mniconjou escort led by his uncle Touch-the-Sky.

At the fort Burke and Lee met them. With the *wasicu* were several hundred warriors led by Spotted Tail. The warriors acted prickly, and Crazy Horse smiled to himself at this. He was protected by an uncle on his blood mother's side and maybe threatened by one on his other mothers' side. Could there be a question of whether Crazy Horse was safe in his uncle's village and in his father's lodge?

He had no chance to talk to Spotted Tail privately. Burke and Lee made everyone sit down outside to talk. And his talk was simple: Crazy Horse had to go back to Fort Robinson tomorrow.

The Mniconjou broke into a hubbub at this. Crazy Horse was pleased—they remembered that he was not only a guest but a relative. When he raised his hand, they fell silent.

"I come in peace," he said. They could see he had come alone, with no fighting men and without his village, just one man with his wife. "I want to live here with my relatives."

He looked across the circle at Spotted Tail. His uncle was the head chief here. His father and mothers had moved their lodge here to live near Spotted Tail, who was their brother. Crazy Horse no longer was sure who his uncle was, the man who knocked thirteen soldiers from their saddle at the Blue Water or the man who played at *wasicu* politics to get ahead. So he was making the oldest and most honored claim to sanctuary: "I come here to live with my family."

At last Spotted Tail spoke up. "My brother, you have roamed like a fire in the north. You are of the Oglala."

You are one of them, not one of us Sicangu! From his uncle. Crazy Horse searched Spotted Tail's face but saw nothing personal there, only the relentless amiability of the politician.

"The Oglala people are yours. Something good should happen to you with them. Instead you have run away like a wolf with its tail between its legs."

Crazy Horse was only half-listening now. His mind began to flood with pictures of his uncle from memory.

"This is my band," Spotted Tail went on. "I do not want anything bad to happen to you here. Therefore, I give you a fine horse as a gift. I want you to take this horse and go back to your people, the Oglala. You will listen to me and do as I say."

Crazy Horse's mind snapped into the present. *You will listen to me, you will do as I say.*

You are of the Oglala, not my people.

You are not welcome in the camp of your mothers' people the Sicangu, or your birth mother's people the Mniconjou.

Most of all, *You will listen to me, you will do as I say.*

His mind rocked up and down with memories like waves in a lake. Spotted Tail's face as he explained that the white men don't understand choice. Spotted Tail as he rode bullet-proof toward the warriors of the Two Circle People, and did it again. Especially Spotted Tail on the day he came back from crying for a vision, his mind made up to throw his life away. Crazy Horse saw again the fun on the face of the doomed man who wanted to singe Flat Club's bottom, and the laughter and tears when it worked.

He looked across at this Spotted Tail, who had somehow usurped his uncle and onetime teacher. Spotted Tail's face changed. The political smile disappeared, and a stony indifference replaced it. Crazy Horse knew there was nothing more for him there.

Crazy Horse felt an odd tingle across his shoulders and down the back of his arms. He could not have said exactly what it was. Not fear, not revulsion, not anger, not bitterness. Sadness, maybe. Sadness at one world lost, gone as far away as one of the star people, and sadness at a new world he didn't want to live in.

He said nothing. Tonight he would send a messenger to his uncle with one sentence: "If this new road turns Lakota against Lakota, Sicangu against Oglala, uncle against nephew, what good can it be?"

Now the two soldiers, the commander and the agent, asked Crazy Horse why he had left Fort Robinson. The Strange Man had lost interest in the talk. He explained politely that this morning the scouts and soldiers had come to arrest him, though he had done nothing but speak for peace. Now he simply wanted to live quietly with his relatives here. But he only murmured all this halfheartedly.

The soldiers insisted that he go back to Fort Robinson and explain to the commander and the agent there.

Must, must, thought Crazy Horse.

If he would go back, the agent would go with him, and an escort of his friends and relatives. They would see that no harm came to him, and the agent would support his request to live at Spotted Tail Agency.

No, thought Crazy Horse, *you don't understand, my uncle has made me unwelcome.*

He saw his youth vision, his own people hurting him from behind.

So Crazy Horse shrugged and consented to go.

To be a warrior was not to predict, only to be ready.

THE BEAT OF THE DRUM

About halfway to Fort Robinson the next morning, His Crazy Horse was riding with Touch-the-Sky and a few other friends and relatives behind the ambulance that carried the agent Lee and the interpreter Bordeaux. Scouts from Spotted Tail Agency, Sicangu, rode up from behind dressed in their soldier coats. Despite the promises of friendship, His Crazy Horse understood that he was now a prisoner, guarded by his own uncle's men.

He had no gun. He and Lee had agreed that neither of them would carry a sidearm on this journey. He did have the new knife in a leather sheath, the one Bradley had given him. It was hidden in his clothing. Since he was alone and surrounded by enemies, it would do him no real good.

He knew his friends found him distracted, mentally absent, not awake to this moment, to captivity, to the danger of imprisonment and death. He would have liked to be easy with them, to talk and joke, to recall better times and smile in comradeship. But his mind was somewhere else. He was listening to the beat of the drum. In it sounded the pulse of his life, and of Hawk, and of all life. In it was the throb of the living earth. It held his mind, his calm attention, his spirit.

As they approached White Crow Butte, the agent sent a message ahead to Clark. Lee said that it included the promises made to the Strange Man, that he would be able to tell his side of the story, especially that Grabber had misrepresented his words, and that he would get to say to the soldier chiefs again that all he wanted was peace. Lee said the note also asked whether His Crazy Horse should go to the agency or the fort.

When the message came back from Clark, it said only that His Crazy Horse should be taken directly to the office of the commanding officer, Colonel Bradley.

The sandy-haired man wondered if these notes were just more scheming, but he didn't know. He paid attention to Hawk, perched there in his heart, and waited for guidance. He listened to the beat of the drum.

Near the fort He Dog came out to meet him, and they rode the last distance together, moccasined feet almost touching, which made the Strange Man feel good. In the clop of their horses' hooves he heard the beat.

On the grounds of the fort the party halted in a tumult of Indians. Everyone had heard that His Crazy Horse was being brought in. The Oglala police pushed up close, Little Big Man among them. His Crazy Horse looked at his friend, but Little Big Man's face was closed. His Crazy Horse knew he had decided to do his duty.

Lots of other warriors crowded the spaces between the buildings, led by Red Cloud and American Horse. A few His Crazy Horse warriors stood to one side. The sandy-haired man looked for Woman Dress and No Water, whose spite had brought him here, but they were nowhere to be seen. He glanced sideways at his uncle Touch-the-Sky. A few Mniconjou relatives meant nothing now. In all this ocean of Lakota people His Crazy Horse saw only one Oglala ally, He Dog, sitting his pony next to the sandy-haired man, legging to legging. In his heart he turned to his true allies, Hawk and the drumbeat.

Agent Lee spoke briefly with a soldier and told His Crazy Horse he must go talk to Bradley, the commanding officer. The Strange Man simply nodded, watching and waiting. He could feel the ugly spirit in this crowd, his own people. He thought the drumbeat was telling him, *The time has come.*

Col. Luther Bradley told Lt. Jesse Lee that His Crazy Horse was under arrest and must be turned over to the officer of the day. He would be detained in the guardhouse tonight and shipped by rail to General Sheridan tomorrow for final disposal. He would not be harmed, but he was a prisoner.

Lee protested. The Oglala leader had been wronged, he said. The interpreter Grouard had mistranslated his words, maybe deliberately. Captain Burke and he had promised His Crazy Horse that if he returned voluntarily to Fort Robinson, his side of the story would be heard.

"It's too late," said Bradley.

"It's unfair, Sir."

"I have my orders," said Bradley. "From General Crook and from General Sheridan." General to colonel to lieutenant—this was the U.S. Army.

"Sir—"

"You have your orders, Lieutenant," Bradley snapped. "Give him to the officer of the day."

Lee thought before he spoke. "There will be trouble, Sir. What shall I tell him?"

"Tell him it's late in the day and we'll talk tomorrow."

"It's unjust, Sir."

Bradley shrugged. He had his orders. It wasn't his fault. This was the army.

"It's almost night," said Lee to His Crazy Horse. "You can talk to Bradley tomorrow. Go with this officer and you won't be harmed."

His Crazy Horse barely managed to hear the words over the beat of the drum. After a brief hesitation he offered Lee his hand, and the lieutenant shook it. His Crazy Horse glanced at Touch-the-Sky before walking off with the escort.

Lee watched the small party move toward a low building. The adjutant's office was there. Next to that was the guardhouse, with cells, bars, and chains. Lee was pretty sure His Crazy Horse didn't know that. The chief was walking between the officer of the day and Little Big Man, troopers behind, Indian police in front. The lieutenant was transfixed. He had the uncanny feeling that the Strange Man was marching to music, funeral music.

Hawk was alert, grasping and letting go with her claws, turning on her perch. His Crazy Horse walked next to Little Big Man and the soldier chief, also alert. He was a warrior again now, aware, ready, calm. He thought sweetly of Hump, the man who had taught him. He thought of his hidden knife. None of it mattered. He would lift and lower his feet to the beat. He would feel its music through Earth herself. He would march wherever the pulse of Earth led him.

They came up to a door in a little building. Surrounded by policemen and soldiers, His Crazy Horse couldn't see it well. The Indian police opened the door and went in.

In the doorway His Crazy Horse saw what it was: the jail. The cells with barred windows, locking doors, cramped and dark. The chains.

At the sight of this death, Hawk lunged.

His Crazy Horse felt his feet upon the earth and heard the beat in his heart. Since his decision had been made long ago, he moved swiftly and easily.

One hand flashed out the new knife.

His body whirled.

Hawk screamed, KEE-ur, KEE-ur! Hawk lifted into the air.

After one step he felt them, Little Big Man's hands grabbing his arms.

His Crazy Horse spun, slashing with the knife. His feet touched the earth rhythmically.

He felt Little Big Man's hands clamp hard.

For Pvt. William Gentles, training took over. He was a soldier. He saw a prisoner wielding a knife. He had been drilled repeatedly in the thrust of the bayonet: Step back out of range. Plant feet, cock shoulders back, step forward, rotate shoulders into the thrust vigorously, shoulders and back and legs propelling the blade.

Some Indian had the prisoner by the arms just enough. The first thrust hit the door facing. Then Gentles had a decent target, the back. He felt the bayonet push against flesh and muscle and finally the resistance of insides. He snapped the blade back out, bloody. He would have guessed it went nearly through from back to front.

His Crazy Horse looked into Little Big Man's eyes. He felt his comrade's arms holding him up. His feet had stopped moving. He said, "Stop, my friend, you have hurt me enough."

He felt Little Big Man's hands let him go. He fell and hit the earth. His blood ran into the dust. The beat of the drum was muffled.

HAWK

A jumble: Pain like a huge wave boiling. A room. The *wasicu* doctor, a needle going into his arm, a strange unreality, pleasant and ugly, like a sour vision. The murmurings of his father, Worm, his mothers, his uncle Touch-the-Sky.

Through it all Hawk was quiet, still, at peace.

More jumble: Lifting on the wave of pain. Doctor. Tears

and lamentations. Cresting on the wave of pain. Vague and intermittent drumbeats. Floating, washing toward death. Tonight his spirit, the one known to him as Hawk, would go beyond the pines. His heart flooded with warmth from Wi, the sun.

Tonight the single eye of his heart would close and his spirit would go to live beyond the pines.

His father wept. His mothers and uncle wept.

He yearned to go.

He tried to speak to them. *"He, he, he,"* he tried to say. Regret, regret, regret.

Hawk felt the wind in her face. She turned into it, and felt its lift. Power, power, the wind has power.

Gently, she raised her wings and rose a little. She hovered. The wind was from the north, and she understood, understood not in words, but in a change in her breast. The wind was growing colder. Yes, it was from the north. She would fly that direction, and on beyond the pines. She would not see the sun rise again.

She rose a little on the wind, feeling its strength. She still felt a wish to hover over this small cabin huddled in the darkness. She heard its human beings wailing, singing one of the great songs of their kind, a song of grief.

It was almost time, but not yet. An awareness held her like a falconer's will, a connection with the man below, a beat.

She rode the wind there in the blackness, waiting.

It came simply. She felt a tug in her breast. It hurt a little, and she knew that the single eye below was closed, and the drum was silent.

She felt her freedom. It was time to fly.

Hawk mounted on the wind a little and turned to the west. She circled the cabin four times, sunwise. The first time she hovered for a moment in the west, where the Wakinyan dwell. The second time in the north, where the white giant lives. The third time in the east, home of the sun. Last she faced the south, the giver of life, as a salute.

She turned slowly back to the north, and felt a thrill at the strength of the wind. She mounted higher and higher into the black sky in great rings made sunwise, higher and higher. When she would have been beyond the sight of human beings even in daylight, she turned for the last time into the north wind, flapped her wings, and began her journey.

Before the sun rose on this earth she would be soaring beyond the pines at the edge of the world, beyond the path of the winds, away in the northern skies where there is no darkness, no sickness or sorrow of any kind can come, and the spirits dwell in peace and beauty.

HISTORICAL NOTE

Most of the characters and incidents in this book are historical. Where I have gone beyond the record, it is an attempt to explore more fully what is known—for example, the nature of Crazy Horse's spirit guide, the texture of the romance between His Crazy Horse and Black Buffalo Woman, No Water's enmity for His Crazy Horse, the details of His Crazy Horse's friendship with Buffalo Hump, what was going on in the mind of Lt. William Philo Clark near the end, and so on.

The major elements of His Crazy Horse's story have come to us from the Lakota people: The light-haired Curly did have the vision described here, did not tell anyone for a long time, and did have difficulty living his vision. He went against the Omaha with his maternal uncle Spotted Tail. Spotted Tail threw down his life and was imprisoned at Fort Leavenworth for a year. Curly rode bullet-proof against the People Who Live in Grass Lodges, and his father honored him with the name His Crazy Horse. His Crazy Horse did become a shirt wearer, did elope with Black Buffalo Woman, was shot by No Water, did have the shirt taken away, did marry Black Shawl, did have a daughter who died, etc.

The broad pictures of the lives of the principal Lakota around His Crazy Horse are also historical, though in places the evidence is slight: It's likely that Curly's blood mother, Rattling Blanket Woman, committed suicide. His father, a holy man, did subsequently take two sisters of Spotted Tail as wives. His Crazy Horse's brother, Little Hawk, and his friend Hump were killed in fights like those described here, and in that year. The characterization of Red Cloud is intended seriously, and in my judgment fits the record.

Likewise the major political and military events here are historical, many of them set down in army records: After the incident with the Mormon cow, Grattan led twenty-nine soldiers to their death in the Sicangu village. Harney massacred women and children on the Blue Water. The battle of Creek of Turkeys, where the Cheyenne bullet-proofing failed, was actual. The great council at Bear Butte was real, as were the massacre at Sand Creek, the battle of Platte Bridge, the Fetterman fight, the wagon box fight, the engagement of the Lakota and Gen. George Crook at the Rosebud, the battle of the Little Bighorn and its military aftermath, the surrender of the Crazy Horse people at Fort Robinson, the subsequent maneuverings, and his betrayal and murder.

The principal characters and large events of this novel come from history. The interior lives of these characters, their emotions, and the meanings of these events to them are imagined.

Principal Historical Characters

LAKOTA

His Crazy Horse's Immediate Family

His Crazy Horse, first known as Light Curly Hair, son of Tasunke Witko (His Crazy Horse), a Hunkpatila Oglala.

Tasunke Witko (His Crazy Horse), father of His Crazy Horse, later known as Worm.

Rattling Blanket Woman, a Mniconjou, first wife of Tasunke Witko and blood mother of His Crazy Horse.

Red Grass, wife of Tasunke Witko, sister of Spotted Tail, born a Sicangu. (Her actual name is unknown.)

Corn, wife of Tasunke Witko, sister of Spotted Tail, born a Sicangu. (Her actual name is unknown.)

Little Hawk, half brother of His Crazy Horse.

Kettle, sister of His Crazy Horse. (Her name is invented.)

Black Buffalo Woman, Bad Face, Crazy Horse's love for many years, briefly his wife.

Black Shawl, Bad Face Oglala, His Crazy Horse's second wife and mother of their daughter.

They-Are-Afraid-of-Her, His Crazy Horse's daughter with Black Shawl.

Nellie Laravie, daughter of a trader, given to His Crazy Horse as another wife at Fort Robinson.

His Crazy Horse's Extended Family

His Father's Side

Long Face (earlier and later known as Little Hawk), His Crazy Horse's father's brother.

Ashes, His Crazy Horse's father's brother.

Bull Head, His Crazy Horse's father's brother.

Spotted Crow, His Crazy Horse's father's brother.

Black Elk, His Crazy Horse's cousin, father to the Black Elk of *Black Elk Speaks* by John Neihardt.

His Blood Mother's Side

Lone Horn, his uncle, a Mniconjou.

Touch-the-Sky, his uncle, a Mniconjou.

His Adoptive Mothers' Side

Spotted Tail, his maternal uncle.

Spotted Tail's wives, Spoon (an invented name) and Sweetwater Woman.

His In-laws

Red Feather, brother of Black Shawl.

Joe Laravie, trader near Fort Robinson, father of Crazy Horse's last wife, Nellie.

His Crazy Horse's Friends

Buffalo Hump, his *hunka,* a Hunkpatila Oglala.

Little Big Man, an Oglala, in this story a Bad Face.

Young Man-Whose-Enemies-Are-Afraid-of-His-Horses, Hunkpatila Oglala, a shirtman, son of the chief with the same name, later leader of the Hunkpatila.

Lone Bear, Hunkpatila Oglala.

He Dog, Bad Face Oglala, a shirtman.

Horn Chips, Bad Face Oglala, a stone dreamer, His Crazy Horse's spiritual adviser.

His Crazy Horse's Rivals Among the Bad Faces

No Water, Bad Face Oglala, brother of Black Twin and White Twin, husband of Black Buffalo Woman.

Pretty Fellow, later known as Woman Dress, son of chief Bad Face.

Standing Bear, brother of Woman Dress and Little Wolf.

Little Wolf, brother of Woman Dress and Standing Bear. (Note Cheyenne leader of same name.)

Black Twin, brother of White Twin and No Water.

White Twin, brother of Black Twin and No Water.

Red Cloud, Bad Face Oglala, war leader, treated by the whites as a major chief.

Red Dog, friend of Red Cloud.

Other Lakota

Bear-Scattering-His-Enemies, a leader of the Sicangu.

Sitting Bull, leader of the Hunkpapa.

Drum-on-His-Back, an Oglala who learned to read. Also known as Sitting Bull the Oglala.

Gall, a Hunkpapa and military leader at the Little Bighorn.

Big Road, a Bad Face leader.

Frank Grouard, Grabber, born to a Mormon missionary and Polynesian woman, adopted son of Sitting Bull, translator for the army, betrayer of Crazy Horse.

Billy Garnett, half-breed son of Confederate hero Robert Garnett and a Lakota woman, translator for the army.

Big Bat Pourier, half-breed son of a Lakota woman, translator for the army.

James Bordeaux, a half-breed trader and translator at Spotted Tail Agency.

CHEYENNE (SAHIYELA)

Morning Star, a leader, also known as Dull Knife.

Yellow Woman, rescued by Curly with her newborn son at the Blue Water, later his host among the Cheyenne.

Hail, a seer, brother of Yellow Woman.

Little Wolf, a leader.

WHITE MEN

Gen. George Crook, in command of U.S. Army forces against His Crazy Horse's Lakota at Rosebud Creek, responsible for the decision to arrest His Crazy Horse at Fort Robinson. Known to the Lakota as Three Stars.

Brig. Gen. William Harney, who attacked Little Thunder's peaceful village on the Blue Water. Known to the Lakota as White Beard and later as the Wasp.

Lt. John Bourke, Crook's aide-de-camp at the Rosebud.

Bvt. Gen. George Armstrong Custer, army explorer of the Black Hills in 1874, in command of the Seventh Cavalry at the Greasy Grass (Little Bighorn) fight. Known to the Lakota as Long Hair or Yellow Hair.

Lt. William Philo Clark, aide to Crook and in command of the Lakota scouts at Fort Robinson. Known to the Lakota as White Hat.

Gen. Nelson Miles, who fought against the Lakota near the Yellowstone River in the winter of 1877. Known to the Lakota as Bear Coat.

Dr. Ferdinand Hayden, leader of a fossil-hunting expedition to the Maka Sica of South Dakota, later a principal explorer of the Yellowstone country. Known to the Lakota as Man-Who-Picks-Up-Stones-While-Running.

Lt. Col. William Judd Fetterman, who led infantry and calvary against the Lakota at Fort Phil Kearny in 1866, resulting in the deaths of all eighty-two soldiers.

Col. Henry Carrington, commander at Fort Phil Kearny in 1866.

Dr. James Irwin, agent at Red Cloud Agency at the time of His Crazy Horse's death.

Col. Luther Bradley, commanding officer at Fort Robinson at the time of His Crazy Horse's death.

Lt. Jesse Lee, agent at Spotted Tail Agency who brought Crazy Horse back under guard to Fort Robinson.

Capt. Daniel Webster Burke, commanding officer of Camp Sheridan, the military post at Spotted Tail Agency.

Pvt. William Gentles, soldier who bayoneted His Crazy Horse fatally.

Principal Imaginary Characters

Plum, Mniconjou, His Crazy Horse's maternal grandmother by blood (Rattling Blanket Woman's mother).

Flat Club, a drunken Sicangu, and his wives.

Porcupine, a *heyoka*.

Benoit, an interpreter for Ferdinand Hayden.

Paddy, an Irish sentry at Fort Phil Kearny in 1866.

A Note About the Names of Lakota People

The Lakota names have been mistranslated often over the years. Tasunke Witko, for instance, should be not Crazy Horse but His Crazy Horse, and Red Cloud might equally well be rendered Red Sky.

One of the errors has been to shorten names into a kind of equivalent of nicknames in English, a custom alien to Lakota people. Their names are often one word made of various words joined, like Elk-Standing-in-the-Water-Whistling, and Lakota people do not shorten this to Elk-Standing in their language. Sometimes this is because the picture made by the words shows some kind of medicine and that element would be lost completely if words were dropped.

Some of the mistranslations are serious. Man-Whose-Enemies-Are-Afraid-of-His-Horses has been misnamed Man-Afraid for a century, and the meaning of his name thus changed completely.

Other mistakes are minor. The Oglala leader commonly known as Big Road, for instance, should be called something like Broad Trail. (What does "Big Road" mean anyway?)

In this book I've tried to strike a balance between strict correctness and convention. When the old translations are truly misleading, as in the case of "Man-Afraid," I've chosen new ones. Where the implication of the name is close to the original, however, I've put the convenience of the reader first and kept the familiar English translation—thus Big Road, Red Cloud, etc., and usually Crazy Horse rather than His Crazy Horse.

This book is first of all a work of imagination.

In the form called the biographical novel the writer must make music in two keys at once, fulfilling the responsibilities of fiction and biography. These sometimes yield harmony and sometimes dissonance, because each seeks a different kind of truth.

The biographer's fidelity is first of all to the particular shape of his subject's life. He studies the record assiduously. First in his mind and then on paper he recreates a reality from it, working analytically, logically, always ready to rethink. He assembles the pieces as an outsider, and gives them the shape his judgment discerns. He restricts himself, more or less, to what can be proven.

The novelist's aspiration, or at least my own, is less to limn the particular form of the life of his subject than to discover the profile of what is permanently human in it. So a story that begins as reportage, then metamorphoses into history, and is transformed once more, this time into myth.

For this transformation the novelist sees the facts as merely an armature for a work of art. And the tools he uses to create are not analysis, logic, and judgment, but feeling, imagination, and dream.

All this requires, absolutely requires, that he see his subject not analytically but holistically, as in a dream. Then he must sing boldly the song of his dream, whatever it is.

Otherwise we have facts but not truth. For no record is complete enough, or trustworthy enough, to give us a person's spirit. That lies within reach only of the artist, not the analyst. In the end it is not right because it satisfies the mind but because it satisfies the spirit.

In this book I have treated the record with scrupulous fidelity. I have read the books and the archival materials. I have consulted closely with Lakota people and studied their oral traditions about their great warrior. Yet I have also gone beyond the record. In the last months of composition I have dreamed of His Crazy Horse many nights. Those dreams, in the broadest sense of the word *dream,* are the breath of these pages, the spirit of the book.

One example: Ethnologists tell us that most Lakota of His Crazy Horse's time had spirit guides, animals who were their counselors or models. That spirit guide was at the center of the person's life. Not to know about a Lakota's spirit guide would be like not knowing that Billy Graham's guide is Jesus of Nazareth.

Though His Crazy Horse, the Strange Man of the Lakota, surely had such a guide, the record only hints at what creature it was. Nor does the record tell us what His Crazy Horse learned from his guide. Striving to reach beyond the facts to the truth, I have given my Strange Man a hawk as a guide, and have put that spirit creature at the very center of his being.

But the reader objects, "We don't know that his spirit guide was a hawk." That's true. In giving him that friend I speculate. I may be mistaken. In my view, however, not to do it would be both error and cowardice. It would falsify his life utterly.

This is the freedom that the novelist claims but the biographer dares not.

Thus: This is a work of imagination. Of dream.

—Win Blevins
Jackson Hole
January 1994

LAKOTA WORDS AND PHRASES USED IN THIS BOOK

Note: These commonsense English pronunciations are very approximate, for some Lakota vowel and consonant sounds do not have equivalents in English. The ⁿ represents one such sound: It is not pronounced but signals that the preceding vowel is nasalized.

Pronunciations have changed over time. The ones indicated here aim at representing neither the very old Lakota nor the contemporary language but the speech of the early reservation period. The expression *hiye haya* is a vocable and so has no translation.

a-i-i-i an expression or exclamation of anxiety. AH-eeee.

ake wancinyankin ktelo literally, "until I see you again"; farewell. ah-KAY wahⁿ-CHEEⁿ-yahⁿ-keeⁿ k'TAY-loh.

akicita tribal police; men of a warrior society delegated to keep order. ah-KEE-chee-tah.

ate father (used to address the biological father and his brothers). ah-TAY.

Canapegi Wi September, Moon When Leaves Turn Brown. chah-NAH-peh-GHEE wee.

Canapekasna Wi October, Moon When the Leaves Fall, Moon When the Wind Shakes Off Leaves. chah-NAH-peh-ka-SNAH wee.

Cannanpopa Wi February, Moon of Popping Trees. chahⁿ-NAHⁿ-poh-pah wee.

cansasa tobacco (the shredded inner bark of the red willow, red alder, or red dogwood). chahⁿ-SHAH-shah.

cante heart. chahⁿ-TAY.

cante ista the (one) eye of the heart. chahⁿ-TAY eesh-TAH.

canupa pipe. chahⁿ-NOO-pah.

ce adult penis. CHAY.

e-i-i-i an expression or exclamation of regret. AY-eeee.

hai an expression or exclamation indicating startlement. HAH-ee.

han yes. HAHⁿ.

hanbleceyapi crying for a vision; vision quest. hahⁿ-BLAY-chee-AH-pee.

hau welcome; a greeting; literally, "I am listening." HAH-oo, which sounds like HOW.

he, he an expression of regret. HAY, HAY.

hecitu welo (or *yelo*) an expression or exclamation of affirmation; literally, "That is true." hay-CHEE-too way-LOH *or* way-LOH.

heyoka thunder dreamer, especially one who, by dreaming of thunder, becomes a contrary, a person who does things backward. hay-YOH-kah.

hinu, hinu a woman's expression or exclamation of astonishment. hee-NOO, hee-NOO.

hokahe a war cry. HOH-kah HAY.

hoye expression or exclamation of assent. ho-YAY.

hu ikhpeya wicayapo an expression or exclamation calling for total defeat of enemy, including buggery. hoo EE-k'pay-yah wee-CHAH-yah-poh.

hunhunhe a man's expression or exclamation of sorrow, astonishment, or apprehension. hooⁿ-hooⁿ-HAY.

hunka relative by choice. The ceremony by which a person is made your relative is the *hunka lowanpi* or *hunkapi*. hooⁿ-KAH.

Hunkpapa One of the seven council fires of the Lakota, Those Who Camp by the Entrance of the Circle. HOOⁿ-k'pah-pah.

Hunkpatila His Crazy Horse's subband of the Oglala. Like *Hunkpapa,* it means "those who camp by the entrance" but does not refer to one of the seven council fires. HOOⁿ-k'pah-tee-lah.

inyan stone, pebble. When capitalized, medicine stone. eeⁿ-YAHⁿ.

isna tipi the lodge of seclusion during menstruation; literally, "alone lodge." eesh-NAH tee-pee. See also *isnati.*

isnati menstruation. eesh-NAH-tee. See also *isna tipi.*

Itazipcola One of the seven council fires of the Lakota, Those Without Bows or the Sans Arcs. ee-TAH-zee-pee-CHOH-lah.

iyotancila I love you. ee-YOH-tah^n-chee-lah.

Kangi Yuha The Raven Owners, a warrior society. kah^n-GHEE yoo-HAH.

kola friend. KOH-lah.

leksi maternal uncle. leh-K'SHEE.

mahpiya sky. Mahpiya Luta, Red Cloud's name, means "colored sky" or "colored cloud." mah-K'PEE-yah.

mahpiyato cloud. Capitalized, it means the Arapaho tribe. mah-K'PEE-yah-toh.

maka earth. When capitalized, Mother Earth. MAH-kah

mitakuye oyasin all my relations, or we are all related, a phrase repeated ritually in almost all Lakota prayers and ceremonies. mee-TAH-koo-yeh oi-AH-see^n, often elided to mee-TAH-kwee AH-see^n.

mni water. MNEE.

mni wakan spirit water, whiskey. mnee wah-KAH^n.

Mniconjou One of the seven council fires of the Lakota, Those Who Plant by the River. mnee-KOH^n-zhoo.

nagi, wanagi soul; spiritual self. wah-NAH-gee.

Oglala One of the seven council fires of the Lakota, Sand Throwers. oh-GLAH-lah.

Oohenumpa One of the seven council fires of the Lakota, the Two Boilings or Kettles band. oh-oh-HAY-noom-pah.

opawinge one hundred. oh-PAH-wee^n-hay.

Paha Sapa Black Hills (of modern South Dakota and Wyoming). pah-HAH sah-PAH.

Pani the Pawnee tribe. pah-NEE.

Pehingnunipi Wi May, Moon of Shedding Ponies. pay-HEE^n-g'noo-NEE-pee wee.

pezuta wicasa healer; herbalist.

pila maya thank you. The ceremonial phrase was *hiye pila maya*. pee-LAH mah-YAH.

Psatoka Crow enemies. *Psa* alone means "crow." Or the Absaroka, "the people of the big-beaked bird" (the raven). P'SAH-toh-KAH.

pte buffalo. p'TAY. The time of *pte*, the time of the buffalo, is one of the great ages of the earth. The bull is *pte bloka*, the cow, *pte winyela*.

Sahiyela the Cheyenne tribe. shah-HEE-yah-lah.

Sicangu one of the seven council fires of the Lakota, generally called the Brulés (Burnt Thighs). see-CHAHn-hoo.

Sihasapa One of the seven council fires of the Lakota, the Blackfoot. see-HAH-sah-PAH.

sinte tail. sheen-TAY.

skan spiritual vitality. SHKAHn.

Taku Skanskan literally, "that which moves all that moves"; spiritual vitality. tah-KOO SHKAHn SHKAHn.

tanke a man's term for an older sister. tahn-KAY.

tasunke his or her horse. tah-SHOOn-kah.

Tioheynuka Wi January, Moon of Frost in the Lodge. tee-OH-hay-NOO-kah wee.

tipsila prairie-turnip. TEE-p'see-lah.

Titunwan Teton, part of the formal name of the Lakota people. tee-TOOn-wahn.

to a vigorous affirmative, like "damn right!" TOH.

tonwan spirit, bad spirit. tohn-WAHn.

tunkasila grandfather (used for the biological grandfathers and for the ancestors generally and for an approximate equivalent of "God"). toon-KAH-shee-lah.

unci grandmother. oon-CHEE.

unse ma la yelo, unse ma la ye a phrase used in prayer—take pity on me. oon-SHAY mah lah yay-LOH.

wakan sacred, mysterious. wah-KAHn.

Wakan Tanka the mysterious, the first principle or supreme spirit, the father-creator. wah-KAHn-tahn-kah.

wakinyan lightning. wah-KEEn-yahn.

Wakinyan Tanka the thunderbird, or thunder being, the power of the west. wah-KEEn-yahn TAHn-kah.

wambli eagle. The *wambli gleska* is the spotted or immature golden eagle, the highest-flying of all creatures and symbol of Wakan Tanka. wahm-BLEE.

wanh an exclamation of pleased surprise. WAHn.

Wanicokan Wi December, Midwinter Moon. wah-NEE-choh-kahn wee.

wanisugna living seed within the shell; creativity. wah-NEE-soo-gnah.

Waniyetu Wi November, Winter Moon. wah-NEE-yay-too wee.

wasicu white man; literally, "one who takes the fat" or "one who brings the message" (of the Church). wah-SHEE-choo.

wasiyuta el unpi those who live among the whites; the loaf-around-the-fort people. wah-SHEE-yoo-tah el oo^n-PEE.

Wasutun Wi August, Moon When All Things Ripen. wa-SOO-too^n wee.

Waziya north; the giant that lives in the north. wah-ZEE-yah.

wi, anpetuwi sun. WEE.

wicasa man. wee-CHAH-shah.

wicasa wakan holy man. wee-CHAH-shah wah-KAH^n.

wicasa yatapika shirtman; literally, "owner of the tribe." wee-CHAH-shah yah-TAH-pee-kah.

Wicokannanji July, Middle Moon. wee-CHOH-kah^n-nah^n-gee.

win a suffix meaning "female." wee^n.

winkte literally, "a man who wants to be a woman"; a psychological hermaphrodite. Such men took women's roles entirely, even married men, had special spiritual power because of their participation in both sexes, and had particular ceremonial roles. wee^n-TAY.

Wipazuka Waste Wi June, Moon When the Chokecherries Ripen, Moon of Ripening Berries, Moon When the Ponies Get Fat. wee-PAH-zhoo-kah wahsh-TAY wee.

witko crazy. weet-KOH.

wiwanyag wachipi the sun dance, or gazing-at-the-sun-pole dance. wee-WAH^n-yahg wah-CHEE-pee.

yaspapi the time of the bitten moon; the first half of the new moon and last half of the old one. yah-SPAH-pee.

LAKOTA PLACE NAMES

The Lakota people naturally had and have their own terms (sometimes multiple terms) for everything modern Americans use proper nouns for—rivers, mountains, other geographic features of the land they lived in, and other tribal peoples. When the white people came, they sometimes adopted these designations and other times used those of other tribes or their own names. Here is a list of place names and the names of other tribes used in this book in which the modern English and a literal translation of the Lakota are different.

Arapaho tribe—Mahpiyato, Blue Sky People.
Badlands of South Dakota—the Maka Sica.
Bighorn Mountains—Heska, Shining Mountains.
Black Hills of South Dakota and Wyoming—Paha Sapa.
Cheyenne tribe—Sahiyela.
Crow Tribe (the Absaroka)—Psa (this word often occurred in the form *Psatoka,* Crow enemies).
Laramie River—Waga Wakpa, Swimming Bird River.
Little Bighorn River—Peji Sluta, Greasy Grass River.
Loup River—Kasleca Wakpa, Split River.
Mississippi River—Hahawokpa, River of Canoes.
Missouri River—Mnisose, Muddy Water River.
Niobrara River—Mnilusa, Running Water River.
Omaha tribe—Oyatenupa, Two Circle People.
Oregon Trail—Canku Wakan, Holy Road.
Pawnee tribe—Pani.
Platte River (North Platte)—Pankeska Wakpa, Shell River.
Powder River—Maka Blu Wakpa, Shifting Sands River.
Rosebud Creek—Onjinjintka Wakpa, Red Flower Creek.
Shoshone or Snake tribe—Susuni.
Tongue River—Tatonka Ceji Wakpa, Buffalo Tongue River.
White River of South Dakota—Make Ska, White Earth (or Earth-Smoke) River.
Yellowstone River—Hehaka Wakpa, Elk River.

I think that we are on the threshold of a great burgeoning of excellent writing about Lakota culture, much of it by Lakota people. Surely among those new books will be a splendid biography of His Crazy Horse, and I hope it will be the forthcoming one by my friend Joseph C. Porter. In the meantime these are the books I have used in writing *Stone Song* and those I suggest for those attracted to the Lakota people, His Crazy Horse, or the time of the Plains Indian wars:

The best beginning is surely Mari Sandoz's biography *His Crazy Horse: Strange Man of the Oglalas,* published in 1942 and still in print more than half a century later, incomplete and outdated but poetic.

A grand introduction to the Lakota spirit is John G. Neihardt's *Black Elk Speaks.* The edition by Raymond De-Mallie, *The Sixth Grandfather* (University of Nebraska Press, 1984), is especially useful. Joseph Epes Brown's *The Sacred Pipe: Black Elk's Account of the Seven Sacred Rites of the Oglala Sioux* (University of Oklahoma Press, 1953) is a fine companion piece.

James C. Olson's *Red Cloud and the Sioux Problem* (University of Nebraska Press, 1965) offers an understanding of the political and military dilemma of the Lakota in the 1860s and '70s and shows a Lakota point of view more accommodating than His Crazy Horse's.

Ruth Beebe Hill's *Hanta Yo* pioneered truly ambitious fiction about the Lakota and captured their mind-set with great immediacy.

The interested reader will want to pursue more specialized works such as Royal Hassrick's *The Sioux: Life and Customs of a Warrior Society,* Eleanor Hinman's *Oglala Sources on the Life of His Crazy Horse,* Semi Nadeau's *Fort Laramie and the Sioux, The Killing of Chief His Crazy Horse,* edited by Robert A. Clark, *Prayers of Smoke* by the Oglala Lakota Barbara Means Adams, William Powers's *Lakota Religion,* and the editions by DeMallie and Elaine A. Jahner of James

Walker's seminal works *Lakota Belief and Ritual, Lakota Society,* and *Lakota Myth.*

These books should be read not only with the analytical mind but with the single eye of the heart.

ACKNOWLEDGMENTS

Twenty years ago, thinking myself an iconoclastic rationalist, I had an intoxicating and wildly seductive attraction to a man named His Crazy Horse, who was a warrior and a mystic, a man who looked at the world through primal eyes. Without knowing why, I craved to understand him. So I started prowling through the literature.

Soon I wondered why more good books about his life were not available. The only excellent biography, for me, was the poetic one by Mari Sandoz. Though His Crazy Horse popped up everywhere as a fictional character, no serious biographical novel had been written. I wanted to write . . . something.

These many years later I know why libraries offer few good books on His Crazy Horse. The researching and writing have been a hard road, inspiring and tedious, revealing and painstaking, exhilarating and exhausting. To come to know this man of another time, another culture, another way of life, in the end I have had to become a different man myself.

I am surprised and overjoyed to be here at journey's end, and extraordinarily grateful to my companions.

These people grandly gave me what I needed most, their encouragement and emotional support over the long years—Martha Stearn, Leeds Davis, Hooman Aprin, Larry Gneiting, my old novelist compadre Max Evans, Michael and Kathleen Gear, Richard S. Wheeler, Jenna Caplette, Lenore Carroll, and W.C. Jameson. You are people to ride the river with.

Martha Stearn, the mother of my younger son, and a novelist herself, was my first reader and made wonderful suggestions. Jane Candia Coleman read the first draft helpfully. Dale L. Walker, a man of big heart, worked and worked and supported and supported. Thanks.

Joseph C. Porter is now writing a biography of His Crazy Horse, one I expect to become the standard life. He has been generous in answering questions, kicking around ideas, and reading my manuscript. Ruth Beebe Hill, author of the pioneering *Hanta Yo* and the possessor of extraordinary knowledge, talked, supported, encouraged, and greatly refined my understanding of the Lakota lifeway.

Dozens, scores, probably hundreds of people indulged my obsession with His Crazy Horse with hour upon hour of fine talk. Lots of librarians and archivists went beyond their job descriptions for me. Sandra Porter helped me with the research in the first couple of years, giving not only time but understanding. In the last several years Ruth Valsing has chased down innumerable leads and skillfully found the answers to innumerable questions. Bert Raynes repeatedly gave me information on the behavior of hawks and other birds. I thank all these people not only for their generosity with time and effort and ability, but for their generosity of the heart.

Some people I met along the way, Anglo and Indian, have become my teachers. I thank especially Frank Caplette of the Absaroka people, Jenna Caplette, and Murphy Fox. Ernie Bulow acted as my counselor. Richard Willow, Arapaho, helped me start on the new path by taking me into the sweat lodge for the first time. Bill Westbrook made a fine gesture. Victor Douville of Sinte Gleska College read the manuscript and gave useful advice. Reginald and Gladys Laubin gave to me of their time, their knowledge, and their hearts.

Several descendants of His Crazy Horse have helped me—Seth Big Crow, Dolores Mills, and especially Barbara Means Adams. Herself the author of *Prayers of Smoke,* Barbara Adams labored greatly. Other Indian friends have contributed to this book in major ways. Many of them have answered questions, have tolerated my white-man impatience with smiles, have treated me to the wonderful humor of Indian peoples, and have let me see the spirit that vivifies them. The painter Itazipico (Louis Bowker) of the Mniconjou and Itazipico Lakota, the Cherokee Ardy

Bowker, and Cherokee novelist Robert Conley have been my teachers. Thank you.

My greatest obligations for this book are to two Indian men who started out as resources for answering questions and ended as not only friends but guides.

Joseph C. Marshall, Sicangu Lakota, author of *Soldiers Falling into Camp* and *Winter of the Holy Iron,* himself in love with His Crazy Horse, has been my adviser on every page of this book. His vast knowledge of both the printed material about his people and their oral traditions and the presence of Spirit in his own life have been my sustenance and my light. When the student is ready, the teacher appears.

For some years the Honorable Clyde M. Hall of the Shoshone-Bannock Tribe has been my teacher in matters of history and scholarship and understanding of Plains Indian peoples, and my spiritual mentor. Thank you, Clyde.

Thank you, all my friends. In helping me find His Crazy Horse, you have led me to myself.

The most personal thanks: During the writing of this book a man of great soul called His Crazy Horse became my most intimate friend, my partner in a dance of spirits. It is difficult for me to lay down the writing and surrender him to the world as a book. Though he will be with me forever, I miss doing our dance every day.

This week I came here to Bear Butte, the sacred place of the Lakota and Cheyenne for crying for a vision. After my own seeking for insight, I prayed and smoked the pipe on the Teaching Hill, where His Crazy Horse is said to have addressed the assembled tribes. I offered my heartfelt thanks, and talked with him awhile.

Pila maya, Grandfather. *Ake wancinyankin ktelo.*

—Win Blevins
Bear Butte,
September 20, 1994